Earlier versions of some c
Confrontation, Kansai Time Out,
International, Chiron Review, and

Permission is gratefully acknowledged from the Hal Leonard Corporation to reprint lyrics from "Turning Japanese," by the Vapors, ©1971.

I would like to thank the Mississippi Arts Commission for financial assistance during the completion of this work, and also my family for a more intangible form of support.

I would like to thank the Mississippi Arts Commission for financial assistance during the completion of this work, and also my family for a more intangible form of support.

CONTENTS

1. Clouds
2. *Kōrogi*
3. A Night in Korea
4. Learning the Language
5. *Bon*
6. The Japanese
7. Eastern Standard Time
8. The Foreign Offensive
9. Timing
10. The Concrete Buddha
11. The Road to Hell
12. Shanghai Ward
13. Encounters in America

Gō ni itte wa gō ni shitagae.

Obey the customs of the village you enter.

1. Clouds

Peering out the window from 30,000 feet up, Cricket Collins thought he could see the vast maternal curve of the horizon. A puffy level of clouds lay below like some mythical land, peopled by creatures of air with heads of smoke and wispy bodies. He stared at the scene until it began to stare back at him, forcing him to look away self-consciously. The man sitting next to him had just gotten up, leaving his breakfast tray in casual ruin: a half-eaten omelette, coffee scummed with non-dairy creamer, and a triangle of toast smothered by a paper napkin.

The sudden change in scale took a moment of adjustment. Focusing on the tray, Cricket saw that the napkin had words scribbled on it, and looking closer, he read the message:

Vast crystalline blue
fractured a hair
by a toy silver plane

It was obviously an attempt at a haiku, apt enough on an airplane bound for Japan. But the syllable-count didn't look right—wasn't it supposed to be 5-7-5?—and even the words themselves seemed slightly suspect. As a writer, though he hadn't written much, Cricket felt he should care about such matters. He glanced out the window again, testing the image. For one thing, there wasn't much blue out there, more a receding haze. He picked up the napkin and was just contemplating the sharp slant of the handwriting when the man returned.

Cricket blushed, dropping the napkin back onto the tray. "Excuse me, I was just reading what you left here." Then, since the man looked annoyed, he ventured an appeasing question. "Are you a poet?"

The man grinned sourly. "Not really, no." He crumpled the napkin into a ball and shoved it into his pocket. He was a tall, stocky individual whose legs pushed far under the seat in front of him when he sat down. Dirty blond hair framed a clear oval face: late twenties, Cricket guessed, though his body was oddly stiff, as if some part of him had aged faster than the rest. His blue eyes looked somehow hollow.

Cricket wondered if the man had been through what *he'd* undergone: a TWA 707 from New York to Los Angeles, a China Airlines connection with a stopover in Honolulu, and now the long flight to Osaka. It was the cheap way to go. In his wake, he was leaving behind Columbia law school, which he'd deferred for a year, and a few incredulous friends. Europe was cliché by now, he told them airily. Anyone could go there to find oneself, so he was going to try the life of an expatriate elsewhere. Japan had beckoned from a bulletin board at college, listing teaching internships in Asia. And he was going to write (which he told almost no one, for fear of pessimism and ridicule).

In Los Angeles, he had grabbed a bite to eat at an airport café and then walked a slalom course around the palm trees lining the access roads. He made some notes in a spiral-bound notebook he'd brought along to use as a journal. In Honolulu about two a.m., unable to leave the terminal, he had bought an Agatha Christie mystery, *And Then There Were None*, and read almost half of it while getting up to stretch his legs every hour. He had been some twenty-two hours in continual motion—him or the plane—and just wished he could sleep in a seated position.

Normally reticent, he was feeling loosened and broken up by fatigue. He figured he might as well offer a piece of himself to his seatmate: his name.

The man hesitated a moment, then extended his hand: "Matthew Harriman." He pursed his lips as if about to add something, but apparently thought better of it. The two of them ducked instinctively as the stewardess came by to collect their breakfast trays.

Cricket decided to pursue the opening. "This your first time going to Japan?"

It was obviously the wrong thing to say. Matthew made no attempt to mask his pained expression. "Not really. I live there."

"Oh."

Matthew reclined his seat and lay back, but Cricket wouldn't take the hint. He was bored of reading the book bought in Honolulu, and Matthew offered a possible diversion. In situations like this, he could become almost belligerent. "Where do you live?"

"Ashiya. It's a small town in Hyogo."

Cricket nodded as if he knew the geography of Japan intimately. In fact, his knowledge of Japan stemmed entirely from a little coaching by a college friend, a Japanese-American named Peter Inoue who'd never been to Asia. Cricket had acquired some basic vocabulary and took pride in what his friend called a fairly credible accent. But it wasn't worth risking here. "Can you speak Japanese?"

"Yes. Maybe not as well as I should." A guarded look, another wrong opening.

"What do you do?"

"I'm a writer. I teach, too."

"That's what I'm going to Japan for. To teach, I mean."

"A lot of people do." Matthew waved a hand as if to brush away a fly. "You'll probably like it."

"Do you?"

A shrug. "Sometimes. You do get attention."

"How long have you been at it?"

"Three years. I just went home for a break, to see if Massachusetts was still there."

"And?"

"It was." Matthew stopped here, but Cricket didn't stop being curious. Matthew gave out information as if holding something back, and Cricket was determined to draw him out. He asked about family (yes, Matthew had one), Japanese contacts (he knew a few), and learning the language (speaking wasn't too difficult, but reading and writing took a while). In fact, Matthew was willing to address this last point for the equivalent of a paragraph. It seemed to bother him that *kanji*, the Japanese ideograms borrowed from the Chinese, had proved so damned elusive.

It bothered Cricket, in turn, when Matthew assumed the same would be true for him. "Oh, I like that kind of puzzle," he remarked, his competitive sense aroused. He'd always been clever at school.

Matthew frowned. "It's not like some jigsaw, you know. It's a whole writing system."

"I'm sure you're right," said Cricket quickly, just to make peace. This small courtesy mollified Matthew, and they went on to talk of loanwords, such as the Japanese for *taxi* (*takushii*) and the price of cantaloupes in department stores. As he listened, Cricket repressed the shadow of a smile. He'd succeeded in getting Matthew to converse.

"You can pay over fifty dollars for some of them—but they're often bought and not even eaten. You just bring them to sick people on a visit."

"Like the fruit baskets in a hospital, you mean." Cricket asked whether it was true that no tipping was allowed (yes), and how deeply one should bow (it depended on the occasion). An elaborate system of politeness governed both word and gesture, from honorifics to smiles. As Matthew began doing more and more of the talking, Cricket's responses were reduced to nods. He felt he was gaining some insight into the country, and maybe into Matthew, though he was also getting extremely sleepy. The heavy drone of the plane engines began to buzz around the back of his head, obliterating half of what Matthew said. His eyelids felt attached to small lead weights, the cabin interior muted to a lethargic gray. He nodded once more—something about Shintoism?—before nodding off entirely.

As the bosom of the horizon receded, a host of clouds rushed silently toward Cricket, the sun glinting down on the fluffy plain amassing. Strange currents stirred the surface, extruding shapes and forms that moved slowly about. Cricket landed without impact and was greeted by a host of cloud-people, their nimbus feet scudding towards him. When they met in the middle of a cloud bank, they exchanged bows and traded smiles. They looked upward, where Cricket pointed to a silver plane impossibly high up and small. They nodded, he nodded, and together they moved off toward the horizon. The journey, he suddenly realized, would take years. It got dark, it got light, and dark and light again, and whenever it was dark a kaleidoscope of faces and gestures revolved in front of him. First came his dead mother, Louise, who'd succumbed to ovarian cancer when he was nine and who still occasionally nagged him. When he sneezed at a puff of dust, she reached into her voluminous handbag, drew out a tissue, and offered to wipe his nose. She was followed by an indistinct Japanese figure wrapped in a black kimono. A pair of wooden chopsticks floated in the hands of the one semi-girlfriend he'd ever known, Sofie, with her slim wrists and cool touch, who did him the favor of de-virginizing him, as she put it. He reached for his pen and jotted down a note on her stomach. As he stretched to touch her lower down, the vaginal softness turned to mist.

Cricket awoke as the plane began making its descent. At first he wasn't sure where he was, but the NO SMOKING and FASTEN SEAT BELTS signs came on overhead, and an accented voice over the P.A. system announced that they would be arriving in Osaka in less than forty minutes. With an effort, he cleared the dregs of the dream from his mind. He looked over at Matthew, buried in a Henry James novel, *The Ambassadors*. The print was so fine, it looked like a pocket Bible.

Cricket cleared his throat, and Matthew acknowledged his awakening with a brief look in his direction. "Back among the living, I see."

"I don't know what happened. I think I was just sitting here—"

"Yes, we were talking." He paused, as if choosing a fork in

the conversation. "Well, you probably needed the sleep. And there'll be jet lag when you arrive."

"What time is it in Osaka now?"

"Seven-thirty." Matthew answered without consulting a watch. "They'll be eating breakfast right now."

Cricket was going to ask a question about the nature of Japanese breakfasts, but Matthew cut in before he could frame the words.

"Sorry, I just want to finish this chapter before we land."

Cricket nodded, slightly annoyed. It was just what he himself might do, which made it all the more irritating. To console himself, he began mentally preparing himself for his arrival, inwardly smiling, running through his small stock of Japanese. *Hajimemashite*, he addressed the plane window. How do you do. *Ha-ji-me-ma-shi-te.* He spread out the syllables and put them back together again, like a trick shuffler with a deck of cards. He repeated the word till it felt right.

Soon the plane was plunging through the surface of the clouds, which turned out not to be fleecy as he'd dreamed but misty and cold-looking. No stratospheric inhabitants greeted him. After a few minutes they were directly above the gray slate of the sea, dotted here and there by a thumbnail-sized boat and its wake of white lace. All too soon, they were over land and descending fast. The roofs of the houses were a bright blue not found in nature, the green rice fields so neatly demarcated they didn't look quite real. Only the surrounding roadways and traffic lent credence to the rest of the picture.

After the plane landed, Cricket shifted his attention back to the interior. Time to fumble through the carry-on luggage and find his passport, the one with the mugshot that made him look like a prisoner. Matthew shut his book importantly as if he had a monopoly on James's novels. But Cricket had read *The Ambassadors* in college, and the fact that Matthew was reading it now made him feel slightly superior. Should he say anything? He wondered whether Matthew's brand of intolerance was made in Japan, and whether he'd be like that, too, eventually.

But what could happen in such a short time? It was the tail end of the '70s, with nothing momentous on the horizon. It was August. The two semesters teaching at Kansai Gakuin would take nine months, and after that—law school? His father, a cigar-smoking lawyer who disguised his aggression through flippancy, had suggested that Cricket go to either Columbia or a good psychiatrist—in fact, they'd had their biggest fight in years over Cricket's planned decampment. The only point they'd ended up agreeing on was that maybe a while should elapse before they saw each other again.

In the meantime, Cricket was at completely loose ends after seventeen years of schooling, capped by a B.A. *cum laude* in English from Cornell. He had nothing like a girlfriend, not since Sofie last year. On the other hand, he had no intention of turning into a virgin again. Ever since graduation two months ago, he felt as if he were floating, almost disembodied. He finally concluded that the dizzying sensation was freedom. For four years he had toiled in Ithaca; now he was on the other side of the world. Recognizing it as an escape, he also saw it as a challenge. His father's final words were a shrugging parody of Horace Greeley's advice: "All right, young man—go east."

An orange shuttle bus took them to a terminal, where Cricket joined one of the lines going through Customs. *Arigatō*, he rehearsed. Thank you. Though Matthew had been right in front of him the whole time, somehow he had switched at one point to a faster-moving line. Going past the Customs desk, he waved imperially to Cricket, who was still several people back. Cricket nodded in return.

He would catch up with Matthew at the luggage claim, he thought. Because he knew no one in Japan, maybe he should ask Matthew's address. But by the time he got to the outer area, a large crowd had formed around the luggage carousel, and Matthew had disappeared. And Cricket realized that he had forgotten Matthew's last name.

Once he had claimed his luggage, a bulging, belted gray suitcase and the carrying case that held his Olympia typewriter, he walked through the main exit area. *Ichi, ni, san*: one, two, three. In his shirt pocket, he had the address and phone number of Kansai Gakuin, though the school had hinted that someone would be meeting him at the airport. He scanned the crowd. Being able to see over so many heads was thrilling. At 5'7", Cricket had resigned himself to a lifetime of looking up to people, but the Japanese stepping quickly around him made him feel tall, almost awkward.

A few people by the exit gate were holding up placards, looking hopefully at the arrivals. One of the signs was an oaktag parallelogram with "MR COLLINS" in slanted lettering. The blue business suit behind it looked at Cricket questioningly, and Cricket heard a voice in his head telling him to ignore the summons, to step outside the plan. He would walk away, fade into the crowd and make his own life here. He would learn his Japanese from the street vendors, get taken in by a beautiful black-haired girl who'd teach him Japanese cooking, karate, and the finer aspects of Oriental love. Sofie would be jealous. In a few years, he'd be able to show people like Matthew a thing or two. Sophisticated stories of the Far East would emerge from his typewriter, studded with arcane knowledge to startle even the Japanese.

He hesitated at the threshold, and the hesitation proved his undoing. Was there any need to abandon what he'd come for? His neurotic need for security came to the fore, addressing him in the tones of his dead mother. A substanceless hand stroked his brow and called him Crick, straightened his posture and pointed him in the right direction. Surely he could work within the system and learn a lot more that way. And wasn't conformity part of being Japanese?

All right, he'd show them just how Japanese he could be. He nodded encouragingly to the man in the suit, who hastened forward to help him with his luggage.

As they met at the far side of the railing, the man proffered his hand and recited in a lilting accent, "How do you do?"

Cricket smiled, bowing from the waist. "*Hajimemashite.*"

2. *Kōrogi*

On his second day in Japan, Cricket moved into the dormitory at Kansai Gakuin. The school had sent a taxicab to pick him up at his hotel, a sleek black Nissan that deposited him at the dormitory gate with his luggage before gliding away. The driver, Cricket noticed, had worn white cotton gloves as if to avoid contagion with the passengers. Now he was alone.

He looked around the landscape, taking in the double row of ginkgo trees flanked by pounded earth, the high, shingled walls that seemed to hold in the very air of the place. The sun entered at the oblique angle of nine a.m., but a late-summer haze restricted it to dappled images on the far wall. No breeze stirred the foliage. The faintest scent of lemon came from the nearby buildings, which rose only a few stories before slanting into blue-slate roofs. Each element of the scene was natural enough, but together appeared stylized, Japanese. It was like the hotel last night, a Best Western knock-off that could have been plunked down anywhere in America except for a few details that were off, such as the cloth slippers at the threshold, or the cramped dimensions of the room widened by room-service courtesy that bordered on the obsequious.

Hefting his new vinyl suitcase and battered typewriter case, he moved toward the entrance, marked by a wooden door with a leather pull instead of a knob. Before he could knock, an old woman in a severe gray skirt and white blouse swung open the door. Her head was small even for her short form, a tidy bun of black hair perched over her pinched features. She smiled and looked down at his feet. "Shoes . . . please," she said in halting English, pointing at the rack of slippers before the interior matting. Cricket understood and laboriously unlaced his American shoes, thinking he'd better buy some loafers. Slipping on a light blue pair embossed "KG," he padded after the old woman, who whirled around to introduce herself. "My name . . . Ogawa Sachiko. You—your name, please?"

"Cricket. Cricket Collins."

"Cricket, ah . . . English?"

"No." He corrected himself. "*Iie. Watashi wa Amerikan desu.*" He suspected it wasn't proper Japanese, but the only way he could improve was by trying. Since yesterday, he'd been cribbing from a ridiculous phrase-book which told tourists how to get to the railroad station and how to ask when the bus left. Now he availed himself of one of the book's more useful phrases: "*O-benjo wa, doko desu ka?*"

Ogawa-san broke into a surprised laugh. "Ah, speak very good . . . Japanese. *O-benjo!*" She led him down the hall, where he had his first confrontation with Japanese toilets, porcelain troughs set right into the tiled floor. She pointed to the sink and showed him the soap, which gave off the same mild lemon odor he'd smelled outdoors. "Wash-ie," she pronounced. Then she turned on the faucet to show him what water was.

She was going to show him how to use the toilet, but he resisted with a firm "*Nai.*" As he squatted precariously over the trough, shifting this way and that, he had a sudden vision of Ogawa-san pointing to the toilet paper and urging him, "Wipe-ie." Cricket had been in Japan just over a day, but he was already confronting the attitude that anyone who doesn't understand the language must also not know the function of simple objects.

Ogawa-san was waiting politely for him outside the bathroom. "Room now," she insisted, bent over by the weight of his book-heavy suitcase.

"I'll take that—uh, *watashi wa* . . . carry."

He tried to take the suitcase, but she shook her head. "*Iie, iie.*" She was wiry and determined. They plodded down a long corridor with a magnificent wall hanging at the end, a bold, black display of calligraphy on a field of gold. With its various fan-tailed limbs, it looked like an image of speed slowed to eternity. Near the end of the hall, Ogawa-san carefully lowered his suitcase onto the threshold and fished a key from her skirt pocket. "Open," she demonstrated, and Cricket nodded his head violently to prevent her from also demonstrating "close."

The room was narrow, but it had a raised bed, a molded fiberboard desk, and a long closet. It also had a wall fan, which Ogawa-san demonstrated for him. "Off." She pressed a square red button.

"And 'on.'" He intercepted her words by pressing the green button himself, filling the room with a soft, whirring sound.

Ogawa-san clucked her tongue, expressing surprise that a *gaijin*, and a young *gaijin* at that, should understand the mysteries of an Oriental electric fan. "*Ikutsu desu ka?* How . . . old?"

Ikutsu happened to be one of the few words he understood, and he wished she hadn't translated for him, since he wanted to show her he knew what it meant. "*Ikutsu? Watashi wa ni-ju-ni.*" Twenty-two. There was no Japanese he knew for "wise beyond my years," even if she got the joke, and he couldn't mime it, so he left it at that.

She nodded and pointed to the fan. "Fan. Off . . . ten o'clock." She mimed a person asleep. "Understand . . . you?"

"*Hai.*" With a fixed smile, he ushered her out the door. He knew when he was being mothered, and he didn't like it.

In another moment, Ogawa-san was back again. "Towel. Showah now? You showah?"

Cricket never showered more than once a day, a ritual performed in the morning after a brief constitutional. He'd had no walk for two days, the lack of exercise contributing to his edginess. Anyway, he'd already hastily showered and shaved at the airport hotel before being picked up. "Ah . . . *ato de.*" Through some miracle of recall, he employed the Japanese phrase for "later."

But Ogawa-san was not so easily dissuaded. She held out the towel and pointed to his slippers, abandoned by the open door like shed animal skins. "Showah . . . now."

So Cricket followed her diminutive figure all the way to the tiled room down the hall, where he took his second shower of the day. Redolent of lemon soap, he padded back to his room in the blue-and-white *yukata* she had provided for him. This time he shut and locked the door.

Cricket already entertained doubts about visiting an unknown country to perform a function about which he knew little. His teaching experience was confined to some tutoring he'd done between his sophomore and junior years. But the guilt he felt was for his Japanese students, about his effect on them. Now he wondered about the effect Japan would have on *him*. "Oh, it'll just take an adjustment," he said to the *yukata* in the voice he used to reassure himself.

He unpacked his toilet kit, clothes, and books, placing every item in a neat little niche that seemed provided for the purpose. Despite its small size, the room turned out to be a marvel of built-in shelves and cupboards, and he spent some time putting all his possessions in order. The flat desk drawer held all his writing paraphernalia, from a package of putty-like typewriter-key cleaner to a bottle of White Out and a hundred sheets of bond paper. His red plastic Seiko travel clock, made in Japan but bought in America to bring to Osaka, fit right on the window sill. The Agatha Christie novel, still unfinished, stood to the side of three short-story anthologies, Strunk and White's *Elements of Style*, and a paperback dictionary. His clothing took up a pitifully small space, so he amused himself by suspending his socks and underwear from hangers. He had just sat down on his bed when he heard the doorknob turning.

Of course, the door was locked. He got up leisurely and walked over to the entrance. When he opened the door, he saw Ogawa-san's worried face. "No . . . lock, please." She made an "opening" gesture with a twist of one gnarled hand.

"*Hai.*" It wasn't worth arguing about, though he'd have to stand up for his rights sooner or later. In any event, the purpose of Ogawa-san's return was innocuous. She had placed a black laquered tea tray by his door and wanted him to know it was there. In the white porcelain teapot was *o-cha*, the green tea that he hadn't quite gotten used to yet, but it was welcome at eleven o'clock. He finished one cup under surveillance and made a gesture of enjoyment. "*Yoii.* Good."

But Ogawa-san was still bothered by something. Pulling him slightly by the sleeve, she sat him down on the bed and explained when he had to eat his meals. "If no eat," she pointed at her breast, "please tell."

Cricket smiled and nodded, inwardly annoyed at another of his freedoms cut off. He'd intended to skip lunch most days, since he never ate much around noontime. He thought of telling her that right then, but realized that he'd better make it to the first meal, at least. Time to look at shops and lay out a walking route later. Before she left him again, she led him to where the cafeteria was and reminded him twice when he was to come. "Twelve . . . not forget."

"*Hai, hai.*" He nodded vigorously to show comprehension, but the tolerant look on Ogawa-san's face showed she knew how absent-minded foreigners were. As if to support her assertion, when he returned to his room, he fell into a jet-lag doze for over an hour. Suddenly Ogawa-san was in his room, tapping him on the shoulder.

"You eat . . . please." He tried to shake off his haziness as she led him down the corridor towards the cafeteria. What bothered him most was that she obviously hadn't bothered to knock first.

At lunch, Cricket met about fifty of the students at Kansai Gakuin, a name they all shortened—affectionately or derisively—to Kanga. Most of the young men had black hair so well combed it was lustrous. All of them had brown eyes which looked curiously at the newcomer. The women were quite pretty: *flower-like* was the term he would use in his notebook journal, and *delicate* in his first letter to Peter Inoue back home. Ogawa-san led him to the front of a table where almost everyone had finished eating and pronounced what was obviously a short introduction. She scurried away for a moment, and he was left to the tender mercies of his soon-to-be students.

One of the young men was nosed forward, the way a crowd produces its leader. "My name is . . . Nomura. Yasuro Nomura. Your name . . . Collins-san?"

Cricket nodded, smiling. *"Watashi wa—"*

"Please. Speak English. Slowly, please."

Cricket smiled and nodded. He was going to like it here, he could tell. With the faintly supercilious air of a teacher, he started a conversation with Yasuro, while the other students watched in fascination. The details, almost invariant for all future introductions, concerned Cricket's full name, his age, the number of people in his family, and what his purpose was in coming to Japan. He tried to think of a way to turn the questions back onto Yasuro, but that seemed impertinent. He was the stranger, after all.

Still, he looked for a way to disrupt the conventions. When Ogawa-san returned a moment later carrying an oblong tray with two sandwiches on it, he grandly got up and used his Japanese knowledge to the fullest extent. *"Nihon tabemono, kudasai."* Ogawa-san looked doubtful again, but Yasuro spoke a few rapid sentences to her in Japanese, and she retreated with the tray.

"I tell her, you likes . . . same we eat. Okay?"

"Okay." One day he'd have to ask Yasuro just what the students thought of Ogawa-san. In the meantime, he astonished everyone by eating broiled fish and rice with the practiced ease of someone who spent a good deal of time in Chinese restaurants. It was his first victory over an alien culture. Soon after he finished, the students excused themselves and hurriedly left.

"Sorry, late," murmured Yasuro over his shoulder, and Cricket realized with a start that they'd all been waiting for him out of politeness. He was just digesting this compliment when Ogawa-san came back to collect his tray. Her pursed lips opened in an *O* of surprise.

"You like Japan food! Very, very good."

He nodded, expecting that now, somehow, he would be shown greater respect. In fact, the only change was that from then on she always served him Japanese fare, from miso soup to *chawan mushi*, a delicate seafood custard. She continued to call for him at lunchtime, and for the first few days she ushered him back to his room after every meal.

During Cricket's first class, the inevitable question about his first name surfaced. "Please." One of the students raised his hand. "Cricket—English name, isn't it?" He swung a phantom cricket bat. "Game with ball?"

Cricket was used to fielding questions like this, and he politely explained that his parents had named him after an insect rather than a game. That always got a good laugh. It got one now, rows of bright young Japanese men and women tittering politely and jotting down in their notebooks, most probably, the difference between *cricket* and *cricket*. A woman in the third row murmured politely that the insect cricket was *kōrogi*, and Cricket mentally filed the word for future reference.

The class proceeded smoothly with a round-the-room conversation, which began with names and might have ended with numbers of family members if Cricket hadn't hurriedly improvised more questions.

"Junichiro Sasaki . . . "

"I am Jun, yes." A teenaged boy in a yellow vest smiled toothily. "Or Pro."

"Really?" Cricket's eyes widened. "What kind of pro?"

"*Pachi-puro.*" Jun's fingers twitched. "I am good at pachinko." The class giggled, and that enabled Cricket to ask all the students their nicknames and hobbies. Everyone had at least one of each, without exception, as if assigned from birth. Yasuro's hobby was seeing American movies, his nickname Romeo. The woman behind Yasuro explained that she "liked to put on fashion." From time to time Cricket would gently correct someone's pronunciation or choice of words.

That was all they expected of him, really, or so he'd been told. Last year's English teacher, talking with him briefly over the phone before he left, had described what it would be like. "Most of them have been studying English since first-year junior high. They can read and write pretty well. It's their conversation that needs help. So they want you to talk with them." The idea was seductively simple, though he resolved to have a definite subject and plan for the next meeting. Already he was sorting American culture into teachable categories: music, food, education, street crime.

At the end of the class, Yasuro, obviously a superior student, waited for him in the corridor. "Please, if I can do something for you, talk to me." He told Cricket his room number in the dormitory, which Cricket promptly forgot. In the coming days, he received numerous such offers, but in the end he acted on none of them. He wasn't exactly being anti-social. Outside the authority of his class, he was discovering in himself a reticence that was almost Japanese.

During his second week, he began to explore Mikage, the well-scrubbed town that housed the college. Compact as it was, it harbored a labyrinthine complexity that was hard to penetrate. A typically narrow street would turn off into an even smaller thoroughfare, branching into two paved footpaths around a clump of storefronts, ending in a back alley with a little door inset at the end. At the local market, the pickle vendor offered him a tendril of seaweed in brine, soaking in green piles alongside the undersea blue of eggplant pickles, the long yellow legs of *takuan* or white-radish pickle, and pink shrunken turnips like anemones. By contrast, the tofu seller was a study in white, straining his bean curd through silk or cotton and submerging the blocks in flowing water. *"Irasshai!"* they cried, the traditional merchant's welcome. The fishmonger in his yellow boots, the fruit seller with her carefully arranged baskets—they were all delighted to see him, though at times he felt like a mere curiosity. Mikage didn't have many foreigners, it seemed.

His Japanese was improving just from constant exposure to native speakers. In the meantime, he could always point. Still, he always brought his Sanseido pocket English-Japanese dictionary with him as a precaution, fearful of getting involved in some situation demanding complex vocabulary. One incident with the local butcher, resulting in the purchase of half a kilo of ground beef, he didn't want to repeat. *"Miru dake,"* Yasuro counseled him when he asked. "Say *miru dake*—'just looking.'" Cricket gave the meat to Ogawa-san, who treated it as a present, bowed deeply, and came back an hour later with a box of five elegant tea cakes. The *quid pro quo* mentality annoyed him, but he ate the cakes anyway.

On his fourth day of walking around, he discovered the railway station, where over a hundred bicycles were jammed into the racks. A few looked as if they'd been abandoned. "Oh yes, many left behind," Yasuro told him airily, giving him the courage to wheel away one of the rustier models for his own use. It was a one-speed red clunker with bent fenders, still serviceable, with the incongruous name of Sky Lancer. From then on he bicycled all around, increasing his radius of known territory from one mile to over five. Not only were the shops and sights fascinating, but being away from his room also meant time apart from Ogawa-san, who was beginning to figure in his dreams. As in life, she had a habit of simply appearing without warning in her old-woman's hunch, carrying that determined dignity. He could never think of her by her first name, Sachiko, or even her last name alone. In his mind, the unbudgeable title was part of her presence: Ogawa-san.

Every night at ten o'clock, she would come into his room in a kimono and slippers to tell him that the fan must be turned off. When he tried to keep it on longer because the night was hot despite encroaching autumn, she somehow knew and came back to shut it off. After that, she operated a master shut-off from another floor that rendered his switch useless. Now when she came at ten o'clock to inform him that the fan was to go off, he felt like using her frail figure as a battering ram against the inactive fan.

She wanted him to shower at night, but he'd resisted on that point at least. He took a shower whenever he came back from bicycling, and since Ogawa-san apparently didn't possess the means to shut off the water, he was safe on that count. From time to time, when most of the students were taking a hot bath at night, she would sorrowfully pick up his towel and ask, "Showah, bath please?," but he would wave his hand and say, "*Iie*," a cross between "no" and "not at all." It was enormously gratifying to say "*Iie*" to Ogawa-san, even if only on a trivial matter.

Of course, they were all trivial matters. It was simply the whole situation that had become unbearable. Whenever Ogawa-san saw him preparing to bicycle somewhere, she insisted he tell her where he was going and for how long. When he finally left, she tugged at his shirt and told him to "be careful, no." He learned to say "*mochiron*" or "of course," and the more Japanese he learned, the more admiring she was. Nonetheless, he was a *gaijin*, a foreigner or "outside-person." As such, he had to be protected from the vicissitudes of daily life. Sourly, Cricket wondered just what his predecessor at the college had been like, whether he had been at all infantile and so given Ogawa-san her views on Americans. Were prejudices like Ogawa-san's endemic to her species?

One day, glancing through some of his papers, he realized that she was rearranging the items on his desk, and he grew furious. The old bitch! Did she treat all the dormitory residents this way? The next day after class, he asked Yasuro about it.

"Ah, Ogawa-san . . . she is kind, but . . . " (here Yasuro used a word not in Cricket's pocket dictionary). Yasuro whipped out his own dictionary, considerably thicker than Cricket's, and flipped through the pages. When he finally found what he wanted, he pointed: "This word, maybe."

He pointed to a short string of Japanese, after which was printed, "protective; maternal."

"Exactly." Cricket was pleased that someone else had Ogawa-san's number. "Does Ogawa-san behave that way to you? To other students?"

Yasuro shook his head, a bit puzzled. "Not so much. Perhaps you, because you—"

"Because I'm a *gaijin*, you mean."

"I think, yes. Maybe, if you want, I tell Ogawa-san—"

"*Kekko desu.* No, thank you." It was Cricket's turn to shake his head. "I fight my own wars. I'll make her understand somehow." When he walked back to his room, he found that Ogawa-san had changed his sheets again and left the usual tea tray by the foot of his bed. Damn that woman! he thought, even as he poured himself a cup.

Maternal, he snorted. His mother, an active woman who often took him shopping when he got home from school, had never been like that—or had she? She insisted he wear ridiculous red snowpants, yet she laughed at him when he fell off his sled. *My little Crick*, she cooed in front of everyone, and kissed him three times in the middle of his forehead. She picked him up when she was wearing her expensive black evening gown and waltzed him around the room, humming "You're the cream in my coffee." Yet she rarely let him go out alone and always made him get to bed early. She showed him her miniature Swiss army knife and even cut his nails with the tiny scissors, but she wouldn't let him play with the blade because he was too young. He hadn't entertained such memories in years. They made him feel unsure of his past, the victim of a constricting hug. Ridiculous, he thought, how a dislocation in space—some 12,000 miles—can move someone back in time. He sat down at his desk, pushed everything aside, and began to work on his next lesson plan.

After a month at Kanga, his daily life settled into a routine. He woke up at seven every morning, ate breakfast at seven-thirty, and then bicycled somewhere, anywhere, as long as it took him away from the dormitory for a while. After he came back, he would take a shower, write in his journal, then prepare his lesson for that afternoon. These days he was teaching short stories from a fat anthology of twentieth-century American fiction. Schooled in reading English since junior high, his students found the stories easy enough to get through. Talking about them was another matter, and Cricket often had to begin the discussions with elaborate lead-in questions. The results were often disappointing:

"Tell me, Kenzo, what did you think of the narrator in 'The Fall of the House of Usher'?"

"Very good."

Socializing with the faculty at Kanga proved equally disappointing. Apart from a welcoming party at the start of the semester, where names and faces passed in a blur of *sake* and polite speeches, he'd been left mostly alone. At the departmental office where he checked in every week, he came to know only the secretaries, who veered between painfully polite and giggly. From time to time, a few students would ask him out for lunch, but they mainly reiterated the small talk developed in class, and he felt as awkward as an off-duty cop walking his beat. After these occasions, they all bowed and hurried away. He didn't want to be an obligation, and since he couldn't exactly repay their hospitality, he tended to shy away from further invitations.

If Cricket had time before lunch, he would type letters to people back home, including even tenuous acquaintances who had no right to hear from him—mostly descriptions of what he saw on his bike rides. Few wrote back, as if the distance from America to Japan were far greater than the other way around. Most of them, he learned, were busy making money. The '80s, an entrepreneurially-minded friend of his wrote, were going to be mega-big financially. Cricket took the hint that this friend would soon become too important to write letters. Stock options, corporate law—it was all so distant from his little room on the other side of the planet. One sporadic but faithful correspondent turned out to be Peter, who was getting ready to start medical school at NYU. As a *sansei*, a third-generation Japanese-American, but with a midwest upbringing, he was a curious mix. Compared to Cricket, he was simultaneously more knowledgeable and less informed about matters Japanese. He inquired earnestly—he was a very earnest type—about everything from sumo wrestling to the condition of the Osaka subway system. "Tell me," he ended one letter poignantly, "are there still geisha girls around?" Unfortunately, Cricket didn't get out much, apart from his daily bike ride, and was ill equipped to answer most of these questions. "It is all an inscrutable mystery," he took to writing back half-jocularly.

He found himself becoming a claustrophiliac, retreating more and more to the semi-private spaces around the school: the insufficient library with its five study carrels, the alcove at the end of the long corridor from which hung the calligraphic scroll. Yasuro had deciphered it for him one rainy afternoon: "*Heiwa*—it means 'harmony.'"

"But there are two characters, no?" Though he still couldn't read or write, Cricket had gotten to the stage where he recognized how the language looked.

"Yes," admitted Yasuro. "That first character, it means 'flat.' The second means 'peace.'"

When he was feeling particularly edgy after another Ogawa-san ordeal, he would go to stare at the two characters until he felt peaceful again, or sometimes just flat.

In the late afternoons, he read some of the classic novels he'd always wanted to get to: *Moby Dick*, *Vanity Fair*. He even found time to study Japanese from a little paperback called *Learn Japanese Today!* He also thought of taking up some art like *chadō*, the Japanese tea ceremony, but felt he needed to know more of the language first. The same was true of his writing: at this stage, his journal entries were mostly jottings about Japanese culture, from abacuses to Zen. "From the countable to the infinite," he scribbled, feeling clever for a change.

From time to time, he thought of the person he'd met on the plane coming over, Matthew Harrison—Harrington, something like that. He'd never seen him again and told himself it didn't matter, yet occasionally he had questions that Matthew might be able to answer, mostly about the status of *gaijin*. More often, Matthew was the shadowy Other, the person he needed to measure his own progress—sometimes, like the Cheshire Cat, reduced to just his sardonic smile. But Cricket didn't know how to look him up, and Matthew H. became a gap, an unaccounted-for detail.

Once on his bicycle he thought he saw Matthew rounding the corner toward the pickle seller's, but it turned out to be a false sighting. Maybe he'd gone back to the U.S. by now. Was there really a Matthew, he began to wonder, or had he dreamed the whole scene on the plane? What did it matter if he wasn't around, anyway?—sort of like Berkeley's idea of a table when no one was present to see it. So why did Matthew persist in his not-being-there? He'd just consigned the blond memory to his mental OUT box when he passed a tea shop along one of the narrowest streets in Mikage, with barely room for his handlebars.

And there Matthew was, his long frame bent over a teacup, framed by the tinted glass window of the shop. He was alone, reading a book—just as Cricket remembered him. He didn't look up.

Cricket got off his Sky Lancer, parking it awkwardly in the adjacent alley. The awkwardness traveled with him as he mounted the steps to the tea shop. "*Hajimemashite.*" No, that was for introductions. "Hi, remember me?" Now how would he render that into Japanese? "Look at me, how much I've learned"—that was what he really wanted to say.

No one seemed to be minding the store, so there was no welcoming "*Irasshai!*" Luckily, Matthew noticed his entrance. He inclined his head briefly, Japanese style, as if he'd been waiting for Cricket to show up. "Hello," he pronounced carefully. "You're—"

"Cricket Collins," supplied Cricket helpfully.

"That's right. I remember the name. We sat next to each other on a plane." Matthew didn't snap his book shut, but at least his attention was directed toward him. "So how's Japan treating you?"

In his imagined reunions with Matthew, Cricket had trotted out all his accomplishments, from teaching and writing to studying Japanese. But now, faced with that wan, ironic smile, he shrugged. "Oh, I can't complain."

"Of course not. It's forbidden."

Cricket laughed, realizing with annoyance as he did so that his old chuckle had somehow been transformed into a polite titter.

"Are you still studying the language?" asked Matthew, as if reading his mind. "Your laugh has become Nipponic."

"Maybe I picked it up from my students." He shrugged. "They learn from me. Why shouldn't I learn from them?"

"Good," replied Matthew, somewhat obscurely. "What else do you do besides teach?"

Cricket looked at Matthew's book, but from his angle couldn't make out what it was. "The same as you, I guess. Read a lot, write some. I'm going to start tea ceremony lessons one of these days. Maybe join an aikido class."

"I'm sure you will. That's the pattern." Suddenly Matthew looked absolutely weary, with runnels in his face like a statue left out too long in the rain. "Listen, I've got to go now." And with that he shut his book and stood up. Cricket could now see what the volume was: a collection by Ambrose Bierce.

Once again he felt at a disadvantage, but what could he do? He was thinking up a rude rejoinder when Matthew surprised him. Instead of a perfunctory nod, he reached out to put a hand on Cricket's shoulder. "Look, be careful," he said. "I mean, take care of yourself." And with that, he left. At this point the proprietress, a squat woman who looked as if she'd just arisen from a nap, emerged from behind an alcove to ask tartly if she could help him. Reciting an apology, Cricket bowed and departed. Of course, by then Matthew was nowhere to be seen.

He tried to put the meeting out of his mind, but instead he kept replaying parts of the insufficient conversation. In a way Matthew reminded him of his father, whom he had tried for years to impress and then tried to hurt, not that he would ever consciously admit to either impulse. In any event, Matthew was gone again, as inaccessible as before. When Cricket rode past the same spot the next week, even the tea shop seemed to have disappeared.

Meanwhile, as one of his students had put it in class, life kept living. Unused to the amount of free time on his hands, Cricket unconsciously ordered his habits as a kind of spell against boredom. Even as a child, he'd been encouraged by his mother to pursue solitary but organized hobbies like stamp collecting. Now he read two novels a week and wrote enough letters home to arouse suspicion whether everything was really going as well as he described. But he'd never been that close to his father, whose legalistic wrangling always made him feel as if he were arguing a losing case. Japan had been a questionable venture, opined Mr. Collins, in his precise, squared-off script. Sooner or later Cricket would realize that he was wasting his time and come back home to start a career. He no longer insisted on law school but urged his son to pursue "a real vocation, not just some temp job abroad." Cricket found his father much easier to deal with from afar, expending two sentences to rebut every one of his father's. For some reason, neither thought to pick up a phone to cross the intercontinental divide. This was the patented Collins style of emotional non-avoidance. From time to time, Cricket realized just how alone he was—though he'd always been that way, sort of.

The one social aspect he missed was the company of women and the flirting that goes on even in the most casual of discussions. These days, he had his eyes set on a twenty-year-old student in his class named Kyoko Sakai, who had legs like calipers and a beautifully shy smile. The trouble was, she was so shy that Cricket couldn't even start a conversation with her. When a comment produced so much as a giggle, she clapped her hand over her mouth. Still, he had faith in his staying power. He had the time to persevere.

He also had the time to plot minor insurrections against Ogawa-san, though most had to be discarded for impracticality. He couldn't possibly poison her food or tie her up in the *benjo*, even if he'd wanted to. In his more reflective moments, he realized that Ogawa-san was just being solicitous, but the irritation remained like a crick in his neck. He could always tell when she had been in his room: his slippers would be leaning against the wardrobe at an acute angle, the items on his desk arranged in neat piles. She changed his sheets twice a week, though Cricket found out from Yasuro that once a week was usual.

"I think she like you." Yasuro was eyeing Cricket with amusement as Cricket vented his rage on an imaginary Ogawa-san. "Last teacher, he . . . not so easy. Made big mess." His delicate fingers described a roll of untidy bedclothes. He placed a hand on Cricket's unyielding shoulder. "*Daijōbu*—don't worry. Take time. Ogawa-san learn."

You mean give way, thought Cricket, but he wasn't sure who'd concede first.

He needed to discuss this problem with someone more articulate than Yasuro. It wasn't that Yasuro was unintelligent—Cricket would never equate fluency with intelligence, as Ogawa-san did—but maybe another Westerner would show a more sensitive ear. No other Americans taught at Kanga, but there was one Englishman whom for some reason Cricket had never seen. Mr. Knye was his name, and Cricket tracked him down one day after class. His unnumbered office was at the end of a winding corridor which seemed to have no other purpose than leading up to that room.

"Hello, my name's Cricket Collins," he announced as he knocked to enter. "I'm one of the other English instructors here—I don't know why I never met you."

Mr. Knye, seated at his desk in a tweed jacket with patched elbows, harrumphed a reply. He put down his pipe, an ugly meerschaum with a cracked bowl. "Yes, maybe an oversight. What did you say your name was—Cricket?" Knye regarded him with subtle disdain. "Strange name for an American, eh?"

Cricket mentioned the unhappy origin of his name, but got hardly a smile. When he explained his predicament with

Ogawa-san, all he got was a vague "Well, why don't you talk to the lady?"

"You know," continued Knye, warming to his subject, "I've noticed you Americans often don't adapt very well to other cultures. Try to meet her halfway, I mean." He added something about the habits imperialism breeds, and Cricket heard the voice of a Britisher with a curiously warped sense of history. There was also something strange about his accent that Cricket couldn't identify, as he let the man speak on and on.

Cricket finally lost his patience. "Do you live in the dormitories?"

Knye spread his hands, slightly offended. "Oh, no, definitely not. I have a flat in town. Been here for over twelve years."

Suddenly, Cricket realized the oddity in Knye's speech. He spoke English with a slight Japanese inflection: the *r*'s were curled under his tongue, the *th*'s blending into a subtle hiss. After years of speaking mainly to Japanese, his language had merged with their own. Inadvertently, Knye had done a good job of meeting the Japanese halfway. Cricket wondered whether the man was aware of his inflection, but decided against pointing it out to him. "I enjoyed meeting you," he told Knye, who clearly wanted to get back to his paperwork.

"*Dō itashi*—ah, don't mention it," Knye corrected himself in mid-phrase. As Cricket left him, he was re-lighting his pipe and looking through a manuscript of some sort.

Because of his visit with Knye and a subsequent cup of coffee in a tea shop, Cricket was ten minutes late for dinner. Ogawa-san had spread plastic wrap over his tray and left it on the table. The other students were nearly finished, but they watched the tray with interest, as if it guaranteed Cricket's eventual presence. Kyoko was there, he noticed when he arrived, sitting next to Yasuro. They smiled and bobbed their heads toward him in unison, as if both were threaded on the same string of courtesy.

He fought down a pang of jealousy. It wasn't as if Kyoko were his property, after all. For a moment, he envied Yasuro's adept handling of Japanese. Though Cricket improved each week, he was still confined to the realm of simple questions and answers. Of course, Yasuro *was* Japanese.

Still, being a *gaijin* had certain advantages. The most obvious one was that Japanese women took an interest in him. Kyoko, in fact, interrupted her conversation with Yasuro to ask Cricket, "How are you today?" She watched admiringly as he wielded his chopsticks over a bamboo trencher of *udon*, the fat slippery noodles that reminded him of white worms. He encouraged her broken English by asking her how she spent her day and casually correcting one or two of her frequent mistakes. He was just about to ask her what she was doing tomorrow when Ogawa-san came up behind them. She spoke a few sentences to Yasuro and Kyoko, who giggled a bit. Then she took up a post beside Cricket and waited for him to finish eating.

"What did she say?" Cricket whispered furiously to Yasuro. "What was so funny?"

"Oh, Cricket, it is . . . hard to say. Maybe no word in English. But mostly . . . she say, time for your bath."

Cricket swore softly to himself, and when Ogawa-san tugged gently at his sleeve, he jerked back. "*Watashi wa kodomo ja arimasen.*" It was his own improvisation: "I am not a child." He couldn't tell whether Ogawa-san understood him. In any event, she put on a near-toothless smile and led him down the corridor he knew quite well, showed him for the fiftieth time the lemon soap and the spigot he must use beforehand, and then left him to bathe in peace.

He had to do something about that woman. She was making life impossible.

He came to this conclusion in the overheated *furo-ba*—why did the Japanese take their baths so hot?—while looking at his submerged white body. Against the blue tiles of the square bathtub, he looked like some pale aquatic creature. And why did everyone have to soap and rinse off *before* entering the water? He fingered the island-shaped birthmark on his left buttock, almost like a brown stain. The Japanese were such nuts about cleanliness. The first time he had taken a bath, Ogawa-san had clearly wanted to preside over the proceedings, but he had objected strongly, enough to give her the worried pout that he often saw in his dreams. Some Japanese were so germ-conscious that they wore surgical masks over their faces to prevent getting someone else's cold—or was that to avoid giving someone else *their* cold? In any event, Ogawa-san's fussing was more disturbingly personal than that.

Once, when he was doing his laundry in the tiny washing machine on the second floor, and in his underwear because all his pants were in the wash, she trudged by in her only other type of dress, a functional kimono. When she saw him that way, his disproportionately long legs and big feet made her face split in an amused smile, the expression he had come to know well. Before the smile, though, he thought he'd detected a certain absorption in her look, as if she were undressing him further, and he had felt like snatching a pair of sudsy trousers from the wash to cover himself. Now, seeing his dark brown eyes reflected in the surface of the water, he wondered whether Ogawa-san was sexually attracted to him.

The idea of the stump-legged old woman in love with anyone or anything was unreal to him. Her interest was more studious than lustful—it was hard to pin down, but whatever it was, it interfered with everything he did or wanted to do. If he ever got lucky with Kyoko, for instance, Ogawa-san would undoubtedly be in the room, ready with post-coital disinfectant. It was—*unsupportable*, that was it. (Lately, he had been groping for an occasional term in English. He hoped he wasn't on his way to becoming another Mr. Knye, and he practiced his elocution in the mirror from time to time.) Unsupportable, yes.

Or was it *insupportable*? The heat of the bath eased the stiffness in his neck even as he half-resisted. He lay back against the tiling and flipped rings of water with his thumbs, dreaming up private insurrections.

The first item he stole was a pair of slippers from the rack that Ogawa-san had shown him the first day. The act was mostly unpremeditated: no one else was in the foyer when he wandered by, and the next moment he had the slippers tucked under his belt. He hardly needed an extra pair, but the theft itself made him feel better. The thought of Ogawa-san confronting an unaccountable loss in her dormitory greatly appealed to him. Even if the slippers weren't missed, he had committed an act of defiance.

He wrapped them in a bag and hid it in his unused suitcase. At night, he thought of the purloined slippers and grinned into the darkness.

Meanwhile, his classes were showing definite signs of improvement. Jun the pachinko pro was lobbing new vocabulary at the rest of the class every meeting. The one student with a mustache, who sat behind Yasuro, no longer mangled all his verbs. Kyoko had stopped ending her sentences with "isn't it?" and had started ending them with an alluring smile. Now he was teaching the class the subtleties of where to place modifiers when used in a series. His text was Steinbeck's *Of Mice and Men*. His class-hours weren't too heavy, he had just received a short note and a brusque check from his father, and he was thinking of buying himself a better bicycle. He even greeted Ogawa-san with a big hello in the hallway that morning. She laughed and bowed low.

But that night, as he was eating dinner with Kyoko amid a small group of admiring students, Yasuro mentioned Ogawa-san's name. "She say you have large . . . " here Yasuro flipped through his pocket-dictionary " . . . *collection* of . . . of magazine." Yasuro's diction grew suggestive. "Female magazine, isn't it?"

Cricket grew red, thinking of that harridan pawing through what lay under his desk dictionary. Besides bringing over thirty assorted paperbacks from America, he had also brought a few *Playboy* magazines—"for emergencies," as he mentally tabbed them.

Better to come straight out with it. "Yes, I have some magazines," he told Yasuro breezily. "They're part of American culture. I'll lend them to you if you'd like."

Yasuro betrayed an almost adolescent eagerness. "Oh, yes. Yes, that is fine, thank you." Out of the corner of his eye, Cricket looked at Kyoko to see how she was taking all this, but she had blushed at the phrase "female magazine" and was looking away.

"What do you think of Ogawa-san's story?" He directed his question to Kyoko.

"Me, I cannot say. But Ogawa-san, she . . . *jama*, I think. Obstacle? Too strong?" It might have come across kinder if Kyoko had known more English, but Cricket got the point.

He went back to brood in his room. Ogawa-san had thoughtfully left a tea tray propping his door open. He kicked it aside and slammed the door behind him.

The next day, after he had finished teaching—and brought two issues of *Playboy* to Yasuro in a large brown paper bag—he took all the soap from the *furo-ba*. It was a childish act, done solely for its irritation value: "furor in the *furo-ba*" was how he thought of it. His take was seven lemon-yellow bars, half of which he dumped in a trash can two miles away from the dormitory. Let Ogawa-san stew over that—and maybe he could booby-trap his desk so she wouldn't go through his things anymore.

He got on his bike and pedaled as far from the dormitory as he had ever been, over ten miles away. The suburbs merged with the country. The road turned into a narrower road, and the narrowed road turned into a path, which reached its natural conclusion in a trampling of grass that disappeared into the trees. The fan-shaped leaves of the ginkgoes were larger than those of the ornamental flora at school. Here they formed a fertile green-yellow bower that arched in the breeze. Cricket got off his bicycle and walked into the woods, where the faint path ended in a tiny brook. The sound of *kōrogi*, like little rasping violins, came from some source invisibly near.

There was somebody by the brook. A small boy lay in the grass, his head on a rock, staring at a near-leafless bamboo stalk which swayed in the wind. Cricket shivered at the sight and sat down ten yards away on another rock. The boy looked up, but neither person said a word. For once, Cricket was glad of the rustling silence in place of deformed English. The boy was entirely absorbed in watching the bamboo, though Cricket imagined an odd affinity with him. An hour passed that way, the boy watching his personal vision and Cricket wondering whether he should leave. Eventually, as it was growing dark, Cricket picked himself up and walked back to his bicycle. He ate a late, quiet dinner and spent the rest of the evening in his room.

Ogawa-san made no mention of the missing soap, and Yasuro returned the magazines a day later with embarrassed thanks, as if overwhelmed by the abundance of sex. Unaccountably, Cricket felt homesick, and that night, he wrote a long letter to his Sofie, his all-too-brief girlfriend. She had taken him in, uplifted him, and humiliated him all in one week, and he would never forget the experience. At the moment, he felt tender toward her. "I wish you could come to Japan," he began. "I think you'd like it here—and besides, I miss you at night." In the morning, he ripped up the letter and scattered Ogawa-san's dried tea all down the hall. He entered his class in a state of resentment.

"Mr. Sasaki, the word is *told*, not *tell*. Past tense. You must speak proper English. I cannot correct your mistakes forever." He looked over their thoughtful faces and saw how ridiculous he was being, but he couldn't help himself. His loneliness masked itself as anger.

Kyoko saw him after class, and for once she made the first move. She touched his shoulder as if exploring a promontory. "Cricket-san . . . something wrong, *ne?*"

"No. Yes. I'm tired, that's all." He reached out for her hand. "Listen, do you want to go for a drink somewhere? Anywhere."

But Kyoko shook her head slightly, her eyes sympathetic. "I am sorry, but I meet someone else. Nomura-san."

Yasuro? He asked her to repeat the name, just to be sure. He nodded, and walked back to his room alone. What an odd relationship Yasuro and Kyoko must have, their intimacy completely submerged in public. Cricket, he thought, you indiscreet American. He decided to exile himself in his room.

In front of his door was the usual tea tray, and on a nearby table someone had left a lacquered pair of chopsticks. Not the double sticks of wood that split down the middle: these were polished a deep ebony, with a trace of inlay down the side. Almost without thinking, Cricket pocketed them. A few minutes later there was a knock at the door.

It was Ogawa-san, and he felt the chopsticks in his back pocket as if they protruded a foot above his head. Maybe they were her personal chopsticks, or maybe she had just seen him take them and was going to report him—to whom? Ogawa-san ran the place.

All she wanted, it turned out, was to ask whether he was feeling *byōki*, sick. He hadn't eaten any lunch, and she must have seen his tray. Now she held out an orange to him, saying in her familiar singsong voice, "Eat, please. Get . . . better."

Cricket might have been touched by the solicitude, but he chose to be annoyed instead. "*Ato de*," he said firmly, and laid the orange down on his desk. "*Watashi wa . . .* " he had forgotten the word, damn it " . . . not hungry." He pointed to his stomach and drew a balloon. Couldn't she ever leave him alone?

Apparently not. That evening, as if to make up for the uneaten orange, she led the protesting Cricket to the *furo-ba*, where she ran the water extra hot. If anyone else had subjected him to that kind of treatment, he would have thought of ten different ways to resist, but she seemed to exercise some strange hold over him. Also, despite her diminutive stature and foolish English, he knew she was an important woman. "Twenty years she run this dormitory," Yasuro had informed him. "She never make mistake." She could also probably have him tossed out, a thought that excited him whenever he considered his next theft.

He stole a set of teacups next, and the sash from Ogawa-san's own kimono, daringly plucked when it lay draped over a stool one day. Everything went into the suitcase in the closet.

He no longer had his gaze on Kyoko. He had recently met an English girl at a bookstore in Umeda, a brown-haired vision with green-blue eyes. The sheer novelty of the combination made him realize how immersed he had been. Her name was Jill, and she had asked him what a particular Japanese word meant when the dictionary was right at hand. He loved her waist-length brown hair and her Liverpool accent, which spoke to him of fish and chips and the Beatles. She was also teaching English, and he had promised to give her a call. He did call, and they went out a few times, and then he invited her to his room.

Ogawa-san wouldn't allow a woman in his room.

He stormed up and down the corridor, unable to move the disapproving figure in front of his door, while Jill stood slightly apart and said, "Listen, Cricket, maybe this is a bad idea. I'll just leave."

"No! She's been interfering ever since I got here!" He didn't care whether Ogawa-san understood what he said.

Jill came up to him. "You're a sweet boy, really, but you don't understood these old Japanese women. They never let go." She touched his cheek with a fingertip. Her soft hair grazed his shoulder. "Look, it isn't the end of the world. I'll give you a call. Okay?" And before he could come up with an answer, she was gone.

Ogawa-san gave him a short lecture in simple vocabulary, but he pretended he didn't understand any Japanese. He dreamed that night of laying waste to an entire army of Ogawa-sans with a sharpened ebony chopstick. For each corpse, he won an orange, which he sent home to his father, who ruled them admissible evidence. He awoke the next morning sated with vengeance, then remembered it was just a dream.

Outside it was raining hard, which meant that he couldn't go bicycling. The room was flooded with a grayness that wouldn't go away. He needed something to cheer him up. As he approached a turn in the downstairs corridor, into the women's section, he heard a transistor radio playing. He slowed his pace and poked his head around the corner to see who was listening.

It was a girl from his class who usually wore black-mesh stockings and a simper. Now she was listening to a Japanese pop singer croon lyrics whose meaning Cricket couldn't catch. Her door was open, the music invading the hall. Whatever work she was doing at her desk gave her trouble, because soon she sighed, got up, and walked down the hall to the vending machines. A slippered thief, Cricket scuttled into her room and was out in a second with the radio under his arm.

He was just shoving it under his sweater when Ogawa-san appeared at the same corner where he had been watching.

In an unmistakable gesture, she held out her hand for the radio. Completely numb, Cricket handed it over, wondering what would happen to him. He saw himself sent home in disgrace, his term unfinished, his father both pleased and disgusted, the prospect of a job dim and hopeless—all because of a stupid radio. Should he beg Ogawa-san to be lenient? Should he try to beat her up and run for it? Now she was lecturing him, though all he understood was the word *haji*, shame.

The girl returned with a Coke in her hand, surprised to see the two in the hall, and even more surprised to see Ogawa-san holding her radio. Ogawa-san turned toward her, but with a different expression. When the girl asked a question, Ogawa-san cut her off with a flurry of Japanese. She spoke so fast that Cricket caught none of it, but soon the girl was laughing, and Ogawa-san was also smiling. She patted Cricket on the head as if he were a little boy and made another reference he couldn't understand. Then she handed back the radio and, pulling his sleeve, walked Cricket back upstairs.

The sudden withdrawal from catastrophe kept him from talking. He let himself be led back to his room, grateful but confused. Why had she bothered saving him? What the hell had she said to the girl? Ogawa-san marched him to his door and motioned him inside.

"Bad boy. Bad." She shook her finger at him, looking so sad that he almost felt sorry for her rather than for himself. She drew back the sheets and motioned for him to take off his shirt and pants. She patted her breast, and suddenly he found the word he was looking for: *okaa-san*, mother. The word tasted bad in his mouth and he wanted to spit it out, but it swelled up and constricted his throat. From the end of the bed, Ogawa-san watched him with stern, patient eyes.

She made him lie down as if he were sick, and in a while she brought him tea and a *sembei*, a rice-cracker. "Lesson, you know . . . cancel. Rest now. *Byōki*, sick." She shook her head obliquely, and Cricket had a vision of Ogawa-san forever ministering to him in his room, bringing him hot tea and rice as he languished there. She was wearing her faded gray skirt and looked formidable, encompassing everything around her. She knew he was a thief, and now he needed her protection.

When finally she left, he unwrapped the *sembei* from its paper. He wasn't going to eat it at first, but he hadn't had any breakfast, so he ended up making two bites of it and washing it down with green tea. He really did feel sick now, as if some virus had invaded his system. Afterwards, he walked over to the window and raised the blinds. It had stopped raining, and a steady wind was blowing the mist away. It was fifteen feet to the ground, a plausible distance to jump, but he was past that now. Slowly, he uncrumpled the *sembei* wrapper and let it fly out the window. It caught the stiff breeze like a sail, at first soaring upwards, then dipping and darting above the pavement. It was like an insect being driven by a human breath, pushed faster and faster by an invisible source. Cricket prayed silently, and it was almost half a minute before it hit the ground.

3. A Night in Korea

It was already past eight in the evening, but still the citizens of Pusan were hurrying home, carrying bundles wrapped in old newspaper or riding ancient bicycles with pipe-tube racks in back, piled high with anything from flattened cardboard boxes to two other Koreans. When the cyclists rang their bells to warn pedestrians, they sounded for long intervals, like faraway phones. From the seedy lobby of the Wang Hotel, Cricket watched one cyclist turn a corner with two huge cartons of toilet paper, nearly colliding with a truck coming the other way. But the cyclist imperturbably swerved as the truck rumbled on oblivious, carrying its load of rusted engines to God knew where.

Since arriving in Pusan, Cricket had noticed that the Koreans seemed to use all objects to destruction. A bent bicycle wheel metamorphosed into a café table-top, the table was cut up to make some sort of metal containers, and the containers were eventually flattened and stacked for scrap. The bus and train tickets all had the milky-gray look of reclaimed newspaper.

Even the people looked reconstituted, as if assembled from some giant vat of parts beyond the city limit. Koreans tended to have broader faces than Japanese, as well as more muscular physiques. Compared to Osaka's well-scrubbed exteriors, from storefronts to foreheads, Pusan's façades were hardened with experience. What they wore also looked poorer, faded dresses and overalls patched and pieced together. The Japanese, on the other hand, seemed to throw everything out that wasn't a valuable antique. Depending on his mood, Cricket found the differences either gloomy or intriguing. Just now, the use and re-use amidst all the deterioration depressed him, and he looked away from the street. He was just waiting for the moment to pass, anyway. He felt like the only stable point in a moving landscape.

The woman who ran the hotel pulled at his sleeve, the way they all seemed to do to get one's attention. "Hello, hello. You sleep tonight, yes?" She tilted her head on her hands to imitate slumber. She couldn't have been more than forty-five or so, but she had the same recycled look of the bicycles and the scarred sidewalk trees. There was an odd tilt to her shoulders, as if a giant hand had patted her too hard on the back. Her eyes were ringed with blue eye shadow, which crinkled harshly around the edges when she laughed. "Korea pretty—*kirei*, eh? Mama-san know, *daijōbu*."

Mama-san, as he'd been told by the girl who cleaned his room, spoke little English and less Japanese. When she talked to him, it came out as a jerky combination of both, accompanied by emphatic gestures. She was such a contrast to the last house-mother he'd endured, Ogawa-san at the Kansai Gakuin dormitory, that he couldn't help marveling. Ogawa-san in her starched kimono was all stern spirit, whereas Mama-san wearing orange stretch pants was the flesh incarnate. Now she pulled him by the sleeve to the hallway telephone and sat him down in a straw-slatted chair. She spread her wide legs and sat down on the table next to him. When she laughed, she showed her gold teeth—which might have been a status symbol in Korea, for all he knew. She patted his knee, letting her hand stray to his thigh. Making a circle with one thumb and forefinger, she thrust her other thumb through it. "You like, eh? *Ichi man en.*" She held up her thumb: ten thousand Japanese yen for an unspecified sexual act.

Cricket leaned forward, finally coming to life. He knew the reputation of this area in Pusan, and in fact he'd brought along twice that amount of money for just that purpose. His motive was cloudy, half horniness and half Western curiosity about the East. Though he'd been working up his courage to ask, now the offer was thrust on him. Reaching into his pocket, he counted about fifteen thousand yen and a few thousand *won*. That was all he had left after bargaining for a flock of cheap shirts that afternoon. Should he haggle for this, too? He held his hand above his head. "*Takai.*"

Mama-san disagreed, pulling at his sleeve again as she picked up the phone receiver with the other hand. "*Yasui*, cheap." The girl who cleaned the rooms came down the hallway at this point. She glided rather than walked, like a somnambulist on skates, but she was awake enough, and Mama-san began talking to her in rapid Korean. Having spent four months learning Japanese, Cricket felt no obligation to another language, but wished he could at least catch a phrase or two. A lot of foreigners went to Pusan when visa regulations dictated they leave and re-enter Japan. It was one way of prolonging a tourist visa.

In Cricket's case, he'd forfeited his work-visa by losing his job at Kansai Gakuin after only one semester. Luckily, he'd found another sponsor soon enough, a large firm in downtown Osaka called TESCO that needed more Americans for its business-English seminars. Being rewarded for speaking English still seemed odd to him, and he suspected that more and more

Anglophones were on their way to Japan for just that reason. In the meantime, as he'd heard so many sports figures tell newscasters, he was "just happy to be here." Only here wasn't there yet. In two days, he'd be going back to Osaka after obtaining his new work-visa, and he didn't anticipate a return visit. Because he knew he'd be leaving, and without traces, he was more excited than nervous. He broke in with a question.

"*Kirei desu-ka?* Pretty?"

"Ah, ah, *sō.*" Mama-san's hands described an improbable hourglass figure, the curve swelling at the breast-line. "Big, big."

The cleaning girl explained in Japanese, most of which he could follow, that a Korean mother and an absent American father were the source. She shifted to English. "Friend of Mama-san's, twenty-five old, right for you," she said, but the hallway was dark and it was hard to read her expression.

Cricket nodded in the precise Japanese manner he'd acquired, all the while feeling in his pocket for the money. His passport and plane ticket to Japan were upstairs in his zipped bag, but he worried about theft. Yet another side of him wanted to be taken for all he was worth, to be seduced and abandoned, left anonymous. Would they discover him on an unrecyclable ash heap out back, his underwear pulled down to his ankles? He shivered slightly.

He snapped out of his reverie when Mama-san pinched his thigh. "I have Japanese money only," he told her. He held out his ten-thousand-yen note as flat as if it were on a collection plate.

"Ah, okay, *daijōbu.*" Mama-san nodded vigorously and fished in her apron for a wad of *won* notes. She tweaked away his bill and counted out thirty thousand *won*, which was only a little worse than the official exchange rate. The notes made an uncomfortably stiff bulge in his pocket, like some lucrative erection. Soon Mama-san got up to check the front desk, while the cleaning girl glided away to make some barley tea in the tiny kitchen down the hall.

Cricket sat there, unsure whether to bolt or sit still. The cleaning girl returned with a mug of tea on a coaster with the hotel's name on it. Since she offered, he accepted it, though the barley tea he'd drunk in Japan always tasted like a bouillon of wet cigarette butts, and the Korean version didn't seem much different. Finding a bonsai pine tree on the nearby table, he dumped his tea the way a non-drinker surreptitiously waters the potted plant with his scotch. Absent-mindedly, he slipped the coaster into his pocket and stared at the map-like crack in the ceiling.

Celibate for over a year and a half, he was usually content with fantasies. His hands were well-practiced mistresses. Having bargained for a woman, he now felt oddly priggish. At least he hadn't paid for anything yet, but this was no dream he was getting into. Experimentally, he pinched his own thigh, the muscles rigid from bicycling every day. The pinch turned into a light massage, his hands traveling up and down his legs, as if half of him were another person.

Outside, the night sky had turned into slate roofing, suggesting that something lay beyond the roof, but no stars showed. The brass clock at the front desk was crawling toward nine. With a sudden belch, the ghost of his dinner came back to him, a mélange of noodles and short ribs, ringed around with saucers of kimchi, the ubiquitous Korean pickles bathed in red pepper and garlic. Like the Japanese, the Koreans seemed to pickle anything and everything, from cabbage to seaweed and even live skinned eels, which Cricket had seen in the marketplace, writhing in a plastic bag smeared inside with red paste. In fact, the whole city of Pusan smelled of red pepper, hanging around the buildings like a haze to lend a little warmth. Compared to Japan and its silken politeness, Korea seemed a colder, crueler society, with steel chopsticks in place of the break-apart wooden ones he knew in Osaka.

He soon got tired of waiting and began to prowl the hotel corridors. Near the second-story landing, three squat Koreans were preparing to bed down on yellow plastic matting, crosshatched in imitation of real tatami. He thought of his own room upstairs, with a queen-size bed, a private bathroom, and a television set that looked like a relic from the 1950's. Tomorrow, tomorrow, it would all be over tomorrow, when he'd return to Osaka to start his new job. TESCO had hired him to teach corporate executives, to lecture in a jacket and tie at eight in the morning. He had already bought five shirts and five ties in expectation of his first class, which began on Monday. But tonight was Friday, and already friendly drunken calls could be heard out on the street. When he looked back to the room with the yellow matting, he saw the cleaning girl reaching behind her back to loosen her bra as she entered the room. She didn't come out again.

Soon the husky Korean who functioned as a bouncer at the front desk came upstairs, flanked by a solid girl in a denim jacket over a black leotard. She passed without a word, barely looking at him. Pausing at the hall mirror, she checked her appearance, combing back her smooth shoulder-length black hair. When Mama-san returned, happy as a matchmaker, she pulled the girl toward him. With a broad wink, she repeated a few words of Korean to the girl, who looked expressionless. "Your room, *heya, heya.*" Mama-san held them both by their sleeves as she walked them upstairs, marching them down the green baize corridor to his room on the fourth floor. She plucked the oversized key poking out from his pocket, opened the door, and followed them both in.

"*O-kane*, now." Mama-san counted invisible money with thumb and forefinger, and suddenly Cricket realized with wonder that he was going to go through with it. He took out the stack of *won* notes and began to count through them all, but Mama-san stopped him at twenty. "Okay, okay. *Kirei*, eh, pretty?" Her nimble fingers made another gesture, thumb through curled forefinger and middle finger, as if playing with variations on an old, old theme. Counting the money once more, smiling maternally, she closed the door firmly.

He was left alone with the girl, who sat down in the only seat the room offered, a faded pink-and-white armchair without arms. He perched on the sagging bed, his legs crossing and re-crossing. Neither said a word.

At first, to break the silence, he tried speaking Japanese to her. He asked her how old she was, and she said twenty-two. "That's how old *I* am," he told her. She smiled but said nothing. When he asked what her job was, though, and whether she was sleepy, she said she didn't speak Japanese.

"Me father American." She pointed to her belly, its trampoline tightness accentuated by the second skin of the leotard. "Korean mother."

"*Sō desu ne.*" For at least a few minutes, he kept replying in Japanese, though it was clear that her nods didn't indicate comprehension. Me father American, too, he felt like saying. Dead mother. Actually, she didn't seem to care whether he was getting through. She just sat there, waiting for him to do something.

When he edged nearer, she didn't move. She looked at herself in the mirror and unwound a bandage that covered the tip of her finger. After inspecting the wound, a tiny red gash, she wrapped it up again. She did this several times. It wasn't the thought of the money spent, but the idea of a wasted night, that eventually made him reach out for her. She made no resistance but didn't help, either, so that he practically had to haul her onto the bed. She was unwieldy with a muscular heaviness, her arms thicker than his, but with her half-cooperation, he managed to get her in some semblance of the right position. On the other side of the room, separated by a distance of two years, sat the memory of Sofie, who with her slim hands had led him completely. Those tapered thighs, rising to meet him . . . . When he turned to look at her, she had been replaced by Matthew, the enigma he would never catch up to. Matthew's mocking expression indicated that he'd gone this route before and done better. Christ, was everyone going to judge him?

He shut his eyes and started kissing the back of the girl's neck, his lips brushing against her coarse hair as his hands slid up and down her shoulders in exploration. Was it Peter Inoue who'd told him that Asians considered the nape the sexiest area of the body? Hers was ridged with a thick tendon, which pulsed lightly when he experimentally licked it. A slight taste of salt. No red pepper. She was his for the night, wasn't she? But when his hands cupped the hard jut of her breasts, she sat up abruptly.

"Take shower first." Was this an echo of Ogawa-san, yet another shade hidden somewhere in this cramped hotel room? In any event, the woman didn't wait for an answer. Strolling to the bathroom, she turned on the overhead hot-water spigot and came back to sit on the chair. Cricket perched on the bed again, wondering what the etiquette was in these situations. He thought that washing was probably a good idea. Bowing absurdly, he stripped down to his underwear in front of her, taking off the last item in the bathroom. He soaped himself liberally with an orange bar that smelled suspiciously of red pepper, making sploochy sounds to reassure her of his presence. A few minutes later, he re-emerged in his underwear again to find her brushing her teeth over the wastebasket.

He took out his own toothbrush from his bag (first feeling for the thin envelope with his passport and return ticket), and she smiled for the second time that night. Her mouth seemed too small for the amount of teeth it contained, like the enigma of a fully rigged ship in a bottle. But the smile brought him to tenderness. He thought of the two of them sitting by the mirror, brushing their teeth together for a while as a prelude to getting to know each other. Maybe they could compare cavities.

"I take shower now." And she ran the water again. Her jeans came off with a whuff of air, and her leotard top peeled upward to obliterate her face temporarily as he watched with what he fancied was clinical detachment. The curve of her buttocks was almost boyish, her bra cups padded and wired. But her thighs were wide and womanly, narrowing to firm calves and slim ankles. Her entire body had a hard sheen to it, as if waxed and buffed in some way. It was the sex-doll look of Oriental stereotypes, toughened for the street. While she was in the bathroom, he inspected his own body in the wall-mirror, flexing his biceps and stretching his legs. He'd always felt short, though not by Asian standards, and in this mirror he had to bend over to see all of himself. Was he worthy? When she came back into the room, his towel wrapped around her body, she found him spread-eagled on the bed, having just touched his toes five times. A strange mood was coming on, and he felt he had to exorcise it.

She walked over to her night-bag on the table and took out a pink pill wrapped in plastic. "Are you sick?" he asked idiotically, but she only shook her head, and he never found out if the pill was for a cold, birth-control, or getting high.

Then she did something with the light switch, and instead of the light going out completely, a dim halo remained from the one low-wattage bulb in the center of the fluorescent ring. Under this weak yellow illumination, she lay down on the bed and pulled away the towel. The dim reflection from her body all seemed drawn into the furred blackness between her legs. She lay perfectly still, eyes closed, legs open, smiling.

When he reached across her chest, she yielded only slightly. He had to use his arm as a lever to force her body sideways, to press her against himself. Her nakedness gave off no heat at all, and for one dazed instant he suspected he was making love to a mannequin. When his underwear brushed against her pelvis, he reached down shakily to remove it, finished taking off the brief with his foot, and dropped it with his big toe so that it fluttered to the floor like a broken-winged bird. He began running his hands all over her smooth skin.

He started lightly over the broad shoulders, then swept down to her breasts, which suddenly felt surprisingly soft, shifting when he touched them as if a breeze fluttered over the surface. His caressing hands moved past her taut belly, down to the fuzzy beginnings of her pubic hair, where his hands hesitated. Each five fingers crouched like an uncertain mule, with the middle finger as the head, bent upwards to look around. The surface above her vagina was hard and muscled, and when he found her opening, he parted the lips like a spelunker entering a cave without a lantern. He lingered for a moment, then ran his fingers all the way around to her buttocks, and still she made no move: eyes closed, hands at her side, no emotion except for that vague smile she held. Her flesh remained cool and undisturbed.

Sofie *tsk-tsk*ed from the armless armchair.

Didn't your mother teach you anything? said nobody in particular.

Foreplay, he thought blurrily, and began with a peck on the girl's cheek. When he kissed her on the lips, which she didn't seem to like, she smelled of something more acrid than tobacco. His lips moved to her neck, then to her left breast, where he sucked hard at the dark brown areola until his mouth was full of puckery softness. Whether she enjoyed it was impossible to tell. Occasionally, she stirred and sighed, but that might have been from restlessness. His lips traveled down her belly, past the saucer-shaped navel, to the fuzzy vee between her thighs. He licked around a bit, catlike, finally inserting his tongue inside: sweat, fish, and something muskier than both.

He tongued her for a minute, trying to drive himself into the deepest part of her anatomy, but still she showed no particular reaction. She opened her thighs to let him get his head between them, but that was it. He wanted her to be weak with pleasure by now. One of his recurrent fantasies, nurtured over the years, was of a strong-legged woman thrashing about, thighs against his neck, as he drove her to a high-pitched wail. This reality was too compliant, and everything was so damned quiet. Someone before him had sucked all the sound away.

Finally he gave up on cunnilingus. Damn, she was supposed to be doing this for him—though he couldn't have asked even if they'd lain there a week. Cold Cricket, Sofie had called him. You just can't open up. And she'd showed him how she could. All right, so it was different for a woman. By now, his erection was beginning to twist under him like a curved scimitar. He raised himself so that his body lay on top and tried to fit his penis in. But he kept missing the spot and for one awful instant thought she had somehow retracted everything. He bent himself like a hook in trying. After several of his attempts, she felt along his thigh to his groin, her hand hard and knowing, and pulled him downward. When she had him safely inside, she pulled back, tightening her thighs.

She set her own rhythm by arching her back. His erection was harder than it had ever been, and he felt that about ten more strokes would do it. He mouthed her breasts, clutched at her buttocks, drove home—

It was no good. After five minutes, he was still at the same tumescent state, unable to get more sensation from the slick walls that brushed against him. In and out, like some dumb piston—it was like work. After over a hundred strokes, he felt how absurd he must look to anyone observing the scene. He looked around just in case.

Standing in the corner, dressed in Ogawa-san's kimono, Sofie folded her arms, clucking her tongue. The same thing had happened with her, an erection without an ejaculation. She had stroked him thoughtfully, told him it didn't matter.

It did so.

Now the girl urged him on by undulating her hips, her strong arms pressing and slackening against his back to increase his thrust. It was no use. He just couldn't get the same motion, the same excitement, as when he masturbated to the vision of a dozen houris, holding him against themselves until they fainted from ecstasy or half-suffocated him against their pneumatic busts. He tried squeezing his face between her breasts, but there was no danger of encompassment, just acquiescence.

After a while he paused, still inside her. She said nothing but stopped arching her back. Imbedded in her, he felt utterly futile. The yellow overhead light made a grotesque shadow of their bodies, and he couldn't help noticing a small cockroach scuttling across the carpet. Instead of romantic sexual visions, he saw his buttocks in the mirror on the wall. They were athletic-looking, at least, which cheered him on to try again.

This time, she gently nudged his thighs together with her knees, then braced her legs against his like a crab. Squeezed tight, he felt titillation rising—but again the same thing happened. After about thirty strokes, bringing him halfway to orgasm, silly myths began to crowd his mind, and he thought about how all prostitutes were supposed to be frigid, and he wondered whether he should have worn a condom to avoid disease. Could you get venereal disease on your tongue? Every time he pressed against her, his excitement gave way to an overseeing vision of how they must look, and how he needed help to perform one of the commonest human functions. The next time he peeked over his shoulder, he saw his own reflection judging him, and that defeated him utterly.

After he failed a second time, she waited quite a while. "I'm—I'm sorry," he whispered. "These things sometimes happen." He tried to sound authoritative, as though it were a tooth that might have to come out, an unfortunate but necessary event.

"What." The girl kept her eyes closed as if she hadn't understood him, which was possible, but after five minutes of disengagement, she rose from her position and turned him on his back.

They tried it with her on top, her hips swiveling around his upright penis like greasing a maypole. The weight of her bearing down on him helped to increase the excitement, making him feel like a real stud. But the vision was too distant from the silent female above him, and after five more minutes, he tapped her on the back to indicate he'd had enough. She tried a little longer and then got off him. Reaching back to where Mama-san had left a roll of toilet paper, she tore off a piece and thrust it between her legs. He also ripped off some and swabbed himself. Two crumpled balls of toilet paper sailed like puffballs over the side of the bed. Was this how Yasuro and Kyoko, the one couple he'd known at Kanga, ended their consummation? The Japanese were always so sanitary; perhaps they simply didn't leak.

When the girl resumed her immobility, he simply lay beside her, wondering what to do. Should he take out the ginseng extract he'd bought earlier in the day? On the way to the hotel, he'd counted almost thirty herbal shops, selling everything from pickled ginseng and dried tea to ginseng jerky and giant blanched roots like fetuses in bell jars. The one store he'd entered was presided over by a mammoth woman who sized him up instantly and handed him a pamphlet in bad English:

> GINSENG, the shining way—
> ** to promote best health
> ** cure gallstones and backacke
> ** increese potency

The list of problems for which ginseng was the solution continued for over a page. After a look around, he purchased the cheapest option, a foil packet of ginseng extract, and stuffed it into his pocket. Of course, he didn't believe any of that nonsense. But (and here he heard his mother) it couldn't hurt.

No. Not now. Floating near the ceiling, Ogawa-san gave him one of her troubled looks.

When the girl glanced at her watch by the bedside, he thought she might be leaving soon, but all she did was pull up the covers to her breasts. Two bodies lying in state. He couldn't stand it any longer. Closing his hand around his penis, which still throbbed, he began stroking himself hard. Three ballerinas filled his mind, around him, under him, on top of him, pressing, pulling, squeezing—until a thin jet of semen came out. He wanted it to splatter on her breasts, but it only dripped viscously on the sheet, and she watched as one might peer at a curiosity in a zoo. Sticky creature.

Even as humiliation weighed him down, some impulse higher up goaded him to action. He had failed, so he had to atone somehow. He had no idea what he would say if she understood his language, but in a way that was a relief. In a little while, she got up, but just to wrap the towel around herself again—his towel, he couldn't help noticing. When he dared to touch her, she tolerated his fingers anywhere but under the towel. Had he exceeded his limit or something?

He fell back against his pillow, wondering whether seduction was always this hard. He wondered what her American father was like—some bull-chested G.I. from the Korean War, maybe, who decided to stay after everyone else had left. Did she even have an American father? What the hell did it matter, anyhow?

The girl yawned, sat up, and turned on the television. Half the stations were impossibly fuzzy, but finally she settled on an adventure series. The main character was a man who knew jujitsu and could stop bullets by deflecting them in mid-flight with his hands. The plot was impossible to follow, but a British spy and a beautiful girl kept chasing him everywhere. Finally, they managed to shoot him by skimming a bowler hat towards him at the same time the girl pumped bullets at his chest. He couldn't see both at the same time and had his mind on the hat. He fell to the ground, and that was the end of that night's episode. At least the rising action ended in a climax, thought Cricket—was it as good for him as it was for me? Yet something in the tone of the closing music made him realize that the jujitsu man had been the bad guy all along. In America, he couldn't help thinking, it would have been the reverse: good guys were always chased. Or was it chaste?

After the program ended, the screen inexplicably turned to snow, but the girl kept the television on. She twisted and untwisted her bandage. Cricket reached out to stroke her hair—she had put some strange vanilla scent on it after taking her shower—using slow, small motions to push her bangs gradually back from her forehead. With his forefinger, he pushed one fragrant lock away, then another, smoothing the surface in what he hoped was a relaxing way. With his other hand, he delicately traced the outline of her eyebrows, her wide sockets, and the bridge of her nose. He circled once around her full lips and cupped her chin, then gently massaged her temples.

"Are you sleepy now?"

She shook her head. But when he looked into her opaque eyes, all of a sudden he saw an uncontrollable tremble. A flicker and they were back to normal. How much she must be concealing, he thought, half-angry at the imposture, half-pleased that they functioned on the same level.

He went back to smoothing her hair, and eventually she yawned. She rose once more, to put her pillow under her knees. He had seen long-distance runners do that, to ease the flow of blood from their legs. He thought of how tired her legs must be from walking the streets, or maybe just spreading her thighs all the time. Suddenly he felt quite tender towards her, and he especially wanted to erase any thought left of his failure. So he added his own pillow to help prop up her legs, and walked on his knees over to her feet.

Lightly pummeling her insoles, he pressed down on each toe in turn—the balls of her feet were rough as sandpaper. He rested them against his chest as he worked upwards, kneading her calves. The last time he had done this was with Sofie, and before that with his mother, lying in pain on what would become her deathbed. He bit his lip at the recollection and almost stopped.

He began to concoct another fantasy. The girl's knees were bony and slightly twisted, as if someone—her angry American father?—had kicked her downstairs one day, for refusing to go to bed with him. So she hobbled away and never learned how to speak proper English, he thought, as he worked his way upward to her thighs. Smooth, thickening poles, two hairless tanned expanses like a fleshy desert with a lush oasis in the middle. But he felt workmanlike, felt he was doing good.

When he finished, she was asleep or at least looked it. Gently stealing his pillow from under her, he crawled back to his side of the bed. His last vision was of her sitting up in bed to check her watch again, examining the dial, which had a Korean cartoon dog on the face. The dog moved about as if confined within the crystal, and when the girl looked up, her eyes were as luminous as the watch. He looked right through her, but after that she clouded up and whiteness settled over everything.

Misty creatures emerged from the bed, bowed elaborately, and whispered in his ear that they didn't know who he was. The British girl he'd tried to sleep with, Jill-something, pushed him from behind—into the waiting arms of Ogawa-san, who nursed him at her breast. When he finally fought free, he had to dodge a fusillade of bullets and hats as Matthew the Mystery *Gaijin* scowled magnificently from above. The cloud creatures clapped and cheered at Cricket's giant erection, but when he looked up they had all gone. A toy plane shot through the blue air.

And then it was morning, the sunlight streaming through the crooked venetian blinds, the girl asleep by his side. He picked up her watch, the cross-eyed dog pawing at ten after seven. He played with the watch until she sat up and stretched oddly: latitudinally. After allowing herself that one luxuriant motion, the rest of her actions were quick. She got up, put on her underwear and jeans, fitting on her bra with a wriggle and a shake. Her clothes pinched her in again, made her look smaller. He opened his mouth to say something but had forgotten the Korean for "good morning." When he tried a grin, she shook her head and reached out to clamp his jaw shut.

She fixed her hair as he wandered into the bathroom, brushing his teeth and tongue to get rid of the taste of her. He just wished that she would say something, or that he had the nerve to say something, but there was no momentum left in the situation. He half-hoped she would miss him because he had been so tender to her, though she might just go down to Mama-san and say with a laugh that the American couldn't perform at all last night. God, he hoped she wouldn't do that. Did she expect a gift? She said nothing.

Outside, across the street, eight Koreans in loose white shorts were playing tennis like people spooning up fluff balls. They would stand in the middle of the courts and glide back and forth as if on runners, only to miss most of their shots with their slow, relaxed swings. They looked so comical that at first Cricket thought he might still be dreaming, but no, the sunlight was too penetrating. Just outside the courts, three soldiers were waiting by a bus stop. But after the bus came by, they were still there, waiting.

The girl had finished brushing her teeth, dressing, and combing her hair. In an oddly lilting voice, she said, "I go home now." Then she turned and left. No kiss, no goodbye, which surprised him, though he'd told himself not to expect anything. Maybe he had deserved more, but what? A final embrace, a keepsake? His fingers strayed to his trousers and found the hotel coaster he'd pocketed the night before.

The door closed behind her with a catch just as he managed to haul up the one phrase he was sure of in Korean, *komp sŭm-*

nida. "thank you." He stared at the door for a long time, as if memorizing its position. When he finally thought to move to the window, to catch sight of her leaving, the street was deserted. The tennis players had all left the courts. Only the sun continued to slant idiotically through the window.

He looked at himself in the mirror and thought, what a waste, what a waste, though it wasn't clear in his mind what had been wasted, other than one night in Korea. This would be one of the blanks in his journal. Still eyeing himself in the mirror, he took a deep breath, expanding his chest and extending his legs. His quadriceps tensed, his calves jutting with muscle. What was a waste? Nothing should be allowed to go to waste. He positioned himself by the window, bare feet straddling the faded blue rug. *Mens sana in corpore sano.* Never mind his mind. *Karada ni taisetsu shite*—take care of the body. Was it Kyoko who'd taught him that, or Ogawa-san? Somehow he had to get rid of these interfering voices, the faces that peered down at him. Slowly, rhythmically, gradually building up speed, he began to do jumping jacks, the city of Pusan rising and falling with each leap, and he didn't stop until he hit one hundred.

4. Learning the Language

After the first few months in Japan, Cricket underwent a sea change and reformed his sedentary habits. Something piquant in the air got him up at seven to do morning exercises before breakfast, accompanied by Japanese pop music on the radio. *"Kimi ni wa, kimi no yume ga ari. Boku ni wa, boku no yume ga ari"*: "You, you have your dream. Me, I have mine." He thought the sentiment meant something, despite living in what one of his new co-workers referred to sarcastically as the Land of Rising Conformity. He believed in new beginnings—hadn't he benefited from one himself? After his abrupt dive from Kansai Gakuin, the TESCO people were like a large, comfortable life raft. They had hired him after only a brief interview which resembled a casual chat. Later, he found out that they simply wanted to check his accent. The degree from Cornell—"Ah, very very good"—had done the rest.

TESCO (the acronym stood for nothing, as far as anyone knew) wasn't exactly a school. It was more a parental agency that loaned out English teachers all over the Kansai area. Because Nippon Electric Corporation wanted its top executives not to make fools of themselves on their business trips to Los Angeles, they called TESCO. When Mitsubishi Auto needed an international division that could chat intelligently over the phone in English, TESCO was the company they thought of. In fact, numerous agencies were springing up to teach conversational English, but TESCO had set up shop over a decade ago, and the Japanese believed in name-brands and longevity.

The list of TESCO clients now ran to ten pages, from corporate giants like IBM Japan to semi-wealthy individuals who could afford private tutorials. And though TESCO now boasted its own seminar rooms and classrooms, most of its customers preferred to be taught on-site. In fact, the main purpose of the large TESCO office staff was to make these arrangements, down to accompanying the anxious foreign teachers to their first class, instructing them where to change trains, and so on. After receiving textbooks and an instruction schedule, most teachers rarely saw the inside of the TESCO headquarters. Instead, they simply showed up for their classes and handed in their time-sheets once a month.

Wary of any long-term employment, Cricket nonetheless enjoyed his job, down to the immaculate trains and taxis that took him to factories and corporate headquarters all over Osaka. Seated at the front of a polished seminar table, he appreciated the attention his students paid him. Even in a society that venerated age, a twenty-two-year-old foreigner who could tell a Matsushita executive how to order a martini at an American bar was listened to with deference. The students ranged from diligent to disaffected—like students everywhere, Cricket supposed. His time at Kansai Gakuin had given him some perspective. But the term *sensei* still commanded respect, even if the teachers weren't always sure what TESCO stood for.

"'Testin' Comp'ny'?" suggested Charlie Sayles, a disgruntled Aussie who apocopated half his syllables. "'Teachin' Engl'sh to Sedent'ry Corp'rate Orient'ls'?" Murase-san, the imperturbably elegant, gray-haired head of the company, a diminutive man always to be seen in a three-piece suit, neither encouraged nor discouraged these remarks. His gift was to run TESCO like a frictionless machine without seeming to lift a finger. He was pleasant enough to the foreigners. Only the Japanese members of the staff deferred to him as if he were a minor deity.

Embarrassed that his students handled English better than he did Japanese, Cricket worked on increasing his range, working toward a more picturesque speech. *Jitensha* was "bicycle," but *charinko* was a rattletrap two-wheeler. *Rokudenashi* meant "scoundrel" and sounded as quaint in current Japanese as its counterpart in English, but he used it for comic effect. In restaurants, he learned to order the dishes he liked by name instead of pointing. *Soba* was "noodle"—though *udon* and *sōmen* were also noodles, and so was *ramen*.

He taught himself the *hiragana* and *katakana* syllabaries with homemade flashcards. Riding the train, he'd turn over a card to reveal what looked like a cockeyed smile-face. "*Tsu!*" he'd say, repeating it several times for emphasis. A proofreader's caret was *he, hi* looked like a "Kilroy was here" nose, and so on. Each syllabary had forty-six elements, identical but for the fact that one set was used only for foreign words—which had unpleasant xenophobic overtones that he tried to ignore. Because every sound had to be a syllable instead of a simple consonant, his own name in the *katakana* for foreign use came out as *Korikketo Korinzu*. Should he have a *hanko,* a name-stamp, made up with that? He still mentally compared himself with his shadow, Matthew H., recalling some confession of difficulty with the language. Any day now, he intended to tackle the Chinese-derived *kanji* ideograms. He hung the scroll he'd swiped from the Kanga dorm in his room and at least learned to execute its two ideograms, *flat* and *peace*.

After four mole-like years at college, he felt Japan was rejuvenating him, and he owed something in return. He trained himself to pick up the last grain of rice in his bowl with his chopsticks. He assigned himself a chapter a week in *Japanese for Today*, a textbook he had picked up at the Kinokuniya bookstore. And he practiced his politeness in the mirror, perfecting a smile that was almost Oriental.

From time to time he dreamed about a Zen temple set vaguely in the countryside, with monks tending the white pebble gardens amid the orderly hum of cicadas. The temple spread itself out against a landscape of trees, the wide roof like a set of wings forever poised for flight. Stone steps anchored the entrance, marked by a sliding panel of cedar with an indecipherable sign written in *kanji*. Sometimes Cricket was a docile monk in a white robe, and other times he was a cicada with a bug's-eye view. No women ever dwelt in the temple, nor did any right-thinking monk ever miss their presence. There was a purpose to this life, a connecting force that linked all his actions. Slowly, a little of his dream began to carry into his waking moments.

Whenever he dropped into the TESCO office, he'd see a few other teachers hanging around for a little professional solidarity or just exchanging gossip. Ted Allen, who wore a necktie even to the pachinko parlor, was leaving Japan now that his Japanese wife was due to have a baby. Charlie Sayles speculated that the child would be born with a Takashimaya silk cravat. Jennifer Hertzl was looking for a new apartment in Kyoto, her fifth in two years. Jennifer was attractive in a leggy, L.A. way, with a smart-ass manner that was kind of fun, at other times abrasive. She also paraded a series of successively dopier boyfriends who strained everyone's tact. The rumor was that she occasionally slept with her students.

Once or twice Cricket had joined in the open discussion of whether Jennifer found impossible landlords, or the landlords found her impossible. Rarely did anyone mention her problem with illicit substances. A prominent notice on the wall of the TESCO waiting room featured an article from *The Japan Times* about Paul McCartney and his recent deportation from Tokyo for smuggling in marijuana. "DON'T LET THIS HAPPEN TO YOU," someone had scrawled underneath. One nameless teacher who'd sniffed cocaine a while back had been given twenty-four hours to leave the country.

But most of the teachers at TESCO preferred legal drugs like alcohol. At times, it seemed that half the teachers were ex-drunks from New Zealand or Australia. Unemployable at home, they'd found steady work at one of the English teaching companies springing up all over Osaka. Unable to get very far in Japanese, they made endless jokes about Japanese English, or Janglish, as they called it.

"'Crispy Gal'—you see that in the Shiseido makeup ad at Umeda?" This was Jack Sims, the ex-Marine who still walked as if he were in the military. He had a bone-crushing handshake and a bow that was somehow its equivalent.

"Not bad," smirked Harry Belton, a Michigan native, "but I saw a T-shirt the other day which tops that. 'Let's Sports Violent all day long.'" Harry, whose paunch preceded him, did a huff-and-puff pantomime of what he thought the intended meaning was.

"Heck, they're trying," said Ted, who was clearly too nice for these discussions. He claimed he'd never taught a class he didn't like. Now that he was leaving, people were more respectful of him.

"*My* favorite T-shirt," declared Jennifer during one of her rare appearances, is 'Jimy and Emiry, Portrait in Love.'" She stretched her tall arms to laugh, flipping her blonde bangs. She was wearing a genuine Stanford University shirt, for which, she told anyone who cared to listen, she'd been offered ¥10,000 downtown.

Rhotacismus, thought Cricket, who'd gotten curious about the continual slippage of *r* for *l* among his students. And *lallation*. On the other hand, he found the Japanese flapped *r* exceedingly difficult to pronounce, especially in a combination like *ryō*.

"Of course," murmured Jack so that the only one who could hear was Cricket, "they'd give her ten thousand only if she took the shirt off in front of them."

Cricket, who lived across the street from an establishment called Mamy's Beauty Saloon, simply used his No. 2 smile on Jennifer—after a more private No. 1 smile at Jack. Then they all wagged their non-learned heads: so much correcting to do, and so futile. Still, it was a job. Either Jack, or someone making fun of him, had put up a joke-poster in the TESCO washroom: "JAPAN—IT'S NOT JUST RAW FISH, IT'S A CAREER." True, some *gaijin* were less than happy with their living conditions: Charlie Sayles couldn't get Vegemite anywhere and looked disgustedly at Cricket when he'd suggested miso as an alternative. When others talked about recalcitrant students, Cricket suggested classroom options like debating or word games. He'd been on his way to becoming unpopular before he learned to nod deferentially, taking his cue from the Japanese TESCO staff.

Jennifer intrigued him but would never go out with him, he knew, because women like that never did. The closest he'd gotten in that direction was Jill from Liverpool, disappearing even before his fall at Kanga. He'd made a few inquiries, but heard she'd gone back to Britain. That was the way: most expats would stay one or two years, then suddenly return home. They missed their boyfriends or fish and chips or the way they used to be, which was probably unrecoverable.

Cricket himself knew only a few people he could call friends, but he was busy, or made himself that way. In an attempt to align his psyche with his soma, he'd started aikido at a local exercise center, and he was currently looking into tea ceremony classes. He'd recently moved into an ascetic apartment in Nishinomiya close to the train station, nexus to all his English classes. The room at least had new tatami matting pliant as skin (if epidermis were made of straw), and modern plumbing, which meant that he didn't have to go to the *sentō* or public baths every night but could shower and soak in his own tiny tub instead.

Not that he hadn't tried the *sentō* at first, as he tried everything he came across in Japan. The one in his neighborhood cost ¥500 and offered a kidney-shaped communal bath that one could enter only after the obligatory wash-up by the tiled periphery. Men squatted or sat on stump-legged stools soaping their backs, using the towels they were issued, the size of cloth napkins, to scrub and rinse themselves. After a few visits, Cricket reluctantly gave it up: too many naked bodies, and he felt watched.

The two-story apartment building in which he lived was presided over by his landlords Mori and Mori, a middle-aged couple he'd begun to recognize as a distinct Japanese type. Mori the wife was parsimonious and sharp-eyed, respectful of her tenants but wary of lease infractions and always the one to collect the rent. When she wished Cricket good morning—"*Ohayō gozaimasu!*"—it was as if she were conducting a lesson, especially since the stock answer was an echolalic repetition, down to the discreet bow. The Japanese like dittoes, thought Cricket, yet he quickly adopted the routine. He appreciated his place in the order and only occasionally wondered whether his rent was higher because he was a *gaijin*.

Mori the husband gently offset his wife's hardness with his

maundering air, peering through thick spectacles and groping as if hidden pockets were sewn outside his pants. His bow of greeting was the opposite of his wife's: a hesitant tilt of the head instead of an emphatic nod. A small man always seemingly at loose ends, he was nonetheless handy with tools and did all the building maintenance. Not that Cricket's apartment had much to fix. Into the empty space he had unpacked his spartan soul, his meager belongings ranged around the room with spurious order. The Moris had provided only a mobile cardboard closet and a low table that forced him to adopt a hunched posture while seated at it.

On days when he had no morning classes, he would proceed directly across the room to his Olympia typewriter, which had recently accepted a Japanese silk ribbon without complaint. Even with two classes a day, his schedule was ridiculously open, and the stimulus of each new day made his writing pour out in endless drafts, most of which never got finished. He got to the middle of a short story he had begun before he left the States, about a psychoanalyst who was slowly going crazy. He began another about twins trapped on identical desert islands, and a third about a dog abducted by pet thieves in Paris. Three pages of an article on palindromes waited patiently in a drawer. He was faithful to his journal, which he brought up to date every three days, and he typed ever-lengthier letters to friends at home until he'd frightened most of them away. Even Peter Inoue, bogged down in first-year medical school at NYU, begged off for a while. The truth was that Cricket had never had more than a few acquaintances. He told himself he was going to be a writer and addressed himself to that end.

The one subject on which he couldn't cohere his thoughts was Japan. It wasn't that he had no observations. They overflowed his letters and his journal, which soon became a daily affair. He explained to his journal what whale meat tasted like (fishy sirloin), set down the principle of the Asian restaurant toothpick dispenser (a salt-shaker with one hole punched in the top), and even devoted a closely typed page to what the Gion festival in Kyoto was like (decorated wooden carts, centuries old, wheeled around a block of streets). He never quite achieved the essence of the thing.

But he kept trying. He took in the yeasty odor of *sake* from the Hakushika brewery near his apartment, the clip-clop of the Shinsei sushi man in his wooden *geta*, and the indefatigable chant of the fishmonger in the narrow shopping lane by the railroad station. He studiously copied the store sign down the street from his apartment so he could show it to Miyamoto, the friendliest staffer in the TESCO office, and learn what invisible merchandise was sold there ("non-moving product," or real estate).

Kenzo Miyamoto, a mild, fortyish, wispy-haired presence whose desk was adorned with Japanese proverbs executed in calligraphic script, had ushered Cricket to several new classes. Of all the staff, he always seemed to be least busy when Cricket walked into the office, and they had struck up a conversational acquaintance of sorts. Most TESCO staffers maintained a polite don't-touch attitude toward the foreign teachers, as if they were drying shellack. Miyamoto shook hands almost too vigorously. He wanted to know about Cornell University, American cuts of meat, and Western proverbs. He'd given Cricket some advice on apartment-hunting that saved over ¥50,000. And as opposed to so many Japanese, who treated *gaijin* like people with special disabilities, Miyamoto generously assumed a linguistic and cultural conversance that they often didn't have.

"Tell me," he asked Cricket on a train ride to an inaugural class in Minami-Osaka, "do you have a proverb like *Nana-korobi, ya-oki* in English?"

"That depends," answered Cricket cautiously. "All I get is the *nana*—seven, right?"

"*Hai, sono tōri desu.*" Miyamoto broke into a grin. "You're right. And the rest?"

"*Shirahen.*" Cricket cheerfully used the rude Kansai dialect form of "I don't know." He found it got more of a rise than polite phrasing.

"Ah, who taught you that?" Miyamoto slapped his own knee admiringly. A few schoolgirls riding on the seats opposite giggled.

"You did."

"*Sō?*" Miyamoto rubbed the bridge of his nose reflectively. "Anyway, *Nana-korobi, ya-oki* means something like 'Fall down seven times, get up eight.'"

Cricket pursed his lips for a moment as the train hurtled through a turn. He used to be good at this, though learning Japanese seemed to rob him of some flexibility in English. "'If at first you don't succeed, try, try again,'" he ventured.

"Ah, I think so." And Miyamoto launched into a discussion of the Japanese national character.

Nana-korobi, ya-oki, rehearsed Cricket silently even as he listened. He wrote it down in his notebook in *Romaji* or Western lettering, then rewrote it in *hiragana* for drill, adding it to his collection of useful phrases and sayings. He sent it home to Peter to cheer him up during his medical exams. And he always kept his ears open on the street for further material. Only he still couldn't put anything together in the form of a narrative except for local color, which he considered a cheap appropriation. He even addressed social issues such as Japanese education (strict until the laxity of college life) or the concept of group consensus, which fascinated and slightly appalled him. To his father, he noted that the Japanese managed their affairs with far fewer lawyers than in America.

Whenever the writing faltered, he relied on his classes for a boost. These days, he was trying to teach definite articles to a quorum of indefinite engineers at Shin Meiwa Aircraft. Since Japanese didn't have any articles, Cricket could sympathize with their frustration. "Last teacher," frowned Mr. Yamazaki, "he just tell us no problem." Privately, Cricket cursed all the laid-back, incompetent instructors floating around the city.

Then there was the opposite approach. One TESCO member in particular, Harry Belton, boasted that he humiliated his students. "Sarcasm to sneering—it all works well in a shame culture," he'd remark with relish. The rumor was that he had no use for women. A scraggly pepper-and-salt beard swarmed around his fleshy carmine lips, and a pair of gold-rimmed glasses that he fussed with gave him the look of a dissipated Santa Claus, complete with overgrown belly. At times, the belly itself had its own swaggering attitude. His smile diminished rather than expanded his face, and his pronouncements on subjects from racism to careers for women left a choking gap in the air. Because he'd been with the company for so long, he had the TESCO equivalent of tenure, but it was clear there'd been complaints. He urged his students to take him out drinking, which they were delighted to do—until they found out the cost of his bottomless capacity. That time at the *robatayaki* bar in Juso, or the Night of the Seven Platters at Sushi-Sei . . . Harry Belton stories were circulated among TESCO staff like collectible coins.

Cricket's initial run-in with Harry started innocently enough over a set of textbooks, *Encounters in America*, which both of them needed for an upcoming class. In fact, Cricket had them first, but when Harry loudly asked for them, one of the more servile staffers, a narrow-shouldered woman named Tani, whispered that Korinzu-san had just taken the set.

"Oh?" Harry podged over to the anteroom, where Cricket's

open-mouthed teacher's bag sat stuffed with the new textbooks. Reaching in ham-handedly, he transferred them to his own bag. Cricket happened to be talking with Dawson, a rangy, cobalt-eyed Indiana man, the only foreign staffer in the TESCO office. His one-man department was called Textbook Development.

When Cricket saw what Harry was doing, he said "Excuse me" to Dawson and marched over to Harry. "Those are mine," he informed Harry.

Harry swung his belly menacingly. "*Were*," he growled. "I've got seniority here—don't I, Dawson?"

Dawson had acquired enough Asian reticence to want no part of this, but he also obviously didn't like Harry. He cleared his throat quietly. "I have seniority over both of you. And I wrote that book."

"So?" Harry puffed his cheeks like a blowfish. "We all know what a piece of crap it is, but it's been assigned for my Tuesday class."

Dawson muttered something in rapid Japanese, then assumed a smile that was all frost. "Don't worry, gentlemen. We have enough copies for both of you." And he led them to a giant steel cabinet at the back of the office to replenish Cricket's supply. Harry snorted as he walked off, and Cricket was intrigued to find that he now had an enemy.

For some reason, both Harry and Cricket always came in on the same day to pick up their paychecks. Harry was one of those *gaijin* who'd picked up only "restaurant Japanese" over the years, and when he wasn't insulting underlings, food was his main topic of conversation. He didn't care whom he addressed, as long as he had an audience. In fact, he seemed to have forgotten the textbook incident, as well as several other slights involving Cricket's pedagogical skills and reading abilities.

One day Harry was wheezing about his latest find, a curry-rice shop down in Nihonbashi that offered refills. Cricket hung a replica of Dawson's frost-smile on his face. He said he cooked most evenings.

"Yeah?" Harry half-stifled a belch. "You'd make a fine wife for some Japanese businessman, kid."

Cricket's smile tightened. He was about to make some comment about overfed Americans when Murase-san glided by like an elegant suit on wheels, seemingly abstracted. Harry took the opportunity to leave, and by the time Murase-san was out of earshot, it was too late for Cricket to do anything but grit his teeth so hard that they ached for a day afterwards. Unfortunately, Miyamoto was away that afternoon, ushering a novice from Ottawa to her first business English seminar in Takarazuka. Living in a politeness culture had made Cricket forget how to deal with bullshit like this. What did the Japanese do?—they smiled and clenched themselves. Cricket's expression on the train home was more a grimace of coat-hanger proportions, but he was dealing with his anger. He imagined various fates for Harry, committing a few to his notebook, but the scenarios were too crude, fatal without sufficient humiliation. And anyway, he knew that nothing could be done. Which was also Japanese—*shikata ga nai*, as Miyamoto had taught him: it can't be helped; no way.

By the time he reached his apartment, he was outwardly calm. Inwardly he seethed with plot. He slipped off his shoes and put the kettle on the gas ring. While the water was boiling, he did fifty sit-ups to relieve the tight spot in his stomach. Carrying a cup of tea over to his typewriter perched on the table by the window, he sat down cross-legged and slammed out an opening paragraph:

Every Saturday, the American instructor would come from the town below Kurosaka to teach the senior students English. They would each pay five hundred yen and, after the lesson, take the *sensei* to dinner. It was a revolving obligation in which each student paid for the teacher's meal about once every two months. Tonight, it was Kenzo's turn to pay for the huge appetite of the *sensei*, huge because he was an *Amerika-jin* with a big belly, but also because he insisted on skipping lunch and riding his bicycle as fast as he could up the hill to work up an appetite. "Please let *Amerika-jin* ride short and slowly today," Kenzo prayed to no god in particular. "I have only five thousand yen for which I have other uses."

(Cricket nodded, took a sip of tea, and smiled faintly. This was his private smile, the only self-approval he allowed himself. He flexed his fingers and resumed typing.)

It was four o'clock, and the *sensei* was due at four-thirty. He was usually a few minutes late, arriving at the school in a screen of tan dust from the roadway, his broad shoulders hunched over the handlebars of his bicycle. It was a five-speed Sky Lancer, an expensive item for most of the townspeople, but the *Amerika-jin* treated it casually, leaving it out in the rain and occasionally getting off and kicking it when it didn't go fast enough to suit him. No one liked the *sensei* much. Most of the time, he treated the class as if it were a joke he had grown tired of. The teacher's name was Mr. Belford, and his Japanese was exceedingly poor, but he did speak native English and was therefore the best teacher to be had within many miles. There are some foreigners the Japanese are civil to because they are pleasant and because they are foreigners, and there are others to whom the Japanese are civil only because they are foreigners. Mr. Belford belonged to the latter class, and tonight Kenzo would grudgingly but politely entertain him.

(Now Cricket frowned. Was the style too restrained, too drawn out? But this is the way I always write, he commented to the critics in his head. Less solemn, though—he intended to have some fun with this.)

Kenzo sat underneath the tree-at-the-top-of-the-hill, waiting for Mr. Belford and wondering whether he could be induced to eat *soba* instead of meat or fish; it was so much cheaper. Of course, the other students, who had all dug deep into their pockets to provide well for the *sensei*, would then be angry at Kenzo. Things would be so much simpler without the English lessons, in fact, without any *Amerika-jin* at all. Happiness with less: it was like the lesson from a Zen fable, and he was just contemplating the idea when the road below produced a miniature cloud, traveling north and moving slower as it reached the hill. From the cloud, like an ill-tempered god on a bicycle, came Mr. Belford.

The sinews in his broad neck stood out as he strained against the hill. He had on a madras shirt and shorts which revealed thick, hairy legs. His yellow beard, mixed with streaks of gray, dripped sweat into the handlebars, and Kenzo noted with sorrow that the *sensei's* belly had gotten even bigger since last week. It was an evil belly, gobbling up meat and shrimp in the same quantities that others ate plain rice. Sometimes Kenzo had the feeling that it was the belly which spoke, rather than the head of Mr. Belford.

"*Konnichi wa!*" Mr. Belford called out in horribly accented Japanese, and Kenzo got to his feet. The other students were already gathering inside the school, bringing nothing with them, since Mr. Belford never handed out anything that he didn't take back at the end of the lesson. And he had no patience with any texts other than his.

Mr. Belford parked his bicycle by the tree-at-the-top-of-the-hill, took his satchel from the rack, and strode toward the school. He was panting heavily, but Kenzo felt sorry only for the bicycle—the poor, abused bicycle and the dry, dusty road. The *sensei* walked heavily, and a few yards before the school he kicked a stone so that it clattered against the outer wall and knocked off a chip of paint. Takahiro, at eighteen the oldest boy in the class, held open the door for the *sensei*. The class rose for the teacher, and Kenzo entered unceremoniously in his wake.

"Hello, class."

"Good afternoon, Mr. Belford. How are you?" chanted ten voices in ragged unison. It was the standard statement and response, so ordained by Mr. Belford, who did not reply to the question. After taking attendance, the *sensei* might call upon a student to answer questions. There was little or no curriculum. The class was conducted according to Mr. Belford's whim, which meant there were stops and pauses, and sometimes a test on verbs or vocabulary when the *sensei* didn't feel like teaching. At those times, he would sit there and read from a book, occasionally picking his nose.

(How the hell *did* Belton teach class, anyway? Cricket wondered. I'll bet he has favorites.)

For two hours, the students would learn under Mr. Belford. At exactly six-thirty, the *sensei* would look at his Timex watch, clap his hands together with a cry of "Class over!" and walk out with the student who had been selected to provide dinner for him that night. He would not speak much after class. Perhaps because he was hired to speak English, he had acquired the habit of measuring out his words slowly, and not wasting any when he was not paid for them.

This afternoon, Mr. Belford decided to have all the students give a short speech about what their fathers did. He stood on the clumsy wooden dais, arms akimbo, and pointed to each student in turn. Takahiro talked about working in a grocery store, and Hideki, the tailor's son, described threading a needle. When it came time for Kenzo to speak, however, he was still thinking about dinner.

"And you, Kenzo, what does your father do?" Mr. Belford eyed Kenzo as if he were going to eat him, an oddly appropriate look. The class waited, silent.

"My father is a *soba*." He meant to say "soldier," but had said the Japanese for "noodle" instead, and the whole class giggled, first at him, then at their own laughter.

Mr. Belford did not laugh, nor did he fly into a rage—these were useless expenditures. Instead, he smiled, showing the fleshy upper lip of a man with a beard. "A *soba*! And what does your *soba*-father do? Does he lie in a pot like this?" Mr. Belford did a ludicrous imitation of a fat, limp noodle.

"Yes, I mean, no—he . . . he is in army, fight." Kenzo meant the *jieitai*, the self-defense forces, but couldn't think of the English. The pressure of embarrassment was suffusing his face a bright pink, and he wished fervently that Mr. Belford, who was still in his pose, were a real *soba*, then he would be eaten rather than eat.

"Ah, you mean a soldier, s-o-l-d-i-e-r." And with a lump of chalk, Mr. Belford drew a stick-figure with a gun on the blackboard. Underneath the drawing, he wrote "soldier." Then he drew a pot with lines inside and labeled it "*soba*." "There is a great difference." This provoked a new wave of laughter from the class, especially from Kazuo the carpenter's son, who was bigger than Kenzo and could therefore laugh as much as he pleased. Kenzo looked hard at Mr. Belford, but the *sensei* was looking elsewhere, and when he turned, Kenzo saw only boorish indifference. Kenzo was quietly furious, but the *sensei* moved on to another boy, and the lesson continued.

On a little pad of paper from his pocket, Kenzo drew a sword, with Mr. Belford's belly run through it like a shoat. Then he drew a huge belly like a gourd with two squat feet. When the teacher caught his eye, he smiled, but only because he was drawing a flaming pit to encompass the belly of Mr. Belford.

After they had finished the speeches, Mr. Belford thought for a moment, then opened a worn composition book. "We will talk about homonyms. These words are spelled the same, but have different meanings. I'll give two examples, 'be' and 'bee,' and 'pair' and 'pear.'" He wrote the four words on the board. "Can anyone tell me some other examples?"

No one could. Kenzo, who thought that possibly "bear" and "bare" might be an example, remained determinedly silent. He would not give the *sensei* the satisfaction of a reply. It would be extremely difficult acting pleasantly at dinner tonight, he was thinking.

Mr. Belford wrote "two," "too," and "to" on the board, but no one volunteered any other instances. After calling on a few hapless victims and getting blank responses, Mr. Belford snapped the book shut in irritation and decided to give the class a spelling test. Paper and pencils came out of the satchel, and Mr. Belford's voice droned monotonously as the class strained to catch the words. "Claw, color, cream . . . ."

The test was over a little before six-thirty, but Mr. Belford was deliberately slow in collecting the papers. When he had them all in his satchel, he looked at his watch and pretended to be surprised. "Six-thirty! Time flies." He stepped down from the dais, which made a sound like an animal whose tail has been trod upon. "Class over. Now, whose turn is it tonight?"

The class waited, all eyes upon Kenzo, who gritted his teeth and slowly, reluctantly, raised his hand.

"So! Mr. Noodle. I hope we are not having noodles for dinner." The *sensei* chuckled at his own joke, patting his stomach appreciatively.

(A rhythmic *skreet skreet* brushed at Cricket's consciousness like a hand scratching his head. He looked out the window to see Mori the husband down below, sweeping the curved street in front of the building with a twig broom. "Broom" was what?—*hōki*. Mori also brushed off the steps and mopped the foyer floor every Thursday. Cricket checked his watch: 5:15. What was Mori the wife doing now? In fact as he watched, she came down the street on her little purple bicycle, her front basket full from shopping. When Mori the husband made some remark, she laughed quietly. He whisked her away with a mock sweep of his broom as she turned to park her bicycle in the alley. For a second, Cricket could see them twenty years ago, just embarking on the rhythms of married life. He shook his head, blocking out the scene.)

I will take him to the water and see if he can float like a fish, thought Kenzo. He looks like a blowfish, anyway. Or I could let all the air out of him like a bicycle tire, *pshht*. I think my dislike for Mr. Belford is getting dangerous.

But he showed none of this. Instead, he smiled. "No *soba* tonight. I take you to place with meat, yes? *Teppanyaki?*" It was a meat and vegetable dish prepared on a sizzling hot griddle.

Mr. Belford grinned from his belly and nodded at Kenzo. So they understood each other. Kenzo led the way to a restaurant near the middle of town, a thought beginning to form in his mind.

The place Kenzo chose was run by a distant cousin of his. It was an establishment specializing in various exotic dishes which were nonetheless cheap, primarily because they used the less desirable parts of animals, such as the organs. Local beef was the only expensive specialty. Kenzo's cousin greeted him as a friend, though he had not seen him in months, and Kenzo indicated that there was a guest with him.

"Ah! I am please meeting you." Kenzo's cousin bowed to Mr. Belford, who bent forward so that his belly seemed to be bowing, as well. Kenzo recalled from the last time he had entertained Mr. Belford that the *sensei* was especially deferential toward things edible or the providers thereof.

They removed their shoes and sat down on the tatami. Kenzo ordered a beer for Mr. Belford and cold barley tea for himself. He casually mentioned the name of a dish to the waiter, who bowed and scurried away. It would take almost all of his five thousand yen, but the results would be—delicious. He turned to Mr. Belford. "Tonight, we eat much meat, specialty of house."

"What?" Mr. Belford looked slightly uneasy.

"Cow, best part, don't mind."

"Ah, good." In a moment, the waiter brought the beer, and Mr. Belford took a large swig from the glass. As they were waiting for their meal, he made a few comments about the weather and asked for another beer. Kenzo, who calculated that he would then have only two hundred yen left, assented with a forced smile.

Soon the waiter came with the griddle and placed it on the table. After a minute, he dropped a spoonful of oil on the surface and watched it sizzle noisily. He left and came back with a large platter of vegetables and meat cut translucently thin, a tasteful orchestration of green peppers, pale onions, fan-shaped mushrooms, carrot medallions, purplish meat, and potato slivers. The carrots and potatoes went on first, then the other vegetables, and finally the meat, all carefully arranged on the griddle and turned with a pair of cooking chopsticks. Mr. Belford smacked his lips. "I will remember this meal!"

"I hope so."

The waiter served the contents of the pan on two large plates, and when he offered Mr. Belford a knife and fork, he was waved away. If Mr. Belford had learned anything from living in Japan, it was how to eat fast and well with chopsticks. The feast began.

(Here Cricket got up to stretch and refill his tea cup. Having skipped lunch, he suddenly realized how hungry he was. He arose from the table to move toward the food cupboard, but lurched and fell sprawling onto the tatami. His left leg had fallen asleep, and he spent the next minute massaging it back to life. The numbness gave way to a prickly sensation that felt eerily like knives rather than needles. Was this what happened during a two-hour seated tea ceremony? Maybe he'd better rethink his plans.

Rummaging around the cupboard and still wincing a bit, he found a cellophane packet of soba, like a piece of his own story penetrating his apartment. He had just set a pot of water on the gas ring when the baked-sweet-potato vendor came calling down the street. He trundled an ancient cart of heat-blackened metal and wood ahead of him, the scent of starch and molasses drifting upward in his wake. His clothing, an odd combination of overalls, padded trousers, and boots, looked older than the man himself. *"Yaki-imo,"* he crooned softly but persistently, advertising his one item, and Cricket had to repress the urge to run downstairs and buy one. Not when he was in the middle of writing, not when he already had water heating up. He waited until the cart had rounded the corner (the *yaki-imo* chant took a block longer to fade) before sitting down gingerly, this time with his legs outstretched. He focused his attention on the typewriter, sticking out its tongue of paper at him. Where was he? He had to backtrack a few sentences before he saw where he'd been and found out where he wanted to go.)

The potatoes were crisp without being burnt, the vegetables were cooked but crunchy, and the meat was done so that the inside was a delicate pink. On the side was a dipping sauce of grated white radish, vinegar, and soy sauce. Mr. Belford ate his portion with rapid shoveling motions of his chopsticks, exclaiming in pleasure at the taste. Everything went in through the beard, like a bushy tunnel. Kenzo ate at a somewhat slower pace, carefully noting what the *sensei* had and hadn't eaten yet. Mr. Belford ate everything.

"Ah, absolutely delicious."

After the waiter had cleared away the dishes and brought the bowls of rice, Kenzo looked almost pleasantly at the *Amerika-jin*. "I think you will be lucky tonight. Eating *kawami* is bringing luck, you know."

"Oh? What is *kawami*?"

Kenzo feigned surprise. *"Kawami*, it is—I thought you knew. It is . . . from the small animal, that high." He indicated a height of about three inches. "It is a rodent, very fast. You eat tonight."

"Tonight? You said it was cow!" Mr. Belford's stomach heaved slightly, his face as pink as Kenzo's had been during the English lesson. "Beef, you understand?"

"Beef, cow?" Kenzo's confusion magically disappeared. "Ah, you must forgive me. I confused words, like . . . '*soba* and 'soldier.' *Kawami* is not cow, no. Is found in sewers, sometimes grow"—here he raised his hand to the height of a foot—"this big."

Mr. Belford's face had changed from a bright pink to a dull gray. He grabbed for his beer bottle, but he had drunk his second beer already.

"I've been poisoned!"

"Oh, no. No think that." Kenzo grew pensive. "Of course, once, twice a year, *kawami* served, have disease. But I do not think this one so. You like him?"

Mr. Belford got up from the tatami with difficulty, his belly at first catching the edge of the table and almost overturning it. "You horrible Japanese, you little bastard, you planned this!"

"Sorry? I am good host, only try please *Amerika-jin*."

"I may die, you mean! I'm getting back home where I have some medicine!" In fact, Mr. Belford's belly was heaving as if he might not need the medicine after all. Without waiting to thank the waiter, he lurched out the door and began running toward his bicycle. It was obvious how much it hurt him to run, especially after such a big meal, but he made it to his bicycle in quite good time. He flung his satchel on the rack and went flying down the hill. A tan cloud of dust showed in the twilight, traveling much faster than usual, accompanied by a barely discernible howl, finally lost in the distance. Kenzo watched from the restaurant window, sighing for anyone who would hear and wondering idly whether there would be an English lesson next week. He rather hoped there would not be.

(The pot of water boiled over on the gas ring, but Cricket didn't notice and kept typing.)

Kenzo's cousin materialized beside him and asked anxiously, "Please, what made him go off like that?"

"I don't think he liked the meat you served."

His cousin grew indignant. "But I serve fine beef from Sapporo!"

"Ah, these *Amerika-jin*, you know. Sensitive stomachs. Not your fault." He patted his cousin's back in sympathy.

The waiter, who had been listening to the entire exchange, now came forward. He seemed hesitant, but finally spoke. "Tell me, please." His hand described first a height of three inches from the ground, then a foot. "I never heard the word before. What is *kawami*?"

After Cricket finished, he felt quietly elated. An approval that seemed to emanate from all four walls descended on him. The ghost of his mother patted him on the head. This was no scrawled haiku on an airplane napkin, he told the absence of Matthew. Double-twist stories are rare.

How come there are no women in the story? Sofie wanted to know. She had never again reached the apparitional heights of his night in Korea, but he still talked to her from time to time.

Because Belton doesn't like women, he replied loftily, and that seemed to satisfy her, or at least silence that portion of his brain. For a moment, he just sat at the table, staring at his hands. If I were typing, he thought, and the writing were going well, I could stay this way forever. They'd have to cut off my legs eventually.

But when the angry sizzle from the remaining water in the pot came through to him, he finally got up and made himself a bowl of soba. He even prepared a little dipping sauce of *wasabi*, soy, and egg, sucking the noodles down the Japanese way, with a slurp at the end. Afterwards, he read for a while (lately he'd been on a Graham Greene jag) and studied some Japanese. *Watashi wa manzoku shite-imasu.* I am content. He unrolled his quilted futon on the tatami and went to bed with a clear head.

Looking over the story the next day, he made only a few changes and titled it "Learning the Language." It read a little like a fairy tale, he decided, or maybe something by Saki. Should he present Harry Belton with a signed copy? Should he slip an anonymous copy into Harry's mailbox at the TESCO office? For a while, he carried around a copy of the story in his teacher's bag, but it seemed to work like an anti-Belton talisman, since he and Harry rarely saw each other at the office again.

Meanwhile he typed up a clean draft, copied it on the Fuji machine at the office, and sent it off to a slick magazine he'd been courting in America. It came back within a month. But that wasn't going to stop him. He typed up another cover letter and sent the manuscript back home again, along with the finally finished manuscript of his desert-island story. Instead of enclosing self-addressed stamped envelopes, he tucked in an international reply coupon, the equivalent of an American stamp, along with a small airmail envelope. "You may discard the manuscript," he wrote, though typing the sentence gave him pain.

In a few instances, an editor would send back more than a form, perhaps taken by the charm of distance if not the manuscript itself. "This is Saki-esque," wrote an assistant-illegible from *Harper's*. "No one writes this stuff anymore. A few do read it," he conceded unhelpfully.

"Doesn't sound like the real Japan," scrawled an editor at a small-press magazine called *Yellow Dragon*.

Told you so, sniffed someone, though probably not Sofie. Cricket didn't deign to reply.

Gambatte, Miyamoto had taught him: persevere; hold out; keep at it. *Gambatte-imasu*, he told himself. I'm trying. He smiled tightly as he walked to the post office, another bright, futile manila envelope in hand.

5. *Bon*

Bon, pronounced "bone" and not to be confused with *bon*, meaning "tray," was the annual festival for the dead in Japan. It took place in late August, when the summer heat was just beginning to recede into the lengthening gray evenings. Everyone from salarymen to street-sweepers would return to their hometowns so that they could venerate their ancestral spirits. Apart from what little family he had, Cricket felt oddly bereft, as if missing something that he'd always professed to dislike. In fact, he'd known about *Bon* since his first semester at Kanga, but had never participated. Now here he was in Hikari, in the prefecture of Yamaguchi, at the behest of his new girlfriend, Reiko.

The idea of a girlfriend made him nervous in general. He'd met Reiko two months ago in a Kobe coffee shop when she was waiting for an acquaintance. He was solo as usual, nursing his loneliness. The acquaintance never showed up. She looked upset, her delicate figure twisted in apprehension. He'd surprised himself by stepping in, using the line "Mind if I practice my Japanese?," which was what everyone usually said to him, but with "English" as the last word in the sentence. She admired his intelligence and American-ness; he liked that she was Japanese and easy to talk to. So one thing had led to another, or *tsugi kara tsugi ni*, as someone—Miyamoto?—had told him, and now he had a certified Japanese girlfriend. They'd been to the movies, where they'd held each other, and they'd been to his apartment, where they'd gone considerably further. She was still fairly virtuous, thought Cricket half-ruefully. Her character was *honorable*, which sounded old-fashioned but in Japan today meant premarital sex was all right if you were committed.

Celebrating *Bon* in her hometown was a real commitment, as far as he was concerned. Though Reiko told her parents that Collins-san was just a foreign friend, he still felt as if he were being sized up—and found wanting. He had never felt more like an outsider, though Reiko tried hard to include him in everything. The ceremonies included prayers, cremation-site visits, feasting, and an odd, lilting dance that she demonstrated for him. "No, first this way, now that," she insisted, as he clumsily tried to follow her movements. With an undinal sway of her arms mimicked by her hips, she looked like a sea wave, whereas he looked as if he were drowning. "Maybe practice," she advised unhelpfully. The *Bon odori*, or festival dancing, would take place tomorrow night whether he was ready or not.

As with everything Japanese, the delicate and the subtle took real work. And it could get quite confusing: for one thing, the *kanji* for *Bon* was in fact the same character as for "tray," so what did that mean? Cricket more appreciated the Japanese trait of ritualizing daily existence through simple repetition and difference: making a cup of tea could become a two-hour ceremony; a pile of polished stones could represent a whole way of life. In fact, he still had dreams about a Zen temple against a backdrop of bamboo and cicadas. During these nights he was a monk tending the stone garden, and when he died he turned into a cicada.

Yet real death in Japan appeared rather complicated. When Reiko's maternal grandmother had suffered a fatal stroke two years ago, for instance, the body was cleansed with hot water and dressed all in white. Then the body was placed with the head facing north and unpillowed, covered by a sheet.

"Why white?" Cricket wanted to know, among other things. They were on their way to visit the local temple, which was Buddhist, and maybe later the neighborhood shrine, which was Shinto—another complication that made only mixed sense.

"White is color of death," Reiko told him.

"Really?" There was so much about Japan that he didn't know, he often felt. In society, he could glimpse tradition in the way an old woman hobbled through the streets, in the precise inclination of a bow or the two pronunciations of one word. In the natural world, the customs and folklore were like myriad white streamers entangled in the trees or scattered by the breeze, ever-present but hard to catch. He could spend an eternity studying Japanese culture—*would* be spending an eternity here if he died suddenly, he thought. The idea made him shiver slightly. "In the West, death is black."

"I know," said Reiko shortly. She didn't like being told things about America that she already understood. Didn't she own two Bruce Springsteen tapes, and hadn't she once memorized all the lyrics to "*Ki-iro no sensuikan*" ("Yellow Submarine")? Cricket was supposed to be a fund of American culture, but he never discussed it as much as he should. Instead, he quizzed her endlessly about Japanese society. That was at least better than when he was flippant, or worse, retreated into a weird inner region that hardly seemed a part of himself. "But also, black is stylish in New York, no?"

"True," he admitted. "But I'll bet white isn't always associated with death here, either." On their right they passed a tennis court, echoing the insistent *pock . . . pock . . . pock* of lobs and returns. A nation of ralliers. He pointed. "There, do those players in white look like ghouls?"

"What's 'ghouls'?" she asked hopefully.

And he patiently explained. She loved it when he was like that: the all-knowing American.

When they arrived at the temple, Reiko approached a shaven-head monk to press an evenlope of money into his hands. Later she bowed her head to intone a short prayer.

"But what does it mean?" whispered Cricket to Reiko, as they filed outside the building. The temple's wooden eaves sloped down like an awning of interlaced cypress leaves, protective yet also restrictive, or maybe it was just his imagination. From his temple-dream, which recurred once a month or so, he retained a profound awe of these structures. They diminished him in a way that he found alternately pleasing and demeaning.

When Reiko said nothing, he repeated his question.

"Hard to translate," she replied, evading his eye. He knew that look—or lack of a look, really. It meant she didn't know, and since she understood that "I don't know" made him impatient, she employed other responses, from polite hedging to silence. Cricket's responses to hers ranged from occasional deference to sarcasm.

"Does it mean 'I respect your spirit, O mighty one'?"

"No . . . ."

"Or maybe 'Here, have a sniff, Grandpa'?"

"Hmm . . . ." Reiko's full lips, pressed together, softened to a smile. He caught at her wrist, and they walked along that way. They had a few more stops to make, mostly food-shopping for the upcoming feast. Hikari was a seaside resort town that was half closed down half the year, blossoming into beach-sport stores and boat-ride concessions during the summer months. A giant chemical conglomerate, Kameda Limited, helped keep the townspeople employed year-round manufacturing fizzy vitamin drinks.

That evening, Cricket met Reiko's father, a *buchō* at the company, now near retirement. He had the quiet but important air that Cricket recognized all too well as the prerogative of Japan's executive branch (yet how red-faced they got after a few too many drinks). Standing erect in his blue business suit, his necktie practically welded to his shirt, he looked like the figure of authority Reiko had described. The two men exchanged bows, Cricket reciting the humble form of introduction he'd been taught.

Only within the apartment, where Cricket would see him over the course of a three-day visit, was he willing to relax in a *yukata*. Cricket himself felt less at ease. His status of "friend" still made him feel a bit like a fraud, and he wondered whether the imposture showed.

"Dzoo you lahk . . . Japanese *bīru*?" Reiko's father asked Cricket the first night, as his wife brought out a two-liter bottle of Asahi draft.

When Cricket bobbed his head, his glass was filled to the brim, and refilled whenever the level sank below some invisible line. Mrs. Hashimoto—for some reason, he couldn't think of them as *san* and *san*—put out a little dish of boiled green soybeans still in the pod, at which the two men picked idly. In pidgin English and Japanese, they conversed about the humid climate and the summer season in Hikari. When Mr. Hashimoto asked about teaching English, Cricket thought he should inquire about manufacturing chemicals (Mr. Hashimoto seemed singularly uninformed about it all, unless that was a pose). Reiko and her mother had disappeared into the depths of their rather shallow apartment, leaving the men to talk. The conversation was innocuous enough, though Cricket was conscious of being judged. Mainly he was aware of having said a lot, his drinking partner little.

"He probably thinks I'm just another noisy American," Cricket observed gloomily to Reiko the next day. The festival dancing was set for that night, and still he danced like a drunk crab, as he put it, thinking the image Japanese.

"Maybe, maybe no." She cocked her head as if considering the option. "Could be like my mother's cooking. Often he complain. When he say nothing, that is good."

Besides bearing the burden of her husband's appraisals, Reiko's mother spoke almost no English and for some reason couldn't grasp Cricket's occasionally over-creative Japanese. He felt sorry for her without feeling much sympathy. In any event, Reiko's parents were both present and absent during his visit, terribly solicitous one moment and reclusive the next. And though they didn't exhibit the xenophobia of other Japanese who'd lived through World War II, he still felt uneasy. How did they celebrate *Bon* in 1945? he wondered.

His own feelings about the dead were conflicted. Since all of Cricket's grandparents were long gone, as well as his mother, he felt the intangibility of his lineage more than most. At times it even held the romance of mystery. On the other hand, his parents had never seemed to care much about family, let alone revering certain members.

"It's the two *c*'s"—his father told him when he was twelve, in one of those comments that came out like a barbed joke. "They ran in your mother's family."

"Which *c*'s?" asked Cricket, the eternal straight man.

"Craziness and cancer."

It wasn't funny then and it isn't funny now, he thought, but maybe there's some truth to it. He thought of the few deceased relatives his father had mentioned over the years. There was a great-aunt named Ida with an almost-maniacal gift for misspeaking. "Nervous insults, that kind of thing," his father remarked. "Near the end of her life, she'd sing at funerals." Then there was his mother's brother, a stooped figure with a chewed-looking mustache and sad spaniel eyes. He'd lived in Detroit and sent his nephew a bunny-rabbit birthday card every year until he died of leukemia when Cricket was in the third grade. How would it be to welcome those two, wherever they were buried, into the unconsecrated space of his apartment?

Of course, much of the dead past was buried in his brain: a set of false teeth, pink and white, resting in a fizzy glass—that was Grandpa Charlie, the one grandparent he had known at all; a pat on the shoulder from Mrs. Hennery, his kindergarten teacher; and innumerable voices, from the imaginary sister he once dreamed up, to the conversations he continued with people he'd met only yesterday. They weren't dead, exactly, just not there. They provided company, though occasionally all he asked was that they leave him alone. Sometimes they did and sometimes they didn't, but they hadn't bothered him much lately.

He shook his head to clear it. They were on their way back from a swim, and he had water in one ear. Reiko, who looked quite attractive in a one-piece, was now modestly wrapped in a towel, which seemed more in keeping with the occasion. Already, lanterns lined the streets, to be lit that night along paths from the grave-sites to the apartment complexes. That way, as Reiko had explained, the spirits could find their way home. After lunch, they were going with Reiko's mother and father to visit the graveyard. For some reason, the rituals fascinated him. "Tell me again what happened after your grandfather died."

"Well, after *tetsuya*—"

"Is that the all-night wake?"

"Yes. Then priest gives him special Buddhist name. Then comes cremation . . . ."

As they walked along the sandy road, Cricket visualized the ceremony as Reiko described it: the body reduced to ashes, the remaining bones picked up with uneven chopsticks and placed in a jar. Seven days after the death, the local priest visited the family's spirit altar, a special construction placed in front of the regular family altar that sat in the living room. The priest came to chant sutras every seven days till forty-nine days afterwards, and then at odd yearly intervals: 1, 2, 6, 12, 16, and 32.

"But why—" began Cricket.

"I don't know—why don't you ask priest?" Reiko shook her head. "'Why,' 'why'—sometimes I feel like talking to small child."

"Sorry," he muttered. "But—"

"*What?*"

"Well, what was your grandfather like?"

"Hmm." Reiko's eyes widened as if allowing something to pass through them. "He was a short man, fat. He gave me chocolate."

So that's how he survives, thought Cricket: as a candy-spirit in the mind of a Japanese woman.

And what about me? . . . and me? . . . and me? sighed the wind from the beach, but Cricket chose to ignore it.

It was at the grave-site of Reiko's grandfather that Cricket succumbed. The graveyard occupied a plateau cut into the hillside, like a field that grew stone slabs and markers instead of rice plants, fertilized by the ashes of the dead. It was crowded, like most public spaces in Japan, but since this was the countryside in Hikari, the stone plain was surrounded by wild grasses stippled with something like buttercups. The cicadas sounded loud but invisible, as if they came from underground.

Earlier that morning, Mrs. Hashimoto had cleaned up the area around the burial spot, swabbing the granite so that the incised characters showed clearly. She was setting out a jar of *sake* by the marker when a late-summer breeze wafted toward them. Cricket blinked, as if registering a sensation he hadn't felt in a long time. His nostrils quivered.

Mrs. Hashimoto recited a long prayer as her husband thoughtfully adjusted the cup for his father-in-law's spirit. Alongside the cup was a bowl of uncooked rice and a spray of something like asters, as if she had laid a stone table for a meal. She was just intoning another prayer when the air around the grave became trembly again, and Cricket could hold back no longer.

"*Aaaachoo! Achoo, achoo!*" Hands flailing, he knocked over the jar of *sake* and almost scattered the rice before Mrs. Hashimoto snatched it away. He sneezed violently three more times (seven in a row was his childhood record) before subsiding. The flat stone marker reeked of alcohol, which had half-drowned the asters. All three members of the Hashimoto family simply stared.

He finally broke the silence himself. "Um, has anyone got a tissue?"

While Reiko fumbled in her purse, he tried to explain about his old allergies. But he couldn't think of the Japanese for *allergy*—it turned out to be a hideously unpronounceable loan-word, *arerugī*—or even for *sneeze*—*kushami*; he would repeat to himself in bed that night, *kushami, kushami, kushami*. Meanwhile, his nose was ripe and juicy, his eyes streaming and itchy. Reiko finally extracted a tissue from the little porta-packs that all Japanese seemed to carry and handed it to him without ceremony. Mr. Hashimoto made a remark that Cricket couldn't catch, but which made the others titter.

"What?" he demanded of Reiko after blowing through the flimsy tissue and receiving two more. "What did he say?"

"Oh, Cricket, it's not so important." She handed him another tissue. "But he thinks maybe his father-in-law doesn't like you."

Whatever didn't like him, Cricket thought resentfully, was probably ragweed. It was already half past August, and this was the right season for it. How could he have forgotten?—but he had, or at least repressed it. It was years since he'd carried around what his father called a snot-rag, a handkerchief of indeterminate origin grown ratty with overuse. Did he even have any antihistamines in his overnight bag? He shut his eyes against the sun and the breeze, and as he did so, the memories returned under the soft cover of darkness.

It was another mid-morning in late August. He was five years old, lying on the overstuffed blue couch in the living room. His mother in her sun-outfit had just returned from the supermarket, her sandals slapping against the linoleum as she put away the groceries. She was humming an old tune, the words to which had rubbed off years ago. Cricket just lay there, quietly sniffling and rubbing his eyes. He was supposed to be playing in the schoolyard, but something in the air outside had made him want to go back inside. It was a while before his mother noticed his presence at all.

"Honey, what's the matter?" Suddenly his mother loomed over him, her face wide-eyed with concern.

"My nose is leaking," he told her solemnly, "and I can't make it stop." It was a line she repeated to his father when he got back from work that day, and after that they took him to a doctor. He remembered a turquoise pill that always made him drowsy, eventually replaced by a tan pill that had the same effect. They didn't even work that well: at the height of the spring allergy season in third grade, he was the one who walked around with a 1,000-sheet roll of toilet-paper in a bag embroidered by his mother, so he'd always have something to sneeze into.

She wrapped her arms around him and wouldn't let him go. The song she sang most had the annoying refrain: "Take good care of yourself, you belong to me." She showed up at school with his medication when he forgot to take his pills. Most embarrassing of all, she wouldn't let him go on the class field trip to the nature center, for fear he might have a bad allergic reaction to something unknown. She bought him books instead of baseball bats, keeping him indoors as much as possible. His father was flippant, dispensing advice like "Don't sneeze too hard or your nose'll fall off."

When he was in the sixth grade, his symptoms receded, and vanished the next year. No more itchy eyes, no more drowsiness—he might as well have been normal. But his outlook on the world had already been formed. He had to be wary (the most beautiful day could harbor an attack); he was cautious (always bring along your survival kit). He'd become insular: sports like baseball and soccer were vaguely suspect; reading indoors was what he preferred. "I think I have an allergic personality," he'd confided to Sofie, who understood all too well, even without his explanation. Had he changed that much since then? It seemed like forever in no time at all.

He blinked and was back in Hikari, dabbing at his nose in front of a woman named Reiko and her family. "Listen, I think I'd better leave," he told her. "Whatever it is, isn't go . . . going . . . *achoo!*" This last sneeze was particularly messy. Reiko diplomatically handed him the whole tissue packet. They left her parents to continue the ceremony alone as they went in search of a drugstore.

"Will this work?" sniffed Cricket doubtfully, examining a blister-packet of yellow pills a little later. They'd also bought three more tissue packets. Leaving the graveyard had helped, but he still felt a little precarious.

"I think so . . . ." Away from her parents, Reiko showed more affection. Now she reached out to pull softly at his nose. "*Warui hana, ne?*" Bad nose, miscreant nose.

Where's your stupid roll of toilet paper? asked a rude schoolyard voice.

The return of the repressed, he thought. He had read Freud in college. And Jung believed in ghosts. "Look, I'd better get indoors. Let's go back to . . . to . . . *achoo! Achooo!*" He scrabbled desperately at the plastic slit in the tissue packet, but couldn't get through fast enough.

Half an hour later, he was lying on a futon in a darkened room, his head propped on a pillow stuffed with dried beans. Reiko was at the kitchen sink, wetting a washcloth to lay over his puffy eyes. A circle of crumpled tissues ringed the pillow like a lumpy halo. The inside of his head felt bruised, from either congestion or the return of his childhood. The vision of his mother had departed as soon as it had come, leaving only a trace of lipstick, a whisper of eau de cologne. He was left alone with himself again.

Life was sad. Yet here was someone. Reiko came into the room, murmuring "*Kawaisō*"—you poor thing. Slowly, as if enacting a ritual, she laid the washcloth across his eyes. The cool dampness soothed the itchiness, and the presence of Reiko's body relieved the loneliness a bit. Reaching out to touch her, he found the smooth inward curve just above her hip. She placed her hand over his, and they sat there for a moment. The moment, which seemed to exist as a pulse between their hands, grew larger and larger until it filled the whole room.

He wanted to say something—an endearment, some jest—anything to break the silence that was growing thick as cotton. But his tongue acted as if it had been put in backwards, and as the moment prolonged itself, he felt himself getting drowsy. At first, he thought it might be the draining effect of emotion, but then a memory stirred inside like a ripple in a pond from an underground current. The lethargy had to be from the antihistamines, he recalled. It was like walking underwater. As he looked toward the blinded window, his gaze slid upwards: the dim white ceiling, the overhead fan lazily revolving like a propeller coming at him in slow motion. Reiko dissolved into a soft gray shape by his side as he fell backwards into a deeper gray, a longer moment.

The house was darker these days, the October days growing shorter and colder as his mother lay upstairs in bed. All that summer something had been wrong, nothing he could really understand except that his mother was always tired, and often away to see doctors, from whom she seemed to come back even more exhausted. Why do you see them if they make you tireder? he wanted to know. She just smiled and patted his head. Crick, oh, Crick . . . .

She wore a faded blue bathrobe that smelled of sleep and her perfume like roses in alcohol. Later his father came home in his brown business suit and explained that she was sick but would get better. These things take time, his father said, smiling and patting Cricket's head in a manner that wasn't at all the way his mother did it. When his father asked him to leave the room, he slammed the door and read on the living room sofa—for three months. When his hay fever came back in the fall, he slept there.

Meanwhile the thing that took time kept taking it. His mother's body was collecting shadows: under her eyes, along her throat, and in the loose skin of her arms and legs. She went to fewer doctors, but that didn't seem to help, either. She only half-answered his questions with a wan smile, while his father grew testy and told him to go to his room.

So he withdrew. He went to school and did his work and came back home and lay on the sofa again to read. He particularly liked books that involved magic and transformation. My mother the witch, my father the dragon. A cold enchantment ruled the house. The few friends he played with no longer came over because he fought with them, but the isolation just made him more determined. If he could simply get absorbed in his own activities—reading, improvising little games—he could break the evil spell for days.

Only now that the cold weather had set in, his mother rarely went out of the house, and occasionally she'd call him on the intercom that his father had rigged up between floors. The bodiless voice would come out of the grid: Crick, can you hear me? Crick, are you there? Could you get me a glass of milk, bring my sweater from downstairs, read to me? Except sometimes he'd merely lie in silence, pretending he wasn't around.

His father paced angrily. Why won't you do what your mother tells you?

I'm busy. Anyway, you told me to go to my room.

His father hit him. Don't be a smart aleck. Your mother won't—

Won't—won't what? he cried in between tears.

But his father left the room without finishing his sentence. The air in the house became cold and thin, taking shape only around his mother, who was losing her voice and eyesight. He kept waiting impatiently for her to get better.

No one told him she was going to die.

When she left in November, he felt like something had died inside his own body, or as if a piece of his heart had been wrenched away and replaced by some cold, metallic part. For almost a year afterward, he carried around this dead matter. His father tried to comfort him through various distractions—a pet collie, a trip to France—but Cricket was allergic to dog dander and sulked in front of the Louvre. Anyway, he saw through the tricks and clung to his grief and guilt. He still talked to his mother, and often she answered back. He treasured her Swiss army knife (which he lost on a camping trip when he was fourteen). And though he eventually found some new friends, he kept a cautious distance. Be careful, said a voice that wasn't his mother's or his father's or even his own; don't get too close because they'll leave you.

He read books all the time now, even during meals when there was often no one else at the table. His father was busy at the office. By the time he entered junior high school, he had lost his plant allergies and acquired an allergy to people. A girl with a crush on him in ninth grade taught him how to relax and paid for it with his panicky withdrawal. Stubborn kid, muttered his father when Cricket told him he was headed for Cornell rather than his father's alma mater, Princeton. He lowered his head. But he grew tired of his own coldness, yearned to open up. You're an Aries, murmured Sofie, running her fingers wherever she liked. I'm not surprised you're so obstinate. The voices told him to beware, but could he trust them?

The years rattled along like empty carts. "Cricket is a very intelligent pupil with an oddly formal manner," wrote his fifth-grade teacher on her evaluation. He was a lonely boy of twelve who talked to himself. He was a scared fifteen-year-old student who took refuge in reading and writing. He was a college freshman who got all A's in his first semester and was crestfallen to meet someone who had actually received an A+. He was a departing graduate who'd decided to leave Western civilization behind. Yet none of this was quite true: he liked the world of the classroom; he had a few admiring friends, whose mothers were always offering to cook meals for him; he wasn't homeless, after all. During one bleak month, his father spent a whole weekend with him at the arcade, at the movies, in a diner. He still made attempts to get along with his son, though they usually ended in Cricket's withdrawal and his father's disgust. Slowly they learned to get along, after a fashion. Civility, insisted his father, was an underrated talent. So Cricket learned politeness, though in the way a pupil learns a lesson. His father was right: it got him places. It got him to Japan.

So why did it all seem so barren in retrospect? It's not what happened, murmured the unidentified voice, it's what you remember, it's what you become. Cricket could put aside his carefully cultivated stiffness, but it was like watching the unbending of someone with joint trouble. It hurt to be vulnerable. Better to preserve the mask.

A grinning *Nō* mask swam by his face. He grinned back at it, carefully measuring the angle of his bow. The cloud creatures descended, and though none of them could help find his mother, they showed him how to write the *kanji* for *mother*, which looked something like a chest of drawers. When he opened the first drawer, he found his Swiss army knife. He opened the next drawer to find the mouth of a long upward tunnel, which he began to climb.

When he awoke, Reiko was gazing down at him, her solicitude all too apparent. "There you are," she smiled. "I wait for you."

"What? Oh . . . thanks." He raised a leaden hand to take the cup of green tea she offered. His mouth was dry, and his head felt as if his brains had been stirred with a long spoon. Side-effects from the antihistamine, or maybe just from climbing through the tunnel. Already the chronology of the dream was fading, merging into one continuous gray scene. Outside, it was just a shade past dusk, and from somewhere beyond the window came the sound of a slow drum.

"Everyone went to festival. I tell them, we come when you wake up." She reached into her store of English to pull out one of her strangely metaphoric locutions: "Are you all out of sleep yet?"

"I . . . guess so." He took a sip of tea. It was *genmai-cha*, with its faint undertaste of brown rice. Not his favorite, but the way he felt, he would have drunk saltwater. He opened his mouth for a long swallow, and the fluid seemed to travel right into his veins. *"Aaaah . . . "* he breathed. But when he rose to a sitting position, his head lagged behind. *"Ooooh."*

"*Daijōbu?*"

"Yeah, I'll be all right."

"Have another cup." Like most Japanese, Reiko believed fervently in the restorative effects of tea. At any rate the caffeine helped, and in a little while Cricket was donning a borrowed blue-and-white-checked *yukata*. It came only to his knees, since Mr. Hashimoto was half a head shorter, but it would have to do. Turning him around like a model, Reiko tied his sash with matronly care. She herself changed into a green kimono with a pre-tied obi.

"You take good care of me," he observed quietly.

She turned away. "You know why." She meant that she loved him, though she knew he didn't like to talk about it.

Why not? she'd asked him the first time he shied away from the subject. I thought Americans always talk about love.

Not this American, he told her. I'm just not very good with feelings.

Ah, you are Japanese.

Privately, Cricket wondered if he wasn't allergic to love. It seemed as good an explanation as any.

Now they were walking to the festival grounds, following the path of multicolored plastic lanterns set into the pounded earth. Here and there an authentic torch blazed smokily against the darkening night. Foodstalls by the entrance offered grilled squid and roasted ears of corn, and Cricket realized poignantly that he hadn't eaten dinner.

Following his gaze, Reiko reached into the sleeve of her kimono and pulled out some money. "Here, I buy you corn."

"No, I—okay." It was childish to protest, he supposed, but that was what he felt like: a child. He still felt lightheaded from the effects of the drug. Clutching his ear of corn, he followed Reiko, who was looking for her parents. The festival was being held in a converted schoolyard with a decorated platform in the center. Lines of dancers rayed out from the platform like spokes on a giant wheel, with onlookers and tourists at the rim. As Reiko moved across the hub, Cricket had his snapshot taken several times by people who'd probably wonder later how a *gaijin* had wandered into the picture.

"We must be in between dances," he remarked, gnawing at his ear of corn. Everyone was milling around, chatting.

"Yes, we are in the middle of things." Reiko pulled at his sleeve. "Finish that corn."

Reiko's mother and father were on the other side of the circle, looking like quaint villagers in their *yukata* and split-toed *tabi*. When her parents greeted them, her father called Cricket *nebō*, sleepyhead. It's a debility, not laziness, thought Cricket with annoyance. If I were an amputee, would he call me "Peg-Leg"? But the Hashimotos just laughed. They indicated a spot to the left where two more people could dance.

As soon as they weren't looking, Cricket frantically finished his corn, but then faced the problem of what to do with the wet cob. Though the sky was now completely black, crepe-paper globe lanterns overhead illuminated the darkness. Whatever he did, he'd be seen. He couldn't very well throw it behind him—he'd certainly hit someone, given the crowd at the rim. Maybe he could bury it—but the hard-packed ground of the schoolyard was as unyielding as a rock shelf.

Suddenly the solitary background drum was joined by a medley of gongs, around which a Japanese flute flew in and out. A singer from the platform began to chant a melody, and everyone began to move in time with the music. Cricket hastily shoved the cob into his left sleeve and began the steps that Reiko had taught him. Right foot forward, left foot joining, sway back, undulate the arms, then clap. The rhythm was slow but graceful, as each point on every spoke of the wheel advanced. The clapping was punctuated by the singer's refrain, intoned by all: *Hikari-o*. To the right, Reiko rotated gently in line with him, her parents just ahead and curving in tandem.

He stepped, swayed, clapped, and for a moment was a part of the ring, in line with the people, the place, and the occasion. This horizontal human Ferris wheel to celebrate the dead moved with him and through him, as if the colored lanterns danced in his bloodstream. The night air smelled of the shore, smoke from the stands, and something else, a scent that flared his nostrils.

"*Achoo!*" He stumbled forth, breaking the rhythm of the dance. "*Achoo, hachoo!*" He reached for the tissues he'd stashed in his sleeve, but came out with the corn cob instead. In sheer frustration, he flung the cob to the side, where it skidded against the sandal of a nearby dancer. The man's mild protest was swallowed up by another sneeze. The lanterns swam in Cricket's vision, and he closed his eyes.

"Here." Something soft was being pushed into his hand. Reiko stood by his side, with a flock of tissues. Gratefully he took three and eviscerated them with one blow. "More?" He grabbed all she had. Gradually they moved away from the rest of the dancers, toward a scattering of spectators by a cotton-candy stand. Like a performer pushed out on stage, he sneezed several times for them. They stared curiously at him, then looked studiously away. Reiko patted him on the shoulder. "You need a new nose," she joked.

"That's not all I need." An alternate set of memories, maybe even a different brain. He recalled a notice that his father had posted during one bad season, when crumpled tissues littered the living-room couch: "If your nose runs and your feet smell, then you're built upside-down." *Am* I built wrong? he wondered. Not for the first time, he ached to be someone else.

Crick, oh, Crick, sighed his mother. Your feet smell fine. It's your head I'm worried about. Go talk to your father.

Who do you talk to when you feel that way? demanded Sofie. You don't talk to *me*.

You showah now, stated Ogawa-san, holding out a tissue big as a towel.

"Are you okay?" Reiko was peering anxiously at him, her usually smooth features screwed up with concern. "Come, I take you home." In the lantern-lit darkness, her hand slid into his and squeezed with the gentlest of pressures. He let himself be led away like an errant toy balloon. At the moment, he was too woozy to feel shame. The festival music receded until it was just a drum in the distance, and then they were back at her parents' place. She rolled out the futon again, made him lie down, and vanished for a moment.

Is this what love is? he asked the low ceiling. How does a family share it? Can death defeat it? Since no one deigned to reply, he kept on: Is it an attachment, an illusion, a force stronger than gravity—or just *evol* spelled backwards?

The window blinds clacked lightly in the night breeze. He sniffled and reached for a tissue, but they were all gone again. From several rooms away, he could hear Reiko moving about in the kitchen.

Is love different in Japan? he queried the futon. Do the Hashimotos love one another? There was a Japanese word he couldn't think of . . . one of those compound verbs that described this whole business, one he learned while at Kansai Gakuin. But then Reiko was back with a glass of water and another antihistamine on a little ceramic tray.

"I don't know if I want that." He raised a hand as if to fend off a scourge of drugs.

She stamped her foot like a little mare. "You must. To get better."

"All right, all right." He took the pill from the tray as Reiko watched approvingly. So he'd get tired again, so what? It was time to go to sleep, anyway. He was just swallowing the pill when the word came to him: *mendō-miru*, to take care of, to look after. Yes, that's it, he thought, as he replaced the glass on the tray. Reiko took the tray and disappeared again, dimming the light. The room was dark, and the ceiling seemed to have crept lower. When he fumbled around for a last nose-blow, he found that she had left two packets of tissues by his pillow. As he lay back with his eyes shut, he thought of a final question: How is it that you can feel lonely even when someone else is touching you?

No voiced response came, but he imagined his mother placing her hand on his brow. She smoothed his hair, brushing it back with her fingertips. The soft pressure of her hand felt so real that he finally opened his eyes—and saw Reiko kneeling over him, doing just what he'd imagined. Wordlessly, he extended his own arm as if to offer something in return. It wasn't right, it was too much, and for a brief interval he vacillated between yearning for her to do this forever and wanting to snatch her wrist away. She placidly laid his hand across her thigh and kept stroking him. He could no longer resist and soon gave up trying.

Outside, the drum for the dead kept to its rhythm, beating till dawn.

6. The Japanese

At the edge of the high-school playing field, Cricket stood and waited, hoping for the sudden appearance of a minor god or a chasm to open under his feet. It was the Year of the Monkey, the start of his third spring in Japan. A bank of cicadas, dormant all winter, wailed somewhere in the grass. Cricket himself felt stagnant and enclosed, which everyone had told him was a chronic problem for expats. Lately his periods of intense concentration and study—tea ceremony lessons, aikido, attending cultural events—alternated with spates of rebellion, days when just riding the immaculate subway system to and from his job grated on his nerves. At the moment, he badly needed a stimulant. Or a depressant. Or something.

Japanese society was conformist, which he'd found both good and bad. It was good in the sense that you always knew what to expect, and people were polite. That was comforting, reassuring in an uncertain world. It was bad because you always knew what to expect, and people were polite—the same damned aspects, fumed Cricket, that were so comforting and reassuring. Sure, the trains ran on time, and street crime was almost nonexistent. But you paid a price for that, at least the Japanese did.

A few weeks ago he'd been riding his bicycle around the south end of Nishinomiya when he passed a typical Japanese schoolyard, basically an oblong field of pounded earth. Eight in the morning, and all the children were rayed out like a sunrise, obediently performing calisthenics. He heard a loud authoritative voice and looked around for the source. It was only when he looked up, in the same direction as the students, that he realized where the sound was coming from: a huge faceless observation tower with a loudspeaker bolted to the rim, blaring out orders. The Japanese used to get their instructions from the divine Emperor, he thought. Now they get them from all over.

Enter a train station your first week here, and you could get lost in the maze of colorful signs and announcements and tracks. Come back after picking up some of the language, and you'd be astonished at how much had changed: the whole station functioned as a grid of information. The overhead signs told you politely but firmly that all passengers must purchase their tickets before boarding, the signs on the right and left instructed you to have a safe and pleasant ride, while the P.A. system was informing you that the Kobe express had just arrived on track 9. Step lively, step right up, watch your step.

Of course, as a *gaijin* he got the best of both worlds, the benefits of a controlled society and the freedoms tossed to an outsider group. The flip side: he didn't belong. It was like trying to get along with Mori and Mori. I've been their tenant for over a year, he thought, and still all I hear is "Good morning" in the morning and "Good evening" at night. No, he reconsidered, that's an exaggeration. We *have* talked—mostly about the weather. They're kind to me, but it's the kindness of strangers.

He'd written some of this to Peter Inoue a while back, trying to explain himself. As a *sansei*, a Japanese-American a few generations off the boat, Peter might understand. But he was also an overworked medical student pursuing the dream his parents had forced on him: chief surgeon or bust. "You sound like you have too much time on your hands," he'd told Cricket in a recent postcard, "maybe even a little lost. Why don't you come back home?" Cricket could just see him saying that, his rimless glasses studying the page in front of him, his lips pursed with just a hint of reproach. Well, he asked himself for the hundredth time, why don't I go back?

Why do I stay? he repeated to the air in front of him. Because I *like* it here. He'd never felt so at home in a country, and that included America, land of his father (which reminded him, his last two aerograms had received no reply). The food agreed with him, the customs suited his sense of decorum, the very streets led him in the right direction. Hell, he thought, I appreciate everything here more than Peter ever would. Maybe it's a cliché, but Japan has been like a mother to me. He shifted from foot to foot. What no one told him was that he'd get tired of mothering from time to time. Then he got these mood swings, and all of a sudden he wasn't Cricket Collins, the obedient adopted son, he was Crick the pain in the neck. The voices he heard in his head changed from authority to disrespect.

He wished, as always, that he had known his own mother better. His father had once hinted that she had a darker, wild side, particularly at parties. But what did that mean? Spiking the punch bowl, insulting the other guests, carving her initials in the table leg with that little red Swiss army knife she always carried with her? Of course, his father wouldn't elaborate. Cricket would have liked to ask her a few questions. He still talked to her from time to time—in his head. It usually calmed him down. Only now he was edgy. He hadn't even written in his notebook for days.

A recent falling-out with Reiko hadn't helped matters. After his semi-disgrace with her parents in Hikari, they hadn't talked much about love and its attendant obligations. Now she was graduating from Kobe Jo-Gakuin this coming year, and she seemed to have no idea what she wanted to do with her future. They'd had a fight last Thursday over that—when Cricket found out that she saw her future as him. They'd spent the weekend sulking separately, a sport he'd grown quite good at. But I know it's my duty to call, he intoned to himself, and I will. He kicked at some loose gravel. Maybe tomorrow.

Usually, he liked to suffer by himself. This time, he'd telephoned for help: a half-friend named Bruce, who happened to live only ten blocks away from where he'd wandered. Bruce was not his usual kind of company. He belonged to the Brit expat colony and ran on Saturday mornings with the Hash House Harriers in Kobe. But he'd gone bicycling with Cricket a few times—and we both live near Osaka in the Year of the Monkey, Cricket snorted, which makes for something in common. Many expatriate bonds depended on a lot less. Like just being non-Asian together. So he felt no compunction when calling from a public phone booth: "Take me anywhere, get me drunk, bring me to a place where I won't have to think about teaching English, learning to bow—any of that. Or about my tiny apartment in Nishinomiya."

"Right. Definitely." Good man, Bruce. "I'm not . . . *sure* about this, but I think there's a party on somewhere in Ashiya. Never mind, we'll find it. We'll go out to eat first. With Grant. He's got the van. See you in five minutes. Ta."

Bruce taught history at the Bromfield Academy, a rich prep school for the children of businessmen and diplomats. Grant taught something else at the academy and had a half-share in the van with Bruce. When I first came here, recited Cricket, explaining his own background to an invisible third party, I taught at Kansai Gakuin and lived in a dormitory. For various reasons, I found that too cloistered. Now I have a job at TESCO and travel all over Osaka to teach company workers how to pronounce *Philadelphia* without the *r*'s. That's what we English teachers do. And we're all in Japan together—that forms a kind of link. He laughed nervously.

He waited at the edge of the field, fingering but not reading a Yukio Mishima paperback he'd bought yesterday, *Confessions of a Mask*. It had established definite eye-contact with him in the used-book racks at the Juso Exchange, a weird second-floor shop off the Hanshin line that he'd recently discovered. The Exchange was part language school, part bookstore, somewhat of a travel agency, and maybe a few other things in back. The proprietor, an old man who looked either Asian or British, depending on the light, didn't talk much. You mostly saw non-Japanese there, which was to say foreigners.

Even used, the Mishima book had cost 1000 yen. It was an investment he felt he could recoup only by loving every sentence, but in his disoriented state he wasn't about to risk it. Instead, while he was waiting, he watched a group of schoolgirls in blue-and-white uniforms stage a volleyball practice. They seemed like cute, dynamic dolls, the way they all did. If Reiko was any guide, they had strong thighs and a lot of energy. Just then they were keeping a ball aloft, thumping it about in a tight circle. The ball, colored maroon and white, looked somewhat bruised.

Soon Bruce came jogging down the field, his unhandsome face sweating. He had huge pores and a long dog's-body, his nostrils always quivering. "Well, shall we go, then? My new flat is just down the road." He'd relocated his apartment, or rather was relocated by the school after his wife had come to Japan, hated it, and returned to England. Since the school supported only married housing, he now lived in bachelor's digs.

They walked down the road, gradually escaping the view of the school. The road soon narrowed but stayed neatly paved, flanked by a concrete sewage ditch protected by a railing. After passing a lot of houses like milk cartons with blue roofs, they came to a row of green metal bunkers. Bruce unlocked one of them. He made a half-hearted attempt to shake off his running shoes before entering, but one of them flew past the recessed area of the *genkan*, and the other got dragged along until he kicked it aside. His 250cc motorcycle stood like a banished pet in the miniature foyer. Cricket shook his head in admonition: he preferred bicycles. Through a doorway on the left lay squalor and an unmade bed. Cricket had the feeling that there'd be more disarray if only there were more room. Bruce motioned him into the tiny alcove on the right, which functioned as a haphazard kitchen.

"Tea? Doughnuts? Peanuts? How about an apple, or a banana? No, yes?"

"Tea?"

"Green or black? I don't have green."

"Whatever."

"Right, I'll make us both a cup. Grant'll be here in a minute, except he's usually late, so he'll be here in ten. Have a seat."

"I think I'll just stand." Cricket balanced on one foot, then the other, as he drank tea, filching peanuts and raisins from a convenient dish. In ten minutes exactly, Grant knocked on the door.

"Hello, Cricket. Hi, Bruce."

"Can I offer you—" Bruce looked anxiously at the pot "—a thimbleful of tea?"

"Nah, don't bother. Been playing rugby and just drank a lot of beer. Let me just get back to my place to change, and then we'll go for sushi."

Bruce and Grant knew of a place down the road that didn't charge them too much and didn't boggle at them for being foreign. One of the delights of being in Japan, thought Cricket sarcastically. After a short wait at Grant's green metal home, which looked remarkably like Bruce's, they left in the van. Grant made up for lost time by trying to beat a motorcycle down the hill, almost crashing into a traffic post when the motorcyclist swerved.

"Crazy bastard there, did you see that?"

They caught up to the motorcyclist again at the next red light, and Bruce leaned out the window to shout "Wanker!" at him.

They jounced farther down the hill, or maybe it was the second hill, towards the sushi place. At a small intersection, Bruce pointed to a small shack with a small blue sign, GYOSAI—why was everything so small in Japan? They parked on the bias, went inside, and ordered. The waitress spoke English. They spoke English. Beer arrived. They talked about the party that night.

"In honor of someone named Reggie Fowler." Bruce took a swig from his glass of Kirin draft. "At least I think it's Reggie. Member of the Kobe Rugby Club."

"What's he done?"

"Done? Nothing—oh, I see what you mean. Old Reg is getting hitched—can't remember her name, but she's Japanese." Bruce's nostrils flared. "Comes from a good family—speaks English well."

"Japanese women," said Grant, as if announcing the title of a thesis. "Easy till they get married. Then they turn into salary-grabbing witches."

They all took a long swallow of beer.

Kokusai kekkon, "international marriage," was big these days. Reiko had pointed this out to Cricket. To solve the problem of language, there were language schools. Around Osaka, the availability of Japanese instruction was outmatched only by the places that offered English lessons. Bruce, it turned out, was being tutored in the language by a Japanese girl who believed in free expression. Grant knew how to say "thank you," "hello," and "goodbye." Both had been here for eight months, but as everyone said, a few phrases certainly went a long way. Yes, that's one of the great things about Japan, Cricket thought of announcing, but didn't.

Their sushi came on a huge red lacquer tray: white sea bream, maroon tuna, yellowtail, translucent squid, salmon roe, sea urchin, cooked octopus and shrimp, and several unidentifieds, with plastic bamboo grass added for decoration. Bruce had a nasty accident with the soy sauce and complained about the lack of elbowroom in Japan. They left early to get to a liquor store, the sushi shop owner being more than usually obsequious because they were foreigners. He beamed when Grant said thank you, then goodbye. At the liquor store, they picked up three miniature kegs of Asahi beer for the party, though Bruce wasn't exactly sure where it was taking place.

"We'll just tool around until we hit it. Supposed to be near the station. I think it's on somebody's roof."

They took fifteen minutes getting to Ashiya, overshot the station, turned back, almost flattened a pedestrian, and parked on the curb. Music and an odd cackling came from a nearby building with lights on its flat roof. A burly Japanese with a mustache waved them away from the stairs leading up. "All down. *Shokuji-chū.*" He made a gesture of shoveling in food, then pointed to the little restaurant occupying the ground floor of the building.

An Australian twang boomeranged out the open window. "Go on, who're you calling a mick?"

Everyone inside was using chopsticks or hands at various levels of proficiency. They kept ordering *okonomi-yaki*, a cross between a Western omelette and a pancake, from the two waitress-cooks behind the grill. A huge rugby player pinched one of the women on the buttocks as she walked by with two plates of food, and she pretended to laugh. A straw-haired man at the far table began banging his chopsticks on the table and got a dishrag thrown at him by a sleeveless girl ten feet away. She missed, and the dishrag sizzled on the grill for a while.

"How the hell are you, Bruce! Take a seat, take two, they're small. Want some food?" A bald man with an eye-patch pointed at the various plates around him, which all had *okonomi-yaki* in one or another degree of consumption. Next to him—Cricket blinked twice—was the great receiving maw, Harry Belton himself. His girth had increased to sumo-size since Cricket had last seen him. If the belly is the spiritual center of the body in Japan, he thought, Harry must be a goddamn Buddha. Harry nodded at all of them, patted his greasy beard with an obscenely dainty gesture, and went back to his meal.

The bald man repeated his offer, but Bruce backed away with British politesse. "Thanks, I think . . . not. We've had sushi. Really fine place, like to take you there sometime. We brought beer." At this, all three of them held up their kegs, and about half the group cheered. Cricket noticed a few of the British girls in summer blouses, too many Australian rugby players, a few nondescripts, and a woman cradling an infant. One of the British girls told them to call her Cynthia and gave them glasses. Another dishrag flew through the air, and someone overturned a beer bottle.

"It's Reggie's birthday party *and* his engagement party." The woman with the baby was using it to gesture. She pointed with the baby to a triangular-faced leggy blonde at the far end of the room, and Cricket realized that it was Jennifer Hertzl, the L.A. Peril. "I think it's her birthday, as well—we bought three cakes, at any rate."

"Oh?" Bruce sat down next to a girl in a pink sleeveless blouse and began to spill beer, while Grant perched on the edge of a table to talk over the day's rugby match with the straw-haired man. Jennifer arched her eyebrows at Cricket, and he sidled over—another departure from his regular self, since he wasn't a sidler.

"*Hisashi buri*," she remarked out of the corner of her mouth, as if taking a drag on a cigarette. *Long time, no see*, translated Cricket automatically, momentarily pleased by the coincidence between the two cultures. Japanese . . . English, samey-same, he sniped back at himself. To Jennifer he nodded, practically a reflex by now. Someone could stomp on my foot in the subway, he thought, and I'd probably nod.

He opened lamely: "Don't see you at the office much anymore."

She blew a plume of invisible smoke, stretching her strong bare arms sexily. "Not much to see there."

He nodded and tried another tack. "You know these people?"

"Some of them. Who're you with?"

"Bruce and Grant. Over there." Only they weren't over there anymore, so he ended up pointing around till he located them.

"Hm. Didn't Bruce's wife fly back to Brit-land?"

"Um, yes. You know him? Her?"

"Not really. But I hear a lot." She put on a distant smile.

"I'm sure." Her ears were as tan as the rest of her, what Cricket's father used to call a year-rounder. "Hey, is it really your birthday?"

"Close enough." She spread her arms again, this time in mock despair. "I can't believe I'm going to be twenty-six."

If this is American-style flirting, Cricket thought, I've forgotten what it's like. "It happens," he murmured, trying to be hip. "So who're you here with?"

"I'm solo. Feels good." She patted her chest, but her grin disappeared in a second. Cricket noted that she was also talking too fast, which meant she was running on something that wasn't alcohol. "Christ, what a creep Jeff was."

He didn't bother asking who Jeff was. Or had been. He just nodded, slightly mesmerized. Jennifer was attractive in a hazardous way, he knew. Kobe was paved with her castoffs. "I'm sure you'll find someone before the night is out," he told her. Then he surprised the hell out of himself by winking.

She smiled acquisitively as she stood up. "Catch you later," she said. He didn't know the precise Japanese for that. As if by design, he let himself drift out of her circuit and into the Aussie caucus. They were talking rugby.

One brick-cheeked man described a flying wedge with his hands. "Some damn good players there today. See those two Japs at the corner table? I can't remember their names, but they're not bad at all. Wish to hell they could speak better English."

Cricket drifted some more. The baby-woman pointed the infant at him like a big microphone and asked what he did for a living. "I teach English at TESCO," he told her with a self-deprecating grimace. Of course, most of the people there—drunks, criminals, rugby players—taught some kind of English. No chivvying about qualifications for that in Japan, no siree!

Someone at the corner table vacated with a screech of chair legs, and Cricket sat down. A man with octagonal eyeglasses was poking at a little sea of *okonomi-yaki*, using his chopsticks like a set of oars. They talked for a while about teaching English. His problem, the man finally confessed, was that he couldn't stand the students.

"All in those dark blue suits, each with the company pin. Me, I just show up in jeans to see their reaction. Never get much response, though. Next year, if I make enough money, I'm going to India."

Cricket nodded: you could go places from here. That was a definite plus about Japan.

Bruce had already gone up to the roof. It turned out that the party had started right after the rugby match, though no one else had shown up until seven. This was the tail end of the dinner hour.

Grant came by, nursing two glasses. "Let's, you know, go to the roof."

"People finishing up here?" Eat-and-run Belton seemed to have waddled off already.

Grant nodded. "That's right. Anyway, the bill hasn't been paid, and there's always an argument with the last people left."

They left through the side entrance, circled around, and clambered up the spiral fire-escape steps. On the paved roof was a homemade bar and an amplifier system, pumping out a recent Japanese pop tune called "My Fine Lady." The straw-haired man ambled by and punched Grant on the shoulder. Cricket tried punching Bruce, standing right in front of him, but missed.

"Just relax." Jennifer was back, or maybe she'd never gone. With a swanlike motion, she poured Cricket a glass of Suntory whiskey. It seemed like a nice change from all the beer he'd been drinking. "Where do you come from, anyway, Cricket?"

"New York." Said in a gruff tone, these words still had an impact in the Far East. So what if it's really Tenafly, New Jersey? whispered an interior voice.

"Never heard of it." She took up what she was doing before, which looked like dancing. She swayed and bobbed, moving to some rhythm that didn't come from the amplifiers. The Japanese kid behind the bar watched Cricket, watched her, watched everyone in a kind of trance, which meant he spilled drinks occasionally. He'd apparently been hired for the night and wore a tuxedo with a Hawaiian shirt underneath.

It's amazing the number of people you can squash together on one small rooftop, thought Cricket. Of course, the Japanese are masters at spatial arrangement. Almost all the people from downstairs were engaged in a slow swirl at the center, eddying toward the edges. The smoggy dusk slowly obliterated any distinctions between west and east until the Japanese kid in the Hawaiian tuxedo reached down to snap on a string of—what else?—Japanese paper lanterns. They swung prettily and created cones of visibility. Cricket spotted Jack Sims in one, looking like an M.P. on holiday, demonstrating his knowledge of *shiatsu* on an Aussie girl.

At nine-thirty, the engaged couple showed up. The three cakes, two for the birthdays and one for the couple, had been set out half an hour earlier. Just a short while after that, Jennifer had sat down on her own cake by accident and gone downstairs to scrape frosting off her jeans. The other two cakes looked badly pecked at—though no one was touching them—and the first intimation that the fiancé had arrived was when a huge bull voice roared out, "Cake!"

A husky figure in a dark suit with a baby's bow tie held up one of the cakes. Most of the icing was missing. The man in the dark suit, who had a lantern jaw and who had to be Reggie the fiancé, weighed the cake and put it down again. By his side was a woman half his size dressed in a formal kimono, the tight hemline allowing her to move only six inches at a time. Cricket couldn't help wondering how she'd gotten up the stairs.

"Don't they make a lovely couple?"

Reggie tilted his head back and let out a huge rooster's cackle. His fiancée had hold of his sleeve.

"They've been together for over two years."

Cricket nodded and helped himself to more beer. Everyone knew couples like that—Larry and Naoko, Daniel and Mariko, John and Junko. On Saturdays, you could see them in the huge underground mall in Umeda, hand in hand, shopping for a sweater that would fit him. They talked in Japanese-English or English-Japanese. They ate rice and pizza. Cricket often wondered what happened to them after they got married. This wondering was turning into a problem. *Ojike ga tsuite-iru*, Reiko had taught him, was the translation for "having cold feet." He'd jotted this down in his notebook, though it wasn't the kind of phrase he was likely to forget. For one thing, Reiko wouldn't let him.

True, Cricket knew a former TESCO teacher named Ted Allen who'd married a Japanese woman, and they were even expecting a baby, but Ted was the most accommodating person in the world. Also, they'd left Japan, so they didn't count. No one counts who leaves Japan—that was the expatriate rule.

But he couldn't help thinking about other couples. Yasuro and Kyoko, for instance, from the days at Kansai Gakuin. Now *they* were a traditional couple: polite, undemonstrative in public, Japanese. He often wondered whether they'd gotten married, wondered with the annoyed curiosity that meant he'd once lusted greatly after Kyoko. She had the kind of shyness that anyone with an ounce of egotism interprets as playing hard to get. But midway through the year, he'd found out she was engaged to

Yasuro. The last Cricket had heard, Yasuro was going to get a job at Mitsubishi after he graduated. So what does that make Kyoko? he wondered. A housewife waiting for hubby to come home drunk on the Hankei line? But she was the loyal type—cruelly he imagined her fetching Yasuro's slippers in her mouth.

He looked over at Reggie's fiancée, who someone told him was named Ayako. Her smile was like a row of tiny pearls, but she wouldn't open her mouth much farther than that. She also seemed surgically attached to Reggie. The Stones' "Jumping Jack Flash" came through the amplifiers, and he found himself in the corner, talking with a woman in a batik shawl. She looked exactly like someone from Cricket's aikido class, except that she wasn't. The music made it hard to hear anything else, so they both had to shout until they got the bright idea of moving away from the speakers. Cricket realized that he was slightly dizzy.

"Last weekend was just like this—another engagement party, I mean. Sometimes I get sentimental about it." She picked at the chocolate icing from one of the cakes, which by then was little more than a vague, spongelike structure. They talked about life in Japan, which is why they were all here, presumably. She said that she didn't like paying 750 yen for a cup of coffee, and they agree there were certain cultural advantages at home.

"Of course, jobs are easier here. I couldn't get a job to save my life at home. Here, I'm an English teacher." She placed a hand on her meager chest. "I speak, and they listen."

Cricket nodded without really listening. The music continued its thumping bass, the whiny lyrics rising to "gas gas gas!," which some of the party crowd chanted as a mantra. This is what deejays at home call a blast from the past, thought Cricket—it's all that most expats know. He wandered around trying to find a haven from the noise. All he could hear were pieces of different conversations which sounded like one strange whole.

"She's no company for him."

"Hasn't been since they moved to Rokko."

"*Why* are these lanterns yellow? Everything's been yellow since I got to Japan."

"My God, who did the decorating here? It's lovely, I really mean that."

"Here, try this bottle, it'll make you forget all about the decor."

"If you don't drink, why'd you come here?"

"I always come here. Where do you end up?"

"You know, you can end up anywhere here. In Kobe, in

Rokko, in Osaka, in a ditch by the roadside. Last week, I ended up in my room. Alone."

Jennifer, re-emerging from below like a flower that had just been watered, asked him to dance. Why the hell not? The Beatles' "Let It Be" flowed around them, which meant that it was slow-step time. Since Jennifer was half a head taller than Cricket, she stooped to fit into his arms. This was as arousing as it was disconcerting: he was so used to looking down at Reiko. Jennifer leaned against him, her breasts rubbing his chest, her body smelling of some familiar clean scent that he later identified as Japanese lemon soap. Their hands full of each other, they somehow managed to talk.

"This," she declared as they avoided the tarry patches on the roof floor, "is more like it."

What they didn't manage to avoid were other dancers, many improvising all over the place. "Sorry!" Cricket called out as they nudged one gyrating dervish with their double-buttocked form. "Excuse me," he mumbled as they cut through a Japanese couple improbably sketching a waltz.

"Just be glad I left my roller skates at home," Jennifer murmured into his ear, her lips so close that he could feel a buzz.

Cricket appreciated this kind of snappy humor, which he hadn't heard in too long. He grinned over her shoulder. "Home in Kyoto or home in America?"

"Here, but it's not Kyoto anymore. I've got a place in Sannomiya now."

That makes how many moves in how many years? Cricket wondered. Expatriates live like transients anyway, let alone having to shift residence every few months. He tried to visualize her Sannomiya apartment—the accumulated objects, what kind of clutter she saved—but he couldn't. I lead too insular a life, he thought for the tenth time that evening. *I don't know enough people.*

"So," he said a little too brightly, "English conversation topic No. 3: What brought you to Japan?" That really *was* the third question most Japanese asked foreigners, after name and occupation.

"You first." She swirled him around as if he were the woman.

"Me?" He had to give this some thought. His usual response was something about the beauty of the culture, but that didn't seem to fit tonight, and besides, he hadn't known about that before he'd arrived in Japan, had he? "I was looking for something different," he finally ventured.

"Wherever you go, there you are." Her perception startled him.

"Maybe, but I never fit in too well at home." He took back the lead, almost driving them against one of the Japanese lantern posts. "Anyway, what about you?"

"Escape." She threw her head back. "The real question is, why do we stay?"

Lack of options? Because they pay me. I'm learning Japanese. I like it here. Inertia. What's there back home? Since he didn't want to tell her his feelings about Japan the motherland, he ended up saying nothing. They continued to move around in a circle.

"You know," she warned, "people change after two or three years here."

This time he decided not to wait till he thought of the right answer. But when he opened his lips, he got a mouthful of Jennifer's honey-blonde hair.

"Hmm . . ." she purred and stuck her tongue in his left ear. The feeling was wet and electric, sexy but such a shock that he pulled back. It was clear that he could end up at her apartment in Sannomiya, but then he thought of Reiko and her slender body, her fierce loyalty and willingness to be his, all combined with that odd delicacy—her Japanessence or whatever the term was. Suddenly Jennifer was a weight in his arms, and they bumped to a stop.

"We need something to drink," he told her, and she nodded, a little puzzled. He came back with two giant Sapporo beers from the rooftop bar, which was just a plank across two overturned garbage cans. "Look, I'm going to mingle a bit." He tried to sound British, as if mingling were an obligation he found amusing in a tiresome sort of way.

"Okay, but let's finish our beers first." This was a cleverer ploy than he realized, since these were liter bottles that took forever to drain. With all the alcohol in his system, he could feel each chug bringing him closer to total liquidity. Jennifer matched him gulp for gulp.

"Okay—*urp*." He finally put down the empty bottle on the roof and waved Japanese style, pivoting at the wrist. In a moment, he collided with one of the Aussie girls. They performed a do-si-do in an attempt to get by each other. In his swing to the left, he almost went over the railing. He recovered by thrusting out one limb—his arm, perhaps. This maneuver made him slightly woozy, and he had to sit down for a minute. The roof had become implausibly crowded, like Umeda at rush hour.

Somewhere in the center of the action was Charlie Sayles, flinging himself about with two Japanese girls who mimicked his every hop and flail as if learning a routine.

He'd managed to lose Jennifer for the moment. But getting to his feet again, he saw someone he'd never expected to see again, not that he'd ever forgotten him—Matthew, the guy who'd snubbed him at Osaka Aiport. Who'd subsequently high-hatted him in a tea shop. *The* American expatriate in Japan, the person Cricket compared himself to whenever he practiced his Japanese, the hobgoblin of his mind for the last two years. He was standing over in the corner, safe from the fracas, sipping a drink. He must be well over six feet, thought Cricket. He'd stand out in any crowd, so why didn't I notice him before? And what's he doing here? This doesn't seem like his scene. Or at least that wasn't how Cricket had imagined him, and he'd been imagining him for a long time. When he'd met him on the plane coming over here, Matthew said he'd already been in Japan for three years, the way you talk about an army hitch. The tea-shop scene, Cricket now realized, had been equally bleak.

The music changed to "Pinball Wizard," and everyone jerked in a slightly different direction. Does he recognize me? wondered Cricket. Should I wave? Christ, he's wearing a really weird expression—moving like a sleepwalker. I'll chance it.

"Hey, Matthew!" Cricket waved so broadly it looked like the all-clear sign after an air-raid.

Matthew waved grimly to him, and Cricket started to move in his direction, but he got blocked by two dancing couples, then by a fat man spilling drinks. When he finally reached the far corner, Matthew was gone. Damn it. That's what happened at the airport, thought Cricket, and everywhere else, too. He just disappears. Hell, maybe I'll see him another year.

He looked around some more. One of the roof amps blared "that deaf, dumb, and blind boy" in his ear. The woman who'd been holding the baby finally couldn't stand it anymore and began to rock wildly in time to the music, rocking the baby with her. After a few minutes, she gave the baby to the man with the eye-patch, who began to dance, too. The baby, which might have been doped because it remained asleep, was eventually taken by a sympathetic Japanese man, who crooned to it. Cricket liked the man for what he'd done, so he walked over and introduced himself. They started speaking in Japanese. The man told Cricket that he ran an antiques store in Kobe and collected foreign friends. The reason he was here tonight . . . Cricket couldn't catch what he said next, except for one word, *kembutsu*, something like "sightseeing."

Meanwhile, the engaged couple, having disappeared downstairs a while ago, reappeared slightly flushed. They were led to the center of the roof and handed a package of presents, heavy with symbolism. Hot dogs, bananas, a tightly furled umbrella, a beer bottle, a folding fan, and a strange cylinder of some kind were dumped out onto a chair, held up to the lights, and variously examined. Then they were thrown in various directions, though Ayako tried to save the umbrella. Somehow Cricket ended up with the fan, which, when opened, showed a gray carp swimming through the panels. The imprint at the bottom read *Nihon Senmei*, Japan Life Insurance. The strange cylinder turned out to be a vibrator. Reggie gave his rooster's cackle again. It sounded more realistic each time.

Grant was climbing the water tower using only his hands. When he got to the top, he pulled down his pants and performed what he called the natural function of a water tower. This event had little to do with the police, who came up the fire escape five minutes later because of the noise. Their English was minimal, but one of the Australian rugby players walked over to try his Japanese. His Japanese wasn't bad, actually, and he managed to be so rude that the head policeman said he was ending the party. Three other policemen were waiting on the stairs, stopping the rugby player from a possible fist-fight. Everyone trundled down the corkscrew steps, with Reggie hoisting Ayako in a fireman's carry after she almost broke a leg descending.

Cricket found Grant and Bruce on the sidewalk with three women. One of them was the Aussie who'd almost whirled Cricket off the roof, another was a stubby girl in blue who kept inspecting her nails, and the third was Jennifer, none the worse for wear. She grinned unmistakably at him. He didn't know what to do—this kind of thing never happened to him. If I write this down tomorrow, he thought, my notebook won't believe it. And what about Reiko?

The van they came in was parked a block down. Bruce raised an eyebrow like a caterpillar. "Well?"

Cricket cleared his throat very awkwardly. "If it's all the same to you, why don't you give me a ride home? First, I mean." He tried not to look at Jennifer.

Grant laid a hand, then both hands, on Cricket's shoulder. "No drink?"

Cricket relented, carefully detaching the hands. "There's a

small place near where I live. Or we can drink in my apartment." Safety in crowds, he thought. And you can drink almost anywhere. The Japanese seem to agree on that.

Without explicit agreement, they all piled into the van. Bruce was pushed into the driver's seat and they pulled away from the curb. Bruce was drunker than he'd let on, and at the first traffic light he came to such a sharp stop that Jennifer got thrown into Cricket's lap. She fastened her hands around his waist as a safety belt. As her nails dug into his buttocks, he groaned, knowing he was done for. It took them a while to drive back to Nishinomiya, during which Bruce wove through two columns of cars and sideswiped a Honda hatchback. Every lurch drove Jennifer further into Cricket until they were practically fused. Her breasts pushed heavily against his face. The girl in blue looked politely away; the Aussie woman leered. Bruce took the last turn too fast and almost demolished a roadside shrine. Japan is a very historic country, thought Cricket drunkenly. They parked on the sidewalk and let all the passengers extricate themselves. Jennifer slowly detached herself from Cricket's side. Grant had somehow wedged himself into the luggage compartment.

"Where are we? Now, I mean."

"Near my apartment." Jennifer looked ready to eat his underwear, but somehow he had to appease this crowd first. "Look, I know a sort of restaurant that stays open late. They serve beer."

"Lead on."

The restaurant, really just corrugated siding set up nightly in front of an alley, was almost full. Most of the customers were truck drivers, eating ramen and drinking beer. They all watched the foreigners intently. They were especially appreciative of a mishap Bruce had with his chair, but they weren't exactly rude. Cricket quickly ordered fried dumplings and beer as they talked about the party.

"I thought Reggie and his fiancée looked smashing."

"I feel sorry for Ayako."

"Someone told me she comes from a good Japanese family."

"Someone told me she rented the kimono."

Jennifer squeezed his thigh under the table.

"*Unnnh* . . . they do that because the kimonos are so expensive. It's a custom."

The discussion about Japanese customs soon petered out for lack of data. The girl in blue confessed that she led a cloistered life. Apropos of expensive clothing, Jennifer made a comment about the TESCO boss Murase-san and his clothes-horse mistress, some Kyoto woman named Mika. "You can tell she belongs to him. And that kind of silk dress costs a fortune—I know."

"So the wife doesn't know?" asked the girl in blue.

"She does and she doesn't," said Jennifer with a shrug. "That's always the way."

Various nods.

How do you know all this, Cricket wanted to ask, and does everyone have this kind of knowledge but me?

Grant, not entirely irrelevantly, chimed in with a crude story about a long-haired girl named Jill, since gone back to England, who'd slept with two friends of his. At the same time.

Jill? thought Cricket frantically. With really long brown hair? He recalled her from the days when he'd lived in a dormitory at Kansai Gakuin. She'd been quite friendly, but Ogawa-san wouldn't let her visit his room. "Did she have a Liverpool accent?" Cricket blurted out.

"That's the one," agreed Grant, looking at him with new interest. Jennifer was now blatantly fondling Cricket. "Did you know her, too?"

"Not really," Cricket admitted, trying to avoid a violent intake of air as Jennifer reached his groin.

The dumplings and beer soon arrived, but no one felt much like eating or drinking. Bruce filled all the glasses anyway, as he talked about the motorcycle races he was going to the next day. He tried to persuade the girl in blue to come with him.

"C'mon, then, what'd you come to Japan for, anyway?"

She yawned into her untouched beer. "I'd rather sleep."

After enough dumplings had been eaten and a few in the group had sipped their beers, they decided to go. The Aussie was vaguely worried about how she'd get back into her apartment. "I forgot my key, and my landlady gets angry when I come back this late. She can't speak English, so I can't explain."

"Don't worry, love, we'll break in somehow." Bruce flexed his arms. "All right, heave-ho."

Grant had fallen asleep, but he soon woke up. Cricket paid the check, though the girl in blue pushed a 500-yen note into his hand after leaving.

"You shouldn't have to pay all that."

Cricket offered a ritual protest, then muttered, "All right—thanks."

Jennifer slipped her hand into his back pocket, as much for support as to cop a feel. He thought of giving her the fan in his other pocket, maybe not now, eventually as a sort of present, but decided he liked the carp design too much. Instead, he gave her a broad smile. The rest of the group seemed to understand instantly. They all piled back into the van (this time Grant was elected to drive), and almost everyone waved.

"Bye."
"Good night, now."
"See you."
"*Sayonara*, mate."
"Ta."

Cricket and Jennifer waved back until the van ran a red light and zoomed unsafely out of sight. Turning to each other, they exchanged a kiss like molten lead. Envisioning the night to come, Cricket couldn't believe his luck or his perfidy. Should I kick myself or pat myself on the back? For the difficulty of it, he tried both and almost landed on the curb. With Jennifer's arms outstretched to break his fall, he suddenly realized that he'd misplaced his Mishima book, God knows where.

"What's the matter?" she asked.
"Nothing. I just forgot something."
"What?"
"A book. I lost a book."

She shook her head despairingly. "You *are* a strange *gaijin*, Cricket." She ran a shivery hand down his cheek. "We'll make up for the loss, okay?"

You always find something to read, muttered a voice in his head. And you'll probably go back to writing in your notebook tomorrow.

So what? He shook his head to clear it.

By now they were only two blocks away from his apartment. Mori and Mori must long ago have gone to sleep, but music from the adjacent *karaoke* bar issued forth as Cricket fumbled with his key, and suddenly the lyrics of a song swelled into the night air. "*Ai dido ito mai uwei*"—the ever-popular Japanese version of Sinatra's "I Did It My Way." The singer was a passable tenor, making real headway against the canned background music. It could be Reggie, thought Cricket, if he were kidnapped at birth and raised in Kobe. But would he still be a rugby player, and would he have attracted Ayako's attention at the Daimaru department store where they first met? Where did Matthew disappear to?

Jennifer tapped her foot just as the music stopped.

Suddenly, a loud belch from the bar broke the silence. It burgeoned outward like the croak of a tree frog perched on the highest branch of a pine tree, or the ripple from a rock in a pond. The breeze carried the sound over the humid street till it thinned into night air. For a moment, Cricket felt in the presence of true poetry. But Jennifer was laughing hysterically, and he soon joined in. After a moment, he unlocked the door, took off his shoes at the entrance, and paused there, halfway home.

7. Eastern Standard Time

He was nearing the end of his voyage, signaled by a grand procession of swirling limbs and faces. Beyond the crowd, white gauzy shapes bowed and beckoned, luring him on as they receded into the clouds. But as the cumuli slowly parted, a yellow warmth settled on his face, tickling the hairs in his nostrils. He opened his eyes gradually to see the slatted pattern where the sun came through the Venetian blinds. The pattern was already halfway up the wall, which meant it was past nine o'clock. Yet the fixity of the light in the silence of the room created an odd illusion, that it had been exactly that time of morning for the past year.

Cricket reached absently toward the other half of the futon, but Reiko was gone. She left early because of her work at the Meishin trading company, an office job that began at eight-thirty. Getting there by train took almost an hour, and she often didn't arrive home until after seven, at his place by eight. She had her own apartment, but her landlord distrusted *gaijin*. That was all right with him: it gave him time for necessary reflection, time to be alone. The more time he had, the more he seemed to need, like an expanding vacuum. Occasionally, though, he wondered whether Reiko resented his own working hours, which were so scant as to be practically free-floating.

Almost any day of the week, he could do whatever he wanted: cook a five-course Japanese meal, go to the American Center to read *The New York Times*, even roller-skate down Ueshima-dori if he'd been so inclined. The English-teaching company TESCO had once linked him up with his assignments, but they'd taken too large a cut from his fee and imposed too rigid a schedule. He also hadn't gotten along well with the other teachers, so nowadays he did only freelance work. Today, a Tuesday, he had a lesson at four in the afternoon, and nothing else until then.

He rolled up the futon, stretched lazily, and padded over to the tiny blue-tiled bathroom that always reminded him of the inside of a fish-tank. In front of the mirror, he rubbed his eyes (puffy), examined his teeth (yellowing a bit), and raised his pajama top to check his waistline. One of the initial attractions about Japan had been the naturally low-fat diet, but lately he'd been putting on weight. For a while, his frame had combatted all outside influence, not just calories but also his desultory attempts at exercise. Lately, something inside had slackened. He was beginning to look like his father, whose bodily contours were largely reined in by mental effort. He shrugged, took off his pajamas, and got into the shower.

After a thorough toweling, he walked over to the small kitchen area and put the aluminum kettle on to boil. He reached into the cabinet for the sack of *sen-cha* and sprinkled a few grams into his porcelain tea pot. Inscribed with a chrysanthemum design, it was a gift from one of his first classes two years ago. The endless stream of offerings—neckties, tea pots, *sake* cups—used to embarrass him, but now he accepted them with indifference. Most Japanese were extraordinarily hospitable if they weren't too shy. They treated *gaijin* specially, like giving him a small cake whenever he walked into Panza, his favorite bakery in Umeda.

Under a packet of *udon* noodles was a gorgeous square box of these cakes, *manjū*, each with its outer layer of pounded glutinous rice filled with sweet bean paste, probably one of the reasons he'd been putting on weight. When he moved in two years ago, he'd stocked the cabinet with seaweed, rice, and dried fish. Along with miso and tofu, that had constituted his main diet, and he'd been stick-thin for a while. But that was before his present sedentary way of life. An observer might have judged him to be over thirty, since he had the growing broadness, the bounceless step, of middle age. Only his head looked young: intense brown eyes perched on a thin nose and lips that sharply drew together the rest of his features: his mother's face, he'd once been told. He took good care of his complexion, washing his face every night with an expensive moisturizer called L'Avale, which Reiko had bought him. As his curly brown hair grew wispy, she passed slow fingers through it to puff it up.

He had his tea along with one cake on a little sun deck, from which he could see the upward sweep of the ginkgo trees in the park. The park formed the grounds of the shrine to Ebisu, one of the seven lucky gods. Ebisu happened to be the god of wealth, extending a plump white hand to protect all the nearby merchants, and at first the idea of this nearby sanctuary had greatly appealed to Cricket. Later he discovered the basis for some of the shrine's wealth, the decorated barrels of *sake* in back of the altar, symbolizing various donations from the local distilleries. Leave it to the Japanese to extract a certain poetry from money.

Only gradually, over the course of the last year, had he discovered the consolations of *aware*, the sweet melancholy that suffused so much Japanese literature, from Bashō to Mishima. It seemed to inhere in the very landscape. When he gazed outward, the branches of the ginkgoes were like a many-level house built by lugubrious insects, and he relied on the trees to give him some substitute for inspiration. He still intended to write, though any incentive was fleeting these days. He looked harder at the leaves. Who was it who'd told him that ginkgoes were also called "maidenhead trees"? Unfortunately, his *aware* wasn't the type that produced disconsolate odes. It was more like a long-term depression that produced nothing. And the nothing wasn't a Zen nothingness but a sort of limbo. "Expatriate existentialism," as Dawson the TESCO staffer had once described it—but Cricket wasn't connected to TESCO anymore, so Dawson had, for all intents and purposes, disappeared.

The end of October was near, the mornings growing chilly. The cicadas and their siren song had long ago departed. From his second-story outlook, Cricket could see the man with the pointed stick picking up trash from the lawn around the shrine. On weekends the shrine was a tourist attraction, and by Monday a circlet of wrappers and paper cups fringed the greenery like a piebald monk. He had been there once or twice in the early morning before there was any life in the park at all. Once on a whim he'd even picked up the trash himself, depositing it all neatly in the wire-mesh receptacle before the puzzled groundskeeper arrived. Now he sat and watched as the man expertly speared each piece of paper, denuding the lawn of its paper crown.

He padded back into the apartment to dress, then took a trip downstairs to see whether the mail had arrived. The few other tenants in this two-story milk-carton of a building were mostly away at this hour, so he had the place all to himself. Or nearly: usually his landlady Mori read all the mail, or at least the available information on the envelopes, before depositing the day's delivery on the table in the communal foyer. He'd seen her at it once or twice, and she'd seen him seeing her, at which moment she'd handed him his mail as if that were the point. As he scribbled in his notebook: "The Japanese are an intensely private people who grant each other no privacy at all." Whenever his thoughts strayed back to that ace busybody Ogawa-san at the Kansai Gakuin dormitory, he felt extremely uncomfortable. Oddly, she still wrote him a card at mid-summer and New Year's, and odder still, in the uneasy grip of obligation, he always sent one back.

Today there were only three envelopes, two with addresses in *kanji* (which he read badly, having put his studies on hold last year), and an aerogram addressed to Mr. Cricket Collins. He picked it up like a fragile artifact, not reading the return address until he was perched on the only seat in his room, a fold-up chair that looked as if it had been stolen from an auditorium. It doubled as his typing chair at his desk, though for the past few days he'd had it facing the autumn light from the window. Almost everything in his apartment was collapsible or temporary, from the bedding that rolled up to fit in a cabinet to the reinforced cardboard dresser that looked like a wrapped present. The one-burner gas ring, the no-legged table—some of the items he had bought himself and others he had inherited from departing foreigners, but all were at the stage where he no longer recognized their individuality save as an extension of himself.

The angular limbs of the chair creaked disobligingly as he settled down to read. "Dear Cricket-san," the letter began in tightly slanted handwriting. "It's been a while since I last wrote you—busy, busy, busy, from the time I get to the hospital at six a.m. to quitting time, which is never . . . ." What followed was a messy précis of Peter Inoue's third-year medical school blues. The irony that someone named Inoue was pursuing this all-American course while his Caucasian friend had traveled to Japan was never lost on Cricket. Mainly it had been an escape from law school, which had already doomed half the people Cricket had known at college.

The initial motive for staying so long had something to do with the pursuit of the Orient. Europe was foreign, but Asia was really different, even in the simplest of acts like eating: chopsticks instead of a fork, two wooden poles as opposed to metal prongs, or pincing versus stabbing. Yet it all worked well. Japanese society had an essential rightness and order, leading him to feel that he'd been led astray by American democracy into a swamp of anomie. Here were thousand-year-old customs instead of unheeded laws, prescriptions in place of shrugs.

But the overriding reason lately was an opposite impulse—if *impulse* was the right word for the way he drifted through his days. Here he had his own state within a state, an island of freedom floating in a sea of regulation. He had access to urban sophistication without crime, and a significant income without breaking his back to attain it. Teaching English was lucrative, with individual tutoring starting at ¥3,500 an hour, and group sessions far higher. The real money was in the few corporate classes he'd snatched from TESCO. In short, he could make it on his own.

His father, who used to wish that Cricket had pursued a law degree, had finally admitted that his son had a life of sorts. Of course, so did his father. Two months ago, he'd quietly remarried after all these years and let Cricket know in a letter. The accompanying picture showed him and his bride, a woman named Annabel with smile wrinkles and a mass of brunette hair, holding each other as if for mutual support. He'd met her last year at a party hosted by the Donaldsons—"You remember the Donaldsons," he wrote to Cricket, who didn't. Annabel was the recent widow of a doctor; no children. They promised to visit, but Cricket doubted they ever would. It was like many of the invitations in Japan: the offer was merely a gesture, and you weren't really supposed to accept.

Anyway, Japan was outside the ordinary American's drift zone. Those who made it here were usually gone for more than a *Wanderjahr*. The easy wages helped prolong anyone's stay. From time to time, the assiduous Peter reminded him that the field of medicine was also lucrative, but Cricket had never answered these appeals. If he went home now, he suspected, he'd be acutely aware of his nonspecific status that friends like Peter only reinforced. The two had suffered no real break in communication, though lately Peter had expressed concern over Cricket's continued self-exile in Japan. "The leaves are turning red and yellow in New York," he had started his last letter in a somewhat Oriental vein, "and I wonder if you're turning Japanese." Peter was now doing a three-month surgery rotation at Mount Sinai Hospital, kowtowing to residents and interns. Buoying him was a steady girlfriend, also a third-year medical student, and a growing interest in moving to the suburbs in Westchester after he married. Privately, Cricket thought his friend was sinking in a bog.

This most recent aerogram offered items similar to the class notes in their alumni newsletter. Stan, the World's Most Ineligible Bachelor, had recently married. Greg, who'd pledged his soul to IBM, had taken up bodysurfing. Peter's own regimen sounded killing: following the nurses at morning call, or helping the resident physicians just before he was due to go home. "I just don't have the time to do anything else anymore," he complained near the bottom as he was running out of space. "It's satisfying at the end of the day, but I get home exhausted, and all I want to do is lie down on the bed and have a beer. Lately, I've even started watching television, and I used to hate it."

In the additional message space on the other side was one penciled question, "What are you doing with yourself these days, anyway?" Cricket put aside the letter. He'd reply this week, but there was no hurry. No sense in giving Peter the impression that he had nothing better to do than answer correspondence.

Over on the desk crouched his Olympia manual typewriter, its guts now half Japanese replacements but still functioning reasonably well. The machine still represented the ambition he had brought over from America, to write as an expatriate. At first he had kept his journal religiously, as well as composing short stories and sending them off to American magazines—along with half the people in the U.S., it seemed. Even in Japan, apart from one or two tourist-type magazines, he hadn't found any outlets. He'd had one story published in a magazine called *Squirt*, but failed to get a second one in, and last year he'd sold a typical "foreigner in a sushi bar" piece to *The Japan Times*. His few attempts to publish something back home all met with form rejections sent in the airmail envelopes he thoughtfully provided, the postage paid for with exorbitant international reply coupons. It was hard, very hard, he told all his friends. *Taihen muzukashii*, he told Reiko, which meant the same thing. A writers' group had formed in Osaka last year, but the inaugural meeting was peopled by half-poets and pseudo-hippies, and Cricket had never returned.

Still, he had a job, so it wasn't as if he were a bum or a recluse. A lot of foreigners, particularly in Kobe, lived from month to month illicitly teaching English and traveling to Tokyo twice a year to renew their tourist visas. Or taking the ferry to Korea to show they'd been out of the country at least once. Then they "visited" Japan again. He'd done that himself once, but now he had a real working visa, an apartment, and a job. Many *gaijin* had been here over five years and still didn't know much of the language. There was so little impetus to learn, unless one cared about the trivialities of occasionally boarding the wrong train, or having to point at dishes in restaurants.

Cricket's initial months of study had amassed into a core of information, and he could usually get around. He even knew some slang, which Reiko delighted in teaching him. But the spoken language, with its easy grammar, sharply contrasted with the *kanji* ideograms. What he knew he learned on his own. The most important terms like *train station* and *exit* weren't too hard: *east*, for instance, the first character in the eastern city of Tokyo, was a sun rising behind a tree. *Big* was a stick-figure with its arms spread wide. Retention depended on how pictorial your mind was—or maybe not: Japanese learned them by rote, stroke after stroke.

Occasionally Reiko grew impatient with his parrot-Japanese and tried to teach him some real grammar or a better way of phrasing something. "I'll go back to it someday," he would announce with a resigned smile and put his arms around her, ending all pedagogy.

Over by the dresser, where an American lover might have flung her clothes, Reiko's underthings for the next day lay in a neat pile. Her panties were a delicate jade green, her bra blushing pink. Reiko herself was petite and wiry, unlike the moon-faced students he often saw on the subways. But she had a fluorescent paleness from all her time at the office, and he worried about her health occasionally. Two hours of overtime wasn't at all uncommon for her. They all worked that way in Japan: it was ingrained in the system, along with morning gatherings and daily exercises before starting work. When polite Japanese asked Cricket what he liked most about Asia, he invariably said the way of life, but he wasn't talking about a typical Japanese existence.

The plastic red Seiko on his dresser blinked 10:30. He liked his little fold-up travel-clock, not that he ever traveled anywhere, but he enjoyed the idea that he could if he wanted to. In fact, almost all the objects in the apartment, from the gas ring to the freestanding cardboard closet, were temporary furnishings in a permanent place, like transients who've overstayed their allotted time. Some days he felt like the only still point in a revolving landscape.

Was it only inertia that could move him nowadays? He prodded his stomach to allay a mid-morning hunger pang. The seat of all spiritual force was in the *hara* or belly. Was he getting too soft? That was a constant worry, though as with any constancy, dulled by repetition. Occasionally he assuaged it through action. So. He knelt in front of the mirror by the sink, took a deep *ki* breath, and launched into the first movement of the aikido regimen he'd learned. The battery of lessons he'd taken during his first two years, from tea ceremony on, had more or less stayed with him.

Aikido was a peculiar synthesis of martial arts and Zen meditation that moved toward neutralization, not just of the opponent but of more shadowy demons. It had regimens like the Exercise of Stillness and helped calm the nerves. But as he reached downward to the floor, he felt a slight crick, a sudden dislocation in his lower back. The novelty of any different sensation almost encouraged him to keep going—until a further twinge stopped him. It was like one of the presences he harbored, an assertive voice.

Here I am, said the pain. Would you like to know me better? Cricket sat quite still. Another time, perhaps. Maybe he should go to the *sentō* tonight, the public bath near the train station. It was friendly, warm, muscle-soothing, and fairly cheap. For a long time he'd stayed away because he felt self-conscious, but now he felt the company might do him good. Meanwhile he contented himself with a few toe-stretches to fight the stiffness.

From his vantage on the floor, he saw his old battered notebook, veteran of a hundred train and taxi rides. It contained practice Japanese dialogues and observations on Hokusai prints, short-story openings without middles and many, many unmatched endings. In the notebook he'd described the sound of crickets, the musical traffic crossings for the blind, the sizzle of tempura dropped in oil, the train conductor's words when the stop was Nishinomiya, and the way a particular Japanese lady had thanked him for returning a dropped handkerchief. But the most recent remark in it was from a month-old meeting with a friend from TESCO days, Miyamoto. At one point, when Cricket had pestered him for an answer to a question, Miyamoto had looked at him levelly and said, "You know, Cricket-san, Americans always think that saying nothing is no response."

The effect on Cricket had first been expansive—he'd never thought of it that way—then restrictive—he tried so carefully to choose his words that none came at all. The notebook sat on a shelf, deliberately hidden from the casual glance. He didn't like to be reminded of writing when he wasn't actually doing it. Only now he had an idea: a catalogue of silences, from a pregnant pause during a conversation to the hush after a rainfall. He reached out for his notebook, flipped to where he'd left off, and scribbled a bit. The stillness of completion, and the ringing silence after a jackhammer finishes pounding. How about the difference between the silences after a question and a statement? The gap in space and time following a slammed door. The silent scuttling about in dreams. Or the horrible calm after a suicide leap.

He stopped writing at that point. The rooftop party in Ashiya had been half a year ago, but it had never entirely left his mind. The swirl of bodies like a human kaleidoscope, the near seduction that he could still feel at odd times of the day, the unexpected appearance of Matthew like a pop-up toy over the crowd—and the fall from the roof to the alley, which no one had even known about until the next day. Cricket had learned about it through Bruce, with whom he was no longer friends. "Poor bugger must've dived for it," he told Cricket the next week. "Might've spoiled a good party if anyone'd noticed at the time."

A small item had appeared in *The Japan Times*: Matthew Harriman, an American who had lived in Ashiya for the past five years, had been found dead in an alley, apparently from a high fall. The police had ruled it a suicide. No interviews with a neighbor commenting, "He seemed like such a quiet man," or friends who said, "Yeah, he'd been feeling kinda down for the past few months." It wasn't that kind of article. Cricket suspected that Matthew had been feeling that way for the past few years but of course couldn't prove anything. Most of the Matthew he knew was simply projection, anyway.

So he'd finally bested him, surviving Japan. Then why didn't the Matthew he'd built up in his mind go away, and why did he feel so guilty, as if he'd had a hand in Matthew's death? Who *had* killed Matthew, anyway? The Japanese?

His head hurt. Pushing Matthew to the back of his mind, he returned to listing silences. The absence of sound in an old-fashioned office, really composed of little pencil scratches canceling each other out, that was a good one. Leaning against the desk, still half in the aikido *zazen* position, the notebook propped on his knees, he covered a few more lines. He was working on a particularly hypothetical case, the silence in your head when you stop talking to yourself, when he realized how quiet it was in the room. Should he take that down, too? And was this activity art or merely observation?

The travel-clock now read 11:00. Depending on how you looked at it, he either was horribly late or still had hours to burn. He'd always had an abstract aversion to a nine-to-five job. Now accustomed to stretches of time in which he could read, walk, and take afternoon naps, he suspected that an office regimen would murder him. It was his own way of life, as a desultory teacher of English, that he valued in Japan. The daily toil was okay—for others.

Not that he didn't have his own schedule of sorts. It was a necessity for anyone staying longer than a year, and this was his third. Nine o'clock was the hour for rising, unless it happened to be later. At ten o'clock it was time to go shopping. It would have to be done after eleven today, but that was all right. Lunch, reading, and time for reflection occupied similar flexible niches. A Westerner living on Eastern Standard Time, that was his self-description. When he'd explained the joke to Reiko, she smiled dutifully, though he could tell she didn't think it was funny.

He walked over to his Formica-top desk, took a ¥5,000 note from the flat middle drawer, and walked back to the tiny vestibule, where his shoes were waiting for him, toes pointed toward the door. That was just one of Reiko's many little touches, along with precisely symmetrical dusting and commandeering his laundry. He reciprocated by doing most of the cooking, mainly because he enjoyed it. The preparations broke up the afternoon after his nap, and it was still a slight thrill to work with *daikon*, the giant radish like a hard white thigh, or the brown sinewy *gobō*, which his dictionary defined unsatisfactorily as "burdock root." His miso soup, with a delicate flotsam of scallion and tofu cubes, was almost elegant. Even his Japanese acquaintances, really just a few TESCO staffers who'd met once for a potluck party, admitted he was good at Japanese dishes.

Tani, the shy staffer with the gazelle shoulders, had particularly liked his *yaki-meshi*, Fried Rice à la Collins, with green pepper and onion. "Cricket-san," she'd told him in an unusual display of feeling, patting her lipsticky mouth, "you are rare bird—is that right idiom?" Poor Tani, soon after eased out of her job because she should have been married already. Whatever happened to her? Then again, what was happening to the others still at work? They certainly had no time for anything but wolfing down a bowl of noodles at some little stand before going home for the night. The same was true for his students: most companies encouraged their employees involved with foreign branches to take English lessons, and this cut further into their free time. One of the sayings on both sides of the world was "*Toki wa kane nari*": Time is money. It was the last proverb that Miyamoto had taught him before he left TESCO. Cricket himself subscribed to this idea and thought of himself as quite fortunate. And he aggressively resisted those who made inroads on his spare time.

For this reason, though he was occasionally asked to take on extra classes, he stuck with his fourteen-hour workweek. As it was, the two ten a.m. classes he had took it out of him, leaving him torporous and spent. The day after, he invariably took a long nap. "I need more sleep than other people," he had explained to Reiko. "Otherwise I can't work, can't write."

Reiko had nodded, looking understanding—she understood quite well. Even in his fits of greatest exertion, he rarely spent more than an hour at the typewriter, and the most he taught any given day was four hours. He earned slightly more than Reiko, though she called him rich. It was another of their well-worn jokes.

Outside the apartment building for the first time that day, he sniffed the air. Someone was burning leaves nearby in a fiery orange ashcan. The sky was roseate blue, like the scarf he'd bought for Reiko this past Christmas. She had gotten him an English-Japanese dictionary.

Reiko said she loved him, and he didn't doubt it. He wasn't so sure about himself. To atone, he decided on a labor-intensive dinner, a sort of Japanese stew called *oden*. Ducking into the alley alongside his apartment block, he wheeled out his almost-new bicycle, a bright yellow model with the logo "Salient" in script along the crossbar. He'd ridden all over the place on his trusty rusty Sky Lancer, but a drunk from the nearby *karaoke* bar had made off with it one night. So he'd gone out and bought the Salient, though he rarely rode more than a dozen blocks on it these days.

As with so many other Japanese vehicles, like the dumptrucks small as old VW vans navigating the threadlike streets, the Salient was a miniature. The frame barely came up to his belt, the wheels like large dinner plates. Straddling the low crossbar gingerly, he shifted his back experimentally: no twinges. He pushed off down the street, past the Kyoen tea shop and the painted sign for "Mamy's Beauty Saloon." The south wall of the park rose high on the other side of the street, a pink-and-gray expanse of stone blurred to one indeterminate color as he rode.

His long legs pumping higher than his waist, he veered down a street that left the main road at an awkward angle, the only way to reach his first destination, a slant-roof shop that sold the freshest vegetables. Daiei, the local supermarket, was filled with tired Japanese housewives carrying babies on their backs, and the sight depressed him. In fact, it seemed as if most of the women he saw shopping, no matter how pretty, were simply baby-making machines to produce more Japanese. They were so earnest about competitive shopping, making themselves attractive for their husbands, and taking care of their children that he often felt he was living in some version of 1950's America. Even the rebellion against conformity was dated, from the motorcycle gangs called *bosozoku* to the mass-worship of James Dean.

At the railroad intersection, he rang the shiny bell on his handlebars, feeling a little like a Japanese housewife himself. Reiko was more modern. She'd slept with him the second time they went out, after an American adventure movie. In a coffee shop after the film, she'd broached the subject of sex, her English almost disappearing altogether. "Strong handsome American man," she called him, and he mentally tabbed himself by the initials. Because he wasn't sure, despite his many protestations of love, whether he could ever give her the satisfaction she wanted, that outmoded American dream of a cozy family with children. The Japanese had such strong family values, though Reiko's parents had practically disowned her for staying with him.

So he did things for her. Four months ago he'd suddenly gotten interested in pachinko and spent all his free mornings amid the whirring and clicking of a hundred machines, punctuated by the steel cascade of ball bearings, the little gains rushing into the shooter tray every few minutes to offset the large-scale losses. When the ball entered the little colored jaws on the playing field, it disappeared into the bowels of the machine but caused a lot more balls to fill the tray below. Cricket kept at it with the dogged persistence of someone who wouldn't admit he had nothing better to do. The ostensible goal was to win a stuffed doll for Reiko.

"No keep eye on ball," the *pachi*-pro Jun Sasaki, a former student, had once advised him. Unfortunately, Jun had never made it clear what you were supposed to watch, so Cricket had evolved his own, probably Western style, with a jittery hand on the ball-release mechanism and a penchant for overshooting. In his freshman year at college, Cricket had whacked the hell out of an old Gottlieb pinball machine in the student lounge, but the upright pachinko machines seemed untiltable. Maybe proper placement had something to do with Zen. Some of the older men seemed to spend all day there, half-sunk in trances. After two weeks, the man in the khaki apron who wandered down the aisles, offering change and greeting some of the other players, began to give Cricket at least a perfunctory nod. Finally, by a combination of luck and maybe a little skill, he'd managed to accumulate over 1,000 balls. He'd exchanged them all for a blue-eyed doll that Reiko thanked him for, though she was clearly upset about something.

"What? What's the matter?" he'd demanded.

"*Pachi*-prize," she'd muttered. A piece of junk when she'd been hoping for a real gift. Still, she enshrined it in her apartment in Koshien, the way she treasured everything he gave her. After he bought her a pair of copper hoop earrings in Kobe, she wore them even to do laundry.

The Salient coasted to a stop in front of the fruit and vegetable store, where everything was arranged not in bins but in bunches of five, each in a green plastic latticework bowl. Five was the number for everything from teacups to ramen-packet specials since four was bad luck. "*Shi* is four," Reiko had explained, "but *shi* is also the word for death." Like so many other Japanese reasons, this explanation was only partially satisfying. Cricket happened to know that *shi* was also the syllable for "city" and "finger," among many others. But he let the matter ride and never bought four of anything.

The diminutive crone presiding at the store greeted him hoarsely: "*erasshai.*" She never appeared to have any help and made change from a cloth pouch hanging from behind the plank counter. Once I'm gone, she seemed to say, this shop will collapse into ruin. Buy my vegetables while they're fresh. Cricket had found her storefront one day by accident, continuing along a wrong turn after the railway crossing. In her faded gray kimono, bent over from age, she stared myopically at the horizon, which seemed abnormally low today.

After exchanging a pleasantry about the weather, he began to examine her offerings. *Jagaimo*, the mountain potatoes like baby Idahos with beards, were the basis for any *oden*. They were five for ¥350 here. He also purchased seaweed, shiitake, and *konyaku*, a gelatinous yam starch that he'd learned to deal with only in the past year. Like most stews, *oden* would take whatever you threw into it, but *chikua* or fish sausage would provide half the protein, so he biked back over the tracks to another store called Kampoya, which specialized in it. His great-grandmother had probably shopped this way: greengrocer, butcher, dry-goods store. Nishinomiya still had old-fashioned pockets that resisted mass-marketing.

The preserved tofu he got at the *tofu-ya*, whose watery white tanks were like sterile aquariums for bean curd. The proprietor reached down with his white rubber gloves to fetch him a sliver of fresh tofu along with his purchase. "*Omake*," said the man, and smiled as Cricket wolfed down the cool white curd. *Omake* meant "something extra" and pleased him so much that he never bought at the *tofu-ya* at the other side of town, though the two shops looked identical. A few more stops, a few more exchanged pleasantries about the weather (which the store owners variously interpreted as sunny, cloudy, and bound to change), and he was done. Heading back to his apartment with a clutch of plastic bags in his bicycle basket, he almost whistled. He had accomplished something today.

Oden was a dish that could simmer, which was good, since Reiko would probably be home late. Her office had to get out some sort of mailing this week—Reiko's English had broken down in the explanation—and so everyone would be working late at least until Thursday.

"It's business." She pronounced the last word with three syllables. "You wait up for me?"

"Sure. Or I'll wait down, if you prefer."

"What?"

"Never mind. Give my regards to all your co-workers."

The group concept vaguely annoyed him, and more than once he'd asked her why she didn't change her job. She just shook her head. He knew that in a year or two, just like Tani, she would be gently eased out of her job by a male supervisor who thought that all women past the age of twenty-five should be married. Worse than the 1950's, Japan was primeval in some ways, and Reiko's imminent plight was all the more poignant to him, the assumed groom-to-be. He'd have to see about that. He'd have to see about a lot of things one of these days.

On his way back, he stopped in a boutique to buy a thin red candle, a final addition to the dinner table. While he was there, he also bought a tiny ivory paperweight, recipient unknown. Ideas for small gifts were always crossing his mind, and he gave and received little objects and edibles far more often than his Japanese friends. He had the time, after all.

His watch showed 11:50, time to catch the end of the American music broadcast on FM Osaka if he hurried, but he chose to wheel his bike home through the park instead. It might cloud up tomorrow, and he wanted to see the shrine in the clear autumn air before the cold rainy weather set in.

At that time of day, the only other person in the park was an old man, sitting on a bench and leaning heavily forward on his cane. As Cricket crunched along the gravel pathway, the man looked up like a tortoise investigating outside his shell, his eyes rheumed with age. You were never sure if you were interesting in your own right, or if you attracted attention simply because you were a *gaijin*. He'd thought of asking Reiko a similar question about sex, but so far had refrained. The Japanese on subways who came up to him to practice their English—that was clearly a different matter, and his Japanese was adroit enough to fend off their attacks. Once he'd ridden all the way to Himeji with a high-school student who wanted with all his heart and body to visit Hollywood and kept quizzing Cricket as to whether his English was good enough. It had made an odd exchange, Cricket talking broken Japanese and the student abominable English, as the train shot along past Kobe and the people sitting next to them pretended to take no notice.

The old man on the bench was equally polite at the moment of passing: just a flicker of the eyelids, then back to staring at the cane. The shrine was unaccountably shut for the day, with a notice pinned on the entrance that Cricket couldn't read. He shrugged and followed the gravel path flanked by three giant stone lanterns to admire the ginkgoes from close up. They didn't sway in the breeze so much as rustle and shiver, their uncountable leaves vibrating like a musical instrument. He had taken a ginkgo cutting a while back, but it never grew in the pot he provided, which was better in a way because then the ginkgoes remained special to the place.

The breeze increased, making him shudder. One gray carp swam around in the pond, peering up from the depths as if it could see skyward. When Cricket looked up, framed in the branches of the ginkgoes was a tiny airplane in the rose-blue sky. Headed to Los Angeles, perhaps—which way was west? Some line about a toy silver plane floated back to him, but he couldn't recall what it was from. He shuddered again, quickened his step, and was soon out of the park, back in his apartment.

Lose the shoes, unpack the bags, put the items in the refrigerator or the cabinet, and find some lunch while he started chopping vegetables for tonight's dinner. Since he wouldn't be home between the hours of 3:00 and 7:00, he had to make a start before he left. If Reiko came back early, she had a key and could wait for him. He reheated some miso soup from yesterday and sipped from it in between slicing scallions. Soon he switched on the radio, and the apartment was filled with the sound of a Japanese fusion group called Yellow Magic.

The tofu, dressed in flour and pepper, sizzled in a frying pan, the music played loudly, and over it the telephone in the corner rang. He put down his spatula disgustedly and walked, didn't run, over to the phone.

"*Moshi-moshi.*"

"Hello, I'm looking for—Cricket, is that you?"

"Yes, it is." Like many Westerners here, he'd developed a

subtle dislike of other *gaijin*, whom he looked upon as interlopers. "Who's this?"

"Um, this is Jennifer. Jennifer Hertzl."

"Oh." The silent pause of embarrassment, thought part of his mind—write that down. "Um, hi."

"'Um, hi' to you, too. You sound a little stiff." Of course, Jennifer had been here longer than he had, but she remained steadfastly American, and that made him uncomfortable in another way. She was also locked in his memory as the woman who dragged him to bed the night that Matthew committed suicide. If he had to lay blame, he would think of her, though the charge was absurd. Right now he thought of her wide mouth, shaped against his ear.

That's not all she did with her mouth, sniffed Sofie.

Oh, Crick, whispered his mother.

Beware the two *c*'s, cancer and craziness, announced his father.

Fighting his way clear of the voices, he addressed the receiver carefully. "I'm sorry . . . you just . . . caught me at an awkward moment."

"Good. Makes it more you. Listen, I just got kicked out of my place in Morinomiya, and I'm staying at the Kobe youth hostel. I was wondering . . . ."

Cricket knew what she was wondering, and it didn't take her long to get to the point.

"My money's running out—I don't mean tomorrow or anything, but until I find another place I've got to rely on friends. I've got an interview for a job at Berlitz, but that's in a few days. You have any space in your apartment?"

Cricket thought for a moment, wondering how she'd gotten his phone number. It was an audible pause. "Look, I have a girlfriend now," he began.

"I know. Reiko, right?"

"Yes." His head felt like a goldfish bowl. Was there no privacy in Japan?

"If you're worried about that one night so long ago, Cricket, it didn't happen, okay?" Jennifer laughed. "Now, can I crash?"

"Well, I can put you up for a night or two, anyway." This was the expatriate chain, after all, the bond of common nationality. And he did owe her, or she owed him, or something. "Do you know how to get here?"

"You can? Great!" Disregarding his question, she thanked him several times, said he was a real friend in need, mentioned that she had to run, and hung up. Cricket replaced the receiver with a puzzled shrug and went back to his tofu. Confused *gaijin*: she'd probably call back in a few hours when she needed directions. Or maybe she was resourceful and would show up at his doorstep that night. But most foreigners, especially people like Jennifer, didn't speak much Japanese, and she'd probably get lost several times even if she did find her way here. And if she slept over, that would create another problem. Even if Jennifer stayed low-key, Reiko would certainly be jealous. She was convinced he preferred American women and stiffened whenever they passed foreign tour groups.

"*Gaijin*," she would practically hiss, and Cricket could hear the deep-rooted xenophobia of a race cut off from other cultures for a few hundred years. Or thought he could hear it. Children on subways often clung to their mothers when he boarded the train. He didn't think it was an instinctive trait and blamed the parents. What had *his* mother warned him about when he was growing up? Mean dogs, playing with knives, too much candy, the great outdoors . . . . It was a long list, but he didn't think it included foreigners.

He glanced again at his watch—despite his leisure hours, Japan encouraged clock-watching, the national habit—and realized he'd have to stop cooking soon. His job that afternoon, teaching at the Kanzaki Seishi Company, began at four, but the company was located in Kuise, half an hour away by train, not including a fifteen-minute ride from the Kuise station. As an accomplished train-reader, he didn't regret the transit time, but today it meant he'd have to leave the broth for later. Above the sink, just in case of a misunderstanding, he posted a large note for Reiko in simple English, and went to change into a white shirt and tie. Japanese expected a certain formality, and he didn't mind. It was almost a welcome shift, a costume that he donned every weekday, a way to get out of himself.

3:05. He had long ago clocked the bike ride to the station: five minutes pedaling fast. Collecting his texts and a manila envelope with pen, paper, and a few other essentials, he approached the door. Just at the threshold, the *genkan* separating home from outside, he dumped everything into a shopping bag and slipped into a pair of black vinyl loafers. The transformation completed from *flâneur* to English teacher, he walked out and down the stairs. He never bothered to bolt his door, just one of the many changes in his way of thinking since he had come to Japan.

He locked his bike at the station lot with a minute to spare. The semi-local arrived exactly on time. The punctuality of Japanese transportation was always a minor miracle, hinting at a brutal efficiency behind the courtesy that no one—save railway workers—need ever see. The same was true of the clean interiors, the well-brushed blue velvet seats—mixed with the casual molesting during rush hour, when everyone merged chest to armpit. On more than one occasion, Cricket had seen a furtive businessman cup a woman's buttock or rub against a blouse. Reiko, who'd been groped a few times herself, told him that the men never said a word and the women rarely complained. Subtlety and stealth versus grin and bear it, the flip sides of a politeness society. It was almost sinister, he thought, how well he fit both aspects.

At this hour, the train was only half-full, the front seats mostly taken up by the omnipresent schoolgirls in their blue skirts and blouses, talking about a class or some boy. In a few more years, they might look like Reiko. In an old photo she'd given him, she radiated schoolgirl charm: the pearly teeth, her long black hair like an endless series of parallel lines, the slight swell of her breasts concealed by the uniform. Schoolgirls in person were less charming. They always seemed to be laughing at some self-generated joke. Staring at him, opposite them with his legs crossed, they erupted into giggles and covered their mouths. Sometimes they irritated him and other times, when he saw a particularly moody expression or a shapely leg, they enticed him.

"*Hora, gaijin, mite!*" A big girl who looked like the class clown pointed at him as he sat down.

The exclamation was all too familiar—"Hey, look at the foreigner!"

But Cricket was nothing if not prepared for the assault. He snapped on a pained expression and swiveled his head. "*Iie, kasei-jin,*" he informed them. No, I'm a Martian.

They left him alone after that, though he did hear one schoolgirl behind him whisper anxiously, "Do you really think he could be?"

He could have pursued that line. Today he was indifferent and opened a book, reading from James's *Portrait of a Lady* until he reached Kuise. Some vague impulse had led him to slide out the bulky Penguin paperback from his expanding private library, which by now occupied three jury-rigged shelves by his desk, most marked by the Juso Exchange's sticky label. He went prospecting there once a month, always taking away, as opposed to other readers who availed themselves of the Exchange's ungenerous buyback terms, or exchanged two of their old paperbacks for some yet-unexplored volume. Not Cricket—he couldn't bear to give away any part of himself. And each wave of departing expats left behind such transparent ambitions for themselves: all those old mysteries, thrillers, and travel books. It became ever tougher to find something worthwhile, though he always did.

Not that he liked James's ornate style, and the cloistered subjects tickled him unpleasantly. "Under certain circumstances there are few hours in life more agreeable than the hour dedicated to the ceremony known as afternoon tea." The Japanese do tea better, he thought. Still, he felt obliged to keep an interest in English literature as long as he was in a foreign country. It had been his major in college, after all. Diligently, but with increasing absorption, he picked his way through the English afternoon in front of him.

It kept out the voices, and it kept his mind off Jennifer.

As the conductor announced Kuise station, Cricket abruptly shut his book and slid it into his teacher's bag. He checked his watch: 3:30 on the dot. Some of the students got off with him, eyeing him blatantly all the way down the station stairs and onto the street. As always, he felt half annoyed, half titillated. This wouldn't occur if he were Japanese. And what would happen if he reached out for one of them? The big girl, the class clown with her inflated figure, looked as if she could take care of herself. The others resembled a squad of raven-haired dolls pacing about aimlessly in between giggle-bursts. But after a minute they all trooped into a coffee shop called Kitano, while he walked rapidly to the bicycle lot by the side of the station.

It took him only a moment to locate his Kuise transportation, locked up at the end of the last row. It looked like a rustier version of his old Sky Lancer, forlorn and unwanted—but he had rescued it five months ago. With a pump, a crescent wrench, and a little oil, he'd made it ridable again. A pliers and a paper clip reset the toy lock that anchored most of the bikes, really little more than a flimsy metal finger that snapped out between the spokes. He'd done the same wherever he was scheduled to teach, and now he had a serviceable bicycle waiting for him at every station. His amateur restoration was a labor of love and expediency, and perhaps possible only in Japan, a country still poor enough to use bicycles as a major mode of travel, yet wealthy enough to junk them by the thousands when they grew battered.

The Cricket Collins Bicycle Reclamation Project saved more than materials. During his time at TESCO, he'd ridden buses and taxis on company money. Cycling saved yen and even extra minutes, provided the final destination wasn't too far from the station. It also set him off as the teacher who arrived on two wheels, a distinction that seemed rather Japanese in its simple self-sufficiency. It provided some exercise, too.

The bicycle almost seemed glad to see him, like the faithful dog he'd never owned. As he wheeled it from the rack, the handlebars warmed to his hands, and he patted the seat affectionately. Then he was skimming down Shinbashi-dori, his tie streaming behind him like a pennant in a stiff breeze. Along the way, he passed one of his favorite noodle stands, whose counterman knew him by name; three identical-looking coffee shops with different prices posted outside; an establishment devoted to *hanko*, the personal name stamps that graced every written transaction from a marriage to a mortgage; a pocket grocery store packed to the ceiling with merchandise that no one ever seemed to buy; an outfitter who sold uniforms for the paper company where Cricket taught; and a whole section of semi-high-rises painted robin's-egg blue. Every few blocks came a repetition of the same stores and apartment blocks, like an endless loop of film scenery. Kuise wasn't on anyone's list for sightseeing. It was more of a manufacturing town, a place that most workers eventually hoped to leave. And it was where Cricket taught Tuesdays and Thursdays.

By now he figured he'd pretty much seen it all. That was the problem with being a long-term expat: either you or the country didn't change fast enough. When Reiko had wanted them to visit a harvest festival in Nara last month, he'd begged off. In his first year, he'd seen seven of them: a lot of colorfully dressed farmers pounding drums, holding rice stalks aloft, celebrating a bounty that these days was mostly machined. And his allergies had returned again this August, reminding him of his disgrace last *Bon*. The longer he stayed, it seemed, the more allergic he was to the past. But past knowledge had its uses: for example, he never got lost anymore. And knowing where he was going made him bicycle faster.

He was coasting through the intersection at Senri-cho, really just the crossing of an alley with the main street, when he almost collided with a two-wheeler gliding toward him at right angles. He slammed on the cheap hand-brakes as he swerved and hilariously bounced off a lamp post. Slightly stunned, he got off and watched as the vehicle ahead continued its stately progress: a sturdy low bike with a back-rack on which a wizened old man in a tuxedo half-reclined, smoking a cigarette with a three-inch amber holder. The boy in front—his driver?—pedaled carefully as the man kept his balance with perfect aplomb. He took a puff and exhaled lazily, giving a general wave to the crowd as the bike disappeared down the connecting alleyway.

A seat of luxury on the back of a two-wheeler—now that, Cricket thought as he remounted his bike, was a vestige of the old Japan. In a way, he envied the few expats who'd been here since the Occupation: geisha, lacquered umbrellas, antique customs involving salt and rice, shopkeepers who used an abacus instead of a calculator, and levels of politeness that verged on the risible. You could still see those scenes here and there, though they were dying out to the point where retro-chic was just beginning. No, the place to look for tradition was in the simplest things: the unchanging cry of the baked-sweet-potato vendor, who would come calling down Cricket's street as soon as the cold weather set in, or the arrangement of soba on a wooden trencher, served that way for centuries. Reiko, he knew, thought Americans delightful but irresponsible: their culture wasn't mature enough.

A left turn, a few more blocks, and the Kanzaki Seishi buildings loomed in front of him like a concrete village. Gliding to a stop in front of the factory gatehouse, he smiled and nodded slightly. The gray-uniformed man behind the glass, with a bullet-shaped head and no-nonsense glasses, knew him and waved him on. He bicycled past the warehouse area, unimpeded. At the companies where he taught, security was tight, and his foreigner's aura sometimes exacerbated rather than eased suspicion, but the words "English teacher" worked magically. Telling the Japanese that he taught English, when each of them had suffered through at least six years of English classes at school, commanded respect.

"Herro," called out a second guard fifty yards on, with a wave that was almost a salute. On the back of his uniform was stamped the company name.

"*Konnichi wa.*" He always tried to reply in Japanese, aware that his accent was good. Of course, sometimes speaking the language simply meant smiling, bowing, and apologizing. At the ultra-polite headquarters of IBM Japan, where he taught on Mondays, he often came back with tired rictus muscles. Places like this were more straightforward: no suits here, and a considerable lack of interior decorating. Parking his bike in a rack, he proceeded first to the employees' bathroom, where he adjusted his tie and combed his hair, then walked to the building where the class was to be held.

Never people to waste space or materials, the Kanzaki Seishi Company had built two concrete meeting rooms which shared one wall with a pallet-building hangar. For a month now, the two-hour lessons had been interrupted by the sound of hammering and the whine of an electric saw. Any day now, he intended to complain about the location—surely they could meet someplace quieter—but he wanted to see whether any students would complain first. So far, they'd been exceedingly polite, acknowledging the noise with only an occasional, "I cannot hear you, please."

He walked into the converted meeting room, now silent as a cave, and snapped on the fluorescent lights. The chairs were already arranged around the rectangular table like a quorum of empty students. He put his shopping bag on the table and extracted a notebook, a pen, and two worn textbooks, *What's That Phrase?* and *Encounters in America*. The texts were from his old days at TESCO, though he improvised where the material was weak. They'd been written by Dawson, probably still firmly entrenched in his staff job there. In his mind, he saw rust-haired Dawson at the back of the office, staring into the middle distance with his abnormally blue eyes as he scribbled away. Was he still turning out a new text every three months? They were all quite similar: short units on idioms, interspersed with "authentic" dialogue that sometimes needed harsh editing—Dawson's ear wasn't what it used to be. But Dawson himself was likeable enough. It occurred to him that he hadn't talked with Dawson in a while. As a matter of fact, it felt like he hadn't talked with anyone in a while.

In some ways, his students compensated for that. To one class, a particularly adept group at the Japanese branch of Ciba-Geigy, he willingly taught words like *hooker*, *porn movie*, and *masturbation*, learning in return their Japanese equivalents. What the hell—terms like that might prove more useful than what Mr. Yamada said to Mr. Mason when encountering him at a business convention (*Encounters*, chapter 11). Reiko could explain to him only some of the words, but Cricket suspected reticence rather than a small vocabulary.

He laid his watch on the table—he liked to pace himself through the lessons—and waited for the students to arrive. Though he always told himself he didn't care one way or the other, it hurt him when they were late or when they skipped a class for more pressing business. He retained a real if waning enthusiasm for teaching English, unlike many of the floaters who kept on teaching because they needed the money, though bored to death repeating the same instructions to ears that couldn't distinguish between an *r* and an *l*.

At five of four, his students began arriving, still dressed in their company shirts, a neat *K.S.C.* embroidered in a gold triangle above their breast pockets. This class was composed of technicians who knew enough English to begin conversations they couldn't end. Cricket was leading them through the dialogues from *Encounters in America*, since straight improvisation rendered them tongue-tied. With a group like this, rigid structure was necessary.

"Goo deefning," said a gold-toothed man with shiny spectacles. Mr. Harimoto. Mr. Harimoto, Cricket recalled, had trouble with the ends of words.

"Good eva-ning," said another student, and Cricket saw that it was Mr. Sakurai, who tried desperately hard to contribute to the discussion every week. Tried but failed, his mouth gaping like a gaffed fish.

"Good evening." That was Mr. Miura, easily the best student in the class, actually a grade above everyone else, though the company insisted that he join in the same group-level. It was a shame, really, since the class was obviously holding him back. Cricket sympathized but could do nothing. Company policy.

He waited until seven of the eight students had arrived and then began the class. "Good evening. If you remember the end of last class, I asked you to do unit six of *Encounters in America* for this week." He held up the book and flipped to the right page. "Did you all have a chance to do the work?"

A few nods, a rueful smile, and one or two embarrassed shakes of the head. It was going to be a typical session.

"Mr. Shinohara, will you please read from where the passage begins, 'Uh-oh, I think I'm going to be late for work.'" Cricket sat back in his chair to listen for mispronunciations as Mr. Shinohara attacked the text. When the whine of a saw cut through the dialogue practice about fifteen minutes into the lesson, the students incrementally raised their voices.

By the time Cricket arrived home, it was almost seven o'clock. The class was over at six, but then there was the bike ride back to Kuise station, and on the way he bought flowers for

Reiko at a little stall that seemed to have popped up in the time between the start and end of his class. "*Shion*," replied the woman when he asked the name of the flowers. They were a delicate blue, and cheap. He resolved to look up the word in his dictionary—which he used to carry everywhere—when he got back home. The bouquet was a little surprise and also for expiation: Reiko would probably be waiting for him, having discreetly let herself in. Maybe she would even have finished cooking dinner. She really tried hard to please him, and he, in return, tried hard to look pleased.

He got off at the Hanshin Nishinomiya station with his flowers and hooked up again with his Salient bike. As he rode home, more leisurely now, he composed a few sentences to say to Reiko when he walked in the door. They all began, "Sorry I'm late, honey . . . ." Reiko adopted most Americanisms she heard and was convinced that all American husbands called their wives "honey." When she went back to her own apartment on weekends, she watched English television programs and would come back with strange quips. "Not tonight, dear—I have a headache" was her latest acquisition, though she promptly dropped it when he explained how it was used. Sexual reticence was not one of her traits.

As he climbed the stairs to his apartment, he realized that Jennifer had never called back—or rather, he hadn't waited around to give her the chance. He pressed his lips together. If it were really important, she'd call back tonight. Foreigners who had just arrived in Japan had a certain indomitable spirit, a capacity for achievement that only slowly dissipated. Jennifer, on the other hand, was an old Japan hand, wise as to how to get by. And what explained Matthew—staying around too long? Was the dying spirit in his eyes that night apathy or conviction? Why did he still carry around Matthew's ghost? Because his pride was wounded on a plane ride three years ago? *Encounters in the Air*, chapter 5. "Excuse me, but you seem to be occupying my seat."

Why wasn't he *doing* more? He thought guiltily of the dusty books on his bookshelf. The unused typewriter didn't bother him so much since he still wrote occasionally and didn't consider that part of himself to be lost. In fact, Reiko still admired him for being an author. When he opened the door to his apartment, though, no one was there to admire him. His note was still taped above the sink, and a whole cabbage still graced the cutting board. He slipped off his shoes at the *genkan*, undid his tie, and stowed his bag in the corner. Then he went to finish his cooking. He had no idea of when Reiko would be home now. She might not come at all if the company really made her work late. In any event, he was hungry. He took his Japanese chopping knife, which resembled a giant beveled razor blade, and began hacking away.

After five minutes, the phone rang. The breathless voice at the other end of the line was Jennifer's.

"Listen, I tried to call you back before, but you weren't in. I got a place for the night, a friend of mine I tried to look up before, but I didn't know where he was staying or anything."

Cricket couldn't resist. "A boyfriend?"

"Sort of. It was a while back. We both agreed that in Japan, things would be different."

"He may get involved with a Japanese girl, you know." He didn't know why he was being so nasty. Boredom, maybe.

"I *know*, I've been here longer than you. Anyway, I got his number and called him and he said it was all right."

"Good."

"I just wanted to let you know, so you wouldn't worry."

He was just about to say that he never worried about matters like that when he realized how rude it would be and changed his reply. "That's okay. Maybe we can get together some other time. See you."

"Sure. Maybe. Thanks again. Bye."

He hung up just as he heard the doorknob turn. He jumped back to his cabbage just as Reiko walked in and slipped off her shoes. Dressed in the blue jumper that all the women in her office wore, she must have come directly from work. Obviously fatigued, she nonetheless preserved a shiny air, like a piece of candy wrapped in cellophane. She stood there, waiting for an embrace.

He came forward, cabbage in one hand, knife in the other.

"*Abunai deshō*! Dangerous, I mean." But she made no attempt to move away from the sweeping embrace. With his arms wrapped around her body, he held the knife at her back and the cabbage alongside her head. It looked as if he'd just severed a grotesque deformity of some kind. Noting the image, he nonetheless kissed her, twice, hard on the lips. Twice because she had to work overtime, and he always felt sympathy for her then. She rarely complained, but at night when she was asleep, he would trace the half-moons under her eyes. During those moments he could convince himself that he felt something deep for her.

Reiko spotted the phone slightly off the hook with a paranoid's eye: the receiver wasn't cradled right. "Who call just now?"

"A friend."

"He or she?"

"You want the truth? A woman I knew from TESCO. She needed a place to stay for the night, but I said no because of you."

"*Hon-ki?*" She still looked doubtful. She needed reassurance.

"*Hai, sō desu.*" He patted her head, meaning to comfort, though Reiko had once complained that it made her feel short. "You're tired, so just sit down and I'll finish making dinner. I got home just a moment ago."

He removed the knife and spirited away the cabbage. He went back to his chopping board and continued cutting. The cabbage actually wasn't for the *oden* but for coleslaw, one of the few American dishes that Reiko really liked. "Very delicious," she would say, her eyes half-closed to help her taste.

She sniffed appreciatively at the pot on the burner. "Mmm . . . *oden*?" She had a true Japanese nose, small and sensitive.

"That's right." He used the same intonation as in talking to a pupil. "I spent this morning shopping."

"Did you do your writing?"

A lie was permissible. "Yes, a little. But I didn't feel inspired today." Getting along without inspiration wasn't too hard. It got easier day by day.

"When will you finish?" She was talking about an old, incomplete draft of a story, a page of which he'd read and carefully explained to her a year ago. It concerned identical brothers marooned on twin islands, and the different ways they reacted to their isolated condition. One was as inexplicably clueless as the other was resourceful, in everything from food-gathering to keeping amused. Originally comic, the tone slowly became sinister. The brothers' characters slowly diverged, and in the end one killed the other, but which was the victim remained unclear till the last page. Or at least that was the way Cricket had planned it. Unfortunately, the South Sea setting was so far removed from his experience that he bogged down in basic details like edible vegetation. Couldn't they make something like tofu? he'd wondered at one point.

For some reason, he still couldn't write well about Japan.

Should he be getting out more? The aftershock of the rooftop party in Ashiya was slowly wearing off, though he retained a slight fear of heights. In fact, he'd heard of a gathering in Suita this weekend, hosted by Ted Allen, back in Japan after a half-year escape to Thailand, Malaysia, and Singapore. He and his Japanese wife had intended to go all the way back to Oregon, but they now had an infant daughter and figured they could use more money. Would Ted still be as insufferably nice as he used to be? Probably a mixed crowd, but maybe worth a shot. With or without Reiko? He looked over at her, aware that she'd asked him something before he'd drifted off. "What did you say?"

Reiko repeated her question exactly. "When will you finish?"

"Oh. One of these days." Most Japanese wouldn't have grasped the expression, but Reiko did. She understood Cricket, so she understood the words. She didn't respond but started rummaging through her bag, which, Cricket knew, contained a host of items, from tissues and Sanseido lipstick to a tiny Boy Scout knife he'd bought for her twenty-third birthday. When he'd started explaining "Boy Scout," she'd informed him that the Japanese had Boy Scouts. But of course they did—that fit so exactly.

Reiko found what she wanted, a small tissue-paper cone, and brought it over to him. "Here, it's present."

Inside was a daffodil, or the Japanese version of one. It was really a gift for the apartment, something to brighten up the place. Unless Reiko was there, he always forgot to water the flowers and they died.

"It's beautiful. Where did you get it?"

"At flower shop. I thought of you."

He kissed her again for it, gently, and this time she wrapped her arms around him. One of these days, he thought as he reciprocated, she's going to leave me and I will be very, very sorry. He was touched by that thought.

The *oden* was ready by eight, and they both sat on cushions on the floor to eat it. After three years, he felt more comfortable with chopsticks than a fork, a fact that bothered him only if he dwelt overlong on it. After the main course, he served cut-up Japanese pears, the kind called Twentieth Century, which were like biting into round crystal globes of pear juice. Reiko ate more than she usually did, leaving Cricket with a half-empty stomach. While she washed the dishes, he played with the gas burner, seeing how far he could turn the cock and still have a flame. He was pleased when he achieved the faintest of blue coronas. Should he thrust his hand into the flame to show his samurai spirit? Instead, he scrounged in the cupboard and found the box of *manjū*. He bit into one and offered her another.

She shook her head. "No, you get fat."

"I am not fat!"

Reiko said nothing, effectively winning the argument. He threw the rest of the cake into the garbage and took her by the waist. When he spoke, his voice hoarsened. "Now?"

Reiko nodded, though she continued to wash dishes. She rinsed off the large pot, carefully laid it on the rack, and turned around in his arms. When they kissed, her tongue darted into his mouth with little curious twists. Pulling her against him, he could feel the firm pressure of her pointed breasts. He almost lifted her feet off the ground as they moved toward the futon he'd unrolled, and Reiko was already making little feline sighs. During sex she was completely a cat.

With little mincing movements of her fingers, she undid the buttons on his shirt. He unzipped her jumper, letting his hands slide down the jut of her thighs. Reiko was strong-legged, and though Cricket liked the extra power, he'd never managed to convince her of that. "*Daikon ashi*," she would always insist—"radish-legs"—whenever he smoothed down her stockings.

He slid her jumper down her legs until a puddle of navy-blue material surrounded her feet. When he stood up again, she returned fastidiously to unbuttoning his shirt, but he growled and pulled the whole thing over his head. That made her laugh—as always—and she wrapped the empty sleeves around his head, cutting off his vision to immobilize him. She undid the belt of his pants with a practiced ease that always surprised him, as he groped for the buttons of her blouse. It was all as well rehearsed as a mime show, and just as silent. What was there to say?

Sliding under the covers, Reiko wore only her bra and panties, and Cricket had on a pair of Happi-brand jockey shorts. When he finally unfastened her bra, an underwire affair, she would always cover her breasts at first, the last vestige of the shy Japanese girl. There was nothing shy about the way she made love, though, clawing him and often climbing on top to mash her hips against his. Cricket happened to like this aggression and felt guilty only about what it betrayed of his own desires.

They ran their hands up and down each other, Cricket trapping his fingers in the tight cleft between her buttocks, Reiko grasping one of his nipples and twisting it a little. They had to be careful since they were both extremely ticklish and could drive each other into frenzies by a light touch on the inner thigh or armpit. The one spot she always lingered on was the brown birthmark on his left buttock, which she claimed was in the shape of Shikoku and therefore meant he was part Japanese. After a few minutes of stroking, she tugged at his underwear with her teeth. Her long black hair brushed his groin and thighs, all the way down to his ankles. When he pulled down her panties, they rolled against his fingers, and he ended up with a wad of fabric barely bigger than the condom in its wrapper, already maneuvered bedside. When he unrolled that, in the faintest of gold lettering, it read "MADE IN JAPAN."

She dug her nails into his back as he entered her, and said something Japanese in a high-pitched voice—absurdly, he thought of reaching for his dictionary. But now she was moaning, "*Ai shite-iru*," over and over again, the first words she had taught him: I love you.

He repeated the words as if they were a mantra, caressing her cuplike breasts. Her nipples were hard buds whose roseate flush crept down both their bodies. As they heaved and rocked under the covers, Reiko bit his little finger. Visions of the schoolgirls on the train surfaced in his mind, juxtaposed with other scenes, other bodies: Sofie's white fingers, the heft of Jennifer's breasts, the unyielding prostitute in Korea, a bar hostess in Juso who half-sat in his lap all evening. He couldn't help but pause at how far away it all seemed. Now he felt as if nothing could touch him.

Reiko hugged him closer, grinding her pelvis against his, her tongue thrusting in a reversal of what was happening below. He gripped her buttocks, filling his hands and mind with flesh, almost reaching orgasm but not quite, never unless he was alone. Still, he pretended he was coming, groaning as if ejaculating all he had into the rubber foreskin of the condom.

He sprawled on top of her like a beached castaway. Reiko lay with her eyes closed, her lips slightly parted. She felt around for his head and began slowly, delicately to smooth his hair, strand by strand.

They stayed that way for almost an hour, past nine o'clock, but the urge to do something finally propelled Cricket upwards, toward the sink.

"Why?" Reiko called from the futon, holding out her arms in a pose she had learned from too many American movies.

"I have to do the dishes." Standing naked in front of the sink, he washed the remaining plates. By the time he got around to rinsing them, Reiko was by his side to help dry. She looked vulnerable in nothing but her panties, and whenever he looked in her direction, she tried to cover her breasts. It was touching, but absurd in a way. She always reacquired her modesty after making love.

Now he found it rather annoying instead of appealing. He splashed some water in her direction, and she squealed when the drops hit her in the chest. He did it till she came over to the sink to get control of the faucet, and he was feeling easy, so he let her. They went on for some time like this, like a young couple still very much in love, though Cricket held back a bit. He was doing something he hadn't done in a while: closely observing himself.

Two hours later, when they were both back under the covers and Reiko was breathing evenly, Cricket lay apart and watched the slatted shadows from the venetian blinds. He recalled the dream he used to have about a temple, with an indoor screen panel depicting a tree under a moon, groping its branches upward but never quite reaching. And Cricket as the renegade monk. Now the almost-full moon cast a strange presence inside the room, as if it were just outside the balcony. He felt a bit like a moon-man himself, alienated from the immediate surroundings. Some nights he asked himself what he was still doing in Japan, and this was one of them.

Peter's latest letter had disturbed him more than he'd realized. It was always a slight shock to be reminded of his background, his Ivy League B.A., and his fellow graduates who'd gone on to more substantial things. Had it been that long?—just three years—not like Dawson or some of the other long-termers, who sometimes looked as if they were physically turning Japanese. Even Jennifer, he recalled, had adopted the Japanese style of makeup that made for apple cheeks and Cupid's bows.

Cricket got up to look at himself in the mirror. Reiko sighed in her sleep and reached out an open hand. From the angle of the bathroom mirror that the moon illuminated, Cricket saw his face, whitened with moon-glow, with narrowed eyes that peered at their reflection and the aquiline nose that so distinguished him from most Japanese. He smiled: narrow lips, not like the Oriental fullness which Reiko complained of but which he loved to kiss. Was that a new slant forming in his eyes? He squinted, popped his eyes, and frowned for effect.

Reiko sighed, reaching out with one white arm for something, not toward his side of the futon but toward the window. After a while, she stopped, but her fingers still extended in supplication.

Cricket padded into the bathroom, propped himself against the shower wall, and masturbated with thirty hard strokes. A host of women, from Ogawa-san to Sofie, whispered disapprovingly from the shadows, but he ignored them. The darkest shadow was his mother, mostly a bent hand held out to him, a worn face telling him things he couldn't remember.

He ended in silence. And did this postcoital hush deserve its own category? He thought of wandering over to his notebook and jotting down a phrase, but in the end put it off till tomorrow. Instead, he stepped over to the *genkan*—he'd suddenly remembered the flowers he'd bought for Reiko, still jammed in his shopping bag. Reaching down to where he'd left the bag, he groped around. The stems were crushed between two books and his umbrella, and when he unwrapped the flowers, they were already faded. The few blue blossoms looked pursed and dry, like disembodied lips. He threw them in the wastebasket, which was oddly illuminated as if by a spotlight from outside. Reiko's gift hung in the dark, already in a russet vase on top of a shelf.

Alongside the vase was a coaster from the Wang Hotel in Pusan, a fan that unfolded to reveal a sad gray carp, a rolled-up wall hanging whose *kanji* read "peace," an unfinished Agatha Christie novel that looked carelessly flung there but was in fact quite deliberately dropped, and a host of other gatherings. Almost absently, but with an underlying fervency, he rubbed the coaster, then traced over it the ideograms for "peace." He opened the fan and sent a light breeze toward Reiko: her fingers clenched slightly and finally disappeared under the covers.

The shadow from an errant branch across the street cast a thin line against the moonglow, the mirror image of this morning's plane against the sky—*fractured a hair / by a toy silver plane*. Something Matthew had scrawled on a napkin, he recalled. He advanced to the shadow of the branch and put out his hand to touch it, at which point it became submerged in the phantom of his own arm. So what would you do? he asked Matthew anyway. Is this what you escaped?

Nothing deigned to reply. Or was that the answer?

Everything was calm and unchanging, not just inside the room but even in the street shadows. The stillness was everywhere. It extended through the dark of the night and into the day ahead, this week and the next. It was like a tunnel with a faint but discernible view.

There wasn't that much to see. Undoubtedly, Dawson would keep working and writing useless texts. Jennifer would call him back, if not tomorrow, then one of these days. Reiko would keep on sleeping, would probably remain unaware of his lax intentions until she ruined herself for him, which would be a pity, he decided, and he really should do something about it, one of these days.

And what's going to happen to *me*, he whispered to the walls, what will I do, who will I see, where will I go? Opening and answering letters from friends who aged faster than he did, drawing further and further away from the possibility of return. He felt a gathering tightness in his chest, the old motherless tension which just as quickly faded, leaving him without support. This was no *aware*, he knew, but something like phantom-limb pain, a feeling for something not there anymore. Other people could sustain him, but he seemed to be losing that need, too. Except for Reiko, who was now lying on her side, facing away from him. Or would he lose her, also?

He squatted on the floor, another of the Japanese habits he had adopted, and tried to think. But thinking was difficult, and soon he began to lecture himself. I must take stock of myself. I must do something. Next month, maybe, when I have more time, I'll assay and investigate. I'll make a list, maybe restart my journal. Force myself to take up that short story again—and for God's sake, he whispered to himself in the naked darkness, no more just getting by.

I will, he answered himself. I will not sink down. He rose from the floor, putting out a hand to help himself up. The stasis of the room broke like a cobweb. He took a deep breath of night air, an October scent of dried husks and a taint of the sewer. Outside was no park but a mesh of green blackness, which he watched for a minute or two before crawling back into bed. The darkness was waiting, and he wasn't sure whether he'd found what he wanted. Then Reiko put her arm around him, pulling him to her breast, and he slept.

In his dream, he was almost at the end of his trip, but suddenly he was held back, as ghostly female hands wrapped around his waist and groin. Matthew, wooden as a ship's prow figurine, fell from the sky. Cricket tried to rescue him by pedaling forward but ran over him instead. The tiny gentleman in the tuxedo nodded and winked from the shadows, which hid women's faces.

Cricket was part of a slow-whirling game that cast him away from the center until he was out of bounds. The cloud figures descended upon him in a protective haze. But the haze tasted curiously of dust, which made him sneeze till his nose fell off. He never reached the finish line.

He arose late as usual when the sunlight slid past his eyes and formed the familiar pattern on the far wall. All that was left of Reiko's warmth was a vague indentation on her side of the futon: she had already dressed and left. What day was it? He checked his watch: Wednesday, and he had a class that afternoon, but right then he didn't feel like getting up. It was warm under the quilt, and it was cold outside, so for a while he just lay back against the pillow at an angle that allowed him a view of the ginkgo trees in the park. Soon, hunger would force him to get up and make himself breakfast. In the meantime, he would savor the mid-morning languor and the sunshine spreading itself over the quilt.

"One of these days," he murmured half-aloud. It sounded like a line from an old song or from his dream. "One of these days . . . ." But he had forgotten the end of the sentence, so he looked at the ginkgo trees instead, their outstretched boughs fanning each other in the light breeze. How Japanese, he thought, in the absence of any other expression. What pretty trees. The sensation filled him like a balloon lazily expanding with gas, and he felt no need to say anything more.

8. The Foreign Offensive

"There are times," announced Guy Lapham, looking at the assemblage of foreigners around him, "when even ordering a drink can be a lesson in international relations."

The group smiled in sympathetic appreciation as he paused for a final swig of his Asahi draft and nodded several times to no one in particular. When the hostess came by, a middle-aged woman with the sturdy forearms of a barmaid, he called out something quick and incomprehensible—at least Cricket found it so, and he suspected the rest of the crowd didn't pick up on it, either. But the woman snorted in amusement and gave a mock bow.

"*Futatsu hō ga ii*!" That Cricket understood—"Better make it two"—and felt happy to be in the circle of cognoscenti. He'd been coming to Akaboshi on the outskirts of Umeda for only a month and still felt somewhat on the fringes. The small, wiry figure in the middle, Guy, was magnificently accepting of anyone who showed up to hear his stories. But a few of the other regulars were clannish, not to mention British, and Cricket had been forced to heap public coals on America to win a grudging acceptance. Guy happened to be an old New Zealander, but Guy and his stories transcended national boundaries.

No one knew exactly how long he'd lived in Kyoto, nor exactly how he supported himself. He had the kind of epicene, tight-skinned appearance that defied age, though occasionally he let slip references that implied a twenty-year sojourn at the least. He called other *gaijin* "short-termers," a term that Cricket tried not to let annoy him. The one-upmanship among expats was as subtle or bold as the individual wielding it, based on anything from language expertise to local employment. As an ex-TESCO teacher, as well as an expat of over three years' standing, Cricket was higher than the one-year contractees but lower than the Kyoto artisans studying woodblock printing or *sumie*.

In any event, they were all united in their derision for certain aspects of Japan, though that, too, ran a gamut. One Aussie was married to a flat-faced Nagoya woman who to him represented all the flaws of the culture. Another, an egg-bald Britisher with the hairiest mustache Cricket had ever seen, like a miniature doormat, held that America should have dropped *all* its A-bombs on Japan. Most of them voiced complaints about the Japanese insider-outsider way of thinking or spurned the elaborate Japanese system of formality. A printmaker from Vermont was unhappy with the enforced humility of his Japanese apprenticeship.

Cricket had lived long enough in Japan to have his own gripes. The latest involved his landlady Mori and her efforts to introduce him to a suitable woman, on the assumption that he ought to be thinking about matrimony. She either didn't know about Reiko (unlikely) or politely chose to ignore her (something the Japanese did quite well, another one of his gripes). Her husband Mori had even made a crude joke the other day about bachelors and their needs. Arranged marriages were still common in Japan—perhaps Mori and Mori hoped for some sort of percentage. Or maybe matchmaking was just a national pastime.

"*Sumimasen ga chotto isogashii*...." This he knew was a standard hedge: "Sorry, but I'm a little busy...."

"*Ah, sō?*"—"Is that so?" Mori the wife had drawn herself up to her full height, a bit taller than her slouching husband. Her smile was perfect. Shortly afterwards his rent had gone up.

Different problems accrued to other foreigners, for whom Cricket felt only a fleeting kinship. Charlie Sayles, the TESCO teacher who'd introduced him to the group at Akaboshi, couldn't abide the Japanese habit of removing one's shoes by the door. The black brogues he dropped by the *genkan* looked like miniature black coffins. "S'bloody nuis'nce, ass'what 'tis. An' then y'j'st heft' put'm b'ck *on* 'gin." His syilable-swallowing was getting progressively worse, and Cricket wondered how his students coped. Whatever you were, Japan led you to become more so, at least for expats. A penchant for privacy, an inclination to overeat . . . from the grapevine, Cricket heard that Harry Belton was now so obese he needed to walk with a cane. Then again, Sayles told him that Jennifer Hertzl had become a lesbian "j'st t'be annoyin'," and he wasn't sure he believed it.

Dawson had once claimed that the expats were more interesting than the Japanese, but he'd used the word *interesting* the way one describes a bizarrely inedible meal or a noxious weed. So Cricket was surprised to find Dawson at Akaboshi one night, taking a solitary seat in back. "Oh, everyone knows Guy," he told Cricket afterwards without supplying any further details. If you wanted to know more about Guy, you simply listened to him, even if not all his stories were credible. Most had to do with resourceful expatriates and their clever ways of coping with Japan. And Guy, whether you liked his style of narration or not, was a spokesman for them all. No women were allowed—it was that kind of group, though Lapham was never as crude as some of the Aussie rugby players, whose group it certainly wasn't.

The group met on Monday nights after nine, so that anyone with evening classes could attend. It was understood that most of them taught English, just as it was understood that they all merely deigned to do it. Entering through the *noren*, the tripartite blue curtain advertising Hakushika *sake*, they would settle one by one into the awkward confines of a tatami room in back. Even Charlie had to remove his shoes, grumbling as he did so. Cricket couldn't help but noticing on the first night how large and knobby most foreigners' feet were, and what foul socks Britishers wore: gray with red clocks, hairy heather mixture, holed in two toes. Cricket was still getting by on five pairs bought for him last Christmas by Reiko, who worried about him from head to foot and patriotically wanted to supply him with Japanese-made goods. The socks turned out to be made in Korea, but at least they were clean and warm.

Cricket's father also sent him clothing, this year a muffler with the arch notation "Knit in Asia, bought in America, sent to Japan." In return, Cricket had sent him some *tabi* split-toe socks along with a pair of *zori*. To amuse himself in idle moments, he imagined his father wearing them. Their relationship was slowly attenuating, as were most of his contacts back home. Recently his ex-girlfriend Sofie had replied to one of his letters, taking up the length of a postcard to describe her current man. Cricket had Reiko, of course, but she seemed to have few friends of her own whom he could talk to. He needed to get out more, and the group at Akaboshi furnished a community of sorts.

The drinking would begin after a few civilities had been exchanged. Guy was invariably the third to arrive and would wait inscrutably until someone bought him a beer. His Japanese was excellent, but what he did with it other than speak to hostesses was unclear. His English, slightly clipped, was almost too good: it lacked any conversational lilt, and it often seemed predetermined. Sipping his drink meditatively at first, contentedly or aggressively as the narration demanded, he would make a few prefatory comments about someone he knew, or a friend of his having overheard something, or a piece he'd read somewhere. Then he would begin.

"The situation I'm about to describe concerns a Japanese businessman named Mr. Fujita. And one other supporting cast member, a foreigner—only I've forgotten his name. That's all right: foreigners have such indistinguishable names, anyway. Have you heard this one? No? Good.

"Mr. Fujita was on his lunch hour when he saw a tall, sandy-haired foreigner trying to buy some silk at a clothing store in Semba. The more helpful the merchant was, the more complicated the negotiations became. The foreigner was using simple English and one or two Japanese words for effect. The merchant first used polite Japanese refusals and then hand-signals. Mr. Fujita, who was always on the lookout to help a foreigner and incidentally practice his English, stepped in here."

Guy took a deep breath as if to get a fix on his character. "Mr. Fujita was a short man with a Matsumoto Company pin and a tendency to tug at his lapels when making a point. He tugged at both lapels of his dark blue suit and explained patiently, kindly, in miserable English, that the merchant was offering the silk for five thousand yen and wouldn't go any lower."

The hostess smiled at Guy as she took away his glass and deposited two bottles and a new glass by his side. It was never obvious how much English she understood, but she could certainly take bar orders. Now, she took two: a flask of Shirayuki *sake* for the mustached Britisher, and a glass of *shōchū* for Dawson. Cricket was nursing his first Kirin draft. Despite the advertisement at the entrance, they didn't serve Hakushika brand here. The hostess had smiled widely to encompass the misunderstanding, showing her two gold teeth. Women at bars like this were either rail-thin with a trace of elegance or else maternal types in aprons. This woman looked as if she would make miso soup for you when you were sick, and for an instant Cricket felt a deep, stabbing pain for his own mother, who still sometimes held his hand in dreams. He'd taught himself to need no one else—that was his solution and that was his problem.

Not your only problem, murmured the people he didn't need in his head. He bit his lip, ordering himself to be still, calming himself with a sip from his glass.

Guy didn't even glance at his beer but simply caressed the first bottle of Asahi in an offhand way. This was definitely going to be a two-bottle story, he seemed to indicate. He poured himself half a glass (no one here practiced the Japanese habit of each pouring for the other) and took a delicate swig. "The merchant," he said. "Yes."

"The merchant couldn't understand the words but was longing for any resolution, and he smiled hopefully. The foreigner smiled and, out of the corner of his mouth, so the merchant wouldn't hear, muttered an imprecation against helpful, interfering businessmen with Matsumoto Company pins. Mr. Fujita's

English comprehension was on the same level as his speaking ability, but the remark needed no translation: it was spoken in emphatic, idiomatic Japanese.

"The foreigner let go of the silk roll and smiled. The merchant took the cloth, bowed, and smiled. The foreigner walked off in the direction of Yodoyabashi and Mr. Fujita, after a moment's thought, hurried after him.

"'What you say, excuse, you are American—?'"

Guy's accent was atrociously perfect. At the Kobe YMCA where he sometimes substituted, Cricket had once met an ex-salesman with a fund of Japanese-businessman jokes, but the dialogue wasn't as exact. With Guy, it was a labor of love.

"The foreigner threw a remark over his shoulder, barely glancing back. 'Better stick to Japanese. That way we can both understand each other.'

"Mr. Fujita considered the logic of this. He began again in Japanese. 'Are you American?'

"'Yes. What is this, Twenty Questions?'

"'Sorry, but you speak such excellent Japanese.'

"'So I'm a freak, is that what you're saying?'

"'No, no.' Mr. Fujita thought for a moment and added reflectively, 'No.' He paused again. 'But why were you using English with that storekeeper back there? You gave him a hard time for a while.'

"The foreigner showed an upside-down grin. 'Maybe that was my intention.'

"'What?' They were walking down the crowded sidewalks of Midosuji-dori, and Mr. Fujita thought maybe he'd misheard.

"'I said, maybe it was on purpose. Maybe I like giving people a hard time.'

"'You do?' The foreigner hadn't slowed his pace, and Mr. Fujita had to hurry to catch up. The foreigner's legs were long and his were short. It was one of those engaging details that set foreigners apart. 'What do you mean?' he asked.

"'What do I mean? I walk through the streets and school kids shout 'Haroh!' at me. I pause for a moment at a street corner, and an old woman stops to ask me if I'm lost. Maybe two old women. I spent years learning Japanese—reading and writing, too—so people would stop patronizing me. And what happens? I start speaking Japanese, and they smile and gargle in English. I happen to like the English language, and they murder it. And they go out of the way to do it, too.'

"'Now, really—'

"'What were you trying to do back there?' The foreigner gestured in the direction of Semba.

"Mr. Fujita blushed, which meant that the tips of his ears turned red. He tried an apology in English. It didn't come out as successfully as he had hoped.

"'There you go again, tripping over yourself.'

"The redness spread from the tips of Mr. Fujita's ears to his cheeks. He switched back to Japanese. 'Since you object—'

"'I do. I get this kind of treatment every day. And sometimes I get back at people. Here, watch this.'

"The foreigner stopped in front of a noodle stand and asked in perfectly clear Japanese for a bowl of *soba*. The old man behind the counter grinned toothlessly and said, '*Nūdoru, ne?*' He gave an imitation of a person eating noodles with a sucking sound. He dredged out the noodles from a big pot and put them in a bowl. He remarked to no one in particular that Americans, too, liked noodles.

"Mr. Fujita saw the foreigner's jaw tighten. The effect was a ghastly fixed smile as he took a pair of chopsticks from the rack on the counter. The old man nodded encouragingly and showed with his hands how to break apart the two sticks. The foreigner took the sticks and broke them not down the middle but in half. The counterman laughed uncertainly, looking a little worried. He took a pair of chopsticks from the rack, snapped them apart, and handed them to the foreigner. He pushed the bowl of noodles forward.

"The foreigner broke the new pair in half, arranged the pieces in a square, and clapped his hands in delight. He dug his hands into the noodles and placed a handful in the middle of the square. He added soy sauce.

"The counterman looked despairingly at Mr. Fujita, who made sure to be looking elsewhere. As a last resort, the counterman actually served himself a bowl of noodles, broke apart a pair of chopsticks, and began eating the model noodles. At this, the foreigner clapped his hands again and pushed the soggy square of noodles in offering toward the counterman. He bowed obsequiously, said '*Arigatō*' in a hideous drawl, and dropped the money for the noodles into his half-full bowl."

Here, Dawson began sputtering over his *shōchū*, which was already filling half the room with its pungency. Cricket had tried it once—the real stuff was fermented from sweet potatoes—and had glumly concluded that certain Oriental pleasures weren't meant for foreigners. So it heartened him that Dawson could knock back the stuff, heartened and nauseated him at the same time.

The hairy Britisher managed to light a Mild Seven cigarette without igniting his mustache. Guy's first Asahi was now empty. He began stroking the second bottle, preparatory to the rite of pouring. The oddity of his speech was that it had no *ums* or *ahs*, Cricket realized, no conversational pausers whatsoever. He might as well have been reading from a script—was the gesture with the bottle planned, too? The sentences themselves all came out as if turned on a lathe. Such regulation made Cricket less wary than envious, as he was lately of any control, artistic or otherwise.

Yes, control yourself, Sofie told him.

Just then, Guy pinpointed him with a look that said 'Stop thinking so loud,' and resumed.

"'There,' said the foreigner when they were several blocks away from the noodle-stand. 'You see what I mean?'

"'That was inexcusably rude.'

"'But fun. And he started it, don't forget. If they treat me like a two-year-old, that's the way I act.'

"'It seems—unnecessary. Why don't you just explain in Japanese?'

"'Then I'm a performing seal who happens to be able to bark out a few words. Ever been abroad?'

"'Once, yes.' Mr. Fujita tugged at his lapels proudly. 'My company sent me to Los Angeles. Very good food. People . . . of diverse backgrounds.'

"'Oh? And did anyone compliment you on your ability to eat with a knife and fork? Did people titter and point at you when you walked by?' As the foreigner spoke, one of those unfortunate coincidences occurred that seems planned by fate. A group of school children passed by on the other side of the street. They tittered and pointed at the foreigner.

"The foreigner's jaw tightened again, resulting in the same forced smile. Mr. Fujita was going to counsel forbearance, but it was already too late. The foreigner beckoned with a wide wave, and the children came rushing over. They told him 'Haroh!' repeatedly, like an echo in an enchanted forest. In stumbling Japanese and English, the foreigner introduced himself as Mr. Smith and offered to teach them some English. He took a yellow sheet of memo paper from his pocket and wrote in elegant calligraphy the Japanese for *school, traffic light, street,* and *store*.

Opposite the Japanese, he wrote several English obscenities, along with their variants. Mr. Fujita's trip to Los Angeles had not been wasted. He recognized the words but didn't know how to intervene without appearing absurd. The foreigner had crowd-control, the children delighting in his slightest action. He wrote a syllabic pronunciation-key over the words and, after a little drill-work, sent the children away. They continued to laugh and point. Many of them yelled goodbye. Others yelled the words the foreigner had taught them.

"Mr. Fujita compressed his lips tightly together. 'You're corrupting Japanese youth.'

"'It'll wear off. They're not your kids, you know. Or do you speak for all Japan?'

"'Americans,' Mr. Fujita sighed, 'have a highly developed sense of irony.'

"'You don't say. Want to know what else I've done?'

"'*No.* Yes. Yes, you might as well confess.'

"'Should I unveil the atrocity exhibit? All right.' They were entering the Hankyu department store, and the foreigner led the way to the up-escalator. As they slowly ascended, he ticked off incidents on his fingers.

"'One of my first acts of office, so to speak, was to drag a businessman fifty miles out of his way. He wanted to show me how to get to Nara, though I was obviously buying the right ticket.' He chuckled in recollection, a tinny sound that made several people behind him look up. 'He was on that train almost two hours, first trying to explain to me about the wild deer at Nara, then trying to practice his English. I let him go on for a while, then pretended I was German. That usually stops them, unless they've taken German in school.' He paused. 'This one had, so after that I pretended I was crazy. I undid his necktie and chewed on it, for one thing. He threw me some money at Nara and ran like hell.'

"They passed the children's clothing department and automatically changed for the next escalator. 'Then there was the woman in Kobe who wanted to show me to her family. Like some goddamn mannequin. It was nighttime, and she led the way down one street, then another, took a turn at a dark alley . . . .'"

Another swig of beer. Guy liked to time his effects. Cricket noticed that they were all, including himself, leaning forward at attention.

"'You didn't. Tell me you didn't.'

"'I didn't—I'm not a rapist, just an irritant. And anyway, by this time, I had my campaign mapped out. I met her family—all of them, including the deaf grandmother. They served me instant American coffee, though I asked for a cup of green tea, and they all crowed in pleasure watching me drink it. It was awful.'

"They passed the housewares department in silence. Mr. Fujita asked, 'That's all?'

"'You mean, what did *I* do? I gave them all packets of American chewing gum, spiced with red pepper. You can buy it at joke shops.'

"Mr. Fujita clucked his tongue. 'That's not the way to treat an aged woman.'

"'Oh, the grandmother. She gave her packet to the little boy, as I recall. Do you know where I can pick up some exploding cigars? For that particular kind of self-important businessman.'

"'I have no idea, and I strictly disapprove.' They walked through ladies' wear. Mr. Fujita grew thoughtful again. 'What else have you done?'

"'Nothing that would interest a bluenose like you. Repeat performances, of course, when I get a good gag running. I have no idea how many people I've gotten lost when they tried to give me directions. Leading people astray, putting people out, being a slob in public places—once, causing an awful lot of players to trip in a pachinko parlor.'

"'What?'

"'Those little steel balls—the box slipped, sort of on purpose. There must have been over a thousand spilled on the floor.'

"Mr. Fujita tried to picture the scene. 'Actually, I like to play pachinko now and then.'

"'So do I. Do you point and gesture to your friends when a foreigner sits down next to you? Do you try to load the balls for him?'

"'No . . . then I can't watch my own machine.'

"'Good for you. I'm glad you concentrate.' The foreigner stopped talking to look around. They were in the kimono area now: full kimonos draped like exquisite corpses, all that hand-woven silk, all tagged with astronomical prices. One kimono featuring a river scene with a boat and two herons was labeled ¥565,000. The others around it were a bit cheaper but still more or less unaffordable. The one saleswoman in the area looked straight ahead with vacuous attention. The foreigner advanced while Mr. Fujita snuck behind an array of bathrobes to protect himself.

"'How much is the most expensive kimono you have?' the foreigner asked in Japanese. In ominous calm.

"'¥600,000. But it's not on display.' The saleswoman looked at him levelly. 'Would you like to see it?'

"'Actually, that's a lot more money than I have. How about *yukata*?'

"'Those are much cheaper, I think you'll find. There's a selection of them over on the right. If you want any help, just ask.'

"'Thank you,' said the foreigner. Mr. Fujita thought the voice sounded grateful. 'Thank you very much.' He moved over to the *yukata* section and pretended to look for a while, incidentally exposing Mr. Fujita hiding behind a pink-checked robe. He nodded to the blushing businessman as he got up from his crouch.

"'That's a very intelligent saleswoman back there. Knows what she's doing.'

"Mr. Fujita's face fell perceptibly. 'You're not going to—to do something abhorrent?'

"'I asked a straight question, I got a straight answer. Why should I cause trouble?'

"Mr. Fujita bowed his head. Comprehension humbled him. 'Ah. I misjudged you. I thought you were simply malicious, but you do have a system. I thought you had no integrity, but now I see . . . no retaliation without provocation. That's fair—almost kind, in a way. Yes, you could be called a kind man. A kind American.' He hesitated. 'I wonder if I could prevail upon you to talk with me a little in English. Since you are kind. Your name, your job, your family, how long you've been in Japan . . . maybe what the electricity business is like in America . . . .' He looked up for a reply, but the foreigner had disappeared. He hurried to the escalator, but the saleswoman ran after him. He discovered he had an embroidered *obi* trailing from the waistband of his pants. By the time he had explained himself and returned the sash, pursuit was useless. Too much time had passed, and the foreigner might already be a subway stop away.

"If he had been more eloquent, perhaps, or swifter in his pursuit—but the *obi* flapping behind him could have been attached by only one person. Mr. Fujita stood on the main floor of the department store and pondered the mysterious ways of the West. When he finally got around to looking at his watch, he realized he had seriously compromised his lunch hour. With a cry of dismay, he hurried out the store entrance and into the gaping mouth of the subway.

"During the afternoon, the image of the foreigner began to blur, and in the days that followed, the incident took on the dimensions of a dream. Surrounded by the usual office staff, the same commuters going home, Mr. Fujita began to doubt that there ever had been such a figure as he remembered. It might have been a phantom brought on by too many beers at lunch time—except that he didn't recall having lunch that day, and anyway, he didn't drink at lunch, and the more he thought about the incident, the less sense it made. He finally gave it up, regretfully, the way a child gives up a broken toy. He concentrated on his work and studied English conversation on the train home at night."

The two Asahi bottles clinked on the table, empty. Cricket's left foot had fallen asleep, but he didn't want to disturb the narrative. Guy took a deep breath amid the cigarette haze.

"Some weeks afterward, as he was leaving the office for the day, Mr. Fujita saw a foreign woman, blonde and not at all unattractive, sitting by herself in the park next to the station. She had a map of the city in front of her and was tracing out a route with one red fingernail. Mr. Fujita moved forward, tugging at his lapels, ready to stammer out an introduction, but as the woman looked up, the words died on his lips. He remembered, or thought he did, an odd scene at a fabric store in Semba, and a ludicrous incident at a noodle stand came back to him like an apparition. The woman looked at him wonderingly, this businessman standing stock-still in front of her. Mr. Fujita bowed from the neck, smiled in a perfunctory way, and moved on with the crowd."

As always, dead silence followed after Guy finished. Or maybe it was a meditative silence, or an inscrutable pause—Cricket thought of adding it to the seventy-three kinds of silences he'd already listed in his notebook since October. This one suggested fullness rather than absence, like the echo after a bell-ringing at the local shrine. Finally the silence was broken by someone knocking over his *sake* cup, a satchel-cheeked newcomer reaching for his pack of cigarettes. Dawson, who had sunk into a Buddha-like trance over his *shōchū*, blinked in surprise. Guy leaned back after his coda, appraising the crowd.

The hostess came by, anticipating another round of drinks. More of the same for most of the group. Cricket, who had downed his half-liter of Kirin, headed toward the toilet at the rear of the bar. After Guy had finished, it was mostly trade talk and gossip, not that Cricket was averse to some of that, but he didn't know most of the individuals mentioned. He kept himself company, his mind peopled with what he called ghosts: his dead mother and his much-alive father, the distant Sofie and the nearby but inaccessible Jennifer, Ogawa-san always trying to take over his conscience, and of course Matthew Harriman, the shade of shades. They whispered asides in his ears and tendered advice he didn't always want. Get a life, said Sofie. Button up your coat, murmured his mother. You wouldn't understand, Matthew told him, looking away. He half-expected that one night Matthew himself might show up at Akaboshi. Maybe they could simply pick up where they'd left off on the plane, pursuing an inconclusive conversation to its logical end.

Since his ghosts had yet to appear in front of him, Cricket would play through both sides of each dialogue himself. The usual scenario with Matthew featured a grudging respect for Cricket's cultural adaptation but an equal annoyance at interloping. The discussion would end in a wedge of silence like a hole gouged out from a hill. It always devolved upon the enigma of Matthew's suicide, driven by something far fiercer than the resentment of Mr. Fujita's foreigner, but what?

It was hard eking out a character with so little to go on. Staring at his face in the bathroom mirror, he wondered how Guy did it. Were the people in his tales based on experience or made up to satisfy a whim? What exactly was the point of the stories, anyway? His own fiction had stalled ages ago, leaving him in a bind: what was a writer who didn't write? It sounded like the question about one hand clapping, or some other Zen *koan*. He washed his hands furiously in the tiny basin, lathering with the omnipresent lemon soap.

When he got back, the Aussie married to the Nagoya woman was explaining to the printmaker from Vermont about proper sushi etiquette. "You don't always have to use chopsticks, you see," he said, illustrating with a pincers move. "In fact, sometimes it's gauche."

The Vermonter pondered this point. "How about with *kappamaki*?"

"Well, now you've entered a gray realm . . . ."

The Britisher with the mustache was arguing with the satchel-cheeked newcomer about when the American Occupation had ended. "It was 1950." He thumped his meaty hand on the table. "It had to be then because you Yanks got involved in Korea in 1950, and you couldn't do it all."

The newcomer shrugged. He looked like the kind of man who wouldn't insist too hard, not even about his own name. "Maybe, but my father was in the occupying forces, and he wasn't released till 1951."

"*Huh!* That's probably what he told your mother." The Britisher got a few chuckles out of that one, even one from Guy, who laughed as if it pained him to do so. A few sessions ago, Cricket had become embroiled in a discussion over the precise meaning of *iie*, usually defined as "no" but which sometimes implied "yes." They'd finally settled on "not at all," but not before two more beers apiece. Cricket wasn't going to fall into that trap again—not at all.

With a brief nod to Guy, he paid his share, waved goodbye to the group, and brushed through the blue curtain separating the establishment from the cobbled street. He was halfway down the block when he realized that someone had followed him outside.

"Leaving early, Cricket? So am I." It was Dawson, fingering his shirt pocket the way he had when Cricket still worked for TESCO, as if the fabric itself were itchy. "Where are you headed?"

"Yodobashi subway line." It occurred to him that he didn't even know where Dawson lived. "You?"

"Oh, it's a fine evening for walking."

Cricket nodded as if this were an answer, and they fell into step together. Passing a gift shop on the corner, he saw two foreigners reflected in the store window and recognized himself. They strolled for a while in the silence of not-speaking. "That was quite a story tonight," he finally ventured. "Really a performance."

Dawson paused before replying. "Yes . . . though it was better the first time I heard it, a while back."

"You mean it's not his story?"

"Oh, it's his, all right—at least I think it is—but Guy goes in cycles. Some of those stories he's retold four or five times." Dawson slowed down as if to reflect on his own words. "The rehearsal effect destroys . . . oh, a certain spontaneity. Sad, really. We're the only audience he has, I think."

I had no idea, thought Cricket. *Ah, so*, he almost said. "I see what you mean," he came out with instead. The silence of semi-closure followed this last comment.

They skirted the edge of a pocket park, deserted this late at night except for one cautious teenage couple. They weren't even vaguely entwined, but they exited hastily when Dawson cleared his throat like a polite dragon. "There's a new group at TESCO these days," he noted, as if he'd just chased away two employees. "Makes me feel ancient."

Cricket had left the company only a year and a half ago, but Dawson's declaration made him feel elderly, as well. How old was Dawson, anyway—late fifties? The rust-colored hair was graying, the blue eyes growing a little paler, perhaps. Impulsively, he asked a question that had been gathering for a while. "How long have you lived in Japan?"

The reply was as soft as it was indirect. "A long time."

"As long as Guy?"

"Not quite." They reached the end of the park, all of five benches long, and for some reason began circling back again.

"What keeps people like Guy here?" Meaning 'What keeps you here?' but he decided against that route.

Dawson looked obliquely away, toward the row of empty benches. "Well, in Guy's case, it's all those gay clubs in Kyoto. I thought you knew that."

Cricket shook his head. He knew next to nothing, he realized. He was wondering whether to apologize in Japanese or Western style when Dawson broke in. "No, not me. I was married once. To a Japanese woman." He blew out his thin cheeks. "It takes some people a long time to get over that."

"I'm sorry."

"Don't be." They went once more around the park as if they'd become wardens of the place. "By the way, Miyamoto-san asked after you the other day."

"Really?" Cricket was touched, but tried to turn his feelings into a joke. "Did he pass along any proverbs for me?"

"Yes, actually." Dawson paused in the middle of the street to recite. *"Kyō no yume, Osaka no yume."*

"'Dreams in Kyoto, dreams in Osaka?' What?—people are the same all over?" Cricket was tired of that kind of cross-cultural propaganda. It wasn't true, anyway.

"Not exactly." Dawson drew abreast as they started walking again. This time they escaped the confines of the park by keeping straight, passing a row of shuttered shops like huddled-together milk cartons. "It's from a literary reference. In the original context, it had something to do with fulfillment, no matter where you lived. Something like 'Wishing will make it so.'" Dawson reached into the shirt pocket whose hem he'd been scratching. "Here, he wrote out a copy for you."

Cricket knew a gift when he saw one. The calligraphy on the

stuff white paper was spidery but elegant, and he could almost see Miyamoto's balding head bowed over the desk, peering myopically but cheerfully at his task. He looked at it for a moment under the street lamp before slipping it into his own shirt pocket. "*Domō arigatō gozaimashita.* Tell him thank you."

"Of course."

A left at the hugely silent Daiwa Bank branch, and in a minute they were at the entrance to the Yodobashi subway line, the stairs descending like a stone mouth. The two of them shook hands and bowed for good measure. Cricket watched Dawson's retreating back until it disappeared around the next corner. A fine evening for walking—but where would Dawson go, and what did he do with his time?

Two office ladies wearing identical green sweaters passed him in their descent. The subway mouth glistened black with night, and though his stop was just a few stations away, he fantasized that the insidious underground train would lead him away from his destination, toward some subterranean terror. The shade of Matthew disapproved—of what it wasn't clear. Poor Cricket, sang Sofie in his ear. Reiko said nothing at all.

Teetering on the lip of the steps, he realized that he used to teach at the nearby NEC building, with a bicycle at the ready for riding there. Slowly he walked around the perimeter of the bike lot, as if searching for an errant pet. There it was at the edge of the lot, a little rustier than he remembered it, but still looking serviceable: another beneficiary, now somewhat neglected, of the Cricket Collins Bicycle Reclamation Project. How far was it to Nishinomiya—five miles or so? The only people nearby were a few blue suits, having compensated for working overtime by over-drinking. Slipping his paper-clip skeleton key from his pocket, Cricket approached the bicycle.

Soon he was skimming through the darkened streets toward Yodogawa Bridge. He rode under a double-horned moon, passing fenced-off factories and car lots, shut-up shops and a railroad crossing, followed by a roadside shrine of a rock covered with cloth and a half-empty *sake* jar as an offering. A bent-over *baba*, an old woman in a faded kimono, was bowing in front of it as he passed. Shintoism: tongues in trees, sermons in stones. *Kyō no yume, Osaka no yume.* What you wish for will come true. Just then he wasn't sure what that might be, but he knew something would come to him. At the same time, he decided not to return to the Monday-night sessions, no matter how captivating Guy was. He didn't need that kind of lesson, that kind of company.

Yodogawa was a narrow trough of a river, spanned by the simplest of trestles. Just after the bridge came a slender stand of bamboo. Without any breeze, the stalks remained motionless, but they were so tall in proportion to the plot of ground allotted them that they looked like writing brushes inking the sky. They rubbed against his soul.

Dreams in Osaka. He tried to picture himself as he might look from a hundred feet up, and for one brief moment was vouchsafed a sweeping view from above. Moving along the darkened street under the moonlit sky, he and his bicycle formed an intimate part of the landscape.

9. Timing

Cricket waited in front of Kinokuniya's foreign-books display in Umeda Terminal, shifting from foot to foot, writhing with the demon of marriage. It was 7:40, according to the meter-high digits of Seiko Watchtime, which glowed in neon-red above a video display for Happy Teens. Every minute, scads of Japanese passed him by: businessmen with impeccable silk ties, a surprisingly large number of women in raincoats, families traveling in squadron formation, prowling college boys on the make, giggling schoolgirls seemingly unaware that they were prey, and a variety of couples whose appearance ranged from simpatico to hilariously mismatched. He could watch them for only so long—it was too painful trying to pick out the one meaningful figure, Reiko, to whom he had proposed that morning.

For over a year now, Reiko had pressed him with her love. Lately she would bring extravagant gifts for him in her Takashimaya handbag—a pair of silver cufflinks for his cuffless shirts, a packet of handmade Japanese paper—and afterwards they would make love on his embroidered futon spread over the yielding tatami. Once a week she wrote him poignantly misspelled letters, in which she claimed she would die for him but preferred to live with him for eternity. She began to talk about marriage whenever they were together, and when he didn't respond, she turned away to cry quietly. Finally, forced to decide by the succession of teary scenes in his apartment, he had blurted out yes, probably, he told himself later, because he couldn't stand to see her cry but loved to see her happy. Afterwards, commuting to one of his teaching jobs, he had been overcome with the consequences of his betrothal, and a million objections clogged his mind. He found himself unable to read on the train or even to think, and the rest of the passengers all looked as if they were in on the secret, while studiously avoiding his gaze. It was a kind of slow-motion panic, kept alive by the reiteration of the word *hanamuko*, the Japanese for "bridegroom." He didn't even want to think about his future in-laws, who probably still remembered him as the sneezing fool who threw a corn cob at the *Bon* festival.

What would Mori his landlady say? he wondered idiotically. Would she be pleased or just raise the rent higher? In an absurd vision, he saw Mori her handyman husband working with bamboo and cardboard to extend his studio apartment into a bridal suite. His friend Peter Inoue might applaud the match—"time to settle down, Cricket-san"—but then why did he feel so unsettled? He slapped at his coat nervously, as if flies had alighted on the lapels. Peter himself had recently gotten married and was probably looking for company, or was that misery? As for his father, now there was an open question. Would he appreciate the symmetry of father-and-son marriages within a year, or show annoyance at not being consulted?—in which case he was a hypocrite since he certainly hadn't asked Cricket before marrying whatsername. Cricket got off the train at this point, though he found it impossible to ditch his train of thought, as well. What difference did his father's opinion make? When was the last time he'd asked his father for advice on anything?

At the Kobe YMCA school where he now taught on Fridays, still afraid and needing someone, anyone, to talk to, he had asked Mr. Otomo, the head of the language department, for advice. Mr. Otomo, a short man in a brown business suit, had only made matters worse with his talk of a lifelong union. Visions of marital prison kept popping into Cricket's mind: a couple chained at the wrist, a man bent over a kitchen table with a red-faced baby glaring at him from the opposite seat.

He walked around and around the office, a small room distinguished mainly by its lack of windows. He felt in no mood to teach functional vocabulary. In fact, he felt completely dysfunctional, his mind refusing to run until an escape route was provided. At two o'clock, he called his *sensei* at the Urasenke School to cancel his tea ceremony lesson—he couldn't imagine squatting on his heels for an hour in this state. Then he regretted the call—tea instruction provided a kind of enforced tranquility that might have taken his mind off the situation—but it was too late. He paced some more, trying to draw on an inner calm that didn't exist. At four o'clock, an hour before his evening class, he put through a call to Reiko at work. Though the connection was bad, and both his English and Japanese were by then semi-coherent, he managed to get across to her that he'd made a terrible mistake that morning.

"I—I don't know why—I mean, what got into me this morning . . . I can't, *can't*, consider being married. *Please*."

The voice that had greeted him brightly sunk into near-silence. "But. This morning. You promised."

"I know, but I *can't*. It's wrong, I—I practically had a breakdown coming to the office, can't work, can't think . . . ."

"Oh." A pause stretched into a sniffle. "Maybe I shouldn't see you more."

Hearing those words, he felt free, unattached, almost floating. A second later, an enormous wave of self-pity washed over him at the thought of saying goodbye like this. "No—I shouldn't do this by phone. How—how about if I meet you somewhere?"

"Why?"

"I have to see you. Please, I don't want it to end like this." He felt as if he were reading lines from a grade B movie script.

Her sniffling stopped as she considered his request. "Okay, I meet you. Where?" One of her faults was that she accepted anything he did. He couldn't live with such meekness. She should have been shouting at him.

He told her to meet him in front of the bookstore at 8:00, after work. He had gone to his evening class ushered out by an *"Omedetō!"* of congratulations from Mr. Otomo. His brain refused to clear, the class had been a mess, and he had actually left fifteen minutes early. Now he was at the designated spot, painfully aware of the passing time. In his canvas teacher's bag was a Japanese language text that he couldn't possibly study right now. He dug around further in the bag, unearthing a mystery novel read only half through, the same Agatha Christie he'd bought over three years ago on his way to Japan. *And Then There Were None*, read the title in black-edged lettering, with the helpful addition "Originally *Ten Little Indians*." A broken statue of a cigar-store Indian stared lifelessly from the cover. How on earth had it gotten into his bag? He tried a page or two, but quickly gave it up.

Having failed to distract his mind, he began torturing himself by reviewing his case. He'd actually begun making a double column of pluses and minuses in his notebook that morning before ripping up the page. Now he tried to summon back the list. First, it was possible that he really loved Reiko, in which case he'd be a fool to lose her like this. He recalled an annoying proverb that Miyamoto at TESCO had once divulged to him: *Horeta yoku-me.* Love's partial eyes. Or maybe Westerners, with their passion for overstatement, had got it right this time: Love is blind.

Meanwhile the crowd in front of him kept dividing and flowing together again like some ambient tide. All those jackets and ties matched by skirts and white blouses. Even more formal was the studied sloppiness of Japanese teenagers in black baggy pants or precisely patched jeans. More often, a pale image of Reiko, her short, slight figure, her uncomplaining features, swam in front of his eyes. The past few weeks had been an exercise in cross-purposes. The more he had shrunk from signs of affection, the more she insisted she loved him. A late-blooming romantic. He looked up at the clock. It was 7:45.

That was one point: she was always late. And if he blamed her, she would humbly apologize. He could never engage in a healthy argument since she wouldn't fight back. At most, she'd be hurt and sulk until he slowly brought himself to make amends. How could he love a woman who always made him feel like the oppressor?

A schoolgirl in a navy-blue skirt passed by and waved, though it turned out she was signaling to a friend twenty feet away. She called out something, half of which Cricket picked up, about a movie date. Which reminded him of the last film he and Reiko had seen together, a fast-talking British comedy that, according to Reiko, was badly subtitled. Not that it was her fault that she didn't speak the language well, but with her poor English and his mediocre Japanese, how could they have what Americans called "a meaningful relationship"?

Work on it, advised Ted Allen, whose cross-cultural marriage was going on five years and whose tiny home in Kobe he'd finally visited. In fact, it was larger than Cricket's apartment in Nishinomiya, but the space was shared among two adults and a rather small child, crawling on the tatami in furry-footed pajamas. If marriage made Cricket agonize over choices, the thought of children terrified him. It's a commitment, Ted had said, even as Cricket noticed that the couple didn't talk much together, at least not in public. Still, Cricket was committed in one sense: devoted to Japan.

As long as he was on the subject of devotion to Japan, whatever had happened to Dawson's Japanese marriage? "It takes some people a long time to get over that"—wasn't that what he'd said? So what was a long time—ten years, twenty?

7:50, and they had agreed on 8:00. She was going to come after the obligatory overtime at her job, though she probably didn't feel like working after his insane, disjointed phone call. *Why* did she force him to make her suffer? She said she loved him. To prove it, she caressed his shoulder, held his arm, or trailed her fingers down his side whenever they were together. He'd been told that Japanese were undemonstrative. As with most cultural generalities, it was and wasn't true. She still wouldn't kiss him in public, for instance, as if some bylaw prohibited it. Occasionally he resented the lack of privacy here—which made the retreat to his own apartment all the more important, and how could he even consider sharing it all the time with someone else? No time to be alone. The Seiko clock stared at him. Or maybe he was always alone here. It was hard to tell sometimes, especially in crowds.

A tall foreigner in an odd bluish tweed crossed in front of Cricket, and for an instant he saw the shade of Matthew. Would Matthew get into a bind like this? No, he'd just jump. Anyway, the facial features were too broad, and besides, the foreign man was followed closely by a horsey foreign woman with flaring nostrils. Of course, they weren't foreign, they just weren't Japanese. American, Australian? Foreign. Was she the man's wife? Reiko was on the short side, and Cricket liked her body, fine-boned but resilient in the right places. Insatiable, though. He had made love to that body almost every night she came over, with her getting hurt and pouting every time he protested fatigue.

You're not romantic enough, sighed his old girlfriend Sofie from somewhere above his left ear.

Ki o tsukete, counseled Ogawa-san, her pinched features smoothing into his mother's soft, protective look. Be careful.

Hell with that! snorted Jennifer Hertzl.

He caught himself wondering what sex would be like with the foreign woman, whom he could still see from the corner of his eye. She had a long mane of chestnut hair that she whipped back and forth, and he couldn't help thinking what it would be like to have it descend upon him like a living canopy. Luxuriant tresses like Jill had, that girl from Liverpool, the one he'd lost and never loved. Was it Grant who'd told him she liked a ménage? Where was the crime in idle fantasy? The vision of Reiko's downcast face inflicted guilt.

Must do something to keep self occupied. He reached into his bag once more and came up with a postcard and a fan. *Shochū o mimai moshi agemasu*, the card began, a traditional mid-summer's greeting from two former students of his at Kansai Gakuin, Yasuro Nomura and Kyoko Sakai. Their news was that they'd finally gotten married. Well, what was so terrible about that? As Miyamoto might have said, you burned that bridge when you came to it—no, crossed it. One of these days he really should reply to the card, which he'd been using as a bookmark for almost a month. He opened the fan, which showed a mournful gray carp, and beat the air in front of him. Suddenly he looked hard at the fan, which on the other side read *Nihon Senmei*, "Japan Life Insurance." Another nuptial souvenir, or close: it was one of the party favors for the bizarre engagement party that fatal night in Ashiya. Some Aussie—what was his name?—took the plunge, and Matthew had leaped off the roof.

I was pushed, insisted a Matthew that Cricket had never heard before. In a sense, I mean.

Sexual coward, murmured Jennifer Hertzl. I could never forgive a man for something like that. Cricket dropped the fan as if it were burning his fingers.

A little girl in a sailor suit picked it up and gravely presented it back to him. He absently tendered his thanks. Shyly, she scuttled back to an older couple who looked more like her grandparents than her mother and father. The man wore the kind of old-fashioned black suit that looked even more dated than a kimono, while his wife was dressed in a brown skirt and sensible blouse. They looked as if they'd just emerged from a family outing that had started in the 1950's. The woman patted the girl on the head, the couple nodded briefly at Cricket, and all three moved on.

He felt a brief stab of envy—the last of his grandparents had died years ago. What had their marriages been like, anyway? Or for that matter, his parents' marriage? He recalled the way his mother would start humming as she heard his father's car in the driveway, and the way his father crooned "Louise . . . " and kissed her with a sound like a friendly smack. But he also had vague memories of his father scowling up the staircase, waiting for his mother to descend so they could go out to dinner. Or the two of them stopping an argument abruptly as soon as he came into the room. For some reason, he couldn't conjure up more than fleeting images from that period, as if the tension in his mind had tightly scrolled up his past.

If his stepmother wasn't another Louise, and he suspected she wasn't, then what was she like? Actually he'd been surprised that his father *wanted* someone for life after all these years. Or maybe most humans felt some biological need to form a more perfect union. Christ, was everyone doing it but him?

A sudden silence seemed to come over the multitude around him as they all refused to answer his question. Watching them was beginning to give him vertigo, to the point where the crowd appeared to be the still point and he was the whirling mass. Stepping forward, he collided with a short businessman in a trench coat, and his Japanese reflexes kicked in. *"Sumimasen!"* they intoned in unison, excusing themselves, as they snapped to attention, nodded briefly, and parted. Cricket watched the man as he scuttled away toward the Hankyu line, half-wishing he were that man with that life going in that direction, or anyone else, really.

As the clock neared 8:00, he found himself hoping Reiko wouldn't come. Wouldn't he be better off without her? He might feel bad for a while, but afterwards? Then what would Reiko do? His imagination showed him a picture of a desperate Reiko, trying to kill herself with the Sanseido razor she used on her legs. Or leaping in front of the Midosuji-line subway. The *Mainichi Daily News* reported cases like that every week. What would it be like to live with a death on his hands? Forget the poetic melancholy of *aware*—this was guilt, guilt, guilt.

The problems with the relationship were mostly his fault, he knew. He had told her that. She knew and didn't care. She loved him. In place of marriage, she offered to go live with him in Tenafly, which was where he was born but to where he had no intention of returning. In place of that, she said she'd be willing to wait a year, two years. No acceptance that they ever might separate. Until now.

Reiko had such wide-open, trusting eyes. And small clever hands that could sew on a button or draw cartoon heads of the people at her office. Or deftly handle a kite string: at Suma, they'd entered the New Year's kite-flying contest on the beach with a curved red samurai model that darted about as if alive, manipulated by Reiko's nearly invisible cord. It was a timeless moment.

It was just like her to be late, though. And the kite-flying had ended in disaster as the samurai had broken loose and flown out to sea. He should leave, but he couldn't. In his mind he saw her duck-head parasol, which she rarely wasted on rain . . . she would be wearing her pleated indigo skirt and penny loafers, black hair brushed back, eyes brimming with tears.

As the clock showed 8:02, a man like a sumo wrestler lumbered out of the bookstore like a locomotive gathering steam. Looking up, Cricket thought he saw Reiko in profile behind the man, but it was another girl, taller and shyer, who smiled brightly only when she saw her boyfriend slouching against the far wall. Reiko's smile was far more gracious, a gentle Cupid's bow that transformed the whole face. Now she might be sobbing, rubbing her small fists against her eyes. Poor, poor Reiko. Why in hell was he doing this to her, anyway? He picked up the fan where he'd dropped it again and whipped it back and forth furiously.

Once more he went over the case against her, but none of the points really held up. If you loved someone, then other considerations didn't matter. She was so loyal. She would even show up to receive a brush-off, come to the train terminal just to be hurt by him. She was so patient. And caring. At 8:04, his affection for Reiko began to expand inside him like warm gas.

She did make him happy often, when they went out anywhere together, supporting each other invisibly against the crowd. It was just a question of freedom against binding love. Would she ever relax her hold? The possibility of marriage, after all he had put her through, after all his imagined torment, descended again. It encompassed him like a soft cocoon. It would make her so happy and it might make him happy, too. He wasn't drawing away from her, actually, but from the uneasy limbo of half-proposing.

He saw himself asking for—no, begging—her forgiveness and being accepted. He'd say that he had been out of his mind, which might even be true, and she would cry a bit, but it would probably be all right. Such a quick reversal appealed to him. It would stop the leaking sensation in his stomach, as though he were bleeding internally. He would walk out of the terminal holding her umbrella.

8:06. Impossibly late. No, he was an idiot. He felt like a character from one of Guy Lapham's fables. It seemed like ages since those Monday night stories, but he'd been the one to leave the group. He was spiraling further and further out, divorcing himself from everything. He needed this chance.

D'ye want to go have some fun then? I know a few birds. That was Grant the Brit, winking so broadly at him that his whole face was contorted.

The Korean prostitute smiled enigmatically and said nothing at all.

It wasn't as if Reiko had pulled him back. No. And yet. To agree to marriage, even supposing she said yes, would mean to be tethered like this forever. Saturday afternoons, with her wanting to take a stroll somewhere and expecting him to make conversation—what would he do when he needed to isolate himself? Say so, and receive one of her hurt looks that made a light gash somewhere around his intestines? No, if she came now, he would try very, very hard to say goodbye. Walk away with a handshake or a bow and not look back. Because if he did, she would trap him with her eyes, which held all the memories of them together.

She could swallow him in her gaze. That had been apparent even at their first meeting in the coffee shop. Under the spell of that look, he couldn't stop himself from talking. She listened with her eyes, which became liquid in their soft intensity. The first night, she'd made him carry her naked to the bathroom and soap her smooth white back, delicately lowering her eyelashes for a thank you. The sight of her firm bottom with its peach cleft made him lightheaded. She had guided him to the bedding on the floor, centered him on her taut belly and heaved upward. How could he leave that body? He would lie cradled in her round arms, thigh against thigh. She liked cossetting his head against her breasts, and he liked being held, and they would be happy together, as long as they didn't have to talk too much.

But she didn't come, and at 8:08 he found himself attacking her again. Her perpetual lateness, her general immaturity, her total lack of—what was the word? Intellect. At first it all seemed charming: her skimpy education at an elegant women's college, her strict devotion to a comic strip called *Yumiko*. But she was childishly romantic. She saw him, for God's sake, as some modern knight, all set to carry her off to America. Where did she get this miraculous conception of America, anyway? Happy faces, open prairies, perfect weather—she wouldn't survive a week in a place like New York City. Stay in Kobe.

He stared at the carp on his fan, gray and silent, but now he recalled the fiancé's name from the Ashiya party: Reggie, that was it, and a woman named Ayako. Were they still together, and if so, how? He would have to ask Bruce about them some day, if Bruce ever called again. When was the last time he'd called? And whatever happened to *his* wife? A steady relationship cut you off from others, or was that just his imagination?

Maybe.

Why don't you call? whispered Jennifer in his ear, which he scratched at vigorously.

The swirling crowd was beginning to thin out, couples walking off to restaurants and theaters, the remaining businessmen catching suburban-bound trains. Cricket looked around without seeing Reiko and thought briefly, tenderly, of comforting her, holding her tightly against a phantom stream of endless, buffeting commuters. If she had come at that instant, he would have said nothing, just held her and trusted in her understanding. When she didn't appear at once, he immediately disliked her, the way she kept him in emotional thrall. He had to detach himself. He should leave. No, he would stay until 8:10, at which point he would walk away—or stay a while longer. He snapped the fan shut and dropped it into his bag. If only his mind would stop shuttling between marriage and taking the next train.

The passing faces now made little sense to him. They were all qualified by an absence of something, a blankness where

Reiko's liquid eyes and full lips should have been. There was no pattern but simple alteration in his affections now, and he stared at the minute-hand of the clock as a reassurance of some forward movement. One minute he loved her, and the next minute he wanted a mercifully brief ending.

At 8:10 he knew he needed her, wanted her to squeeze his hand comfortingly and lead him away. At 8:11 he felt the same hand pulling him through a domestic horror forever. At 8:12 he suddenly realized that an existence without Reiko would be barren, ridiculous without the woman he loved. He had to change his mind again at 8:13, unable to bear the thought of living so closely with anyone, no matter what the circumstances. He stood numbly looking up at the red numbers of the clock, his future switching back and forth like some pendular insanity. Even the voices in his mind had quieted down as if motion-sick.

It was 8:16 when Reiko arrived, carrying her duck-head umbrella furled under her arm. She was sniffling slightly, her eyes enlarged as if she had been crying, which he suspected she had. He felt pity and sadness, and would soon have drawn back from the feeling except that it was an even-numbered moment, he had oscillated once more, and at that moment he loved her more than ever before and wanted to marry her. He stammered out a proposal, and she, putting down her umbrella and wrapping her arms around him, accepted before the minute was up.

10. The Concrete Buddha

They were returning to the outskirts of the city, back to the realm of enclosed spaces and the end of the tour. The taxi seemed to bend around the narrow, curved streets as the driver steered with one hand, gesturing with the other. He was balding and wore heavy black glasses, which he kept pushing up with his forefinger. Just then he was wrapping up his travelogue, a personal though clumsy version of the canned speeches on the tour buses. "That was the last of the boiling lakes. We stop soon. You should buy red clay from the blood-hot spring—it cured my mother of rheumatism ten years before."

Cricket sat in the back seat, saying nothing because he could think of nothing to say. Here he was in northern Kyushu. Soon he'd be gone, having gathered his few impressions. He'd spent the day in Beppu, where the entire mountain slope seemed alive. The landscape was dotted with thin plumes of steam like a collection of giant kettles buried underground. The area produced naturally hot springs, which the Japanese called "hells" but touted for their powerful curative properties. Tourists paid high prices to enter the nearby bathhouses where they simmered for an hour or so. But Cricket didn't think the baths could cure him since he wasn't sure what he was suffering from. Maybe it was the burning sensation whenever he urinated, which might have been from a one-night stand in Juso last month. Can you get the clap if you don't get your money's worth? he speculated. Or maybe it was delayed action from that night so long ago in Pusan, or the pained guilt from both, or everything and nothing in general. Maybe his bike seat was all that needed adjusting.

Reiko wasn't along on this trip because she couldn't get away from her job, but that wasn't the whole reason. Cricket's engagement slightly terrified him. When Ted Allen and his wife threatened to throw him a celebration party, his answer was an adamant *no*. Maybe that scared them, he mused. They're so normal and I've become so strange. Or maybe he was just the kind of person who needed to put some distance between himself and the object of his desire. As it happened, this was also one of the rare periods when he'd fallen out of love with Japan: weary of bowing and smiling, annoyed at always being the *gaijin* in a crowd. He'd even grown a little tired of eating rice. Yet he was sure the feeling would pass. It always did.

Meanwhile, his teaching was turning sour, something he'd

realized last month when the students began to resemble each other. Freelance work offered no advancement, no job security, not even a raise. But what else could he do, where else could he go? He'd just had a long-distance fight with his father after telling him that he wouldn't be back for another year. "Is that what you're going to be, a professional expatriate?" his father had asked, puffing on that pipe Cricket could still hear and smell across 12,000 miles, though he claimed to have given up smoking last year.

"No," Cricket had said to himself rather than to his father, "I think I'll just drift away." Which was certainly easy enough to do. Half the teachers he knew worked till they got together a stake and left for India or someplace. Then they reeled back here like yo-yos. Charlie Sayles had blown his savings for living in Sydney on a two-week trip to Hong Kong that he still wouldn't talk about. God knows how much of Jennifer Hertzl's salary went up her nose—though she claimed she'd been clean for months. And Matthew, stuck in his private grudge against humanity—gone but damnably unforgettable. If American advertising and foreign English teachers are all that most Japanese know of the West, thought Cricket, no wonder they have a skewed opinion of us. Even square old Ted Allen had been headed home to Oregon with his pregnant wife, but they'd never gotten there, and after a few months in Bangkok resettled in Kobe.

Cricket had discussed some of this with Miyamoto, the best Japanese friend he had. Even though Cricket had quit TESCO ages ago, Miyamoto had invited him to dinner at home, which both startled and touched him. In a country where everyone lived packed together, most social occasions took place outside the home. In advance, he'd tried to imagine what Miyamoto's living conditions were like, given his probable salary at TESCO. It turned out that he lived in Koshien, the same as Reiko, but in what the Japanese called a rabbit hutch, in an apartment complex like a giant honeycomb. The apartment itself was laid out like Chinese nested boxes, each room bigger than the one before. A tiny entryway opened into a slightly larger kitchen, which led into a standard four-and-a-half tatami-mat bedroom, adjoining a not-exactly-spacious bedroom for two boys aged five and seven.

Cricket had met only Junichiro, who showed the shyness of a five-year-old already wearing glasses. "Police tsu mitsu," he told the foreign visitor, coached by his father, Cricket assumed, and then withdrew. The seven-year-old—Kotaro?—was studying that night at the *juku*, taking evening prep classes so that one day he could get into a decent university. Miyamoto's wife Yoshiko worked for a travel agency to bring in more money, and probably also to get out of the apartment.

Dinner was served in the dining area, basically a table in an alcove, just the way the living room was a television set near the bathroom. But the food was excellent: broiled sea bream, spinach with soy and sesame, and steamed rice, everything arranged precisely on a tray. During the meal, the space miraculously expanded so there was no cramping at all. Then Yoshiko went to play with her younger son, and Miyamoto brought out a bottle of Super Nikka whiskey. When he asked Cricket how things were going, Cricket tried to be stoically Japanese, but Miyamoto said so little and they drank so much that he ended up complaining more than he'd intended. Miyamoto half-nodded all the while in confirmation. Do you know what it's like, Cricket finally asked him, always being an outsider?

For once Miyamoto had no proverbial advice but said, with that rueful look of his, that he didn't think he'd like to be a *gaijin* in Japan. Later Cricket realized that he hadn't even asked how things were going with *him*. There he was, drinking Miyamoto's whiskey and acting like a selfish American. It was then he'd decided that he needed to get away. From himself.

That's why he was on this trip to Kyushu, now that he was in between classes for a week. He hadn't asked anyone else to go along with him. Away from his mental and physical routines, he was a nobody, and that was all right with him. He didn't have to act. He'd let the overnight ferry from Kobe churn him to Oita. From there, he'd taken a green-line train to Beppu, the first spot on his listless itinerary—because the "hells" sounded interesting. Here he was simply an observer, having hired a cab at a fixed price for the afternoon. If anyone asks me where I went, he thought, I can tell them I went to hell.

At one of the hot springs, the temperature was listed at $102^{\circ}C$, and the water glowed green from radium salts. He pulled out his gray-carp fan to keep the heat at bay. At another fissure, the mud bubbled up in a series of angry belches, spattering onto the protective fence around the perimeter. The mud bath was particularly violent today, the cab driver had told him, or else he'd have seen the bubbles form slowly in the shape of a priest's head.

At yet another hell was a geyser that erupted every twenty minutes, smashing against an overhanging cliff before dying down again in a cauldron of rocks. Cricket forgot the legend attached to it soon after he heard it—after a while, one hot lake began to resemble another, and the sulfurous fumes fogged his mind. Or was this evidence of a subtler derangement? he wondered. It wasn't syphilis he really worried about, but rather something accreting in his head like limestone layers, preventing him from concentrating. Not to mention the voices that kept him company.

Jack Sims, who knew all about discipline from his hitch in the Marines, said it was the third-year lulls. It happens in marriages, he told Cricket, and it happens in stays abroad. So what's Jack's excuse? thought Cricket irritatedly—he's been living in Amagasaki for the last four years with no plans to return stateside. Lately Jack had been practicing sword-handling, samurai style—Cricket had seen him demonstrating in a bar in downtown Kobe recently. He'd even taught Cricket a few moves with a kitchen knife. Get physical! he roared, briefly boosting Cricket's adrenaline level tenfold.

But getting physical didn't really help the numbness he felt. It followed him everywhere like a pet shadow. His landlady Mori actually got so concerned that she brought him a pot of miso soup. It was still in the refrigerator where he'd left it.

Kawaisō, murmured Ogawa-san. You poor thing. The kimono she wore was the same one she had on the day he'd left the school, a green willow pattern in strong brocade with a matching obi. You'd swear she'd have switched it by now, thought Cricket, but some things never change. Like the image of his mother, permanently arrested in the memory of a nine-year-old. Since the recurrence of his allergies, now dormant again, she'd come into sharper relief. A widow's peak above a strong brow, a nose she fingered the way some people tug their hair forward, a smile that at times seemed broader than her mouth. But the only tactile remnant, fifteen years after her death, was the vague, restraining pressure of her hand. It wasn't something you could capture on film. Sometimes it just rubbed against his mind the way Reiko ran her hands through his hair. Yet it wasn't always pleasant. When these sensations got too strong, he leaned back to tilt them out of his head, and sometimes that actually worked.

Now he was beginning to feel as if he'd been in this taxi too long, sightseeing in hell. One place the driver took him had no spring at all, just a thatched farmhouse leaning into the wind at the top of a hill. There, a mud-splashed man in an improbably clean shirt and a golf cap showed him two snakes under a hand-labeled placard labeled "SERPENTS." They were each over six feet long, but one was dead-white, dosed with formaldehyde and coiled with its tail in its mouth, preserved in a tank like a portrait of eternity. The other was alive but completely immobile from having eaten a chicken over a week ago. "*Shoka-chū*—digest now," explained the golf-cap man, pointing to his own stomach. As it turned out, the place wasn't a snake farm, just a sort of shrine for these two. The man gestured to an altar inside, where tourists could buy postcards and genuine snakeskin charms. There was also a guest book to sign, its pages of cheap rice paper pressed flat on an old music stand. On an impulse, he'd signed as "Matthew H." with a made-up address in Ashiya. Matthew's shade smiled frowningly, or frowned smilingly, at his handiwork.

The more alone I am, he reflected, the more I feel as if I'm playing to an invisible audience. Everyone is in my head, so I don't have to explain things. They see what I see. While traveling he resolved to take no pictures and buy no souvenirs. He hadn't even brought his notebook. It was a rule he'd just made for himself, that he should carry his past inside himself, because he wasn't too sure of the future. But he'd broken down and bought some stuffed snakeskin charms for Reiko and a few acquaintances (the Japanese habit of gift-giving had taken him over) before he remembered that Reiko hated snakes. Should I tell her that I'm a bit of a snake myself? he pondered. Or do I mean worm? The woman in Pusan years ago seemed to sense that. The prostitute in Juso just flattered him. He could still hear her laugh like a toy piano, a sound so at odds with that strong body, her pelvic grip like a fist, pulling him into her. He didn't even remember her face.

Be careful, said Matthew.

Beware the two *c*'s, proclaimed his father.

If it was just sex, why did he feel guilty? No, it had to be shame. *Haji o shire!* he heard Japanese parents tell their children: "Shame on you!" Shame was guilt turned inward. All this time in Japan had turned him into a monster of introspection. As for why he was in Beppu at all—it was on the way to Nagasaki, which was one reason for stopping, besides viewing hell. Maybe the horrors of Nagasaki would shock him out of this torpor. Or provide more shameful guilt. It was a little past three in the afternoon, and he thought he should head back to the train station.

The tour by taxi had been shorter than planned, mainly because he hadn't stayed as long at the hells as the regular tourists, who were mostly Japanese. Something in each location had hurried him on to the next, until he'd run out of places to visit. He felt he was running out of time, as well. They were past the hills now and winding through streets of two-story shacks, vegetable-stands, and cheap variety stores. The driver recommended a place to eat *fugu*, the perilous blowfish specialty of Beppu, but Cricket had already tried it the night before. It was at a small restaurant that specialized in all parts of the beast: *fugu*-fin soup like a fish consommé attacked by a shark, *fugu* sashimi in slices of translucent thinness arranged in the shape of a fish, broiled *fugu* filets teriyaki style, even sautéed *fugu* liver, which was really dangerous since they could never completely detoxify it. That was how a famous kabuki actor had died a few years ago. People said it started as a tingling that turned into widespread numbness, beginning around the chest and moving upward. By the time you realized what was happening, it was already too late.

Cricket wasn't exactly sure why he'd done it, but something in the Japanese psyche loved trials and sacrifices, the thrill of self-obliteration. He could understand the seduction all too well.

Did I seduce you? asked Sofie.

Not that way.

He got into an argument with her that went nowhere, as usual. When he next looked up, the driver was talking to him again. Another lost moment. Hesitating, the driver asked if he'd enjoyed the tour.

"Yes . . . I'm sure I did." Cricket's Japanese was perfectly adequate by now, but sometimes his voice lacked conviction. Of course, the driver kept stumbling along in English, though Cricket had asked him several times to stick with Japanese. Charlie Sayles had a theory that all foreigners had *GAIJIN* stamped on their foreheads when they arrived in Japan and were treated accordingly. That always reminded Cricket of Guy Lapham's tale about the *gaijin* on the offensive, though he'd been told that Guy himself cut a smooth swath through Kyoto's sex clubs. Why couldn't people ever mean what they said?

The taxi stopped at a traffic light with a double file of schoolgirls in blue uniforms marching by, holding hands. They stared at the foreigner in the car, but they didn't giggle or shout the way so many of them did. After they'd passed, a stillness hung in their wake, as if they'd used up all the life in the street. This was the silence of depletion.

The driver checked his watch, pushing up his glasses at the

same time. He seemed like a well-meaning type, anxious to give good money's worth. "Hmmm ... still early. This is the last tour, anyway. You haven't seen the *Daibutsu* yet? Big statue?"

Cricket hadn't been aware that the city had a Buddha or statuary of any kind. Beppu, he'd been told, was the kind of place where the local museum was closed half the week for lack of revenue. Hot springs, *fugu*, and a notorious red-light district represented local commerce. In fact, the driver had originally suggested another kind of tour entirely, but Cricket had declined twice, considering his experience in Juso, and after that the man had stopped asking. Still, the Buddha sounded vaguely intriguing, and Cricket told him so.

"Okay, we go there. If you have time. Free. I like to see it again myself." He twisted back to look at his passenger, smiling politely. "I must stop off at my house for a minute—nearby."

Cricket had no objections. He had no feelings one way or the other, was what it amounted to. If he didn't take one train to Nagasaki, he'd take another. If I return to Nishinomiya intact, he thought, I guess my future is sealed. He heard himself say yes, and settled back in the green plush backseat.

The driver pinched his thumb and fingers together in the Japanese version of the OK sign. Then he drove on, soon veering onto a road even narrower than the one they'd been on. Some of the old wooden buildings, sagging toward each other, almost met above the middle of the street. It looked like a scene from an impoverished Third World country in comparison to downtown Kobe. Cricket made up an invisible notebook entry: "Japan makes up for the smallness of its country by wide local variations just a few miles apart. In deepest Shikoku, the dialect becomes almost impenetrable. In Kyoto, it's the women who are impenetrable. That's why salarymen travel to Juso."

Oh, shut up.

The taxi cab again seemed to bend sinuously around the turns, as they took two lefts, then a right. The driver parked just outside a two-tiered apartment building with sheet-metal sides painted forest green. Leaving the motor running, he jumped out of the car and called up to the second floor. A plump woman in an apron labeled "ME & YOU, YOU & ME" came out and accepted a flat, heavy envelope he tossed up to her. Probably his earnings, observed Cricket. That's the way it works in Japan: the man is lord and master only outside the house. His wages are unceremoniously handed over to his wife, who doles out an allowance to him.

There. I *won't* shut up.

She tucked the envelope in her apron pocket and patted her side. Her sleeves were rolled up to the elbow, her hands dusty with rice flour. She looked capable, with the air of someone who took care of others: cooking someone's favorite meal or fluffing up a pillow for someone's head. Was this what they meant by "mothering"? The only incongruous aspect was her round doll's face, which made her look oddly breakable.

When the driver mentioned that he was going out again, she frowned. But then he pointed to Cricket in the back seat—who opened the door and waved as if on cue. The driver launched into a long explanation in rapid-fire Japanese that Cricket couldn't catch, and finally she smiled down at Cricket, bobbing her head. Cricket bobbed back. Around the neighborhood, he noticed, a group of old men and women sat on wooden stoops lined with corrugated cardboard seats, sucking their gums. Two kids were playing with an orange plastic bat and a crumpled ball of aluminum foil. Somehow, they all seemed to be staring, as if he and the driver and his wife were all putting on a scene for the entire street. Lately, Cricket felt watched a lot. Not always by the living.

Don't put on airs, sneered Matthew. Cricket tilted his head back, and Matthew slid away.

Cricket asked if the Buddha was far, envisioning a half-hour ride into deep countryside. It reminded him of his temple dream. There, amid green shade and the hum of cicadas—but the driver shook his head. He got back into the car and they began street-bending again. After five minutes, he remarked, "Just nearby." They turned left at a telephone pole, the only marker for the intersection, and jounced straight ahead for two blocks. This street had craterlike potholes, with an old woman angrily poking her umbrella into one of them. Her limbs looked as frail as calligraphy strokes.

One last turn, and the driver glided to a stop. Something tall lay behind the surrounding tenements, but it was hard to see. A crumbling concrete path led up to a concrete altar, draped with a few blossoms so big as to look artificial. Surrounded by a rusted cyclone fence was a great concrete plinth, and seated on the platform in displaced serenity was the great Buddha. The figure was huge, about sixty feet high. It had an odd history, the driver informed Cricket: just forty years old, it was built of concrete and people's bones. The bones were contributed from the local crematorium just before World War II. The driver took off his glasses in awkward reverence.

The Buddha sat in the classic cross-legged position, hands folded in lap, with a mystic third eye in the center of his forehead. From above the surrounding roofs, the eyes stared at everything and nothing, taking in the stunted row of tenements or possibly dismissing them from existence. Sneaker prints up the left flank suggested that a few kids had tried to climb to the same eminence as the Buddha. A water fountain and a bench stood by a wooden shack on the left, but the cab driver and Cricket were the only spectators. A second fence began around the knees of the Buddha, indicating an opening in the Buddha's side. The driver told Cricket that when he was young, people could enter the statue, but they'd sealed off the main access years ago. There was a rumor that a child was buried somewhere inside.

They both stood in front of the altar, considering the rumor, maybe considering the nature of rumors in general. In a small incense bay, sunken into the concrete altar, someone had deposited, like talismans, five pull-tabs from soft-drink cans. Cricket felt he might pray if he believed in that sort of thing. Neither of them said a word. The driver seemed to be communing with the concrete while Cricket was studying the Buddha's pressed-together thumbs, looking for cracks in the structure. The thumbnails were dirty but unbroken. The Buddha's expression was impossible to read.

Finally, the driver put his glasses back on and started walking to the car. Cricket followed him, looking back only once to see, shocked, that the Buddha was flat. From the side, you could see that the depth extended only five or six feet, where the builders had obviously decided to save on materials. The revealed façade gave the statue an odd appearance, as if cornered against an invisible but inevitable wall, trying to protect the street from itself. And who, in turn, protected Buddhas? The statue was to be torn down next year, the driver told Cricket, because the private owners wanted to sell the lot. An apartment building would be put up in its place. This, considered Cricket sourly, was what they called the new face of Japan.

When the driver asked where to drop him off, Cricket said Beppu Station. The taxi bent around the twisted streets once more, passing a series of open sewers and a man sleeping alongside one. A boy was playing a *shakuhachi* on one corner, but a woman came out of the building behind to drag him back by the ear. This is the old face of Japan, Cricket realized, one that not many foreigners saw. They went up a last rise marked by a pickle vendor, and the train station hove into view. The driver stopped with a slithery braking motion in front of the station entrance, where Cricket paid him the agreed-upon fee of four thousand yen. He flicked his glasses, smiled, and drove off toward the red-light district, the opposite direction from his home. A dirty blue plume of exhaust followed him.

Why do people so often betray one another, Cricket sighed, even themselves? He thought about the driver's wife in her apron and wondered whether she'd burn tonight's supper on purpose when he didn't come back in time. Or would she go pray to the great Buddha, and what would she bring as an offering? He saw a snapshot of the scene in his mind, but it was out of focus. He thought of Reiko, waving to him for almost half an hour until the ferry from Kobe was out of sight. She had said she'd visit his apartment every day he was gone.

On to Nagasaki. The guidebook he'd bought at the Juso Exchange described it as "inherently Japanese, a city with almost fatal charm," but was that before or after the bomb was dropped? If the site of the explosion was the prime attraction, did that mean Hiroshima and Nagasaki competed for A-bomb tourists? This destination had seemed like a good idea when he'd been half-planning the trip, but now he had little desire to go. Inertia would carry him along, as it had so many times in the past. His fate was back in his apartment, waiting for him. It's all a matter of choice, he supposed, but that can be an illusion. Oedipus had a choice and it didn't help him much.

What do *you* know about it? sneered Sofie, seconded by Jennifer Hertzl.

Leave my darling alone. His mother ran a hand through his brain.

Reiko looked at him with her liquid eyes, saying nothing.

He paced the platform, trying to retrace his steps each time around. If he kept the same pattern, maybe nothing would ever change. Or was that just another version of hell?

Two minutes before the train was due, he decided to enter the station souvenir shop. He quickly found what he wanted: a small plaster Buddha, three inches high. It was an uncanny replica of the concrete original, flat and stunted as it was. Even the vague smile had the touch of a sneer. He asked the salesgirl not to wrap it and just slipped it into his bag. Then he got on the train, placed the Buddha on the opposite seat, and focused on the smooth features, the serenity just a breath away from torpor, as the station slowly receded behind him.

11. The Road to Hell

It was ten o'clock on a Saturday morning, and a long, slanting ray of light stabbed the blackboard in the conference room. The light seemed to transfix everything, a stasis matched by the torpor of the pupils in the room. Cricket stared at his five students for a moment, cursed silently, then walked to the blackboard to illustrate the point he was trying to make. He enunciated slowly, as if talking to children. Weekend intensive-English camps seemed to be growing in popularity, probably because they were cheaper than a set of lessons over half a year. But even with all this drill-work, conversational practice, and role-playing, what could be done in just a few days? In some ways, Japanese were even more optimistic than Americans.

He tried to recompose his face so that it was a mask. Unfortunately he was in a foul mood, or worse—an accumulation of all his foul moods since he'd arrived in Japan almost four years ago. Actually, he was angry a lot these days, though partly with himself. Reiko offered him cups of tea and backrubs but mostly kept her distance. *"Gambatte ne,"* she'd told him, waving a white dishcloth at him as if he were going off to war. There was that phrase again, always popping up in adversity: "good luck, persevere, don't give up."

It didn't help that he knew half the other teachers at the camp. Jennifer Hertzl looked more alluring than ever in a black scoop-neck dress that was completely inappropriate for teaching. "I hear you're engaged," she grinned, and Cricket replied shortly that he heard she wasn't. Ted Allen, in a checkered cardigan and vest that said *family man*, seemed so glad to see Cricket that he pumped his hand five times. And there was Harry Belton for God's sake, now wheezing with the bulk of three hundred pounds covered by a tentlike white button-down shirt. It was almost like a TESCO reunion.

In fact, a new outfit called EKTAR seemed to be running the show. They had called him specially, not divulging how they'd gotten his name. It was all a little mysterious, but the work paid well: ¥67,000 for two and a half days of teaching office workers from Kobe Steel. Where EKTAR seemed a little weak was in organization. Only after the teachers had arrived at the camp were the sections assigned: Cricket got one of the intermediate groups, and so did Jennifer. Belton bullied everyone to get the advanced group. And Ted walked off with his beginners, his enthusiasm not so much infectious as annoying. He was the kind of teacher who used chants in the classroom. Cricket was the kind who most emphatically did not.

He nodded at the blackboard and at his group, as if introducing them. "The purpose of this drill is to get you to think *and* speak at the same time." He drew a thinking head, some words above it, and an arrow connecting them. "I'll put a sentence on the board to show you what I mean. For example, I may write, 'Last night, I worked until nine,' and then I want you to talk about working late. Okay?"

More than half the heads nodded, and Cricket was encouraged to continue.

"So. One of you will pretend he worked late, and the other person will ask him things. *'Why* did you have to work late?' 'What were you working on?' And so on. Ten questions in all."

A hand rose like a flag being hoisted. "Please?" Mr. Tamura the worrier, whose automatic pencil looked as badly chewed as his fingernails.

"Yes?"

"What do other students do?"

"All right. Two of you will be reporters. You'll take notes on the questions and answers. At the end, I want you to read back what you've written." This was a drill prepared by EKTAR, which claimed suspiciously high results from it. He looked around the room warily. He had begun to categorize his students as traits: worried, shy, distracted. Just then Mr. Maenaka was hiding behind a blue notebook, and Mr. Inagaki was looking out the window. "Whoever doesn't have a role, please listen carefully, since it will be your turn next."

In the ensuing pause, Cricket moved back to his chair at the head of the table to pick up the list of starter sentences. Since the call for the intensive-English camp had come late, and the preparation sheets handed to him only upon his arrival at EKTAR's training center, he wasn't as prepared as he liked to be. Idly, he fingered his frayed maroon-and-silver necktie and wondered how Jennifer was handling her intermediate section. That black dress was clearly her attention-grabber, especially in an all-male class. He suppressed the desire to find her classroom in corridor 10A, wherever the hell that was. EKTAR's training center was what you might call a labyrinthine building—except that *labyrinthine* implied "complex," whereas the interior of this building was maddeningly uniform, with row upon row of identical hallways that met at the back and front.

"I don't know, you've erected some kind of wall," she'd told him last night during the communal dinner.

"A Great Wall," Ted had chuckled. Harry, several seats down and mis-hearing it as a reference to his own girth, had glared at them all. Cricket half-admitted that he'd isolated himself, but it was more like dislocation: in any given place, he wished poignantly that he were elsewhere. Now he wondered gloomily whether his students felt the same way. Still, he had to preserve the mask. One student at Shin Meiwa last year had called Collins-*sensei* inscrutable, which Cricket took as a high compliment.

He paused to consider his situation. Teaching from EKTAR's *All about Idioms* yesterday afternoon had been a failure. Most of the students hadn't yet gotten used to his speech, and the only idiom Cricket managed to teach in a whole hour was "in one ear and out the other." That night, an EKTAR sentence-pattern drill had revealed only that the students had difficulty with English sentence patterns. And the free discussion in the lounge afterwards had degenerated into a drinking binge. Alcohol had at least loosened their tongues. Now there was no drink, and everyone looked either bored or nervous.

The boredom particularly irritated Cricket because he still considered himself intriguing, a good talker with a perceptive outlook. Despite his brusque façade, he always took his teaching personally—what other way was there to take it? And he had experience, knew all the tricks: repetition and interjection, feigned interest. He could swap teaching stories: the time that a viciously fluent student had started hitting on the one female student in the group; the Friday a whole class at Meijiya had disappeared (a company outing that no one had informed him about). It all gave him a certain perspective, backed by a fertile imagination. That was what these Kobe Steel students lacked, imagination. Their lives revolved around the steel business, their wives and children in satellite orbits. He wanted to jolt them.

Unfortunately, the sentences to start each question-and-answer session weren't calculated to jolt anyone. Damn EKTAR. Whoever wrote the textbooks for them was no Dawson, who at least allowed a puckish sense of humor to show through occasionally. Even the look of the text, in round-faced type with a lot of white border that was supposed to seem friendly, simply came across as bland. The sentences themselves ranged from "Yesterday I lost my watch" to "I want to go to Hawaii for my vacation."

He selected one at random, sighed subvocally so that the students couldn't hear his displeasure, and walked to the blackboard. "LAST NIGHT, I WENT TO SLEEP LATE," he printed in neat block capitals. He stepped back and surveyed the group.

The classes he was assigned always had one superior student, and here it was Mr. Aoyama, who stared back at Cricket through steel-rimmed glasses. He wore a well-cut blue suit and had his American Parker pen poised to take down whatever came next. In wretched contrast, Mr. Tamura nervously bit at the push-down top of his automatic pencil. He tried to write down everything Cricket or the other students said. Mr. Maenaka, who was short and squat and probably had a short and squat wife, continued to use his notebook as cover. Mr. Inagaki, usually silent, remained true to form. Only Mr. Kurashige, who at twenty-five was the youngest person in the room, ventured to say anything.

"Who answers questions?" Mr. Kurashige took the necessary risks of a junior member, wanting to show everyone that he was talented but careful not to show off (for which he wasn't quite good enough, anyway).

"Mr. Tamura will. And another student, let's say you, Mr. Inagaki, will ask them. Mr. Aoyama and Mr. Kurashige, why don't you be reporters?" Cricket stepped back. "All right, Mr. Tamura, repeat the sentence on the board—no, don't tell me, tell Mr. Inagaki."

Mr. Tamura intoned the sentence in a sepulchral tone. "Last night, I went to sleep late."

Mr. Inagaki wrinkled his brow. "Why did you go to sleep late?"

Mr. Tamura looked wildly at Cricket, who maintained a neutral look. For once, he didn't have time to use his pencil. "Ahhh, mmm . . . I had headache." Mr. Aoyama and Mr. Kurashige diligently took down the exchange, and the questioning proceeded.

"Did you . . . have medicine?"

A pause. "Yes, I took aspirin."

"Did it help?"

"No."

That seemed to end that line of inquiry, but since Cricket had asked for ten questions and ten answers, Mr. Inagaki corrugated his forehead again in three parallel lines, an act he performed with facility. Silence was really his forte, the kind that Cricket would categorize simply as a pregnant pause except that nothing much came of it. The silence of stillbirths? The hush of cogitation? After fifteen seconds, he came up with another question.

"When did you sleep?"

Mr. Tamura was ready for this. "Three in morning." There was a pause, and he decided to elaborate. "My wife sang to me."

Cricket pictured Mr. Tamura, in the long underwear that most of these businessmen wore from October to March, lying face-down in bed while his wife smoothed back his hair and sang to him. It was an amusing image, and the other students, judging from their smiles, thought so, too.

"Does you wife . . . like to singing?"

Mr. Tamura considered the question from all angles, tilting his head first one way, then the other. "Y-yes. She belong to chorus once."

Ideally, this was the way the question-and-answer exercise was supposed to work, eliciting information the students wouldn't normally volunteer. Cricket found himself wondering what Mr. Tamura's home-life was like. What did Mrs. Tamura think, being married to a man who bit his pencil all the time? It required only a little effort to see the cramped apartment they lived in, Mrs. Tamura washing the dishes at the small sink after dinner, while Mr. Tamura surveyed her from behind and wondered, nervously, whether to grab and kiss her. Or would he would remain forever frozen in hesitation?

Cricket's own situation came to mind. Just the other day, Reiko had asked him in Japanese what he was going to do. She'd simply meant that Saturday afternoon, but he'd misinterpreted it as a question about his future. The horrible part was struggling to find an answer. Was paralysis caused by guilt or torpor? Reiko encompassed him with her large, liquid eyes, saying nothing.

Reiko has your number, muttered Sofie. Can't even discuss your future.

No one has my number, he remarked coldly. And anyway, Japanese has no future tense.

Ogawa-san's troubled countenance filled his mind. This might be one of his bad days. He tilted back his head to clear it.

The last questions in the series were automatic and did little to fill in the description Mr. Tamura had embarked upon. Cricket interrupted only to correct an occasional error.

"When did you woke up—"

"*Wake* up."

"When did you *wake* up . . . this morning?"

"I woke up at seven o'clock a.m."

"Are you tired?"

"Yes, I am. I want a nap."

There were a few sympathetic nods around the table.

"Do you often have nap?"

The authority bore down. "*Naps*. With an *s*."

"No, not often. No time."

"Mmm . . . does you wife have naps?"

A shrug. "I don't know. Maybe."

Cricket broke in. "This is the last question, Mr. Inagaki. Make it interesting."

Mr. Inagaki rested his chin on an upended fist while he thought of a plausible ending. "How many years did you marry?"

Mr. Tamura couldn't answer at once. He seemed to be counting on his fingers. "Twelve years, I think." That ended the series, after which the reporters gave their muddled summary. According to the notes, Mr. Tamura couldn't get to sleep last night, had gotten to sleep at three, had taken aspirin, had gotten up at seven to his wife's singing, wanted a nap, and had been married twelve years. Cricket pedagogically pointed out missing facts and explained how to condense several answers into one sentence.

Despite the bad grammar, the results had exceeded his expectations. At least something had happened. For the next round, he chose Mr. Aoyama to ask questions and Mr. Kurashige to answer them. Mr. Tamura and Mr. Maenaka, who could no longer hide behind his blue notebook, were instructed to make summaries—though Mr. Maenaka complained he couldn't do it, and in fact that turned out to be the case.

For a starter sentence, Cricket looked down the list of possibilities and finally chose something acceptable. He wrote it in large block capitals on the board: "ON THE WAY TO WORK THIS MORNING, I SAW A CAR ACCIDENT."

Mr. Aoyama was quick, delivering his questions in the manner of an interrogation. Mr. Kurashige, whose English was at a much more basic level, required some time in answering.

"How many cars were in the accident?"

Mr. Kurashige shut his eyes, counting the retinal images. "Three, I think."

"Was anyone killed?"

There was another pause while Mr. Kurashige debated with himself. He made a grand samurai gesture. "They were all killed."

"Really? How did it happen?"

This was too complex for Mr. Kurashige to handle directly, so Cricket waited until Mr. Kurashige's lips formed soundless words, and finally intervened.

"Mr. Kurashige, did one car hit the others?"

"Mmm . . . yes. One of the drivers was not looking."

Mr. Aoyama pressed the attack. "Was he drunk?"

"Maybe. Maybe he didn't get enough sleep last night." The class laughed at Mr. Tamura, who looked away. At least they were getting involved, thought Cricket, who imagined himself as a traffic fatality. A car shooting out of a narrow street in Osaka, the frightened, foolish face of the other driver—a deafening collision. Lying on the ground, neck twisted at an awful angle. How would he feel? Stupid question—nothing, of course. He'd be dead.

Just resting, whispered the shade of shades, Matthew.

Be quiet, he murmured between clenched teeth. Not here. He sat with his hands fisted in his pockets while Mr. Aoyama and Mr. Kurashige hammered out a fairly coherent story. The final details came from the reporters, who submitted that a drunken driver who possibly needed a nap had hit two other cars on the corner of Sakurabashi Avenue. All three drivers were killed. The time was ten in the morning, the wives had been told, and the three were already cremated. Cricket, who had his own idea of how the story should have progressed, was grudgingly satisfied. Matthew frowned but forbore to comment.

Because of the pauses between questions, each series had taken over ten minutes, including summaries. The next sample statements generated more complex stories and took fifteen minutes apiece. They revealed, among other things, that Mr. Inagaki was a passionate golf player and that Mr. Kurashige wanted a girlfriend more than anything else in the world. Cricket could see Mr. Inagaki using his furled umbrella to make chip shots while waiting for the subway home. As for Mr. Kurashige, with a wife and more stability, in a few years he'd start slowly moving up the ranks, a company man who'd retire thirty years later as a *buchō*, a department head.

The others also began to take greater shape and clarity. Mr. Maenaka's shyness now seemed eminently reasonable, based not on his short stature but on a simple lack of ability. If he was indeed good at something, maybe it was mah-jong or pachinko. On the other hand, Mr. Tamura would soon drop dead from hypertension, despite his wife's gentle efforts to calm him down. In *manga*, the Japanese comics that Cricket read with increasing frequency, Mr. Tamura would be the one with a private raincloud that followed him wherever he went. Or an anvil, or a sword.

Mr. Aoyama was less easy to analyze, displaying the guarded

confidence of a superior mind in a group-think company, though something was hidden there. It showed in interludes of lip-biting. Oddly, most complex of all were Mr. Inagaki's silences, which now ranged from irritating to minor works of art.

It was now eleven, and there was some question as to whether he should go on with this exercise or switch to the next unit, an unappealingly titled drill called "Where do you go when . . . ?" Should he dispense with it entirely? No, he reflected, EKTAR seemed like the kind of company that liked to tick off stages. "Our #3 group has finished with Level Four locational idioms," they would write in their progress report, "and advanced to Five."

Cricket decided at least to stick with the question-and-answer session for a while longer, since it kept the students' interest. Something about it stirred him, as well. He made a stop sign with his hand. "There'll be a short break now, for about ten minutes, and then we'll continue." For the first time, the students looked more hurt than relieved. Mr. Tamura, the pencil-chewing ace reporter, looked particularly peeved. He lit a Lucky Seven cigarette with a nervous flick of a match and smoked toward the window.

Opening the seminar room door was like knocking down a wall, letting out stale air and a certain claustrophobic presence. Cricket stretched the way stiff-necked Japanese commuters did, twisting his head up and down, side to side, and diagonally for good measure. The buzzing in his brain faded. Much better, though his legs felt a little cramped. Time for a short walk. Nearing the other rooms, Cricket heard Ted's class loudly chanting, *"Can you tell me how to get to! Can you tell me how to get to!"* Presumably they'd soon add on a place-name and be on their way. Of course, they'd need a lot more vocabulary to make sense of any answer they got. That was the problem with these drills: too far from reality.

From the open door of room 8A, he could see that Belton's group was already on its break, maybe even already done. Harry had finished early last night, too, claiming that the advanced group needed less work. The truth was that he favored cafeteria drill over conversational work. "Awful food," he'd complained even as he helped himself to thirds of fried fish and rice. Ted had dutifully praised the pickles or something.

He was circling the corridor when he heard Jennifer's heels clacking around the bend and darted back the other way. He felt sure she was going to ask more questions about Reiko, questions he felt as reluctant to answer as his students faced with another EKTAR drill.

Why haven't you said anything about her before? Is she cute?

Usually quite.

Those two words together make an awkward combination in English. We say one or the other, not both.

Jennifer's heels seemed to be following him. Cricket fled toward the men's room, which happened to be occupied by Mr. Maenaka. He stood next to Cricket, his short figure not much taller than the top of the Western-style urinal. The two nodded perfunctorily, then returned to the business at hand. The scent of lemon soap wafted over from the sink area. Eyes straight ahead, Cricket slowly regained his composure.

"We flush now?" Mr. Maenaka reached out to pull down the chromed knob, clearly pleased to demonstrate some knowledge, even the nomenclature of plumbing. Cricket nodded approvingly and followed suit. There was something comical about these students, no matter how important they were outside the training center. Put them in a situation where they had to speak English, and they became awkward, even childish. Was Mr. Maenaka staring at him? He zipped his fly, sloshed water on his hands, and exited a discreet interval after his student. He looked around warily for Jennifer but saw and heard nothing.

What are you afraid of? mocked Sofie.

He chose to ignore that. Turning his head, he cut across the passageway from corridor four to corridor two and found himself back in corridor six. When he tried to retrace his steps, he entered an irrelevant alcove, and it was a minute before he made his way back to the seminar room.

Before opening the door, he took three deep breaths and adjusted his tie. It happened to be a gift from Reiko, who admired it because the maroon and silver stripes looked like British school colors, which made him slightly afraid of getting caught out as an impostor one day. Kobe was full of Brits, though he'd lost touch with Bruce and Grant a while back.

Losing our touch, are we?

He shook his head vigorously to clear it again. Think English-teacher thoughts. Grammar and syntax.

The students unconsciously came to attention as he re-entered the room. They put out their cigarettes and stopped talking in Japanese, which Cricket couldn't understand well at that speed, anyway. They looked toward him silently, respectfully, waiting for his words. By now, the lively atmosphere from before had dissipated, pulling everyone down to late-morning doldrums.

I'm baaack....

"Well, I hope you all had a chance to collect your thoughts during the break."

Mr. Aoyama nodded sharply. Mr. Kurashige favored him with a nervous grin. Mr. Tamura looked vaguely terrified.

"Yes? No? Anyway, let's pick up where we left off, and we'll finish off this exercise before noon." After a suitable pause, during which no one said anything, Cricket approached the blackboard to write another sentence. He needed something to get them going again, something to work them loose from their surroundings.

Huh.

He thought for a moment and then wrote, "TODAY, I WOKE UP AND COULDN'T REMEMBER MY NAME." He assigned Mr. Maenaka to ask questions and Mr. Tamura to answer them. The idea of amnesia soothed him. He liked his sample sentence and simply thought it a shame that Mr. Maenaka's English wouldn't do justice to it.

"What is your name?"

"I can't remember." Laughs collided around the room, but Mr. Tamura squeezed his eyes shut. "I can't remember anything." His pencil began to roll off the table.

Mr. Maenaka leaned forward, pointing his thumb at his nose. "Do you remember me?"

"No, not at all."

"Are you—marriage?"

Mr. Tamura studied his hands, with short tapered fingers, one of which wore a gold band. "Maybe," he conceded.

Mr. Maenaka wrung his hands. "Do you remember *anything*? Please."

Mr. Tamura had adopted a more relaxed, almost somnolent look. He took some time in answering. "I remember ... a lake somewhere." He focused on a spot on the far wall. "And trees. Maybe, a white house."

Mr. Tamura, Cricket recalled from last night's introductions, lived in a small apartment in Ibaraki.

"What about house?"

"Many, many rooms. And maybe long tunnel."

"Where did tunnel go to?"

"I don't know. Inside, was very dark."

Mr. Maenaka, halfway through a tunnel, paused in his questioning. A different tack was needed. He thought for a moment and smiled. "Why are you *here* now?"

"Yes, why?" Mr. Aoyama, from the back of the room, also wanted to know.

Cricket leaned forward. It was an apt question, and he wanted to hear what the amnesiac would say. Mr. Tamura wore a perfectly blank expression and didn't seem to know what to do with his hands on the table. He retrieved his pencil from the floor, laying it down with exaggerated care on the table, where it started to roll again. He picked it up and held it like a chopstick.

"Where is here?"

"Here is EKTAR company training center. Do you know?"

"Maybe in a dream . . . ."

"This is no dream!" Mr. Maenaka spoke a few rapid words in Japanese.

"What?" Mr. Tamura looked puzzled.

"Mr. Maenaka, ask your questions in English. Mr. Tamura has lost his memory and can't understand Japanese."

Mr. Maenaka didn't smile. "Mr. Tamura, have you . . . " he hurriedly flipped through his pocket dictionary " . . . 'take leave of senses'?"

"Have you *taken* leave of your senses?" He corrected the sentence mechanically. But in his mind he saw a river bank, a dark figure on the bank with the water slowly washing away the sense of touch from the fingertips. His mother drew her long white hands over his brow, assuaging the frustrations of the years since she had died. The loneliness was countered by the people he talked to in his mind. Only lately they'd started talking back and even appearing in front of him. The first time had been at the Wang Hotel in Pusan when the shades presided over his one-night stand. The darkened room, the unsmiling girl . . . . He blinked—back in the seminar room. He managed to repeat his last sentence as a means of recovering himself.

The rephrased question was met with a relaxed look of non-comprehension. Mr. Tamura opened his hands, and his pencil fell to the table with a rattle and a roll. "Maybe, maybe . . . ."

"What happens to your family, your job?"

Mr. Tamura spread his palms. "I don't have to answer questions."

It was the tenth response, and the series was therefore over. Cricket waited a bit, then called for the reporters' version of the questioning. Mr. Inagaki, the first reporter, began his account in broken English, but stopped at the point where Mr. Tamura had claimed his version of insanity. He looked up at Mr. Tamura, who wasn't looking at anyone but rather at a tree outside the window. His hands described the wings of an origami crane.

Cricket called upon Mr. Kurashige, the other reporter, to finish the summary, and then, to snap Mr. Tamura out of it, he assigned him to be a reporter for the next round with Mr. Maenaka. The statement was "I HAVE ONLY TEN MORE DAYS TO LIVE." Mr. Inagaki was the interrogator, Mr. Aoyama the answerer. Cricket noticed as soon as the questioning began that Mr. Tamura was writing not with his pencil but with his finger.

"Are you—painful?"

"Yes, I feel pain. Great pain." Mr. Aoyama grimaced.

"Where does hurt?"

"It hurts in my midsection." And Mr. Aoyama unbuttoned his jacket to clutch his stomach.

Mr. Tamura had cautiously picked up his finger from the paper and was now licking it. Mr. Inagaki averted his eyes for a moment, creating a silence of avoidance. Finally he recommenced, "When did pain start?"

"For years now. Recently, it's hurt very much."

"Do you see doctor?"

Mr. Aoyama nodded vigorously. Clearly, he had seen many doctors, each delivering the same verdict. "They all tell me the same thing. 'You will die.'" He looked down at the table.

"Does . . . your wife know?"

"No." The voice became defiant. "She must not know. Children, too."

Mr. Kurashige, from the back of the room, murmured "*Kawaisō*" out of sympathy. Mr. Inagaki, who if nothing else was practical-minded, asked about insurance.

"Yes, I have. But who will support my parents?"

Cricket was thinking, how noble of Mr. Aoyama to be learning English at a time like this, when he caught himself. Was the game going too far? To hell with it—let it go farther. He sat back and let Mr. Inagaki continue.

Mr. Inagaki thought, opened his mouth, and shut it: the quiet of a carp in an ornamental garden pond. He changed his subject slightly. "What is your . . . disease?"

"Stomach cancer."

There was a sharp intake of breath among the class members. Cricket, preoccupied by cancer and craziness, felt his emotions being exploited. A faint scent of ether occluded his nostrils, and he became slightly ill. Maybe the next round would be the last.

"Do you have pills? To stop pain, I mean."

"Yes, I have." Miraculously, from an inner pocket of his jacket, Mr. Aoyama produced a vial like a film canister. He pried off the top and shook out several white pills onto the table. Cricket hoped very, very hard that they were for an ulcer.

Mr. Inagaki went through his mouth-flapping and then stopped. "I have no more questions," he whispered, and Cricket didn't object. No one seemed inclined to say anything. Mr. Aoyama slowly put the pills back into the vial, and the vial back in his pocket.

There was a respectful pause while Mr. Aoyama straightened his tie, re-clicked his pen, and looked up again, ready to write down what the teacher would say next. Mr. Maenaka and Mr. Tamura, the supposed reporters for the round, said nothing. Mr. Maenaka was possibly too stunned, but Mr. Tamura's attention was drawn elsewhere, toward his thumbs, which he twiddled clockwise, then counterclockwise.

Cricket decided to start a new round immediately as a distraction. He practically vaulted out of the chair to get to the board, assigning roles over his shoulder as he wrote the new sentence. It had to be something that would jar but also uplift. A sort of counter-diversion.

Quickly written on the board: "I FEEL TEN FEET TALL TODAY." And quickly assigned roles: Mr. Maenaka to answer questions, Mr. Inagaki to ask them. Mr. Kurashige and Mr. Aoyama to record them—it was useless asking Mr. Tamura to do anything.

"*Why* do you feel ten feet tall today?"

Mr. Maenaka, his feet barely touching the ground in his black leatherette swivel chair, looked up at the lie on the blackboard. It was too great a leap for his imagination, bridging such a gulf of frustration. "I don't feel tall. Feel like . . . rat." His whisper barely broke the silence.

A lifetime of shelves above his reach, women too lofty for him, suffering others' armpits during rush-hour on the subway, and tiptoeing to reach urinals. Mr. Maenaka sat slowly rotating in a half-circle while Cricket entered his life. How did it feel when a big woman practically sat on him in the train? Cricket felt himself small, breast-high to a lady in a blue dress on his right. Her breast rubbed against his cheek, the odor of her sex temptingly near—a shiver ran down his thighs. Ogawa-san shook her head in admonition.

"What kind of rat?" Mr. Inagaki the inquisitor cut through Cricket's fog.

Cricket intervened just as Mr. Maenaka said something to the table in Japanese.

"That is not a good question." Cricket rose to use his voice of authority. "In fact, I'm sorry, but I gave you a bad statement. Mr. Maenaka, you don't have to answer any more questions."

Mr. Maenaka, sullen, said nothing. Mr. Inagaki looked put out at being told to stop. A pall was descending around the room. Mr. Aoyama stared at Cricket, then looked away. Mr. Tamura focused on a point just above Cricket's left shoulder. Something had to be done soon, but nothing suggested itself. What did they want, damn it?

Clouds began to form in Cricket's mind, scudding in from the dreamscape where they usually congregated. They coiled and re-formed in strangely familiar shapes, bowing and nodding. *"Sumimasen,"* they hissed: "Excuse me." As they receded, Matthew drifted into the classroom with a ghastly pallor framing a forced grin. His eaten-away body shimmered as he waved grimly. Behind him stood a vast maternal shadow, flickering at the edges. *No*, thought Cricket. He focused on an image of Harry Belton, fatly infuriating, and that led him back to the situation at hand. He shook his head free of the vestiges of others and realized the worst: he was left alone with himself. He was it.

The shift was breathtaking. Now they were all staring at him. He felt himself the recipient of Mr. Tamura's amnesia, Mr. Aoyama's disease, and Mr. Maenaka's miserable stature. Mr. Inagaki, frustrated by a language he couldn't speak properly, turned his resentment on Cricket. Mr. Kurashige pretended—Cricket easily saw through the guise—to be unconcerned. They said nothing, but they wanted him. In their own, unresponsive way, they were indicating that it was his turn. As the realization dawned on him, sudden possibility crowded his brain. He would show them he could be inventive. Make them think, at least.

"All right, we'll reverse the situation!" He heard his voice rising. "Now you ask *me* questions. I'll put a sentence on the board, okay?" He saw he had them now, and before the atmosphere could dissipate, he hurried to the board and wrote the first words that occurred to him: "I USED TO BE A PROFESSIONAL THIEF." That should have the right effect. The chalk broke in two as he finished writing, but he didn't bother to pick up the pieces. He faced his audience, hands on hips. "All right, now. Questions."

Mr. Kurashige was the first to understand the import of the message. Unsure of what was expected of him, however, he gripped the conference table in support. "When—when were you thief?"

"Oh, about five years ago. It was a good living, but I'm in Japan now." Teaching English, said a lower, submerged voice. He suppressed it.

"What . . . items did you steal?" Mr. Aoyama, precise as usual, was staring at him with fascination—the way someone looks at a snake, Cricket thought.

"It depended on where I broke in. In some places, I took straight cash or jewelry. Other places, stereos or televisions." You mean stupid items like chopsticks and soap, said the voice, more nastily this time. Ogawa-san clucked her tongue. He rubbed his forehead to aid his new recall, elaborating for Mr. Aoyama's benefit. "Once I stole three mink coats."

Everyone's eyes were fastened on him now. The feeling was exhilarating, like breathing pure oxygen. At the same time, he felt a certain contempt for anyone who would believe him. *Gullible*, that was the word.

"Who did you thief from?" Mr. Maenaka, the ideal victim, asked the question from a safe distance. He pursed his meaty lips disapprovingly.

"I don't remember too many faces, and it doesn't matter, anyway. I just picked their names out of a telephone book." Paunchy businessmen who slept in monogrammed pajamas, the wives with cold cream on their faces. He had always disliked that class of people. Dislike was such an easy, casual feeling. He didn't even like Reiko at times, though she supported him no matter what he did. She was a bit too eager, and anyway, she'd been in Japan too long—ha ha. And didn't he despise these students?

He caught Mr. Tamura looking glassily in his direction and speared him in his gaze. "Don't you have a question, Mr. Tamura? Come on, let's hear it."

Impelled by fear, Mr. Tamura's pupils shrank back to normal size. Cricket kept staring at him as Mr. Tamura swallowed nervously. "Wh-when you come to Japan? No, no, why, I mean. Why?"

"To escape." Cricket smiled pityingly at him. "To get away from what I'd done. I don't like the past, Mr. Tamura, do you?" Sofie's voice, eerily echoing from somewhere outside his head, insisted that he'd been grinding away at final exams before coming to Japan, but he knew that was just an excuse. There was blood on his hands. Really, what was he doing teaching English when he was importantly guilty? Mr. Tamura, bobbing his head like a toy wind-up bird, obviously agreed.

Mr. Aoyama whispered across the table to Mr. Kurashige, something in Japanese that Cricket couldn't catch. "No interruptions, Mr. Aoyama. And Mr. Inagaki hasn't spoken yet, have you?" Mr. Inagaki looked more or less composed, which annoyed Cricket. Cricket rapped his fingers on the table, getting out of his chair to stand tall again. "Come on, we don't have all day!"

Whether Mr. Inagaki understood was doubtful, especially since Cricket had been talking at normal speed without choosing his words. Though Mr. Inagaki made movements with his lips, he said nothing. He wouldn't look at Cricket. The other students all drew closer to Mr. Inagaki as if in mutual support. Finally, he ventured to speak.

"Why are you English teacher?" He looked down again and was silent.

The question took Cricket off-guard as if someone had uncovered his secret vice. They knew he was no thief, but a down-at-the-heels instructor, a job offered to anyone off the streets whose native language was English. He tried to explain, speaking quickly and without pattern. "I teach because I have an avocation to teach—maybe that's not true, exactly, all right, but at least I do better at it than some of the people they employ here." He looked about him, saw the same stares as before, and became more truculent. "Look, I teach and you've got to try to listen, because this is a class, after all . . . ."

No response. Or were a few of them edging away from the table? Where did they think they were going?

Go on, go on.

"All right, because I'm better than you and I can do what you can't—because maybe I enjoy seeing your foolish faces when you can't talk—do you understand?" He stamped his foot for emphasis, then vaulted onto the table as the students began to withdraw in a group. It was peculiar how they seemed to be heading for the door.

"Where do you think you're going? Don't you see how I dislike you—stay, damn it!—you can't even talk straight, and I have to teach you how. Doing exercises for morons, and you lap it all up, while I smile and try again. I'll never be any good—no, *you'll* never be any good, and it's no use complaining because I'm the teacher. That's it, I'm the English teacher and you work through me. I tell you what to say, what to do, isn't that right, Mr. Inagaki?"

There was no answer. There was only a faint rush of air, leaving Cricket with his head tilted upward, haranguing the far wall. The silence closed in, and Cricket slowly, dazedly, got down from the table. A trembling weakness began somewhere around his knees and traveled upwards. He was aware that he'd done something reprehensible, though he wasn't clear as to what. Some serious indiscretion, something to jeopardize his teaching career. Back at the company office, a formal complaint lodged . . . irresponsible behavior. Or maybe he should be grateful for the outburst that had made continuing impossible, no longer necessitating the pretense of teaching. Was this it? No one raised an objection. He sat down in his chair with his head in his hands, waiting for a response from somewhere, anywhere.

Seconds and minutes passed. The passage of time began to have a restorative effect. After a while, he heard the scraping of chairs, the sound of throat-clearings. He looked up and saw the students through narrowed vision, sequentially. First, Mr. Aoyama, prim in his blue suit, followed by Mr. Kurashige, looking sideways as usual, followed by Mr. Maenaka, Mr. Inagaki, and Mr. Tamura. Their expressions were neutral, and though they said nothing to Cricket, they exchanged a few comments in Japanese. Mr. Maenaka adjusted his tie, Mr. Tamura took out his pencil, and Mr. Aoyama cleared his throat. Casually, but with polite smiles that made it all the more awful to anticipate and then actually see, they glanced at each other, looked toward the front of the room, and held their poses.

They were waiting for Cricket to continue.

12. Shanghai Ward

The table fan in the ten-man dormitory looked and sounded like a bit of green fuselage, whistling through the night. Upwards in the darkened room, above the reach of the fan, a mass of air hung stagnant like a hot, breathing presence. From the open casement came occasional whiffs of the Shanghai Canal, smelling of rotten vegetables and raw sewage. Sporadic sighs surfaced in the chamber, but whether they came from the sleepers or the city itself was unclear. Anyway, not everyone in the room was asleep: on the cot in the far corner of the room, Cricket lay patiently, preternaturally awake, waiting for the next rumbling of his bowels.

The problem had started in Guangzhou with something he'd eaten at lunch, a gray, gelatinous slab that he knew was bad even as he chewed it. That night, riding in what the Chinese called a hard-seat train, his guts began to rearrange themselves into unfamiliar positions, glands and ducts all combining as if to form some anatomical funnel. Then everything began sliding down the funnel, and he'd started losing sleep. He had medicines but discovered they were no good. He had stamina but was losing it steadily. The course of his trip to China began to take on a bizarre interior impulse: in trains, hotels, and waiting rooms, to locate the bathroom as soon as possible, and to replenish his supply of toilet paper. He kept hoping for improvement, like a change in the weather, but the days remained hot and humid and he continued to lose weight.

He'd spent so long in Asia that to get sick on his way to America seemed a ridiculous irony. Yet China was another world from antiseptic Japan, in turn opposed to the glitter and lushness of Thailand. In Bangkok he had chewed raw sugarcane from the food stalls and viewed palaces with gold-thatched roofs. Hong Kong offered him everything from custom-tailored suits to double-decker buses, vestiges of the British empire, but with a mercenary zeal that was entirely Chinese. If he hadn't been careful, he might've ended up with five new wristwatches, a portable TV, and a bag of glass eels to take home for dinner. As it was, he'd stayed at the Kowloon YMCA and eaten dim sum for most of his meals.

Bangkok and Hong Kong and Shanghai were all stopping points on a route that would eventually lead to New Jersey. After almost five years in Asia, Cricket resisted the term "homecoming," as his father had put it, but he was at last headed westward.

Reiko would follow him in a matter of months. Yet during the last few weeks on the road, he'd been uncertain whether he was escaping again, losing himself, or returning to an earlier stage. His distrust had slowly transferred itself to his surroundings: merchants trying to cheat him, room accommodations that ruined his sleep.

Finally his food had tried to poison him, injecting him with this humiliating disease. At first he told no one, or rather wrote no one: his main method of communication was to scribble Chinese characters on a notepad he carried and hope for a sympathetic audience. Most Chinese could speak no English. His spoken Japanese from his years in Osaka did him little good here—Chinese pronunciation he garbled hopelessly—except that he could write after a fashion. In Hong Kong, on the first leg of his journey toward the interior, he had combed through a pocket dictionary, looking for tourist words. *Room fee, train ticket, rice bowl.* Over and over he had copied the words, drawing on the calligraphy lessons he had once taken in Kobe. He felt the ghostly fingers of Reiko over his, guiding him through the practice strokes for radicals like "little roof," "man," and "water."

He now had two dictionaries and realized poignantly that he should have brought a phrase book and shown it when in doubt, like other travelers. Possibly his pen strokes were inexact, or the Chinese stroke-order was different. Sometimes people understood, sometimes they laughed. His pad contained, amid many starts and finishes, one conversation with an old man in Shaoxing, pages long, which ended in a long string of incomprehensible characters.

The fuller his pad became, the sicker he got. By the time he reached Shanghai, he'd had no sleep for four nights, and what had started out as an adventure in China had turned into a prolonged nightmare. Getting a place to stay in Shanghai had been hard enough. Every place was booked, and he'd been lucky to find a spot in a hotel dormitory. Tomorrow, he told himself—though lately he addressed his remarks directly to his stomach—in the morning, when you've survived one more night and it's obvious you're not getting better, then you go look for help. His fingers in the dark sketched out the two characters for *hospital*: "doctor-institution." A schematic arrow inside an enclosure, a double curve like a B, the little-roof radical . . . drawing the pictograms cheered him minimally, though the word *hospital* in any language made him feel afraid. His fingers traced out other words: *door, bicycle, girl.*

Bicycle + *girl* led him to an image of Reiko, pedaling along Fujiwara Road. Her large eyes were moist when she kissed him goodbye, but he'd had no choice after the scandal at EKTAR. Belton must've been the one who ratted on him—his students were too polite for that. Or maybe Jennifer had insinuated something, or Ted had overheard the shouting. Conduct unbecoming an English teacher. Employment opportunities dried up overnight, and he woke up one day realizing he had to leave. Of course, he'd told none of this to Reiko; rather, he'd explained his pledge to enter English graduate school in the States and become a real English teacher.

"Welcome back!" wrote Peter Inoue, now a pediatrician in training and the proud father of a newborn girl. "It's about time," wrote his father, who offered to put him up for a while until he located his own place to stay. "And what about Rayko?"

Reiko = *rei* + *ko*, spirit-child. She had taught him that.

Ogawa-san plucked at his sleeve, reminding him to bathe.

He looked up from his ghostwriting. The red travel-clock by the edge of his cot read 2:00 a.m., its digits glowing an evil green at night. It was the made-in-Japan clock he'd bought in New Jersey, brought to Nishinomiya to perch on his dresser, and was now bringing back. Did that represent the wholeness of return or a vicious circle? The clock dropped a digit, and as it did, his guts constricted violently.

The cramps now came on the hour. They seemed to arrive with ever-increasing frequency, like labor pains, but always heralded by a liquid rumbling. They came now, moving with alluvial swiftness. Before the real pain could set in, he was out of his cot and into his shoes and with an invalid's delicacy was padding out the door, down the hall to the communal washroom.

The toilet was Western-style but hopelessly clogged. The bathroom itself, like the entire hotel, was a relic of the Shanghai of the 1930's. Now the wooden moldings were swollen with moisture and the doors wouldn't shut. In the rooms, the fixtures had been ripped out incompletely: a chandelier hole above a repainted escritoire, a bit of wallpaper with an art-deco fish hanging in mid-hallway.

Cricket wedged the bathroom door in place and sat down heavily. The room, through frequent visits, was already familiar. The bathtub was a cast-iron monstrosity with a lion's head for a spigot, a runnel of rust down the interior. In the scalloped marble sink, a mass of gray laundry floated like an island. The tilework, where it wasn't whitewashed over, was flecked with gold and black. In a moment, the lion's head merged with the tiles and the sink as the whole scene swam together. Cricket groaned and succumbed to another body-wracking cramp.

He o hitte, shiri tsubomu, counseled Miyamoto from the ceiling. No use scrunching up your buttocks after a fart.

Cricket bent forward and did considerably more.

His ex-landlord Mori kindly offered to fix his plumbing.

Afterwards, he felt purged but even weaker than before, his thin white legs splayed out like two appendages that no longer belonged to him. His Kobe YMCA T-shirt was soaked in sweat, his shorts hopelessly soiled. Without any clear transition, he was back in the dorm room again, lying down on the hard bedding, and this was the third, or maybe fourth time tonight.

The fan whirred, the vague sighs continued. Alone in the dark, the premonition of the next rumble keeping him awake, he began to resent the others, just inches away yet slumbering unaware. For him, sleep seemed a great distance off—a thousand miles away, maybe, in Nishinomiya with its curving narrow streets and shrine to Ebisu, the *tofu-ya* and the tea-seller's stall, the patchwork roofs bluer than the sky.

You can't go home again, murmured Sofie almost pleasantly.

You can't go home, barked Harry Belton, that son of a bitch.

You can't go, said Reiko with her eyes alone.

You can't, admonished Ogawa-san, plucking at his shirt.

You, breathed the rotting stench from the canal.

Then came the darkness of nothing, settling on him like a shroud. He tried to see what time it was, but twisting around from his present position was too painful. At this hour in Osaka, Reiko would be curled up on her futon. She now worked for Nippon Electronic Corporation downtown, slowly saving up money for her transcontinental flight. And wasn't he going by steerage? She kidded him that teachers couldn't afford to travel on any high scale. "And then you must spend money to write to me." He'd sent her something just yesterday, a brief postcard mentioning he'd come down with something, though he wasn't explicit. He couldn't be when he still didn't know what he had.

Where does it hurt? murmured his mother, or someone like her.

The cot seemed to poke through parts of his body, though the mattress was hard and flat. He shifted onto his side, but his belly complained, building toward another ominous rumble. He was so tired—if he could only fall asleep, he'd be all right for a while, unaware of his body, oblivious like those in the cots around him in this crowded dormitory. He'd talked to only one of the nine others, a long-faced Scotsman who'd offered him a digestive biscuit when Cricket lightly referred to his illness. Most were the backpack-and-tin-cup type of globetrotter, their bags now at the bases of their cots like tombstones. The sleeping figures were so still.

Cricket took a deep breath and tried hard to imitate the others. He stretched out his legs, adjusted his breathing, and shut his eyes. He pretended he was at a tea ceremony with his teacher Otani-*sensei* presiding. First the humble entry on one's knees, then the bringing forth of the tea utensils: the ladle, the whisk, the cup to be turned precisely two revolutions. Time was slowing down, coming to rest on a pale wedge of pottery flecked with a seed-pod design.

Just then his stomach protested violently, the familiar sensation tugging at his bowels. The porcelain in his mind split into ten shards. He was about to get up again, to begin the long trek down the hall once more, when another spasm doubled him up under the sheet. With the clarity of a dreamer who comprehends the past and future, he saw that he wouldn't make it to the morning. He simply couldn't take any more of this. There was even the possibility, not worth thinking about for more than a few seconds, that he might collapse right there. He would lie draped over the bed—a final spasm would do it—and no one would notice till morning.

He looked at the clock, glowing 2:52, and thought of the people he'd wake up downstairs, the havoc that a sick American would cause in the hotel. Or maybe they wouldn't care—you couldn't tell. Since he'd arrived in China, he'd been stared at for minutes on end and completely ignored at other times. In a way, it was the other end of the world from Osaka, and certainly from Tenafly, which was beginning to re-enter his consciousness like a half-remembered dream.

He was just ten, browsing forever through the paperback racks in Spencer's, the corner bookstore on Dubrow Avenue. He lay on the plump belly of the overstuffed love seat in the living room, where he read hour after hour. His mother was dead, a white shadow on the bed. Had he always been this lonely? His bereaved father disappeared upstairs to his study, leaving him mostly alone to do whatever he wanted. Was this what life offered, a continual retreat from his origins until he ended up in a darkened room in a strange city where no one even knew his name?

To remain so isolated in such a crowded city was an art. Shanghai by day was packed with humanity, ten to twenty people wherever you'd expect one or two in a normal city. Huangpu Park had its benches filled with couples, and four more behind the ginkgo trees, two more half-concealed by the Crouching Puma Rock. Walking in the street, he'd been jostled with incredible ferocity, but it didn't seem directed only at him, and on another occasion, he'd been helped onto a bus. This was just after one of his attacks, and it had cheered him at the time, though they gave him a seat at the expense of an old woman with a twisted leg.

The clerk at tonight's hotel had refused him a place three times before finally admitting there was a bed open. The mixed treatment was built on a little logic: he was a novelty item like a gaudy but malfunctioning mechanical toy, alternately encouraged and kicked as he slowly wound down. But to get help, real medical assistance, he needed a friend—or at least one attentive reader.

He hurriedly packed a plastic bag with his dictionaries and passport, shorts, and a change of shirt. Considering that he might be stuck in some waiting room, he added his journal, then rummaged around till he found the old Agatha Christie novel he'd never finished and stuffed that in the bag, too. At the last moment, he snatched his Japanese fold-up fan from his knapsack: any talisman might help. Walking toward the door, he retraced the well-known path, but he must have stepped differently this time because one of the floorboards groaned like a beast. Someone sat up in bed muttering; someone else rolled over in the yellow awning of light from the hallway. Cricket shut the door and made his way toward the stairs. Accommodations tonight were so jammed that people were sleeping in the far corridor. He saw them now, motionless flat bodies on flat cots. The wraith of Matthew flapped from somewhere overhead. He hurried by like a ghost himself.

He descended a flight of grand ballroom steps, a curved expanse with a marble balustrade, then another and another. Waiting at the bottom, however, was no orchestra ensemble but a man sleeping on a scarred wooden bench against the main door. His hand was over his eyes, and he snored like a horse. Cricket approached him, pen and paper in hand.

He tapped the man on the shoulder and, when he got no response, shook him lightly. The man rolled over on the bench and muttered something in Chinese. He was the caretaker, maybe, or the night watchman, guarding the premises with his own body against the gate. Cricket shook him once more, almost violently, and said aloud, "Wake up, will you? I'm sick!"

The man stirred in his undershirt and looked up, his eyes meeting Cricket's. Now was the time to act, to explain. Holding his stomach, he grimaced in pain. Shoving his pad under the man's face, he wrote out in laborious Chinese, "I . . . am . . . sick-condition."

The man looked at the characters on the pad suspiciously. He pointed back up the stairs, talking in Chinese. They all thought that because Cricket wrote he could certainly speak.

Cricket's comprehension of the language was limited to "thank you," "yes," and a few other words, and this was none of them. In any event, he had no intention of going back upstairs. He shook his head long and slowly, pointing to the pad. Underneath his first message, he wrote, "I . . . go . . . hospital." The word *hospital*, which he had traced over and over on the bedsheet, came out elegantly.

The man read the words and barked out a sentence. Cricket gave an exaggerated shrug, the man said something more, and so Cricket printed out the only full, grammatical sentence he knew in the language: "I cannot speak Chinese."

Another suspicious glance. This could go on all night, the way one waited for a room, for a train ticket, the way everything in this country seemed opaque, intransigent. The two men stared at each other. Cricket flipped through his dictionary, found the word *necessity*, and jotted it down next to the hospital-sentence. He presented the pad again.

When the man began talking once more in Chinese, Cricket pointed to his mouth and shook his head violently. "Hospital," he wrote again. His limited Chinese was useful for only one type of arguing: repetition.

Finally nodding, the man got up from the bench, unlocked the huge hasp on the outer door, and gestured down the road. Catching on to Cricket's restricted form of communication, he used Cricket's pad to write out "hospital." He pointed proudly into the dark.

So Cricket was supposed to walk there, but who would guide him, who would give him directions? He shook his head again and sat down on the bench. In any other country, he felt sure, a sick foreigner would be given more attention. He wanted at least an escort. Sketchily, he began to write "you and I," but the man grabbed his shoulder, pointing again.

"One person ... no walk!" Cricket wrote shakily, hastily—had he written *walk* or *run*? He rubbed his stomach with his hand to bring the issue back to illness. He moaned—credibly, he hoped. He wasn't the dramatic type. Worse than Japanese, Reiko now said. You never show what you feel. But he no longer even knew how he felt himself. And all he had for company these days were the voices.

Cricket is a bright boy, but he must learn to share with others, wrote Mrs. McClelland, his third-grade teacher.

I'll say, snorted Sofie, lying back naked on the couch.

He blinked to clear his mind. "Two go," he penned below his last effort.

The man responded in Chinese, striding down to the reception area. For a moment, Cricket thought he'd overdone it and was being deserted, but the man was waking up someone else. He came back with a young man in tow, wearing a rumpled white shirt, trying to rub his eyes with his glasses still on. The older man pointed to Cricket, nudging, explaining in rapid-fire syllables. He took Cricket's pad—Cricket had just found and finished writing the Chinese for *diarrhea* and showed it. The two nodded, and the older man took Cricket's pen and triumphantly wrote "hospital" again in the unused margin.

So he had a guide, or at least someone to accompany him out the door. Getting up from the bench, he had a strong urge to go right back to the bathroom, but clamped down on himself. Stiff-legged, with the man in glasses ahead of him, he walked out the entrance.

Outside, a postage-size moon hung over the canal, the streets black and half-empty. They took a right along the main road, and as they passed one long warehouse, Cricket could hear the sound of high-speed drills. The graveyard shift. They staggered the work around the clock, he remembered reading, and even now, blue sparks flew from the grated windows, escaping a controlled hum. In the distance rose three spires that looked like watch-towers built for some elongated species of alien. For the first time in as long as he could remember, he felt homesick, but for where exactly he couldn't think. As if sensing the drag in Cricket's thoughts, his escort picked up the pace.

Cricket dutifully walked faster, but that made the pains come faster, too, and he had to stop. The man kept on walking, oblivious. "Wait!" Cricket cried out, at least snaring the man's attention. Hobbling forward, he wrote the verb *wait* on his pad and shoved it forward. The pictogram combined *going* and *tem-*

ple—"think of going there to wait," Reiko had suggested when they were going through character-strokes together. But *temple* itself combined *soil* and three strokes meaning *tiny amount*—it was all so complicated, but after a while the correct strokes were automatic—in your wrist, not your head. Japanese schoolchildren learning *kanji* traced out strokes jerkily with their fingers, making them look autistic.

The man looked at the message, shrugged, and offered a hand. Cricket scribbled again. "Hospital . . . far . . . near?"

The man borrowed Cricket's pen and with one neat swirl circled "near." He motioned forward as if encouraging a child. They trudged on.

After four more blocks, they came to a large white building set off from the road. A billboard in front had a red cross in the center, and Cricket recognized the word *hospital* underneath. The man stopped, borrowed the pad, and wrote what Cricket translated as "Number One People's Red Cross Hospital." The place looked deserted. In the front clearing, an acre of rust-streaked earth had been leveled and a pile of bricks lay on a scaffold. A glass-paned door, already set in its frame, opened onto nowhere. For one wild moment, Cricket thought they were going to go through an elaborate charade in this phantom building, but they moved on, past a gate where a night guard slept watchfully. Cricket's escort nudged the guard in the ribs.

The guard woke up at once, and the escort pointed to Cricket, explaining in a flurry of Chinese. He strained his ears but could make out nothing. After all his days of listening, Mandarin still sounded like someone talking with a large cud in his mouth. Cantonese sounded like someone chewing a large cud with straws up his nose. The escort pointed at Cricket's stomach, which growled obligingly—and suddenly he had to get to a toilet.

He had no chance. The escort marched Cricket not toward the white building but to a sort of annex on the left. They walked through an empty lobby, and the man frowned at the elevator in back, stabbed a button. The elevator was a long time in coming. Cricket crossed and recrossed his legs in an effort to hold back. To divert himself from the pain, he flipped through the English-Chinese dictionary and found the word for *stomach*, which he painstakingly copied out on the pad. He couldn't think of the word for *weak*, though it was one he had written out before. Instead, he prefixed the word *evil* to *stomach* and showed the pad to his escort.

For the first time, the man smiled. He patted his own lean midsection, his glasses gleaming in the dim light of the lobby. He took Cricket's pad and wrote out two characters that Cricket deciphered as "fourth level." The fourth level of pain, the fourth level of understanding? As the elevator door opened, he realized that "level" was "floor," where there would be help.

Prepare to die, intoned Matthew.

Cricket frowned into the darkness.

Inside was an elevator operator, perched on a bamboo stool, another sleepwalker minding his job. He stirred long enough to have a brief conversation with the escort, both smiling and nodding when they regarded Cricket. He let them out on the fourth floor, his head drooping again as the doors swallowed him up. Cricket wondered whether he trapped himself between floors and slept there.

Down a short corridor was a glassed-in partition with red-glazed lettering. *Outside*-something and *clinic* were the only characters he recognized, illuminated by a dull yellow light from behind the door. They passed right by, however, and were soon walking down a long green corridor, Cricket halting every few steps because he was desperately close to another spasm. His gait was practically a dance.

Finally, halfway down the corridor, a white-kerchiefed nurse popped her head from a room and beckoned them in. Inside was what looked like a consulting area, with a scale, a table and chairs, and a medicine cabinet. Beneath a cracked blackboard in the corner was a shadowy array of bell-jars filled with translucent white shapes that made Cricket even queasier. Another nurse, also wearing a kerchief, motioned him to a chair.

Cricket shook his head. He pointed to his pad, on which he had just written the word *bathroom*. There were two words for it that he knew of: one politely signified a hand-washing place, the other bluntly stood for toilet, and he chose the second.

The first nurse read what he wrote and smiled—what was so damn funny about his illness?—and said something to his escort. Before they let him go, she gave him a small cardboard pillbox and wrote with elegant care on a slip from his pad a character that bristled incomprehensibly. He had to look it up; he also had to get to the bathroom, and he hurriedly guessed at the main radical, counted the strokes—this was the only way to use the Chinese-English dictionary—and on page 319 he found the character, faithfully reproduced and labeled *feces*. Clutching the specimen box, he nodded and followed his escort to the bathroom.

The glasses-man seemed more impressed with Cricket now

that he had the official status of a patient. With a deferential wave of his hand, he indicated the facilities and waited as Cricket entered the cubicle. The toilet was the usual trough, though the tiled expanse around it was shiningly clean. Of all Asians, the Chinese seemed able to squat for hours, anywhere, on any occasion. It was the world's cheapest seat, completely portable and free. As he bent over, he envisioned Reiko's round white buttocks—thoughts of sex came to him at the oddest times, or maybe the unblemished expanse of curved porcelain was suggestive. Cricket now squatted the same as the Chinese, though feeling as if he were folding himself over the exact area of pain. The spasm lasted for almost a minute, leaving his legs rubbery. When he finally hobbled out, he showed the filled specimen box to his companion, who nodded without speaking and followed him out.

Back in the examination room, the first and younger of the two nurses took the box in a clamp of toweling and padded off with it. The older nurse motioned him to a chair, where she handed him a pen and a form to be filled out. Hospitals, it seemed, shared certain similarities the world over. What was the Chinese for Blue Cross? The form was all in Chinese but decipherable through context and the various characters he knew. There was *name*, and below it something like *domicile*. *Record-country* presented more of a problem: should that be the U.S.A. or where he felt most at home?

"Japan," he wrote, the nurse looking over his shoulder. Then, as a supplement, he wrote the characters "sun-origin," the Chinese for *Japan*. *Age* and *sex* were also characters he knew. Below that were a few closely written lines with blanks that would have to remain empty. When he tried to look up the first two characters, they didn't seem to be there, which was what you got for buying a cheap pocket dictionary, he reflected. Suppose his disease wasn't listed either?

The nurse took the form and walked out of the room, leaving him with his escort. The man sighed and rubbed his eyes. *Tired?* wrote Cricket on his pad and shoved it toward him.

The man looked surprised, as if discovered in a secret vice. *Not so*, he returned. He penned again, in painfully exact calligraphy, *You are sick.* Cricket answered with a short affirmative, and they passed the pad back and forth among them for several minutes before the doctor arrived. His escort, he found out, was twenty-five years old and unmarried, a native of Shanghai. He liked the city. These were questions that Cricket knew how to write, answers he could understand. He would surely have been out of his depth with *long and tortuous love affair*, or *live a quiet but desperate life.*

Half of speaking a language is knowing the culture, wrote Peter Inoue earnestly from Mount Sinai Hospital, wondering if he'd ever get to Japan.

Half of speaking a language is knowing yourself, sniped Jennifer Hertzl.

Cricket acknowledged the truth of these voices even as he tried to keep focused on the matter at hand. Handling disclosure, his own or others', wasn't exactly a strength, and Japan had only encouraged a courteous façade. *Shitashiki naka ni mo reigi ari,* Miyamoto had taught him: "There are formalities between even the closest of friends." So what did that imply when dealing with strangers in the middle of the night?

I love you, said Reiko with her eyes. Now what kind of tact was that?

If only he didn't feel so damned vulnerable! When the glasses-man asked politely whether Cricket's stomach still hurt, Cricket replied politely that it still did. With a mannerly gesture, the man reached for Cricket's fan, poking out from Cricket's bag. He snapped it open and created a light breeze for the two of them. The gray carp on the front of the fan spread to full length, undulating as if moving beyond its flat world into the dark blue outdoors.

The doctor entered just then, white-coated and stethoscoped, looking closely at Cricket before advancing. Short and reedy, apologetically balding, he nonetheless carried himself with the confidence of a professional. Placing a faded pamphlet on the table, he sat down on the chair next to Cricket's. The title read in English, *Glossary of Medical Terms*, with multicolored organs arranged in a circle below.

Opening to the first page, the doctor scanned a Chinese index and flipped forward. "Do you . . . " he murmured, keeping one eye on the page, "have pain . . . here?" He poked lightly at Cricket's abdomen.

Cricket nodded, and the doctor continued his probing. He palpated Cricket's chest, arms, and stomach, which rumbled in response. At one point, he concentrated on the lower gut, looking to the correct page and asking twice, "Hurt . . . when I rebound finger?" It didn't hurt, and Cricket was relieved to answer all the rest of the doctor's questions in the negative. No itchy scalp, no dizziness, no vomiting—they were quite insistent on the last point, and both the doctor and the nurses chimed in on that question. The glasses-man contributed a creditable mime of a patient throwing up.

Cricket changed the subject. After six days of running to the toilet, he was both exhausted and dehydrated. He found both words in the dictionary and wrote them out on his pad. *Dry. Lost . . . 2, 3 kg.*, he added before showing everyone his latest work.

They led him out then, across the hall to a separate room. The entire ward was deserted, which seemed strange, until he realized that they were probably isolating him. They showed him by turned-over palms that he should lie down on the hospital cot. The younger nurse walked in bearing a cup with three pills inside, two saffron yellow and the other an eggshell blue. The other nurse entered then—it was like being royally attended—bearing a glass of water on a tray. His former landlady Mori stood in the corner with her ceramic pot of miso soup. They watched with approval as he swallowed everything. The doctor had already disappeared; now the nurses left, and Cricket was left alone with the glasses-man. He was perched on an armchair, thoughtfully regarding Cricket like a relative who has brought an expensive basket of fruit for a patient. He had gone to the trouble of bringing him here, making sure Cricket got taken care of, and now he was going to watch over his investment.

Cricket lay back against the white sheets, staring at the white ceiling. The rumbling in his bowels was quieting down, the lava drying up. The sensation he'd felt for days, that of perching before a void, unable to relax his guard, began fading away. He might almost be home in Nishinomiya, with its blue-roofed houses and well-guttered streets. Friends and relatives might be in adjoining rooms. No, not relatives—they were back home, or rather, back in America. He had left different parts behind in different places. He told the fishmonger in Nishinomiya, the one with one leg shorter than the other, that he'd be back. The man stumped forth to give him a mackerel. *Saru mono wa hibi ni utoshi*, Miyamoto warned him the last time they saw each other: "The person who leaves is forgotten day by day." But he'd presented Cricket with a calligraphy brush to remember him by, and told Cricket to practice. His last class had chipped in to buy him a hand-dyed silk necktie the color of amethyst. At the Ebisu shrine, he'd bought one of the paper fortunes to hang in the votive tree. He worried what would happen to his flock of bicycles.

Don't let me forget any of this, he thought, in as close a mood as he ever came to praying. But he was getting sleepy, possibly from one of the pills he'd swallowed.

Hazily, he reached for his pad. The man had hold of his Agatha Christie novel and was peering doubtfully at the dead Indian on the cover. *You remain?* Cricket wrote, holding the message up so it could be seen.

The man replied with a set of characters that Cricket couldn't read. *Sleep?* wrote Cricket, indicating the other room.

Sleep, wrote the man, pointing to Cricket, who suddenly felt extremely tired. It was just past sunrise, and a border of light filtered through the gauzy white curtains. The beginnings of traffic noise invaded the chamber: the rattle of carts, a truck starting up. He listened to the sounds for a minute, and when he turned back to write a question, the glasses-man had gone. A breeze moved the curtains, as if to suggest a possible exit route.

Suddenly the nurses were back in the room, scuttling silently across the floor like crabs. They mimicked an injection. It turned out they meant an intravenous tube, connected to a plastic sack hanging from what looked suspiciously like an old hatrack. The label on the sack was in Chinese, but the first character looked like *mother*—no, that was just the base, with the fringe on top of the character it meant *poison*, they were trying to murder him.

Always remember proper survivalist tactics! ex-Marine Jack Sims shouted at him. Don't get caught lying in bed!

Suddenly he was struggling, shouting—and the nurses gripped his arms. He'd already tipped over the I.V., and when he grabbed at the starched front of the first nurse's uniform, she called out to someone in the corridor. The next minute flew by in a flash of limbs and then someone was holding down his arm, injecting him with a needle, wheeling him away into another ward.

They had strapped him down, and the giant digital clock was ticking his life away. Guy Lapham mouthed a "9" at him as they entered a club together. All the expats clawed at their cages, trying to get at him, as he struggled himself, held fast between the Korean girl's thighs. She carefully wrapped his head, recycling it into a lamp. Reiko nodded at something beyond his view as she turned on the lamp. Bright lights and voices illuminated the inside of his skull. Then silence and nothingness.

He woke up in the-silence-after-sleep, but when he stirred, the starched uniforms came in to put him back to sleep again. This happened repeatedly for days, in and out of the same dream. He was aware only of being drugged.

You won't die yet, Matthew pronounced solemnly one day. Not here.

He was alone in the white room again, apart but growing invisibly better, an incalculable distance from the alien streets filling up with people. He thought of the river that ran through the city, of himself walking along the bank and peering over the parapet into the heavy green depths. A lone carp drifted near the surface like a gray shadow. He stared at it with longing as it slowly swam from sight. When he looked upwards, a jet hung in the sky like a toy silver plane. The ginkgo trees climbed toward it, forming a man-sized hedge around the rock garden that he tended ceaselessly, the white pebbles like pearls. The great Buddha with Ogawa-san's face gazed over it all, concrete hands pressed together, always presenting the same aspect to avoid revealing the scuff marks up her eastern side.

Finally when the cloud creatures descended, he was ready for them. He matched them bow for bow, smile for smile, offering up a piece of himself for every gift they presented. They hovered about him, stroking his scattered body with their nimbus fingers, and carefully swept up the remains. *Banzai!* they whispered. May you live ten thousand years. Or at least until tomorrow.

They had brought the rest of his belongings from the hotel. The doctor had said he could leave within a week. "Had . . . disturbance," he murmured, not meeting Cricket's eye. "Required rest."

He was at the river again, peering in. The depths of the current drew him down under. Then the water moved like a tide against the backs of his eyes, and he lay back on the cot and slept. In a minute, he was home. A boy playing the *shakuhachi* blew his sad notes off a windy rooftop. Cricket's father welcomed him, bowing from the waist.

13. Encounters in America

Herbert got up at seven-thirty without the alarm, showered and shaved, dressed, made breakfast, then sat around reading the newspaper because he had no job. It was smack in the middle of the economic boom, which made his situation all the more poignant. The want ads weren't much help. Names were what you needed, and Herbert knew almost none. He felt pointless just staring at the paper for an hour, so after a while he went back to his bedroom and tried to organize the mess on the floor. He stopped only after he realized that he was just shifting his tape collection, books, and clothes piles like a slow-motion three-card monte game.

He checked his gray suit in the closet. It was still there, the jacket hugging the pants in a way that cried out for pressing and ironing. Soon, soon. He had an interview at a bank scheduled for next week. In the meantime, he was lucky to be sharing this cheap apartment in Brookline, lucky that Cricket Collins, a friend of someone named Peter Inoue, who knew an acquaintance of Herbert's, had been looking for someone to split the rent.

Cricket had been disarmingly frank about himself at their first meeting. He was short with curly dark hair and deep-set brown eyes, yet obviously older than he appeared, like an old man wearing a boy's mask. He was also fiercely earnest. "One thing I should tell you is that I write. Mostly freelance stuff—it's not a living yet, but it's a commitment. I'm also doing some studying. You don't smoke, do you?"

"No. I don't have any habits, really."

"Good. I mean, there won't be any problems, then. I don't have late-night parties, or play loud music or anything, but I do type a lot." He paused, as if about to reveal a great curiosity. "For a while, I was a night writer, but lately I've found typing in the morning gives me the same feeling I need. I just pull down the shades and turn the lights on. Anyway, I'll be typing then."

"That's okay. I wake up early anyway." Which wasn't entirely true, but Herbert wished it were. And anyway, he wanted to be obliging.

"Fine." They shook hands on it. Yesterday, Herbert had moved his bits of furniture into the spare bedroom. The apartment was close to the second-floor landing, just across from a motherly type named Mrs. O'Hara. She looked in her mid-seventies, with the bright, wrinkled features of hopeful age, her white hair combed over a shell-pink scalp. She'd already come by with a plate of brownies. Cricket had politely refused just as Herbert was about to accept, but Mrs. O'Hara said she'd be back sometime. There seemed to be some invisible friction between his roommate and his neighbor, though they couldn't have known each other very long. Just whose side should he be on?

He had entered into a realm of unknown quantities. Home, with his parents in Camden, was now five hours away. Yet having lived near there during school at Rutgers, he found the distance liberating. Boston was in a different state, both emotionally and physically. When he looked at himself in the mirror, he saw someone on his own, a sandy-haired young man a bit too jowly for twenty-two, but still promising. He practiced his smile for the upcoming interview.

Cricket, who had a large Oriental scroll hanging in the alcove, had recently returned from Japan. After four years of teaching English in Osaka, he'd come back because, as he told Herbert, "I want to be a real English teacher. I'm applying to graduate programs now." A cinder-block bookshelf in the corridor seemed to contain a lot of literature, not the kind of books that Herbert usually read. Yet a certain amount of Japan still clung about Cricket. In the L-shaped living room were arrayed a folding fan, an odd statuette of a Buddha, some beige sticks of incense, and for some reason three cakes of lemon soap in a tiny pyramid. Even some of the novels in the bookshelf had sticker-prices in yen, stamped "Juso Exchange." A plastic red travel clock sat on the window sill, seemingly thirteen hours off but actually set to Osaka time—just as a reminder, Cricket told him.

The most obvious aspect were shoes, or the absence of them. Cricket insisted that everyone who entered the apartment remove "all footgear," as he called it, at the door. He mostly padded around the apartment in slippers, of which he had three or four pairs, maintaining a feverish, antiseptic activity, though it wasn't always clear what he was doing. Because Cricket was the lease-holder, Herbert acquiesced to leaving his shoes on the welcome mat, though he didn't like the sight of his own lumpy stockinged feet, and he occasionally forgot.

Like Herbert, Cricket was currently jobless. But while Herbert was in that post-college phase where friends become young professionals, complete with office space and colleagues, Cricket seemed more dislocated, as if the time abroad had jostled him off some track. Herbert was curious about what Cricket intended to do for a living, but could postpone his curiosity for a while. Later on, he might have some questions about Japan (he'd heard that a drink in Tokyo cost more than anywhere else in the world). Right now, he went back to reading the comics in the *Globe* while Cricket typed on top of his bedroom cabinet with the panel doors open to fit in his knees.

From eight to eleven that Monday morning, Cricket typed away on an old Olympia manual machine. *Tappety-tap* for a few sentences' worth, then nothing. *Tap-tappety-tap*, arrested by a thoughtful throat-clearing. Occasionally he talked to himself. The two bedrooms were linked by a common door, which, though taped shut, seemed to amplify all sounds. At eleven, the typing stopped abruptly, and Cricket left for what he termed "a brisk walk," during which he apparently combined exercise and errands. At noon he was back with the mail, making himself an odd fish paste and seaweed concoction that looked like his habitual lunch. (Herbert had spotted an assortment of Japanese foods in the cupboard, including a huge sack of rice.) He ate this mixed into some leftover noodles, poling up everything with a nimble pair of chopsticks that acted as fork, spoon, and occasionally knife. The dishes washed, he repaired to the living room. Sitting in front of the radio by the window, Cricket opened a notebook filled with neat paragraphs of insect-writing and began to add to the latest page with evident concentration. He was pale-skinned and wiry, and the cords in his forearms flexed when he wrote.

"I'm still keeping up my Japanese," he explained to Herbert, who was just going out. "I don't know whether I told you—I have a fiancée in Japan. She wants to come to America." He opened a textbook and a dictionary.

This was an unsuspected side of Cricket. "Does she speak English?"

"Let's say she's more fluent than I am in Japanese. But it's hard sometimes, having to communicate that way. We practically lived together for a while."

"When are you getting married?"

Cricket looked startled. "Married? I'm not sure. Her parents don't know much about the real situation. She wanted to come back with me, but I told her to wait."

Herbert paused, confident that Cricket would fill the gap.

"Well, it *is* a burden, when someone's in a foreign country, totally dependent on you. No . . . no, she had an office job, but now she's applying to business schools here, once she passes her TOEFL exam." He showed Herbert his notebook. On closer inspection, the Chinese insects on each page still looked like insects. "In the meantime, we write to each other a lot. So I still practice my Japanese."

"Hmm. That looks difficult." Herbert wanted to show he was impressed.

"Yes, but it's doable. You could do it, too. 'Even a thousand-mile journey begins with a first step,'" he recited. "That's an old proverb. It has to do with persistence."

Herbert nodded, thinking of the border between determination and idealism. He also had another, more practical thought, which he suppressed. Studying Japanese like this was non-profitable, and writing almost was, so what did he do for money? How about his family? Herbert figured Cricket would tell him soon enough. Meanwhile, he had an interesting roommate, with a far-off romantic interest, someone he could tell stories about. It would pad out his own life, add a touch of Oriental mystery.

None of his friends was married yet. His own experience with women was more hopeful than helpful. They weren't attracted to a build that his mother still called "pleasingly plump." Nurturing types like Mrs. O'Hara would offer him food, but that was about it. Only once, after a drunken college party, had he woken up with a woman in his bed. He lived with the memory and was on the lookout for love or a reasonable facsimile. As he was going out, he thought of one last question.

"What's her name?"

"Who?" Cricket had the radio on as he transcribed, something semi-classical.

"Your Japanese fiancée."

"Oh, Reiko. Reiko Hashimoto. Her family name means something like 'bridge-origin.'" He looked up as if reflecting on what he'd just said. "She doesn't like her last name."

"Oh." He thought about Japan as the apartment door locked after him: short, fragile people in kimonos, tea from flowered cups, mountain landscapes with slanted rain. The scene hovered just on the edge of believability. Outside, the sky over Boston was heavy white. Soon it started to drizzle. November cold was setting in, and the sweater and coat he wore made him feel fatly drab. He walked about in the rain, looking around Brookline. The Coolidge Corner cinema was playing *One Flew Over the Cuckoo's Nest*. The bagel store on Harvard Avenue was selling three bialys for the price of two.

For a while he watched the passersby, most of who seemed to be going in the opposite direction, as if he were headed away from a giant department-store sale or moving toward a burst water main. One old woman in a pink bonnet so low that it obscured her nose paused to wave at him—mistakenly as it turned out, since a block later she hailed someone who took her arm. For a while longer, he explored the side streets, but for some reason he kept ending back on Beacon Street. And without something concrete to do, he felt stupid. He wandered about till 2:30, eventually buying an ice-cream cone to give some point to his outing, and then returned to the apartment. When Mrs. O'Hara beckoned from her doorway, a paisley shawl draped over her housedress, he stopped for a moment to chat about the dreary weather. Mrs. O'Hara was of the opinion that it would clear up by tomorrow. Herbert said he sincerely hoped so.

The next morning, as Cricket was typing away, Herbert took out his own typewriter, an old Smith Corona electric from college, and began pecking out letters to banks. The typing in the other room hesitated, stopped, then started up again faster than ever. Whenever Herbert paused or slowed down, Cricket triumphantly typed even faster. It was like two messages in code, hopelessly snarled. When Herbert finished, Cricket resumed his normal speed. Later, when they both happened to be making lunch, Cricket looked annoyed.

"What were you typing?"

"Oh, just some application letters. Have to get a job."

"Not as a typist, I hope."

"No, don't worry." He smiled reassuringly, and Cricket slowly nodded.

"I just got some part-time employment myself, proofreading for a small academic publisher. I have my writing, I have my savings from Japan—I didn't spend much while I was there. Anyway, I'm applying to graduate programs in English, so it can't be too much of a commitment. It's just two afternoons a week."

"You seem kind of busy, anyway."

"I *am* busy." Cricket was suddenly defensive. Herbert seemed to have struck a nerve. "I write, I study Japanese, and I'm getting back to English literature at night. I cook for myself. I also send out a lot of letters, mostly to Japan. I don't waste time at all."

"I don't mind if I waste a little time. But I need the money, and I want a nine-to-five job." Living on summer job earnings and parent support, Herbert felt strongly about this. He made himself a sloppy peanut butter and jelly sandwich. "Have you gotten the mail yet?"

"No, but I looked twice already. Sometimes it's late."

"I'll check it." Herbert went downstairs, realizing that the only mail he might get would be a note from his mother, asking if he was eating right. This embarrassed him, but he figured that all mothers were that way. As it turned out, the box held nothing for him but three letters for Cricket, including a bulging airmail envelope from Japan. "Does your mother . . . harp on what you eat?" he panted to Cricket after re-climbing the creaky staircase.

"My mother's dead." Cricket regarded him suspiciously, as if Herbert were offering to provide a replacement.

"Oh." Herbert shifted from foot to foot. "I'm sorry."

"Don't be. She died seventeen years ago. And I really don't remember what she told me about nutrition."

"Hm. Is your father still living?" It sounded like a lame follow-up even as he uttered it, but he was determined to draw out his roommate a little.

"Yes. He's remarried." Cricket compressed his lips briefly into a hard line. "We don't talk much anymore." He reached out for the envelopes Herbert held. "Are those for me?"

"Hm? Oh, yeah—here." Herbert handed them over, having already scanned the outsides. One was a mailing from a charity, and the other looked like a bill. But the handwriting on the airmail envelope was delicately slanted, feminine, the lower loops like teardrops. Reiko apparently lived in a place called Koshien and wrote messages on the back flaps of envelopes. This one read, "Will you love me with the lights out?" enclosed in quotation marks, with an explanation: "From new radio song."

Cricket spent the next ten minutes reading through all the flimsy pages of Reiko's letter. "She writes a page every day, and then at the end of the week she sends it all."

"In Japanese?"

"Well, half and half. She's supposed to be increasing the proportion of Japanese. She'd actually rather write in English, but I insisted. For practice. Funny, I'm beginning to read it better now than when I was in Japan."

Herbert was about to leave again, to mail his application letters and get the hell out of the apartment. It was already one o'clock, and he felt confined. But what could you do at an hour when everyone else was at work? "Do you write her often?"

"As often as I can. I know it looks like I've got a lot of time, but I really don't. I'm starting *Ulysses* next week."

"Isn't that by Homer? I think we read that in high school."

"Well, you probably mean the *Odyssey*." Cricket suddenly

wore a teacher's smile, tolerant but corrective. "This one's by James Joyce. It's all about Ireland, but he wrote it when he was abroad. Sort of a self-imposed exile."

"Really? Why's that?"

"Good question." Another smile. "He needed the right perspective, and for that he needed to see it from outside. It's an amazing book."

"Hmm. Maybe I should catch up on my reading, too." Cricket made him feel as if he should be doing something constructive every minute. "Need anything mailed?"

"No, thanks."

"Well, uh, tell Reiko hello."

"I will. I'll put it at the end of the letter." As Herbert walked out, Cricket turned up the radio, uncapped his pen, and started to write in Japanese. His features smoothed into blankness as his hand traveled down the page.

Later that night, Herbert passed Cricket's room when the door was open. He sat cross-legged on a cushion, holding his book outward, which read "King James Version" in red-gold letters across the spine. Every once in a while, he paused to make a note on an index card.

"Is that the Bible?" asked Herbert, suddenly worried that he'd thrown in his lot with a religious fanatic.

Cricket looked up briefly. "Uh-huh. Someone told me it was good preparation for English graduate school. You know, it's remarkable, the warring tribes in the Old Testament. China's first peaceful dynasty lasted five hundred years."

"Hm." Herbert waited for him to elaborate, but Cricket dropped his head to start reading again. So this was the studying at night, and without even course credit. To have such control, to be able to live on an internal schedule—maybe it was a trait Cricket had acquired over there. Everyone knew the Japanese believed in discipline. Feeling like a soft American, Herbert went out again for a walk and ended up at the Pick-a-Chick deli, eating potato salad.

On Monday, he went for the first of his interviews, wearing the gray suit he'd forgotten to have pressed. His parents had given it to him as a graduation present. The personnel man at First National of Boston was an overnice dresser who made Herbert feel rumpled. He didn't dwell long on Herbert's qualifications, and he said they'd let him know. The interview on Wednesday went better: the man had some relatives near Camden, and they talked for a while. The accounting department had an opening, but they preferred someone with more banking experience. Had Herbert taken any computer courses? Maybe he could take a night class somewhere.

After that, all he could do was send out more letters and wait. He had a distant cousin living in Back Bay whose husband sold bonds, and he got some names from him. The days passed in uneven sameness. He acquired a depressing familiarity with the streets of Brookline, including the cut-off time for Coolidge Corner matinee prices and a comprehensive knowledge of all the blend-ins offered at Steve's ice cream parlor. He had a few brief chats with Mrs. O'Hara, who he learned had been a widow for fifteen years.

"I don't get out as much as I used to," she told him, "especially not with my rheumatism. But I try to be friendly to the people around me."

Herbert nodded and smiled comfortingly. They were both downstairs, waiting for the mail.

"Your roommate doesn't seem too outgoing, I must say. What's his name again?"

"Cricket. Cricket Collins." Again, Herbert found himself forced to take sides. "He's not so bad, really. Just a little . . . distant."

"Hmm, maybe so," said Mrs. O'Hara, stumping away.

When the phone rang, it was almost never for Cricket. Once when Herbert answered, it was Peter Inoue, whom he remembered as the link that had gotten him the apartment. But when he got Cricket to the phone, there was only a brief exchange. "Look, I'll send you a letter," he heard Cricket tell the receiver and then hang up.

The calls for Herbert were mostly maternal. "Family," he explained with some embarrassment after his mother left Cricket a message to pass on about coming home for the holidays. "My older brother, Gary—he's been married for three years, and he gets the same deal."

Cricket smiled thinly. "My father left me mostly alone. I guess I should be grateful."

"What'd he think when you moved to Japan?"

Cricket tilted his head back as if he'd never thought of this question. "I'm not sure."

"Well, what'd he think of Japan?"

"I don't know. He never visited me there."

"Huh. What was it like, anyway, where you lived?"

Cricket's eyes became unfocused. "Peaceful. Narrow streets

and little neighborhoods with blue-roofed houses. Shops with personalities—the tea-seller, the bakery, the hardware store." He blinked. "The same as America, I guess, but different. I used to be bothered by some of their conformity, but a society needs standards. Japan has a lot of well-mannered people in a small space, and it works."

It sounded a little too ideal. "No kamikazi types, huh?"

"That's *kamikaze*, and sure, there's some of it. But even they don't cause much trouble. The Japanese believe a lot in personal honor."

"I guess. I had an uncle who fought in World War II. He said they could be pretty vicious."

"Really? Ever visited Nagasaki?" He glanced at his watch. "I have to get to my job. But if you want, I've got a few books on the subject."

The next Saturday, Herbert decided to explore farther away. He took the T to Cambridge and spent the afternoon around Harvard Square, watching the people. Though he knew no one there, the surge of the crowd made him feel befriended. In the middle of the square was a blind blues singer, squeezing an accordion and shaking a plastic cup. Another performer was dressed like a jester, complete with droopy cap and bells, juggling three apples and a pear while his female partner mimed the passersby. Students walked around pretending they were townies and vice versa. Herbert stood at the periphery, holding a cup of hot chocolate for warmth.

A young Japanese couple with twin backpacks and a camera took a picture of the juggler, making Herbert wonder what impression all this made on them. Or they looked Japanese—how could you tell the difference between them and Koreans, or Chinese? What did Reiko look like, anyway? Without clarification, she was beginning to turn into several different women, and Herbert realized he was lonely.

He was therefore glad to see Cricket when he got back to the apartment. Cricket could be prickly or brusque, but talking to him about Japan gave Herbert a certain vicarious pleasure. The words in turn made Cricket come to life. With only minimal prodding, he would describe the bells and ball-bearing cascades inside a pachinko parlor, or the way a woman walked in a formal kimono. "Very slowly," he laughed, with a mincing step that made him look like a female impersonator. But Cricket mostly had his routine to keep him occupied, up early typing and muttering, studying Japanese followed by one of his brisk walks, or maybe exercising as he studied, Herbert wasn't sure. He talked to himself, sometimes in Japanese.

He took baths so frequently that the rusty drain stopped working, and a week elapsed before the super, a broad-shouldered man named Mahoney, came in to repair it. Cricket said nothing as Mahoney elbowed his way into the bathroom and clanked around with a pipe wrench, but afterward he complained to Herbert. "Mori, my Japanese landlord, could've fixed that in fifteen minutes. He could fix *anything* in fifteen minutes." But clearly it was Mahoney's delay in coming, the unavoidable break in the bath-taking routine, that bothered him.

Occasionally a gap would open in the sequence of activities: half an hour before he was to leave for his proofreading job, he'd be finished with lunch. Or he'd come home early from a round of errands and not know what to do with himself until it was time to prepare dinner. The worst was when the typing stopped for too long an interval, as if Herbert's roommate were caught forever between sentences. At these junctures Cricket would look lost, sometimes wandering around the apartment, other times standing perfectly still, looking abstractedly out the window onto a single ficus tree growing in a sidewalk plot.

"You okay?" Herbert asked once or twice.

"Yes, I'm fine." Then he'd busy himself in the kitchen or sit down with a book. Since he didn't play much music apart from his lunch-time break, the apartment was often shadowed in silence. The street itself led into a dead end two blocks down, so any sounds from outside were minimal. We need more background noise, thought Herbert wistfully, though he didn't think Cricket would look kindly toward any contributions in that direction, and Herbert's snowy-screen television remained in his bedroom.

Once he even bumped into him outside the second-floor landing to the apartment. He had blended into the newel post in the gathering dusk. "Sorry," Herbert apologized. "You were so still."

"Was I?" Cricket's eyes turned ceilingward. "You know, I once spent three weeks in a hospital ward in Shanghai. Being still."

"What was wrong?"

Cricket's voice, usually so self-assured, grew vague. "I'm not sure, exactly. For a while, I was really sick." Was it his chest or his head that he gestured to as they went in?

Meanwhile the letters from Japan kept arriving. Not all were from Reiko, but it was clear which ones were hers. They were like plump pillows crackling with onionskin paper and little enclosures that would find their way about the apartment: a newspaper clipping, some photos of Japanese castles, a set of colored labels—once a bamboo letter opener popped out of an envelope. When Herbert asked, Cricket showed him two snapshots of Reiko (she'd sent him five so far). Reiko turned out to be a petite woman with long black hair and high cheekbones, smiling a bit too obviously for the camera. In one photo, she stood against a high stone wall with crocuses at her feet; in the other, she was seated at the foot of a curved Japanese bridge that spanned a pond. She looked delicate but abiding, the kind of woman who would wait for a man. The bridge photo was signed, "To Dear Cricket, with all love, Reiko."

"She really cares about you," Herbert observed quietly. After all he'd heard, he felt a little possessive about Reiko, with almost a shared sense of affection.

"That's what this . . . " Cricket gestured at the hanging scroll, the Japanese texts and notebooks " . . . is all about. It helps me feel close to her. You know, I really miss her now that she's so far away." He looked wistfully around the room, as if he expected one of the objects to start talking to him.

Herbert nodded, feeling as if he now understood why Cricket surrounded himself with Japanalia: to keep alive a long-distance romance, though there was something weirdly fetishistic about the whole business. The bars of yellow soap in the living room, were they the brand Reiko showered with? Did Cricket keep a pair of her panties somewhere in his room, and were they any different from American lingerie? And as Herbert wondered about these details, he also mused about which was harder, being separated from someone you loved or having no one to love at all.

In terms of sheer time, Cricket's greatest devotion seemed directed toward his writing. "Fiction," he told Herbert when asked what he was working on. "Stories about Japan, mostly."

"Can I read one?"

Cricket fixed him with a look that Herbert was beginning to recognize as his "no" expression. "You can . . . " he began, "if it gets published. We'll just have to wait and see." In the meantime, he kept typing, adding to a plasticized blue folder in his room. Every once in a while he'd go to a copy shop to multiply his output, then send out material in manila envelopes with red-bordered mailing labels.

All that activity and so little to show for it. Herbert couldn't quite tell whether Cricket was succeeding, but judging from Cricket's increasing irritation, he didn't think so. For one thing, he figured Cricket would let him know if something made it into print. For another, envelopes that Cricket had obviously addressed for the return of his manuscripts kept coming back in the mail. After Herbert handed him five returns in one day, Cricket's typewriter was dormant the whole next morning. It started up at night, sputtered like an outboard motor that had failed to catch, and lapsed into silence again.

But what is the sound of one hand clapping? thought Herbert, to whom Cricket had taught a few Zen *koans*. What is the noise of not-typing? It would've been funny if it weren't so grim. In a few days the typewriter recovered, but it proceeded at a slower and more erratic pace than before. In between bouts, Cricket paced around in his shoddiest slippers, always stopping at the alcove where the hanging calligraphic screen overlooked the corridor like a giant inky eye.

And then Herbert went out one day and returned to find the living room divided by a folding screen. The screen was six feet high, a wood-and-paper barricade that laddered across the beige carpet. From behind came the sound of deep breathing. Herbert thought of tiptoeing around the side, but felt it would be like peeking at a model changing behind a scrim.

"Cricket, is that you?"

The breathing deflated. In a moment, Cricket popped his frowning face around the left edge. "Who else would it be?" He was wearing shorts and a T-shirt with Japanese writing on the front, and he was sweating slightly.

"Sorry." Herbert found himself apologizing more and more to his roommate these days. He always seemed to be interrupting something that required intense concentration. "What're you doing?" he asked anyway, knowing that Cricket liked to explain himself.

"Aikido." He flexed his forearms in an odd snakelike motion, bending his legs as he did so. "Some people call it one of the martial arts, but it's really more like a mind-body discipline. I just felt I was losing my edge." He stood up abruptly. "Here, let me show you. Stick out your arm."

"Um, all right." Herbert extended his right arm, feeling like an overstuffed scarecrow.

"Now I'm going to try to push it down, but you resist." Cricket reached out and placed a hand over Herbert's biceps.

As Herbert nodded, Cricket exerted sudden pressure, and Herbert's arm was shoved downward. "Wait, I wasn't ready," he protested.

"All right, we'll try it once more." Cricket waited till Herbert said to start, but the same thing happened again.

"Well, you've got the leverage, that's why."

"That's only part of it. To stay rigid, you need what aikido calls mental extension." Cricket backed off and raised his own right arm. "Try it with me."

Herbert advanced confidently. Cricket's arm was tendon-ridged, but he was two inches shorter and a lot lighter. Without waiting for Cricket to signal the start, Herbert heaved downwards.

Nothing budged. Cricket was gazing not quite at him, not quite anywhere. Herbert grunted and pushed harder, but Cricket's arm remained steady as a crossbeam. He tried two sudden jerks and finally gave up. It rattled him, though he tried to make a joke of it. "What've you got, an iron rod sewed up your arm?"

"Sort of. But the iron is up here." Cricket tapped his forehead. "You should try it sometime."

"Maybe." Maybe in another life, he thought. He was still annoyed at losing this Japanese arm wrestling match. He stepped back as if surveying the living room for the first time and gestured at the screen. "What about this?"

"*Shōji*. It's a folding screen."

"I can see that." Herbert casually whapped a panel, almost knocking the whole thing over. "Oops, sorry. I mean why'd you get it? Our living room's small enough as it is."

"Actually, the *shōji* extends space. We now have two living rooms."

"Sure, each half the size of the old one."

"The mental space is what's important." Cricket shut his eyes briefly as if focusing on innumerable folding screens. "It's the same with the *genkan*, the area around the door where you remove your shoes (which I see you forgot to do again)."

"Oh, sorry." Herbert clumped to the door and began to unlace his brogues. "But hey, why bother?"

"Because it's important to preserve distinctions. Because there's an inside and an outside, and the divider is where you take off your shoes." He pressed his lips together. "It's also more sanitary and saves shoe-leather."

"Yeah," said Herbert, dropping one heavy shoe onto the mat. "Yeah, all right, I can see that. I guess."

"Wait a minute," said Cricket, disappearing behind the screen, his voice growing fainter, finally sounding from his bedroom. "I've got something for you." After a brief rummaging noise, he came back. "Here, try these on." He held out a pair of black slippers with thick vinyl soles. "They were too big for me, but they might fit you."

"Oh, that's okay, I don't—"

"Just try them on."

"No, really, I—"

"*Try them.*" Cricket dropped them on the floor in front of him, and Herbert figured what the hell. When he slipped them on, they fit perfectly. Like a glove, or whatever you said for feet.

"All right," he said, pretending he was in a shoe store. "I'll take 'em." He padded into the kitchen to get something to eat. "Oh, and thanks." But he spoke to the air: Cricket had gone behind the screen and returned to his slow-motion calisthenics.

Herbert had a dream about Japan that night, though he'd never been farther than San Francisco. It was a bizarre vision: the Japanese were all working in rice paddies, their hair blowing in the breeze like black corn silk. They traveled from one field to another by gliding about on a layer of sandals. At the end of the far field their progress was stopped by a large folding screen. He bowed at them from the other side of the screen, but when he tried to reach across it, the Japanese bent his arms downward. When he tried to reciprocate, they dissolved into cloud shapes. Pushing ahead, he encountered only mist and soon slid on a yellow cake of soap. He flailed about till he found himself floating upward, back into semi-consciousness.

He felt defeated, stopped just before some destination. Night-gloom hovered in his room, reflecting the gray pre-dawn sky outside the window. His eyeballs itched, and the covers were half-off his bed. As his vision adjusted to the dark, the ceiling seemed to lower ominously, so he focused on the walls. There wasn't much: a dog poster and a famous-dates calendar, along with a face-sized mirror above his dresser that he didn't like to look at too often. Finally, he lulled himself back to drowsiness by concentrating on Cricket's Japanalia, from the folding fan to the statuette of the Buddha with its serenely opaque features. His last image before sleep was the door between his bedroom and Cricket's, looming like a coffin lid. He thought he heard voices from behind it, but figured he was already dreaming. He awoke some hours later to the familiar morning song of the typewriter.

The month of December passed with bits of Japan arriving regularly in the mail from Reiko. Herbert read the envelope flaps if anything in English was written on them. "You are my everything" she must have heard on the radio. Once, there was a long string of Japanese, with "LOVE" starred and underlined in the center. Underneath, she wrote that he was the only man for her, and begged for a photograph of him. At Christmas, she sent him a package of little cakes called *manjū*. Cricket ate one a day from a blue ceramic plate, in between sips of green tea. When he offered his roommate a taste, Herbert was initially cautious.

"What's in it?"

"*Mochi* and *azuki*."

"Which are—?"

"Glutinous rice and sweet red bean paste." Cricket put the piece back on the plate. "Look, if you don't want it, just say so."

"No, my father told me you should try everything once." Herbert didn't feel it necessary to mention that his father's taste in food ranged from meat to potatoes and not much further. Gingerly, he reached out for the slice of *manjū*, closed his eyes, and chewed. It was something like an unsweetened marshmallow stuffed with fibrous jam. "Not bad," he said, leaving open the possibility of "not good."

Cricket shrugged. "*Jū-nin to-iro.*"

Herbert looked up questioningly.

"Ten men, ten tastes. It's an old Japanese proverb."

Nodding, Herbert went back to his room and turned on the television. As his tongue flicked a last bit of bean paste from between his teeth, he smiled unconsciously. He had eaten something of Reiko's.

Herbert went home for Christmas and New Year's, a long-overdue visit that turned into an overlong stay. His mother embraced him, saying that he'd lost weight (not true), and served him some eggnog so rich and thick it had to be spooned. His father punched him on the shoulder, told him that he'd gained weight (also false), and inquired about his job opportunities. Herbert mumbled about a few likely prospects, though he was beginning to worry about that himself. At the moment, he was living precariously off graduation-gift money and savings from past summer jobs. Maybe, he thought, he should have gone to Japan to teach English like Cricket.

For a week, he slept in the spare room—his old room redone

in beige—and didn't have to worry about meals. The atmosphere was as homey as it was dated. Everyone he knew in Camden had moved away a while ago, except the few who had stayed, and they were boring. When his parents asked about his roommate, he gave them a thumbnail description of Cricket that included words like *shōji* and aikido, calling him "intense."

"Your uncle Larry fought against the Japs, you know," his father reminded him.

"What's your point, that they brainwashed my roommate?"

His father grinned uncertainly, and Herbert realized that he could now handle himself at home. Now all he had to do was make something of himself in Boston.

When he came back on January 2nd with a care package of food from his mother, he found Cricket had made a few changes. A twenty-five-pound sack of Kokuhō rice leaned like a fat child against the pantry door, and the refrigerator smelled of something yellow and fishy in the lower drawer. A set of odd-looking utensils marked "TEA CEREMONY" lay on the low-lying table in the living room, where Cricket was hanging up a red Japanese fighter-kite, a fiercely mustached samurai scowling on the front. Reiko had bought it for him at the Hankyu Department Store in Umeda. He spoke over his shoulder as he hammered in a nail.

"This is just like the kite that we flew on the beach in Suma. They do that on New Year's—it's a custom called *tako age*."

Herbert imagined the scene: the cold hard sand, Cricket's imperious instructions, Reiko's windswept hair as she ran behind. "Can she fly a kite well?"

"*Very* well. She has small hands, but they can move so quickly, do so many things . . . ." He stopped hammering and stood quite still for a moment. He turned away. "I'm sorry. It's just that I haven't seen her in a while."

"Well, you sure don't have to apologize."

"I miss her so much because she's not here."

At the time, Cricket's statement made so much sense it sounded like a truism. Was that why the travel-clock was set to her time? It was slowly losing a few minutes a week, but Herbert didn't want to tell Cricket. Did he think of her whenever he took off his shoes before entering the apartment, or preparing those odd meals with tofu, miso, and bony fish? Did the soul of Reiko reside in his red-lacquered set of chopsticks, or in the origami crane that now perched on the window sill?

Just from thinking about her, Herbert had slowly developed a clearer feeling for Reiko: her patient brown eyes, the button nose over a mouth that looked modest but capable of passion—those soft lips. She would be fine-boned but sturdy, soft but firm in the right places, her body concealing the kind of sudden strength you saw in martial arts experts. Her breasts were small but round, cool to the touch—in his dreams. Her voice was high and almost musical, he decided. The one point he was unsure of was how she remained so affectionate toward Cricket. That, he decided, might be something peculiarly Japanese.

He walked over to the low table, the tea ceremony utensils arrayed on it with a surgeon's precision. He reached over to stroke what looked like a straw whisk. Two ceramic jars flanked a bamboo dipper and a bowl with a bronze-leaf design. "I've heard of this kind of thing, sitting for hours. Isn't it a lot of trouble for a cup of tea?"

Cricket lowered his head sharply. "That's really not what it's about at all."

"I know, I know. Just a joke—"

"It has to do with austere elegance . . . ." Cricket groped for something beyond English. "*Wabi.*"

"What?"

"*Wabi*, it's—" he shrugged. "I can't translate it."

"Then how'd you learn it?"

"Me?" Cricket's eyes shifted as if he were considering the question from three or four angles. "I was in Japan."

Herbert gave up his quibble. He walked into the kitchen to forage for one of his mother's chocolate-chip cookies, his secondhand sandals slapping against the linoleum. From back in the living room, Cricket was still talking but not to him, Herbert knew. He did that from time to time: carried on half a conversation with someone who wasn't there. "The Japanese believe in ghosts—*obake*," Cricket had told him, the one time he'd asked about it. "These are . . . people I once knew."

"To keep yourself company?"

He hesitated. "Sort of."

Soon the living room fell completely silent, which in a way was even eerier because someone was still occupying the room. Cricket eventually entered the kitchen, not to continue the discussion but because it was time to start preparing dinner. As Herbert rummaged around in a forest of aluminum foil and plastic bags, Cricket approached the sack of rice, crouching as if to converse with it. Then he carefully punctured its neck with a penknife, bleeding the outpouring into an empty juice bottle through a plastic funnel.

"Rice again, huh?" Herbert smiled broadly as a coat hanger to let his roommate know he was kidding.

"To start the new year, I'm eating rice three times a day." He walked over to the counter where his rice-cooker stood like a bald gnome. With the skill born of repetition, he quickly poured in equal amounts of rice and water and turned it on. Herbert had seen him perform the ceremony many times, but was always impressed by the ingenuity of the system. For him, cooking rice was a complicated affair, with half of it sticking to the bottom of the pot. How ingenious of the Japanese to reduce it all to a few easy steps.

Cricket moved to the refrigerator to retrieve some odd-looking vegetables, which he laid on the scarred wooden chopping board. From the silverware drawer, he drew out a brilliant wedge of a knife that Herbert had never seen before. It sliced, or rather slid through, what looked like a fat white carrot.

"Where'd you get *that*?"

"I bought it at a restaurant-supplier in Osaka. I was saving it for something, but then my old knife snapped, so I unpacked this last week." He held it up in the last of the afternoon light. The edge looked like one long beveled razor blade, with three Japanese characters incised in the steel. "A *hōchō*. It's made the way they used to forge samurai swords. It'll cut through anything."

"I'll bet." He watched Cricket chop-chop-chop through a sort of elongated cabbage. What was once a head of tough-looking stalks became green-white flecks. "Nice technique."

"Hm." He didn't look up. "I learned it from a *gaijin*, actually—I mean a non-Japanese. An ex-Marine named Jack Sims. He practiced knife-moves."

"Maybe he was just on K.P. duty a lot," joked Herbert.

"What?" Cricket looked up, his brow furrowing.

"Nothing." To change the subject, he asked, "So, what are your other New Year's resolutions?"

Cricket tapped his head. Half-shutting his eyes, he recited, "*Dō, gaku, jitsu*. Discipline, study, practice." Nodding, though not to Herbert, he picked up his knife again. "I've been slack too long. I need to change my life."

Me, too, thought Herbert. I need to get a job. But all he did was nod soberly as Cricket wielded his knife. At about the time that Cricket hauled a block of tofu from the refrigerator to frown at, Herbert knew what he wanted. Returning to the box of foil and plastic, he searched till he found the roast beef sandwich his mother had made for the trip back.

After dinner, he headed for his room to watch some television while Cricket brought out an inkpot, a thin paintbrush, and a sketchpad to the living room. And though his favorite sitcom had just started, Herbert couldn't help looking in to watch his roommate. Sitting cross-legged on the floor, Cricket held the brush out in front of him, dipping it into the ink pot and executing a series of swirls and serifs that in the end looked like fish skeletons. The brush was a gift from a friend back in Hyogo named Miyamoto, he commented in his non-explanatory way. Beginning today, he was devoting three hours a day to Japanese, almost as much time as his writing. Dip, swirl, pause. After a few minutes, Herbert went back into his room to catch some of the television he'd missed. By the time he emerged an hour later, two sheets of openwork fish were laid out to dry. Cricket had put away his brush and ink, propped his airmail pad on top of his English-Japanese dictionary, and started writing another letter to Japan.

Cricket's new routine solidified over the course of a week. Trying to forget his unemployment, Herbert went to see a lot of movies and began a Robert Ludlum novel. Cricket was again self-possessed, so absorbed that he began to get on Herbert's nerves. They didn't snap at each other so much as retreat to opposite corners of the apartment, separate sides of the folding screen.

Only a few things seemed to disturb Cricket, mostly the wrong noise or people at the wrong time. Recently Cricket's father had called up, a gruff voice demanding to speak to his son. Cricket was writing one of his interminable letters, but Herbert decided that his roommate would have to handle this for himself. Cricket picked up the receiver, said "no" about ten times in one minute, and finally ended the call with a loud *"No!"*

"If he calls back," Cricket warned Herbert, as if he knew what it was all about, "tell him no again." But there was no repeat call.

A week later, Cricket walked back into the apartment and shut the door so firmly that the array of "footgear" by the threshold shook. "That Littlefield woman," he pronounced, stepping out of his step-in shoes. "She bothers me."

"Who?" Herbert had dragged a chair to the end of the corridor and was staring at the wall hanging, hoping it would bring serenity. It hadn't so far.

"Littlefield." Cricket gestured impatiently. "It's what O'Hara means in Japanese, 'little-field.' That's what I think of whenever I see her."

"What's the matter? Did she force brownies on you again?"

"No, it's not that. Well, it *is* that. I mean, she reminds me of some other women I've known. I don't like to be mothered."

Herbert took his eyes away from the wall hanging, giving up on inner peace for the afternoon. "I know what you mean, I guess. But I do like her brownies."

The days dragged on. But January finally yielded some more job possibilities. Herbert was half-promised a badly paying job doing administrative work for a start-up magazine and was on hold with three banks. On January 11th, after a good interview with American Express, he was invited back for the second round of questioning. Slowly his month-long pall began to lift. He even called up his cousin in Back Bay and let himself be persuaded into coming over for dinner.

A late January snow covered Brookline in white for about two days. After that, it turned into city snow, tarred with car exhaust and soot. The final phase was gray slush, seeping into Herbert's good black shoes as he walked to the T for another interview at another damn bank. The interview was tedious and, as it turned out, unnecessary. When he got back in the afternoon, Cricket was at work, but had left a message to call Mr. Walters at American Express. He telephoned, all the while beating down his hopes so he wouldn't be disappointed. After a short hold, Mr. Walters gave him the news: he had a job offer. As assistant to a Ms. Lauer in the audit division, he'd be exposed to all phases of the operation, a yearlong training program. Mr. Walters congratulated him.

Herbert was so elated at being wanted by somebody, anybody, that he didn't ask too many questions about benefits and salary. That could come later. He hung up finally with a greater sense of self-worth than he'd felt in months. His expression in the hall mirror showed the old Herbert grin, an impish curve of the lips that made his whole face tilt upward. Even the increasingly Oriental shadows on the wall looked lighter, and he passed through each room of the apartment as if he were floating.

Stopping by the refrigerator, he opened a beer, and drinking from the can, he walked into Cricket's room to look at the Japanese objects piling up. Reiko had recently sent Cricket a calendar for the Year of the Rat, an inflated dried blowfish, and an inch-high doll wearing a rakish kimono. Cricket had just bought a hollow wooden apple and pear from Bowl & Board to send back: they sat atop a cardboard mailer for imminent export. His thin English-Japanese dictionary lay athwart his massive Chinese-character index on the dresser. Propped alongside the two books was something that looked like a well-thumbed textbook, entitled *Encounters in America* and stamped "PROPERTY OF TESCO." Unable to resist, Herbert reached out to take a look. The chapters were simple and to the point: dialogues in a restaurant, a bank, a train station, and so forth, usually featuring a businessman named Mr. Tanaka. So this was what Cricket had been teaching in Japan?

A sudden noise made him start guiltily, but it was no one, just a creak from the doorframe. As he looked up, a miniature woodblock of a hermit's cottage in the mountains gazed down from the nearby wall like a portal through space. Each individual leaf was visible on the mountain trees, along with the bubbles in the stream that ran by the cottage. On the window sill next to the bed was the bridge photo of Reiko, neatly framed. When Herbert smiled at Reiko, she smiled back—it was their secret. Her soft hair was almost real enough to touch, her lips raised for a kiss. He stared at the picture from the doorway, then from where Cricket slept on his futon on the floor. From the last angle, a trace of sadness showed in her expression, but it might have been the lighting.

When Cricket came back from work and Herbert told him the news about the job, Cricket insisted on making dinner.

"No, really, you shouldn't." And Herbert meant it—he'd intended to go out for the evening.

"But this is a special occasion. Besides, you don't eat right most of the time. I'll show you how." The meal took a while to prepare: a cloudy soup made from bean paste, rice with several kinds of pickles, and some kind of white fish broiled with scallions and ginger. The *hōchō* chopped and scraped with brutal efficiency as Cricket kept up one of his non-illuminating monologues about each part of the dinner. "Pickles. *Tsukemono.* The Japanese will soak almost anything in brine, but this is *takuan.* Here." And on through the last course, which was a simple cup of green tea and a sliced-up orange. The problem was that the meal wasn't filling enough, and at ten o'clock Herbert had to sneak out for a hamburger. He wondered if he'd be happy eating in Japan, though he'd heard they had hamburgers there, too.

The radio was on when he got back, and since Cricket was already in his room, he shifted the dial to get his regular haunt, WBCN. The afternoon deejay, a big-voiced guy named Chet Warren, had gotten Herbert through a lot of slow hours. Now

Noel the Night-Owl was doing a request-hour, "sending out the *best* to all you night-owls in radio-land."

As Herbert retreated to the threshold to put on the sandals he'd forgotten, a new song came on. "I've got your picture, / Of me and you," it began. "You wrote 'I love you.' / I love you too. / I sit there staring and there's nothing else to do." A twangy beat accompanied the words, followed by a punctuationless monotone refrain that went on and on like a tape loop:

> I'm turning Japanese I think I'm turning Japanese
> I really think so.
> Turning Japanese I think I'm turning Japanese
> I really think so.
> I'm turning Japanese I think I'm turning Japanese
> I really think so.
> Turning Japanese I think I'm turning Japanese
> I really think so.

Herbert turned up the sound, listening happily until Cricket came out in what he called a *yukata*, glaring at the radio as if it were some obnoxious pet. He looked like some renegade monk.

"That was 'Turning Japanese,'" announced Noel, "by the Vapors. Special request for Rhonda from 'You-Know-Who.' This song is climbing to the top of the charts! Our next number—"

Cricket switched off the radio. "Look, I'm going to sleep soon. Do you mind?" Without waiting for an answer, he shuffled back into his room and this time shut the door.

Herbert shook his head gently, still too amused to be upset. Odd song, but catchy. He tried to hum it, but he couldn't carry a tune well, and anyway the lyrics were what made it. Crossing over to the Western side of the living room, he puttered around a bit, went back to his room to read a little Ludlum, and finally went to bed. In the following days, when "Turning Japanese" came over the airwaves with increasing frequency, he simply turned it down low. Cricket seemed to be around the apartment more and more, or maybe it was just his imagination.

His job started on the first of February, and from then on he left every morning just as the typing began from Cricket's room. He got home after Cricket had finished with his second Japanese shift and was in the middle of preparing dinner. The letters from Reiko now came two a week, sometimes all in Japanese. Cricket preferred this.

"When she writes in Japanese, I can read it, and it's interesting. *Omoshiroi.* Her English is—well, it's childish, but it's also boring. You know, a lot of the point to a conversation is the way you put things. *Zengo-kankei.* You can make a trip to the supermarket sound fascinating if you describe it right." Cricket had begun dropping more and more Japanese phrases into his sentences, few of them understandable from context.

"What kind of things does she describe?" Herbert was spreading mustard for his third ham sandwich of the week. He told himself he didn't have time to cook anything now that he was working.

"That's another problem. Japanese talk about your health, their health, the weather . . . . She tells me about her errands and her English class." He shook soy sauce into some kind of soup he was making. "She passed her TOEFL test, did I tell you?"

"No, but that's great! Is she coming, then?"

"She applied to Mount Holyoke and a few other places, but she won't hear from them until April."

"You must be excited."

"Yes, I must be . . . ."

This last comment Herbert didn't quite hear, since he was running hot water over a stubborn jar of pickles. Cricket cleaned up after dinner, did Japanese until nine, and then sat on a floor-cushion with a book by Kawabata Yasunari called *The Dancer of Izu*. Reading literature was difficult, he let it be known, flipping through his dictionary and jotting down words, but he was getting there. Afterwards, he would play one of the tapes that Reiko had sent: original *samisen* music from Kyoto, and some *shakuhachi* solos that Cricket listened to while absolutely motionless.

Herbert didn't ask, figuring it was yet another kind of training. He no longer felt guilty about living with a studious roommate now that he had a job. He had worked all day, and now he felt like relaxing. Since Cricket was reading, Herbert went over to a friend's apartment in Allston to watch television. Mike, a Rutgers buddy now working for First National Bank of Boston, had just moved into the area. Over a couple of Rolling Rocks, Herbert discussed his job and living situation.

"Cricket, huh? Is he British or something?"

"Nah. His family's from Newark. But his fiancée's Japanese." At a loss to characterize his roommate further, he went on to describe Reiko.

"Man, she must really love him to hang on like that." Mike grinned. "He going out with any other girls?"

"No, I don't think so. It's like a religion with him. He's sort of a monk these days. Letters go back and forth, she sends little packages .... Last month, he sent a tape that was just him talking in Japanese."

"That's love. Makes you do all sorts of things." Mike rose from the beat-up couch to get some more beer. He leered back from refrigerator. "I'm in favor of *in*-fi-delity." His apartment, a third-floor walk-up that he shared with nobody, looked as if it had already entertained several female visitors, at least the bathroom did. Mike was from Tennessee and the Southern tradition. At Rutgers, Herbert recalled, he'd been known as the Prom King. "So he works on being Japanese, huh?" He mouthed a couple of lines from "Turning Japanese": "No sex, no drugs, no wine, no women, / No fun, no sin, no you, no wonder it's dark ...." The song seemed to be all over the place these days.

"He might not be that way if he had a full-time job." Herbert could now afford such comments. He had to get up at seven tomorrow and stand for half an hour in a crowded subway car. His bachelor life would never be as glamorous as Mike's was, or as full as Cricket's. He felt unmistakably jealous and suppressed it with a belch.

"I wouldn't mind getting to know a girl like that. She'd take care of me real nice." Mike winked as he handed Herbert another beer. "Besides, aren't Oriental women supposed to be crazy in bed? Something in the diet, maybe."

"I don't know, Cricket never said anything about that." Herbert had a sudden image of ploughing through paddies of Japanese women. Those delicate limbs like white stalks, the flowing tresses of soft black hair. "He hasn't gone out with anyone here, though."

"No comparison, huh?" They both laughed, and then Mike told an improbable story about a Chinese woman in a cathouse. Herbert countered with one he'd heard at work about an Asian woman with two vaginas. Suddenly Herbert felt either very young or very old, he couldn't tell which. After one last beer, he left, wandering home unsteadily around one a.m. Cricket had already gone to sleep, and the apartment was dark. As he flicked on the kitchen light, though, he saw Cricket had put up a little sign on his door. Herbert tried to focus on it, but it remained incomprehensible. Finally he realized that it was in Japanese and started chuckling. He was in good humor all the way to the bathroom, entering his room, and sliding into bed, where he promptly fell asleep.

Because he'd forgotten to set the alarm, he woke up later than usual the next day and had to hustle to catch the train. Cricket was up at seven-thirty as usual, and at eight Herbert slammed the door on Cricket's morning typing. Such a clean, ascetic life—what was the point? Would Reiko really appreciate all this? Maybe he'll die in her arms when he sees her again, he thought. The late start and a headache soured the morning for him. At work, he put on a falsely bright smile, adjusted his tie, and managed as best as he could. He'd been assigned to the project of an internal audit on the computer division, which would take at least a couple of weeks. The great advantage of the job was that it took him over and prevented him from brooding. Contrary to his hopes, he still hadn't met anyone he felt he could ask out. He wondered if living with a roommate didn't send off bad signals, but he couldn't afford to move at this point. And Cricket was company, after a fashion. Herbert was even beginning to learn a little Japanese from sheer proximity.

But as spring neared, Cricket began turning odder. He muttered imprecations against Mrs. O'Hara, though he didn't seem to have had any contact with her at all. His talking to himself became more pronounced, usually accompanied by a tilt of the head as if he were listening in return. Occasionally Cricket seemed to walk right by him in the corridor without seeing him. If Herbert wanted to talk to him at any meaningful length, the best time was during his dinner preparations, which grew increasingly elaborate. To the *hōchō* was added a wicked-looking cleaver, as well as a paring knife that Herbert borrowed once to slice an apple, cutting his finger instead.

One night as Cricket was carving flowerets from ginger root, Herbert asked him what he'd heard from graduate schools so far.

Cricket looked away. "I've changed my plans," he stated. "I'm going to apply to Asian studies departments. Harvard has a good Japanese program, at least that's what I've heard." He paused, tilting his head. "It does so," he answered, though Herbert hadn't made any objection.

"I'm sure it does," supplied Herbert politely, wondering whether Cricket had been rejected from English graduate school. Since he was rarely the first to see the mail anymore, he wouldn't know.

"*Mochiron.*" Cricket had regained his poise, though it wasn't clear to whom he was speaking, and Herbert stole away as Cricket picked up the cleaver and began reducing chicken thighs to boneless strips. That was his habit of talking to himself or carrying on a two-sided conversation as if it were a three-cornered one. Usually the effect was a non sequitur, but sometimes it was eerie, like half a ventriloquist's act. Ghosts, that was what he'd called those other voices. Does that mean he believes in them, Herbert wondered, or is it really some kind of Japanese custom? Whatever it was, it was growing worse. He had an aunt who occasionally talked to people who weren't in the room, but Aunt Marian was eighty-four and lived in a nursing home.

Soon afterwards, Cricket brought home a bicycle, a rusty Fuji ten-speed that leaned against the railing of the landing for a few days before he brought it into the entrance-way. Mrs. O'Hara frowned hard at it before shutting her apartment door. As far as Herbert could tell, her annoyance seemed only to please Cricket. The bicycle was rusty and beat-up, the front wheel bent out of shape, but he went to work on it with oil, a rag, and a pair of pliers, rendering it at least ridable.

"Looks like you brought in a stray," Herbert kidded (he hadn't given up on joking yet). "Where'd you find it?"

"Oh, around," Cricket gestured vaguely. "No one seemed interested, so I rescued it."

"You mean you just—took it?" 'Stole it' had been on the tip of his tongue.

"No. I mean, yes, I took it. But it was abandoned. They do that in Japan, you know—leave old bikes around." He finished adjusting the seat-post and tested the saddle. "This way someone else can use it."

"Sure . . . I guess." And if the cops come calling here, I don't know you, he thought. But the bicycle seemed to make Cricket happier. He fitted it with a basket and used it mainly for shopping. When it was back in the apartment, it stayed alongside the shoes by the door like a dumbly loyal dog.

What exactly *did* Cricket do with his days lately? Now that Herbert was gainfully employed, he found keeping abreast of his roommate's activities difficult. When he left the apartment in the morning, Cricket was typing or busy not-typing. At other times during the day, he was doing aikido, practicing his brush-strokes, making lunch, or writing another letter to Japan. When Herbert came back in the evening, Cricket was reading Japanese literature or preparing dinner. On Saturday mornings, he left for

Chinatown on a shopping expedition, but in general he seemed to occupy himself more and more inside the apartment. Occasionally he referred to it as his temple.

Only after a particularly hectic day at the office did Herbert come to a realization: Cricket must have lost his job at the publishing house. Not that he would have noticed his roommate's extra hours—when he was away at work, Cricket could've been performing satanic rites in the basement, for all he knew—but Cricket's routine no longer seemed to include outside influence. When Herbert asked him about his proofreading, holding off as long as he could, Cricket replied shortly that he'd had a disagreement with the management.

"Yeah, I know what you mean." Everyone at AmEx resented the management, even those who were clearly part of it.

Cricket pursed his lips. "The Japanese have lifetime employment. It's a different way of thinking."

"Uh-huh." Herbert shrugged off his raincoat and carefully removed "all footgear." One of these days he'd need a new pair of slippers—the pair Cricket had given him had almost no sole left.

"You, too. I mean that." Cricket spoke at him rather than to him, but Herbert was getting used to that. Sometimes the references were direct: a girl named Sofie, a woman named Ogawa-san, his mother Louise—except that Cricket had said his mother was dead. Was that what Cricket meant by ghosts? In any event, a man named Matthew also intruded with some odd remarks, judging by Cricket's response to them. Even when it was subtle, you could tell what wasn't directed toward you by the angle of his eyes.

"Right," said Herbert. This was usually a safe response.

Cricket nodded in agreement with himself and headed toward his trusty bicycle. "*Ittekimasu.* I'm going shopping."

It was almost six o'clock. "Why now?"

Cricket leaned forward conspiratorially, as if to shut out all interference. "I have to go right now because"—suddenly he looked panic-stricken—"I'm running out of rice."

By the end of March, the weather in Boston was finally improving. Blue skies moved into town, bulbous clouds scudding above the upper limits of buildings like giant zeppelins. It was warmer but windier. One morning Herbert saw an old man's beret sail off his head and get promptly run over by an outbound T. Bikers began appearing, coincident with the daffodils. Even the traffic lights looked greener. Herbert's spirits rose with the temperature, and the next week he asked a woman in Accounting named Donna Harnett out to dinner. Donna had a pleasant face, blonde hair, and a seductive laugh, all of which he interpreted hopefully. At a nouveau Italian place called Gianni's, they sat at a doily-sized table and talked about the long arm of American Express and a few personalities at the office. When the conversation flagged a bit, Herbert introduced the subject of his eccentric roommate.

"Really?" Donna leaned toward him, almost bumping heads across the table. "You mean everything he does is Japanese?"

"That's right. I think he started it to feel more in touch with his fiancée, but now it's gotten a little out of hand." He didn't bother telling Donna about the ghosts and some of the odder rituals. They would only have complicated a good story.

"So, have you picked up any Japanese?"

"A little," he confessed. "For example, do you know what the Japanese say when they answer the phone? *'Moshi-moshi*!'"

Donna laughed, showing all her teeth. "How about when they hang up?" Herbert told her all he knew, embroidering in spots. In return, she taught him some Spanish slang from a long-ago summer in Acapulco. It was a fun evening, and Herbert intended to follow up. Unfortunately, Donna's almost-exboyfriend reappeared the next week, and for a while Herbert was plunged into the gloom of unrequited overtures. A Japanese woman, he couldn't help thinking, wouldn't have acted that way.

For company, he went out and bought a Sanyo radio-cassette player for the living room, though he kept the volume low whenever Cricket was in the apartment, which was almost all the time these days. The week before, Cricket had come back from one of his shopping expeditions on foot, shaking his fist. *"Kono yarō dorobō!"* It was a while before he would explain what had happened, which was that someone had swiped his bicycle. The idea of re-stolen goods made Herbert smile—or would have, if the implications hadn't been so serious. Now Cricket seemed to leave the apartment only when he absolutely had to. He spent a certain period each day kneeling in front of his Buddha statuette—he told Herbert he was practicing motionlessness. An increasingly involved aikido regimen was Cricket's only exercise, along with knife-work that began to verge on the acrobatic for his nightly dinner preparations.

It must have been during this period that Cricket started carrying around a book by someone named Yukio Mishima, *The Way of the Samurai,* pausing in the corridor or the kitchen to declaim passages from it in Japanese. For his part, Herbert borrowed *And Then There Were None,* an Agatha Christie novel from Cricket's bookshelf, and went through a chapter each night to combat the lonely evenings. Occasionally Cricket would look up from his reading or one of his interminable letters to Japan and meet Herbert's gaze from across the room. Sometimes they'd engage in a conversation, though every once in a while Cricket would pursue some dialogue that sounded like one half of a phone call with the man named Matthew. Another ghost, Herbert figured. When Cricket did speak to him, he learned to respond with "*Hai,*" the all-purpose Japanese word for acknowledgement.

The letters to Japan went out and crossed with the letters from Japan in the noon mail. Finally, over dinner one night, Cricket made an announcement. "Reiko wrote me, she got into Boston University, and she's coming here at the end of June."

"Hey, you mean I'll finally be able to see her!" Cricket's room now boasted more than a dozen photos of Reiko, and one of her in a sleeveless green spring dress particularly caught Herbert's eye: those smooth bare arms ending in such delicate wrists. Her brown liquid eyes glistened. She looked so feminine, so charming and understanding. Holding out her hand, she practically pulled him into the picture, as if he could reach Japan that way. He remembered the first day she had smiled at him. She still did sometimes in odd scenes from dreams. It was a brave expression, turned up hopefully at the corners, and Herbert was comforted whenever he thought about it.

Cricket reflected. "Yes, you can see her, I guess. I'm not so sure where she's going to stay . . . ."

"Won't B.U. have dorm space? Anyway, she can stay here for a while."

"Her semester begins in the fall. She's coming this early just to be with me." Cricket shoveled up some rice with his chopsticks. "*Komatta ne* . . . . I'm not sure how much time I'll have—I'm taking an advanced course in Japanese this summer."

Herbert was indignant. "How many months has it been since you've seen her?"

"Well, since last September, it'll have been . . . about eight months. That *is* a long time, isn't it?" He looked worriedly out the window, at the encroaching night and the fuzzy blue-black space between the slender tree branches. "In her last letter, she said she cared for me more than—more than—it's hard to translate what she said."

He paused, his face contorted with the strain of emotion breaking through rigid facial muscles. Herbert didn't press him. In the uncomfortable silence that followed, Cricket finally muttered something about love.

Around the end of May, Cricket's schedule began to fray at the edges. He wandered from one activity to another, leaving his books on the living-room table to go read a Japanese magazine in the kitchen, or stopping an aikido routine to go look out the window for minutes at a time. A large batch of his manuscripts came back in their return manila envelopes, and the typewriter sessions in the bedroom finally shut down. He brought home a long Japanese root vegetable one night and managed to slice his thumb viciously while cutting it, all the while jabbering at the ghost who made him do it. The *hōchō* was shoved into a drawer with blood still on it. He pushed Herbert aside when Herbert made a kindhearted attempt to clean the knife. The next day, he looked stricken and tried to explain himself.

"Sorry about yesterday." He bowed low. "*Dōmo sumimasen deshita.* I'm just not in my right—not in the right mood these days." They were standing in the living room, where Cricket had transferred some more Japanese items to take care of the overflow from the bedroom. A miniature folding screen one foot high stood on the coffee table, depicting a scene of insects like grasshoppers leaping in a field. A globular doll that was all head stared with ink-spot eyes at the origami crane perched on the far window sill. The folding fan that had been shut for so long was opened to depict a gray carp swimming in space. The Buddha statue now shared its floor-space with a deck of Japanese scenery cards and guarded Herbert's Sanyo cassette-radio with its back. Cricket gestured at the air. "It has nothing to do with you."

"I didn't think it did. You don't have to explain."

"It's just—" Cricket flung out an arm instead of a word, and Herbert stepped instinctively backwards. He heard a crunch. He looked down.

"God, that was dumb." The Buddha had broken into so many pieces that it looked like a white plaster mess on the rug. Herbert bit his lip; Cricket said nothing. "Look, I'm really sorry—can I replace it somehow?"

For a moment Cricket looked as if he might cry, but he swallowed hard instead. Finally he shook his head. "No, you can't replace it. I can't get another one like that." His expression hardened. "But it wasn't your fault."

"At least let me pay—"

"No. That's okay. You leave things out, they get stepped on, that's all. *Owari.* Right?" He tried a laugh that wasn't much of a success. Then he went to get the dustpan and broom, with Herbert apologizing a second and third time.

For a day or two, the breakage seemed to jar Cricket loose from his surroundings, but it was only a brief gap in his relentless routine. Herbert bided his time and simply tried to steer clear of his roommate. This didn't prove hard in the narrow apartment since they circumnavigated each other like ships on completely different courses. When Cricket was practicing Japanese in his room, Herbert was playing a tape on the right side of the screen in the living room; when Cricket was wielding his *hōchō* in the kitchen, Herbert was shaving in the bathroom; and when Herbert was scrounging in the kitchen, Cricket was doing something fierce on the left side of the living room screen. When he started throwing over-the-shoulder comments to Herbert again, Herbert took this to mean that he was forgiven.

"Mishima wrote that all Japanese should sacrifice to the spirit of their ancestors." He raised his *hōchō* like a sword. "*Wakarimashita?*"

"*Hai,*" responded Herbert, thinking of his late Uncle Louie, who worked as a Sunday school teacher until they caught him terrorizing his students.

Cricket nodded perfunctorily, sheathing his sword in a cardboard tube, and retreated to his room. The bedroom door stayed mostly closed nowadays, but an occasional glimpse when it was ajar showed a weird combination of barren Zen cell and Japanese storehouse. An altar of sorts had been erected in the corner, with a rice bowl, a *sake* jar, and a corn cob as offerings. Last month's addition was a pair of *geta* that Reiko had sent him, wooden clogs he tried on briefly, adding three inches to his height and making him clop like a horse, before they joined the silent procession of Japanalia in his room. The latest arrival was a flurry of small fan-shaped leaves, which Cricket had scattered like coins on the bare floor area. He now had two calligraphy brushes lying on his desk. For greater writing practice, he had recently started keeping a journal in Japanese. He still hadn't figured out where Reiko would stay for the summer. Herbert was toying with the idea of sending a letter to her himself when she called from Japan.

The call came in the morning, which meant it was night in

Japan, and Herbert was getting ready to leave for work. All he heard was Cricket's voice, speaking abnormally slowly, emphasizing his words. "*Yes.* I can hear you, per-fect-ly." There was a pause. *"Iie, kore wa dameo"*

"Is that Reiko?" Herbert mouthed, and Cricket nodded yes. As Herbert left for the office, he could hear Cricket speaking Japanese into the phone, the receiver clenched in his hand.

When Herbert came home that night, he asked if Reiko had any news.

"Well, she's coming the end of June. *Roku-gatsu.* She's crazy to get to America, but I still don't know my plans for next fall. I'm not so sure about graduate programs anymore. I may want to do something else with my Japanese." He was doing translation these days, he explained, working backwards from a book for Japanese high-school students. He was also working on something he used to teach from, and he held up the *Encounters in America* text that Herbert had seen in his room. "See, I'm trying to turn it into *Encounters in Japan* for Americans."

"That's what I'm living through."

"What?" One of Cricket's voices—Ogawa-san? Matthew?—seemed to be causing interference. He shook his head, listened again, then nodded. He looked at his watch. "You're right, I have to get back to work. There's a whole chapter I have to finish before I go to sleep."

Herbert shrugged and called up his friend Mike to ask whether he wanted to go out. That was fine with Mike, and they met at Luck King Palace. Getting out of the apartment helped deflect his mind from the situation and from his vision of Reiko, a darkly fluttering butterfly. Drink also helped. After dinner, they went to a bar where the waitresses had perfected the art of smiling just for them, and the evening finished late.

When Herbert got back, though, Cricket was still up, his door open, the wall-light on above his futon. One of Reiko's many pictures was taped to the opposite wall, this one with her black hair swirling around her. Cricket was reading a Japanese comic book, occasionally jotting down words in a little notebook. Dressed in his blue and white *yukata,* he looked up, still in Japan.

"O-kaeri nasai. Yoru wa dō deshita ka?"

"Huh?"

"How'd the evening go?"

"Pretty well. Yours?"

"Warukunai—not bad. You know, I really should get out some more. But there's so much to do right here." He took a sip

of barley tea, which he claimed was an acquired taste—hadn't liked it till after he'd left Japan, as a matter of fact. He'd offered some to Herbert a while ago, but Herbert had decided it tasted like bilge water. Cricket took another sip and repeated himself. "There's so much to study, so much to know about Japan. Do you know what *ba-ji-tō-fū* means?"

"Of course not. What is it?"

"'East wind in the ear of a horse.' Like talking to a wall, in other words. *Masaka*. Some people never listen. All that in just four characters." He said something else in Japanese, and Herbert nodded, moving toward the kitchen. Cricket interlaced more and more of his conversation with Japanese, and it could get annoying. Except that Herbert now knew what *"Ohayō gozaimasu"* meant. It meant "Good morning," and Cricket said it across the breakfast table every day. Reiko, Herbert supposed, should be happy to have such a diligent lover. But when he tried to imagine their sex-life, he came up with something blank and pitiless.

Herbert was given a slight raise in June. He was coming along nicely, said Ms. Lauer—he might lead an audit project himself in a few months. Herbert wondered how Ms. Lauer, with her hair dyed raven-black, would look pressed into a kimono, her high heels replaced with *tabi*-socks and *zori*. Cricket had infected him.

In mid-June Herbert started some much-needed exercise, getting out a few T stops before Coolidge Corner and walking the rest of the distance. Cricket, on the other hand, spent more and more time quiescent, with occasional bursts of furious energy. He stomped around the apartment, muttering half-Japanese, half-English threats against their neighbor—O'Hara-san, as he called her. But mostly when Herbert came home from work, he would see Cricket in his *yukata*, seated at the low table in the living room and writing something in Japanese. He offered Herbert a homemade scroll, which Herbert accepted warily.

"What's it say?"

"Hibi kore kessen." Cricket looked defiant.

"All right, I'll bite. What's it *mean*?"

"'Fight the battle every day.'" Suddenly something slithered in his features, and in the moment before he tightened up again Herbert saw a hint of terror. "It's essential," he continued. "I consider myself"—he whirled about—"a *ronin*, a samurai without a master."

Herbert stepped back. "Okay. I mean *hai*. So where do I hang it?"

"At your office."

So Herbert actually took it to his cubicle at work, where it functioned as a conversation piece for a few days. Back at the apartment, Cricket continued to prowl about, sometimes chopping with his *hōchō* even when there was nothing to cut. His eyes were glazed, his head cocked as if listening to a two-way radio. Several times Herbert thought of calling in a doctor, but what would he say? Maybe when Reiko came, she could snap him out of whatever it was. In the meantime, he let it ride.

Since Cricket had stopped getting the mail every day, sometimes Herbert brought it up. In late June, a telegram came from Japan, which Cricket read quickly before using it as a bookmark in his text.

That night, Herbert heard Cricket talking loudly in his sleep, a voice from the floor murmuring something which sounded like "Reiko" and something else which could have been Japanese or garbled English. The voice, which must have been droning on for a while, died out soon after waking Herbert. Herbert turned on his side to look at the clock: three in the morning, and he felt oddly lightheaded. The name "Reiko" had stirred him, and now he reached out toward the night table next to his bed, fumbling under a stack of magazines for what he wanted. Pulling out the photo, he held it up to the pale moonlight, cropped by the tree branches from outside. Reiko smiled delicately at him, her lashes lowered demurely. Cricket had so many pictures that he wouldn't miss one, and he intended to give it back soon, anyway. But just now it soothed him, imagining Reiko as a near, alive presence, as she trailed her fingers through his hair, breathed on his chest, and led him to sleep.

Near the end of the month, Brookline turned into a June dream, the days as clear as a baby's face, cool nights with sunset long after eight. Herbert was walking his extra blocks home from work when he stopped at the Star Market to pick up some prepared food. These days he occasionally did Cricket's shopping, too, if there wasn't much to get. Despite the inviting weather, Cricket had been in his room for the past few days, immersed in Japan. His latest demand was that he be called *Kōrogi*, the Japanese for "cricket." "Unfortunately," he said almost humorously, "there is no Japanese for 'Herbert.'" Then he withdrew again. Only once had he gone out, to buy another airmail pad and some more envelopes. When Herbert had last talked to him, Cricket shut his eyes, asking for soy sauce and aspirin. He complained that he was suffering from bad allergies, though he wouldn't say to what.

Herbert patrolled the supermarket aisles in his suit, picking up some paper towels and a frozen lasagna entrée for his supper, as well as the items Cricket wanted. He carried the shopping bag in front of him as he strode home, skirting into the one-way street and whistling as he walked. Life was good—something would turn up. The sun had only just begun to sink, leaving an hour or more of light left, the breeze through the green-leafed trees picking up like the lightest of warnings. Nearby, the high-pitched song of the cicadas was dying down in the bushes.

Before he'd gotten halfway up the walk, he saw her. She sat near the entrance steps, flanked by two heavy suitcases. Herbert thought she was staring at him, but her gaze was fastened on something farther. He saw that when he moved. As he got closer, he could see she'd been crying, delicate tears from the soft brown eyes that he knew from Cricket's pictures. She was shorter than he'd imagined. Dressed in a pleated blue skirt and a white blouse, she was the one out-of-place element in the landscape. She gazed up as he reached the foot of the steps, her lips parted to say something. Nothing came.

"You're Reiko, aren't you."

She nodded, dabbing at her face with a handkerchief. Her black hair was loose, blowing a bit in the breeze. "Are you—Her-bert?"

He nodded, putting his package down. "Is Cricket still out? He's usually in at this hour. Did you press the buzzer?"

"I did—press. I speak to him." Her face contorted again as a sob racked her chest. "He won't let me enter, he won't—won't—won't t-talk to me." She buried her face in her small hands, hiding her shame.

Oddly, Herbert's first thought was of Cricket, alone in the apartment in his robe, concentrating on his aikido moves. Or seated in his room, writing another letter to Japan. Maybe looking up occasionally at a photo.

"Hm, that's not right." Herbert attempted a lightheartedness he didn't at all feel. "I think he's just not in his right head—I mean not in a good mood."

Reiko shook her head. "So *angry*. At me." She began to sob.

Suddenly a jabber of Japanese sounded from above, followed by loud footsteps. A screech came from the second landing—

Mrs. O'Hara? It was followed by a loud thump and another shout in Japanese. Reiko cringed reflexively. A clang rang out like a sword against a radiator, transmuting into a bleat that died in a gurgle. Oh, God, oh, God. Herbert imagined the blood, but whose? He'd just have to go up there and see what was going on. Or maybe he should find a phone, call the police.

But not just now. The immediacy of his vision confronted him. Reiko sat crying softly, her black hair hanging down around her like a shroud. She cried without rhythm, as if all expectations had been dropped, forgotten. When she looked up, her eyes were liquid, her hair glistening where a few tears had fallen. Herbert moved one of the suitcases and sat down beside her. She turned toward him, a momentary lapse in her grief. He looked directly at her, compassionately—knowingly.

"*Daijōbu?*" he asked Reiko, his tongue sliding a little uncertainly over the word. It was something he'd picked up from Cricket, something along the lines of "Are you okay?" As if he'd been waiting months for this moment, he put his arm around her, comforting her, holding her, stroking her long black hair.